DOROTHY ALLISON

BASTARD
OUT OF
CAROLINA

Ⓟ

A PLUME BOOK

PLUME
Published by the Penguin Group
Penguin Books USA Inc., 375 Hudson Street,
New York, New York 10014, U.S.A.
Penguin Books Ltd, 27 Wrights Lane,
London W8 5TZ, England
Penguin Books Australia Ltd, Ringwood,
Victoria, Australia
Penguin Books Canada Ltd, 10 Alcorn Avenue,
Toronto, Ontario, Canada M4V 3B2
Penguin Books (N.Z.) Ltd, 182–190 Wairau Road,
Auckland 10, New Zealand

Penguin Books Ltd, Registered Offices:
Harmondsworth, Middlesex, England

Published by Plume, an imprint of Dutton Signet, a division of Penguin Books USA Inc.
Previously published in a Dutton edition.

First Plume Printing, March, 1993
30 29 28

Portions of this book first appeared in the author's collection of short stories, *Trash.*

 REGISTERED TRADEMARK—MARCA REGISTRADA

LIBRARY OF CONGRESS CATALOGING-IN-PUBLICATION DATA
Allison, Dorothy.
    Bastard out of Carolina / Dorothy Allison.
        p.   cm.
    ISBN 0-452-26957-1
    I. Title.
PS3551.L453B37   1993
813'.54—dc20   92-32330
                                            CIP

Printed in the United States of America

For Mama
Ruth Gibson Allison
1935–1990

People pay for what they do, and still more, for what they have allowed themselves to become. And they pay for it simply: by the lives they lead.

—JAMES BALDWIN

1

I've been called Bone all my life, but my name's Ruth Anne. I was named for and by my oldest aunt—Aunt Ruth. My mama didn't have much to say about it, since strictly speaking, she wasn't there. Mama and a carful of my aunts and uncles had been going out to the airport to meet one of the cousins who was on his way back from playing soldier. Aunt Alma, Aunt Ruth, and her husband, Travis, were squeezed into the front, and Mama was stretched out in back, sound asleep. Mama hadn't adjusted to pregnant life very happily, and by the time she was eight months gone, she had a lot of trouble sleeping. She said that when she lay on her back it felt like I was crushing her, when she lay on her side it felt like I was climbing up her backbone, and there was no rest on her stomach at all. Her only comfort was the backseat of Uncle Travis's Chevy, which was jacked up so high that it easily cradled little kids or pregnant women.

Moments after lying back into that seat, Mama had fallen into her first deep sleep in eight months. She slept so hard, even the accident didn't wake her up.

My aunt Alma insists to this day that what happened was in no way Uncle Travis's fault, but I *know* that the first time I ever saw Uncle Travis sober was when I was seventeen and they had just removed half his stomach along with his liver. I cannot imagine that he hadn't been drinking. There's no question in my mind but that they had *all* been drinking, except Mama, who never could drink, and certainly not when she was pregnant.

No, Mama was just asleep and everyone else was drunk. And what they did was plow headlong into a slow-moving car. The front of Uncle Travis's Chevy accordioned; the back flew up; the aunts and Uncle Travis were squeezed so tight they just bounced a little; and Mama, still asleep with her hands curled under her chin, flew right over their heads, through the windshield, and over the car they hit. Going through the glass, she cut the top of her head, and when she hit the ground she bruised her backside, but other than that she wasn't hurt at all. Of course, she didn't wake up for three days, not till after Granny and Aunt Ruth had signed all the papers and picked out my name.

I am Ruth for my aunt Ruth, and Anne for my mama. I got the nickname Bone shortly after Mama brought me home from the hospital and Uncle Earle announced that I was "no bigger than a knucklebone" and Aunt Ruth's youngest girl, Deedee, pulled the blanket back to see "the bone." It's lucky I'm not Mattie Raylene like Granny wanted. But Mama had always promised to name her first daughter after her oldest sister, and Aunt Ruth thought Mama's child should just naturally carry Mama's name since they had come so close to losing her.

Other than the name, they got just about everything else wrong. Neither Aunt Ruth nor Granny could write very clearly, and they hadn't bothered to discuss how Anne would be spelled, so it wound up spelled three different ways on the form—Ann, Anne, and Anna. As for the name of the father, Granny refused to speak it after she had run him out of town for messing with her daughter, and Aunt Ruth had never been sure of his last name anyway. They tried to get away with just scribbling something down, but if the hospital didn't mind how a baby's middle name was spelled, they were definite about having a father's last name. So Granny gave one and Ruth gave another, the clerk got mad, and there I was—certified a bastard by the state of South Carolina.

Mama always said it would never have happened if she'd been awake. "After all," she told my aunt Alma, "they don't ask for a marriage license before they put you up on the table." She was convinced that she could have bluffed her way through it, *said* she was married firmly enough that no one would have questioned her.

"It's only when you bring it to their attention that they write it down."

Granny said it didn't matter anyhow. Who cared what was written down? Did people read courthouse records? Did they ask to see your birth certificate before they sat themselves on your porch? Everybody who mattered knew, and she didn't give a rat's ass about anybody else. She teased Mama about the damn silly paper with the red stamp on the bottom.

"What was it? You intended to frame that thing? You wanted something on your wall to prove you done it right?" Granny could be mean where her pride was involved. "The child is proof enough. An't no stamp on her nobody can see."

If Granny didn't care, Mama did. Mama hated to be called trash, hated the memory of every day she'd ever spent bent over other people's peanuts and strawberry plants while they stood tall and looked at her like she was a rock on the ground. The stamp on that birth certificate burned her like the stamp she knew they'd tried to put on her. *No-good, lazy, shiftless.* She'd work her hands to claws, her back to a shovel shape, her mouth to a bent and awkward smile—anything to deny what Green-ville County wanted to name her. Now a soft-talking black-eyed man had done it for them—set a mark on her and hers. It was all she could do to pull herself up eight days after I was born and go back to work waiting tables with a tight mouth and swollen eyes.

Mama waited a year. Four days before my first birthday and a month past her sixteenth, she wrapped me in a blanket and took me to the courthouse. The clerk was polite but bored. He had her fill out a form and pay a two-dollar fee. Mama filled it out in a fine schoolgirl's hand. She hadn't been to school in three years, but she wrote letters for everyone in the family and was proud of her graceful, slightly canted script.

"What happened to the other one?" the clerk asked.

Mama didn't look up from my head on her arm. "It got torn across the bottom."

The clerk looked at her more closely, turned a glance on me. "Is that right?"

He went to the back and was gone a long time. Mama stood, quiet but stubborn, at the counter. When he came back, he passed her the paper and stayed to watch her face.

It was the same, identical to the other one. Across the bottom in oversized red-inked block letters it read, "ILLEGITIMATE."

Mama drew breath like an old woman with pleurisy, and flushed pink from her neck to her hairline. "I don't want it like this," she blurted.

"Well, little lady," he said in a long, slow drawl. Behind him she could see some of the women clerks standing in a doorway, their faces almost as flushed as her own but their eyes bright with an entirely different emotion. "This is how it's got to be. The facts have been established." He drew the word out even longer and louder so that it hung in the air between them like a neon reflection of my mama's blush—*established*.

The women in the doorway shook their heads and pursed their lips. One mouthed to the other, "Some people."

Mama made her back straighten, bundled me closer to her neck, and turned suddenly for the hall door. "You forgetting your certificate," the man called after her, but she didn't stop. Her hands on my body clamped so tight I let out a high, thin wail. Mama just held on and let me scream.

She waited another year before going back, that time taking my aunt Ruth with her and leaving me with Granny. "I was there," Aunt Ruth promised them, "and it was really my fault. In so much excitement I just got confused, what with Anney here looking like she was dead to the world and everybody shouting and running around. You know, there was a three-car accident brought in just minutes after us." Aunt Ruth gave the clerk a very sincere direct look, awkwardly trying to keep her eyes wide and friendly.

"You know how these things can happen."

"Oh, I do," he said, enjoying it all immensely.

The form he brought out was no different from the others. The look he gave my mama and my aunt was pure righteous justification. *"What'd you expect?"* he seemed to be saying. His face was set and almost gentle, but his eyes laughed at them. My aunt came close to swinging her purse at his head, but Mama caught her arm. That time she took the certificate copy with her.

"Might as well have something for my two dollars," she said. At seventeen, she was a lot older than she had been at sixteen. The next year she went alone, and the year after. That same year she met Lyle Parsons and started thinking more about marrying him than dragging down to the courthouse again. Uncle Earle teased her that if she lived with Lyle for seven years, she could get the same result without paying a court-house lawyer. "The law never done us no good. Might as well get on without it."

▪   ▪   ▪

Mama quit working as a waitress soon after marrying Lyle Parsons, though she wasn't so sure that was a good idea. "We're gonna need things," she told him, but he wouldn't listen. Lyle was one of the sweetest boys the Parsonses ever produced, a soft-eyed, soft-spoken, too-pretty boy tired of being his mama's baby. Totally serious about providing well for his family and proving himself a man, he got Mama pregnant almost immediately and didn't want her to go out to work at all. But pumping gas and changing tires in his cousin's Texaco station, he made barely enough to pay the rent. Mama tried working part-time in a grocery store but gave it up when she got so pregnant she couldn't lift boxes. It was easier to sit a stool on the line at the Stevens factory until Reese was born, but Lyle didn't like that at all.

"How's that baby gonna grow my long legs if you always sitting bent over?" he complained. He wanted to borrow money or take a second job, anything to keep his pretty new wife out of the mill. "Honey girl," he called her, "sweet thing."

"Dumpling," she called him back, "sugar tit," and when no one could hear, "manchild." She loved him like a baby, whispered to her sisters about the soft blond hairs on his belly, the way he slept with one leg thrown over her hip, the stories he told her about all the places he wanted to take her.

"He loves Bone, he really does," she told Aunt Ruth. "Wants to adopt her when we get some money put by." She loved to take pictures of him. The best of them is one made at the gas station in the bright summer sun with Lyle swinging from the Texaco sign and wearing a jacket that proclaimed "Greenville County Racetrack." He'd taken a job out at the track where they held the stock-car races, working in the pit changing tires at high speed and picking up a little cash in the demolition derby on Sunday afternoon. Mama didn't go out there with him much. She didn't like the noise or the stink, or the way the other men would tease Lyle into drinking warm beer to see if his work slowed down any. As much as she liked taking pictures, she only took one of him out at the track, with a tire hugged against his left hip, grease all over one side of his face, and a grin so wide you could smell the beer.

It was a Sunday when Lyle died, not at the track but on the way home, so easily, so gently, that the peanut pickers who had seen the accident kept insisting that the boy could not be dead. There'd been one of those eerie summer showers where the sun never stopped shining and the rain came down in soft sheets that everybody ignored. Lyle's truck had come around the curve from the train crossing at a clip. He waved at one of the pickers, giving his widest grin. Then the truck was spinning off the highway in a rain-slicked patch of oil, and Lyle was bumped out the side door and onto the pavement.

"That's a handsome boy," one of the pickers kept telling the highway patrolman. "He wasn't doing nothing wrong, just coming along the road in the rain—that devil's rain, you know. The sun was so bright, and that boy just grinned so." The old man wouldn't stop looking back over to where Lyle lay still on the edge of the road.

Lyle lay uncovered for a good twenty minutes. Everybody kept expecting him to get up. There was not a mark on him, and his face was shining with that lazy smile. But the back of his head flattened into the gravel, and his palms lay open and damp in the spray of the traffic the patrolmen diverted around the wreck.

Mama was holding Reese when the sheriff's car pulled up at Aunt Alma's, and she must have known immediately what he had come to tell her, because she put her head back and howled like an old dog in labor, howled and rocked and squeezed her baby girl so tight Aunt Alma had to pinch her to get Reese free.

Mama was nineteen, with two babies and three copies of my birth certificate in her dresser drawer. When she stopped howling, she stopped making any sound at all and would only nod at people when they tried to get her to cry or talk. She took both her girls to the funeral with all her sisters lined up alongside of her. The Parsonses barely spoke to her. Lyle's mother told Aunt Alma that if her boy hadn't taken that damn job for Mama's sake, he wouldn't have died in the road. Mama paid no attention. Her blond hair looked dark and limp, her skin gray, and within those few days fine lines had appeared at the corners of her eyes. Aunt Ruth steered her away from the gravesite while Aunt Raylene tucked some of the flowers into her family Bible and stopped to tell Mrs. Parsons what a damn fool she was.

Aunt Ruth was heavily pregnant with her eighth child, and it was hard for her not to take Mama into her arms like another baby. At Uncle Earle's car, she stopped and leaned back against the front door, hanging on to Mama. She brushed Mama's hair back off her face, looking closely into her eyes. "Nothing else will ever hit you this hard," she promised. She ran her thumbs under Mama's eyes, her fingers resting lightly on either temple. "Now you look like a Boatwright," she said. "Now you got the look. You're as old as you're ever gonna get, girl. This is the way you'll look till you die." Mama just nodded; it didn't matter to her anymore what she looked like.

A year in the mill was all Mama could take after they buried Lyle; the dust in the air got to her too fast. After that there was no choice but to find work in a diner. The tips made all the difference, though she knew she could make more money at the honky-tonks or managing a slot as a cocktail waitress. There was always more money serving people beer and wine, more still in hard liquor, but she'd have had to go outside Greenville County to do that, and she couldn't imagine moving away from her family. She needed her sisters' help with her two girls.

The White Horse Cafe was a good choice anyway, one of the few decent diners downtown. The work left her tired but not sick to death like the mill, and she liked the people she met there, the tips and the conversation.

"You got a way with a smile," the manager told her.

"Oh, my smile gets me a long way," she laughed, and no one would have known she didn't mean it. Truckers or judges, they all liked Mama. Aunt Ruth was right, her face had settled into itself. Her color had come back after a while, and the lines at the corners of her eyes just made her look ready to smile. When the men at the counter weren't slipping quarters in her pocket they were bringing her things, souvenirs or friendship cards, once or twice a ring. Mama smiled, joked, slapped ass, and firmly passed back anything that looked like a down payment on something she didn't want to sell.

Reese was two years old the next time Mama stopped in at the courthouse. The clerk looked pleased to see her again. She didn't talk to him this time, just picked up the paperwork and took it over to the new business offices near the Sears, Roebuck Auto Outlet. Uncle Earle had given her a share of his settlement from another car accident, and she wanted to use a piece of it to hire his lawyer for a few hours. The man took her money and then smiled at her much like the clerk when she told him what she wanted. Her face went hard, and he swallowed quick to keep from laughing. No sense making an enemy of Earle Boatwright's sister.

"I'm sorry," he told her, handing half her money back. "The way the law stands there's nothing I could do for you. If I was to put it through, it would come back just like the one you got now. You just wait a few years. Sooner or later they'll get rid of that damn ordinance. Mostly it's not enforced anymore anyway."

"Then why," she asked him, "do they insist on enforcing it on me?"

"Now, honey," he sighed, clearly embarrassed. He wiggled in his seat and passed her the rest of her money across the desk. "You don't need me to tell you the answer to that. You've lived in this county all your life, and you know how things are." He gave a grin that had no humor in it at all. "By now, they look forward to you coming in.

"Small-minded people," he told her, but that grin never left his face.

"Bastard!" Mama hissed, and then caught herself. She hated that word.

Family is family, but even love can't keep people from eating at each other. Mama's pride, Granny's resentment that there should even be anything to consider shameful, my aunts' fear and bitter humor, my uncles' hard-mouthed contempt for any-thing that could not be handled with a shotgun or a two-by-four—all combined to grow my mama up fast and painfully. There was only one way to fight off the pity and hatefulness. Mama learned to laugh with them, before they could laugh at her, and to do it so well no one could be sure what she really thought or felt. She got a reputation for an easy smile and a sharp tongue, and using one to balance the other, she seemed friendly but distant. No one knew that she cried in the night for Lyle and her lost happiness, that under that biscuit-crust exterior she was all butter grief and hunger, that more than anything else in the world she wanted someone strong to love her like she loved her girls.

"Now, you got to watch yourself with my sister," Uncle Earle told Glen Waddell the day he took him over to the diner for lunch. "Say the wrong thing and she'll take the shine off your teeth."

It was a Thursday, and the diner was serving chicken-fried steak and collard greens, which was Earle's excuse for dragging his new workmate halfway across Greenville in the middle of a work day. He'd taken a kind of shine to Glen, though mo-ment to moment he could not tell what that short stubborn boy was thinking behind those dark blue eyes. The Waddells owned the dairy, and the oldest Waddell son was running for district attorney. Skinny, nervous little Glen Waddell didn't seem like he would amount to much, driving a truck for the furnace works, and shaking a little every time he tried to look a man in the eye. But at seventeen, maybe it was enough that Glen tried, Earle told himself, and kept repeating stories about his sister to get the boy to relax.

"Anney makes the best gravy in the county, the sweetest biscuits, and puts just enough vinegar in those greens. Know what I mean?"

Glen nodded, though the truth was he'd never had much of a taste for greens, and his well-educated mama had always told him that gravy was bad for the heart. So he was not ready for the moment when Mama pushed her short blond hair back and set that big hot plate of food down in front of his open hands. Glen took a bite of gristly meat and gravy, and it melted between his teeth. The greens were salt-sweet and fat-rich. His tongue sang to his throat; his neck went loose, and his hair fell across his face. It was like sex, that food, too good to waste on the middle of the day and a roomful of men too tired to taste. He chewed, swallowed, and began to come alive himself. He began to feel for the first time like one of the boys, a grown man accepted by the notorious and dangerous Black Earle Boatwright, staring across the counter at one of the prettiest women he'd ever seen. His face went hot, and he took a big drink of ice tea to cool himself.

"Her?" he stammered to Earle. "That your sister? That pretty little white-headed thing? She an't no bigger than a girl."

Earle grinned. The look on Glen's face was as clear as the sky after spring rain. "Oh, she's a girl," he agreed, and put his big hand on Glen's shoulder. "She's my own sweet mama's baby girl. But you know our mama's a rattlesnake and our daddy was a son of a gun." He laughed loud, only stopping when he saw how Glen was watching Anney walk away, the bow of her apron riding high on her butt. For a moment he went hot-angry and then pulled himself back. The boy was a fool, but a boy. Probably no harm in him. Feeling generous and Christian, Earle gave a last hard squeeze to Glen's shoulder and told him again, "You watch yourself, son. Just watch yourself."

Glen Waddell nodded, understanding completely the look on Earle's face. The man was a Boatwright, after all, and he and his two brothers had all gone to jail for causing other men serious damage. Rumor told deadly stories about the Boatwright boys, the kind of tales men whispered over whiskey when women were not around. Earle was good with a hammer or a saw, and magical with a pickax. He drove a truck like he was making love to the gears and carried a seven-inch pigsticker in the side pocket of his reinforced painter's pants. Earle Boatwright was everything Glen had ever wanted to be—specially since his older brothers laughed at him for his hot temper, bad memory, and general uselessness. Moreover, Earle had a gift for charming people—men or women—and he had charmed the black sheep of the Waddell family right out of his terror of the other men on the crew, charmed him as well out of his fear of his family's disapproval. When Earle turned that grin on him, Glen found himself grinning back, enjoying the notion of angering his daddy and outraging his brothers. It was something to work for, that relaxed and disarming grin of Earle's. It made a person want to see it again, to feel Earle's handclasp along with it and know a piece of Earle's admiration. More than anything in the world, Glen Waddell wanted Earle Boatwright to like him. Never mind that pretty little girl, he told himself, and put his manners on hard until Earle settled back down. Glen yes-ma'amed all the waitresses and grabbed Earle's check right out of Anney's hand, though it would take him down to quarters and cigarettes after he paid it.

But when Earle went off to the bathroom, Glen let himself watch her again, that bow on her ass and the way her lips kept pulling back off her teeth when she smiled. Anney looked him once full in the face, and he saw right through her. She had grinned at her brother with an open face and bright sparkling eyes, an easy smile and a soft mouth, a face without fear or guile. The smile she gave Glen and everyone else at the counter was just as easy but not so open. Between her eyes was a fine line that deepened when her smile tightened. A shadow darkened her clear pupils in the moment before her glance moved away. It made her no less pretty but added an aura of sadness.

"You coming over tonight, Earle?" she asked when he came back, in a voice as buttery and sweet as the biscuits. "The girls miss you 'bout as much as I do."

"Might be over," Earle drawled, "if this kid here does his job right and we get through before dark this time." He slapped Glen's shoulder lightly and winked at Anney. "Maybe I'll even bring him with me."

Yes, Glen thought, oh yes, but he kept quiet and took another drink of tea. The gravy in his stomach steadied him, but it was Anney's smile that cooled him down. He felt so strong he wanted to spit. He would have her, he told himself. He would marry Black Earle's baby sister, marry the whole Boatwright legend, shame his daddy and shock his brothers. He would carry a knife in his pocket and kill any man who dared to touch her. Yes, he thought to himself, oh yes.

Mama looked over at the boy standing by the cash register, with his dark blue eyes and bushy brown hair. Time was she would have blushed at the way he was watching her, but for that moment she just looked back into his eyes. He'd make a good daddy, she imagined, a steady man. He smiled and his smile was crooked. His eyes bored into her and got darker still. She flushed then, and smelled her own sweat, nervously unable to tell if it came from fear or lust.

I need a husband, she thought, turned her back, and wiped her face. Yeah, and a car and a home and a hundred thousand dollars. She shook her head and waved Earle out the door, not looking again at the boy with him.

"Sister Anney, why don't you come over here and stand by my coffee cup," one of her regulars teased. "It'll take heat just being next to your heart."

Mama gave her careful laugh and pulled up the coffeepot. "An't got time to charm coffee when I can pour you a warm-up with one hand," she teased him back. Never mind no silly friends of Earle's, she told herself, and filled coffee cups one at a time until she could get off the line and go take herself a break.

"Where you keep that paper, Ruth Anne's birth certificate, huh?" they'd tease Mama down at the diner.

"Under the sink with all the other trash," she'd shoot back, giving them a glance so sharp they'd think twice before trying to tease her again.

"Put it away," Granny kept telling her. "If you stopped thinking about it, people would too. As long as it's something that'll get a rise out of you, people're gonna keep on using it."

The preacher agreed. "Your shame is between you and God, Sister Anne. No need to let it mark the child."

My mama went as pale as the underside of an unpeeled cotton boll. "I got no shame," she told him, "and I don't need no man to tell me jackshit about my child."

"*Jackshit,*" my aunt Ruth boasted. "She said 'jackshit' to the preacher. An't nobody says nothing to my little sister, an't nobody can touch that girl or what's hers. You just better watch yourself around her."

You better. You better. You just better watch yourself around her.

Watch her in the diner, laughing, pouring coffee, palming tips, and frying eggs. Watch her push her hair back, tug her apron higher, refuse dates, pinches, suggestions. Watch her eyes and how they sink into her face, the lines that grow out from that tight stubborn mouth, the easy banter that rises from the deepest place inside her.

"An't it about time you tried the courthouse again, Sister Anney?"

"An't it time you zipped your britches, Brother Calvin?"

An't it time the Lord did something, rained fire and retribution on Greenville County? An't there sin enough, grief enough, inch by inch of pain enough? An't the measure made yet? Anney never said what she was thinking, but her mind was working all the time.

Glen Waddell stayed on at the furnace works with Earle for one whole year, and drove all the way downtown for lunch at the diner almost every workday and even some Saturdays. "I'd like to see your little girls," he told Anney once every few weeks until she started to believe him. "Got to be pretty little girls with such a beautiful mama." She stared at him, took his quarter tips, and admitted it. Yes, she had two beautiful little girls. Yes, he might as well come over, meet her girls, sit on her porch and talk a little. She wiped sweaty palms on her apron before she let him take her hand. His shoulders were tanned dark, and he looked bigger all over from the work he had been doing with Earle. The muscles bulging through his worn white T-shirt reminded her of Lyle, though he had none of Lyle's sweet demeanor. His grip when he reached to take her arm was as firm as Earle's, but his smile was his own, like no one else's she had ever known. She took a careful deep breath and let herself really smile back at him. Maybe, she kept telling herself, maybe he'd make a good daddy.

Mama was working grill at the White Horse Cafe the day the radio announced that the fire downtown had gone out of control, burning the courthouse and the hall of records to the ground. It was midway through the noon rush. Mama was holding a pot of coffee in one hand and two cups in the other. She put the cups down and passed the pot to her friend Mab.

"I'm going home."

"You what?"

"I've got to go home."

"Where's she going?"

"Trouble at home."

The cardboard box of wrinkled and stained papers was tucked under the sheets in the bottom of Aunt Alma's chifforobe. Mama pulled out the ones she wanted, took them into the kitchen, and dropped them in the sink without bothering to unfold them. She'd just lit a kitchen match when the phone rang.

"You heard, I suppose." It was Aunt Ruth. "Mab said you took off like someone set a fire under you."

"Not me," Mama replied. "The only fire I got going here is the one burning up all these useless papers."

Aunt Ruth's laughter spilled out of the phone and all over the kitchen.

"Girl, there an't a woman in town going to believe you didn't set that fire yourself. Half the county's gonna tell the other how you burned down that courthouse."

"Let them talk," Mama said, and blew at the sparks flying up. "Talk won't send me to jail. The sheriff and half his deputies know I was at work all morning, 'cause I served them their coffee. I can't get into any trouble just 'cause I'm glad the goddam courthouse burned down."

She blew at the sparks again, whistling into the phone, and then laughed out loud. Halfway across town, Aunt Ruth balanced the phone against her neck, squeezed Granny's shoulder, and laughed with her. Over at the mill, Aunt Alma looked out a window at the smoke billowing up downtown and had to cover her mouth to keep from giggling like a girl. In the outer yard back of the furnace works, Uncle Earle and Glen Waddell were moving iron and listening to the radio. Both of them grinned and looked up at each other at the same moment, then burst out laughing. It was almost as if everyone could hear each other, all over Greenville, laughing as the courthouse burned to the ground.

2

Greenville, South Carolina, in 1955 was the most beautiful place in the world. Black walnut trees dropped their green-black fuzzy bulbs on Aunt Ruth's matted lawn, past where their knotty roots rose up out of the ground like the elbows and knees of dirty children suntanned dark and covered with scars. Weeping willows marched across the yard, following every wandering stream and ditch, their long whiplike fronds making tents that sheltered sweet-smelling beds of clover. Over at the house Aunt Raylene rented near the river, all the trees had been cut back and the scuppernong vines torn out. The clover grew in long sweeps of tiny white and yellow flowers that hid slender red-and-black-striped caterpillars and fat gray-black slugs—the ones Uncle Earle swore would draw fish to a hook even in a thunderstorm. But at Aunt Alma's, over near the Eustis Highway, the landlord had locked down the spigots so that the kids wouldn't cost him a fortune in water bills. Without the relief of a sprinkler or a hose the heat had burned up the grass, and the combined efforts of dogs and boys had reduced the narrow yard to a smoldering expanse of baked dirt and scattered rocks.

"Yard's like a hot griddle," Aunt Alma complained. "Catches all the heat of that tin roof and concentrates it. You could just about cook on that ground."

"Oh, it's hot everywhere." Granny never agreed with Aunt Alma, and particularly not that summer when she was being paid a lot less than she wanted to watch Alma's kids. And the little Mama threw in to pay her for keeping Reese and me didn't sweeten her attitude. Granny loved all her grandchildren, but she was always announcing that she didn't have much use for her daughters.

"My three boys worship me," she'd tell everybody, "but my girls, Lord! I've got five girls and they never seem to appreciate me. It's how girls are, though, selfish and full of themselves. I shouldn't expect any better."

"Your granny means well," Mama told me before dropping us off to stay the day over at Aunt Alma's, "but don't pay too much attention to the things she says. She's always loved her boy children more. It's just the way some women are." I nodded. I believed anything that Mama said was so.

Almost the first thing I remember is Aunt Alma's house and yard, back behind the tiny roadside store she and Uncle Wade were trying to manage. It was the summer after Reese was born, which means I must have been about five years old, only slightly bigger than Little Earle, Alma's youngest. But Little Earle was a fat toddler still chafing in rubber pants and grabbing at everything with his unfailingly sticky hands, while I was a solemn watchful child with long thin bones and a cloud of wild black hair. I looked down on Little Earle as a lesser creature and stayed well out of reach of his grubby fingers and pushed-out baby lips. That was the summer it was so hot the katydids failed to sing and everyone spent their evenings out on the porch with large glasses of ice tea and damp hand towels to cool the back of the neck. Alma wouldn't even start cooking until after the sun had gone down. Twilight came on early, though, a long-drawn-out dimming of the heat and glare that made everything soft and magical, brought out the first fireflies, and added a cool enchantment to the metallic echoes of the slide guitar playing on Alma's kitchen radio. Granny would plant herself in the porch rocker, leaving Alma's girls to pick through snap beans, hope for a rainstorm, and tease her into telling stories.

I always positioned myself behind Granny, up against the wall next to the screen door, where I could listen to Kitty Wells and George Jones, the whine of that guitar and what talk there was in the kitchen, as well as the sound of Aunt Alma's twin boys thumping their feet against the porch steps and the girls' giggles as their fingers slipped through the cool, dusty beans. There I was pretty much safe from Little Earle as he ran back and forth from Granny's apron pockets to the steps, where his brothers pitched pennies and practiced betting against each other. Little Earle would lope like a crippled crawfish, angling to the side, swaying unsteadily, and giggling his own wet croupy babble. The boys would laugh at him, Granny would just smile. Oblivious and happy, Little Earle would pound his fists on Grey's shoulders and then twirl himself around to run all out toward Granny, Temple, and Patsy Ruth. Naked, dimpled all over, fat and brown and wide, his stubborn little body bulged with determination, and his little-boy prick bounced like a rubber toy between his bowlegged thighs as he whooped and ran, bumping his head on Granny's hip. He was like a windup toy spinning itself out, and his delight only increased when everyone started laughing at him as he jumped up again after falling plop on his behind next to the tub of snap beans.

Granny covered her mouth with one hand to hide her teeth. "You ugly little boy," she teased Little Earle, almost laughing between her words. "You ugly, ugly, ugly little thing."

Earle paused, crowed like a hoot owl, and rocked back and forth as if his momentum were too strong for him to come to a full stop without falling over. Temple and Patsy Ruth shook their wet fingers at his fat little belly while Grey and Garvey smacked their lips and joined in with Granny.

"Ugly, ugly, ugly, ugly! You so ugly you almost pretty!"

Earle squealed and jumped and laughed full out. "Ug-ly," he parroted them. "Uggg-lly!" His face was bright and smiling, and his hands flew up and down like bumblebees, fast and wild up near his ears.

"Ugly. Ugly. Ugly."

"You are just the ugliest thing!" Granny rocked forward and caught her hands under Little Earle's arms, swinging him up off his feet and directly before her face. "You dimple-belly," she called him, "you little dimple-butt." She pressed her mouth against his midriff and blew fiercely so that her lips vibrated against Little Earle's navel—a bubble-bubble roar that made him shriek and bounce and giggle a high-pitched wail of hysterical laughter. He drew his knees up and cupped his little hands around his sex, which only made Temple and Patsy Ruth laugh louder. Granny swung him back and forth a few times and then dropped him down on his feet. He took off immediately for the shelter of his older brother's armpit.

"Dimple-butt," Grey snorted, but pulled his little brother in tight to his side. "An't so ugly maybe." He rubbed his knuckles across Little Earle's nearly bald head and sang out, "You just tall, that's all." Grey laughed at that while Granny wiped her eyes and the girls poured cool water across the beans.

I edged forward until I could put my hand on Granny's chair, fingers sliding over the smooth, worn trellis of woven slats to feel the heat of her body through her cotton dress. The laughter echoed around me, the music, truck brakes ground up on the highway, and somebody started shouting far off as the dark descended and the fireflies began to flicker past the boys' heads. Granny put her arm down and squeezed my wrist. She leaned over and spat a stream of brown snuff off the side of the porch. I heard the dull plopping sound it made as it landed in the dusty yard. I slipped under her shoulder, leaned across the side of the rocker, and put my face close to her breast. I could smell wet snap beans, tobacco, lemon juice on her neck, a little sharp piss scent, and a little salt.

"Ugly," I repeated, and buried my face in her dress, my smile so wide the warm cotton rubbed my teeth.

"Pretty ugly," Granny whispered above me, her fingers sliding across the back of my head, untangling my hair and lifting it up off my neck. "Almost pretty. Oh, you're a Boatwright all right, a Boatwright for sure."

I laughed up into her neck. Granny was ugly herself, she said so often enough, though she didn't seem to care. Her wide face was seamed and spotted with freckles and long deep lines. Her hair was thin and gray and tied back with one of the little black strings that came off a snuff pouch. She smelled strong— bitter and salt, sour and sweet, all at the same time. My sweat disappeared into her skirt, my arms wrapped around her waist, and I breathed her in like the steam off soup. I rocked myself against her, as happy and safe as Little Earle had felt with her teeth on his belly.

"You know, Bone, your mama's gonna be late," Temple told me. "These hot nights, they take forever to clean up down at the diner, and old Glen's gonna be there hanging over the counter and slowing her down. He's pure crazy where your mama's concerned."

I nodded solemnly, hanging on to Granny. The radio sounded louder, the boys started to fight. Everybody was busy, everybody was talking, but I was perfectly happy at Granny's side, waiting for Mama to come home late from the diner, take Reese and me back to the tiny duplex she had rented downtown. If the heat continued into the night Mama would put us out on the screened porch on a makeshift mattress of couch cushions and sheets. She would sit up by us out there, humming and smoking in the quiet dark, while the radio played so soft we couldn't make it out.

The world that came in over the radio was wide and far away and didn't touch us at all. We lived on one porch or another all summer long, laughing at Little Earle, teasing the boys and picking over beans, listening to stories, or to the crickets beating out their own soft songs. When I think of that summer—sleeping over at one of my aunts' houses as easily as at home, the smell of Mama's neck as she bent over to hug us in the dark, the sound of Little Earle's giggle or Granny's spit thudding onto the dry ground, and that country music playing low everywhere, as much a part of the evening as crickets and moonlight—I always feel safe again. No place has ever seemed so sweet and quiet, no place ever felt so much like home.

I worshiped my uncles—Earle, Beau, and Nevil. They were all big men with wide shoulders, broken teeth, and sunken features. They kept dogs trained for hunting and drove old trucks with metal toolboxes bolted to the reinforced wood sides. They worked in the mills or at the furnace repair business, or sometimes did roofing or construction work depending on how the industry was going. They tinkered with cars together on the weekends, standing around in the yard sipping whiskey and talking dirty, kicking at the greasy remains of engines they never finished rebuilding. Their eyes were narrow under sunbleached eyebrows, and their hands were forever working a blade or a piece of wood, or oiling some little machine part or other.

"You hold a knife like this," they told me. "You work a screwdriver from your shoulder, swing a hammer from your hip, and spread your fingers when you want to hold something safe."

Though half the county went in terror of them, my uncles were invariably gentle and affectionate with me and my cousins. Only when they were drunk or fighting with each other did they seem as dangerous as they were supposed to be. The knives they carried were bright, sharp, and fascinating, their toolboxes were massive, full of every imaginable metal implement. Even their wallets bulged with the unknown and the mysterious—

outdated ID cards from the air base construction crew, passes for the racetrack, receipts for car repairs and IOUs from card games, as well as little faded pictures of pretty women who were not their wives. My aunts treated my uncles like overgrown boys—rambunctious teenagers whose antics were more to be joked about than worried over—and they seemed to think of themselves that way too. They looked young, even Nevil, who'd had his teeth knocked out, while the aunts—Ruth, Raylene, Alma, and even Mama—seemed old, worn-down, and slow, born to mother, nurse, and clean up after the men.

Men could do anything, and everything they did, no matter how violent or mistaken, was viewed with humor and understanding. The sheriff would lock them up for shooting out each other's windows, or racing their pickups down the railroad tracks, or punching out the bartender over at the Rhythm Ranch, and my aunts would shrug and make sure the children were all right at home. What men did was just what men did. Some days I would grind my teeth, wishing I had been born a boy.

I begged my aunts for Earle's and Beau's old denim workshirts so I could wear them just the way they did when they worked on their trucks, with the front tucked in and the tail hanging out. Beau laughed at me affectionately as I mimicked him. Earle and Nevil raked their calloused fingers through my black hair and played at catching my shirttail as I ran past them, but their hands never hurt me and their pride in me was as bright as the coals on the cigarettes they always held loosely between their fingers. I followed them around and stole things from them that they didn't really care about—old tools, pieces of chain, and broken engine parts. I wanted most of all a knife like the ones they all carried—a Buck knife with a brass-and-stained-wood handle or a jackknife decorated with mother-of-pearl. I found a broken jackknife with a shattered handle that I taped back together around the bent steel tang. I carried that knife all the time until my cousin Grey took pity and gave me a better one.

Uncle Earle was my favorite of all my uncles. He was known as Black Earle for three counties around. Mama said he was called Black Earle for that black black hair that fell over his eyes in a great soft curl, but Aunt Raylene said it was for his black black heart. He was a good-looking man, soft-spoken and hardworking. He told Mama that all the girls loved him because he looked like Elvis Presley, only skinny and with muscles. In a way he did, but his face was etched with lines and sunburned a deep red-brown. The truth was he had none of Elvis Presley's baby-faced innocence; he had a devilish look and a body Aunt Alma swore was made for sex. He was a big man, long and lanky, with wide hands marked with scars. "Earle looks like trouble coming in on greased skids," my uncle Beau laughed. All the aunts agreed, their cheeks wrinkling around indulgent smiles while their fingers trailed across Uncle Earle's big shoulders as sweetly and tenderly as the threadlike feet of hummingbirds.

Uncle Earle always seemed to have money in his pockets, some job he was just leaving and another one he was about to take up. His wife had left him around the time Lyle Parsons died, because of what she called his lying ways. He wouldn't stay away from women, and that made her mad. Teresa was Catholic and took her vows seriously, which Earle had expected, but he had never imagined she would leave him for messing around with girls he would never have married and didn't love. His anger and grief over losing her and his three daughters gave him an underlying bitterness that seemed to make him just that much more attractive.

"That Earle's got the magic," Aunt Ruth told me. "Man is just a magnet to women. Breaks their hearts and makes them like it." She shook her head and smiled at me. "All these youngsters playing at being something, imagining they can drive women wild with their narrow little hips and sweet baby smiles, they never gonna have the gift Earle has, don't even know enough to recognize it for what it is. A sad wounded man who genuinely likes women—that's what Earle is, a hurt little boy with just enough meanness in him to keep a woman interested."

She pushed my hair back off my face and ran her thumb over my eyebrows, smoothing down the fine black hairs. "Your real daddy . . ." She paused, looked around, and started again. "He had some of that too, just enough, anyway, to win your mama. He liked women too, and that's something I can say for him. A man who really likes women always has a touch of magic."

There weren't any pictures of my real daddy, and Mama wouldn't talk to me about him—no more than she would about the rest of the family. It was Granny who told me what a pissant he was; told me he lived up near Blackburn with a wife and six children who didn't even know I existed; said he sold insurance to colored people out in the county and had never been in jail a day in his life. "A sorry excuse for a man," she called him, making me feel kind of wretched until Aunt Alma swore he hadn't been that bad, just pissed everybody off when he wouldn't come back and ask Granny's forgiveness after she ran him off.

"Eight days after you were born," Aunt Alma told me, "he came around while Granny was over at the mill to settle some trouble with one of the boys. Anney wasn't sure she wanted to see him at all, but Raylene and I persuaded her to let him see you while she stayed in the back bedroom. That boy was scared shitless, holding you in hands stained dark green where he'd been painting his daddy's flatbed truck. You just looked at him with your black Indian eyes like he wasn't nothing but a servant, lifting you up for some air or something. Then you let loose and pissed a pailful all down his sleeves, the front of his shirt, and right down his pants halfway to his knees! You peed all over the son of a bitch!"

Aunt Alma hugged me up onto her lap. Her grin was so wide it made her nose seem small. She looked like she'd been waiting to tell me this story since I was born, waiting to praise and thank me for this thing I didn't even know I had done.

"It's like you were putting out your mama's opinion, speaking up for her there on his lap. And that boy seemed to know just what it meant, with your baby piss stinking up his clothes for all to smell. He passed you right over to me like you were gonna go on to drown him if he didn't hurry. Took off without speaking to your mama and never came back again. When we heard he'd married another little girl was already carrying his baby, Earle joked that the boy was just too fertile for his own good, that he couldn't plow a woman without making children, and maybe it's true. With the six he's got legal, and you, and the others people say he's got scattered from Spartanburg to Greer, he's been a kind of one-man population movement. You got family you an't ever gonna know is your own—all of you with that dark dark hair he had himself." She grinned at me, reaching out to push my midnight-black hair back off my face.

"Oh, Bone!" she laughed. "Maybe you should plan on marrying yourself a blond just to be safe. Huh?"

Granny wouldn't talk much about my real daddy except to curse his name, but she told me just about everything else. She would lean back in her chair and start reeling out story and memory, making no distinction between what she knew to be true and what she had only heard told. The tales she told me in her rough, drawling whisper were lilting songs, ballads of family, love, and disappointment. Everything seemed to come back to grief and blood, and everybody seemed legendary.

"My granddaddy, your great-great-granddaddy, he was a Cherokee, and he didn't much like us, all his towheaded grandchildren. Some said he had another family down to Eustis anyway, a proper Indian wife who gave him black-haired babies with blue eyes. Ha! Blue eyes an't that rare among the Cherokee around here. Me, I always thought it a shame we never turned up with them like his other babies. Of course, he was a black-eyed bastard himself, and maybe he never really made those other babies like they say. What was certain was my grandma never stepped out on him. Woman was just obsessed with that man, obsessed to the point of madness. Used to cry like a dog in the night when he was gone. He didn't stay round that much either, but every time he come home she'd make another baby, another red-blond child with muddy brown eyes that he'd treat like a puppydog or a kitten. Man never spanked a child in his life, never hit Grandma. You'd think he would have, he didn't seem to care all that much. Quiet man, too. Wouldn't fight, wouldn't barely talk. Not a Boatwright, that's for sure.

"But we loved him, you know, almost as much as Grandma. Would have killed to win his attention even one more minute than we got, and near died to be any way more like him, though we were as different from him as children can be. None of us quiet, all of us fighters. None of us got those blue eyes, and no one but you got that blue-black hair. Lord, you were a strange thing! You were like a fat red-faced doll with all that black black hair—a baby doll with a full head of hair. Just as quiet and sweet-natured as he used to be. You didn't even cry till you took croup at four months. I've always thought he'd have liked you, Granddaddy would. You even got a little of the shine of him. Those dark eyes and that hair when you was born, black as midnight. I was there to see."

"Oh, hell," Earle laughed when I repeated some of Granny's stories. "Every third family in Greenville County swears it's part of Cherokee Nation. Whether our great-granddaddy was or wasn't, it don't really make a titty's worth of difference. You're a Boatwright, Bone, even if you are the strangest girl-child we got."

I looked at him carefully, keeping my Cherokee eyes level and my face blank. I could not have said a word if Great-Great-Granddaddy had been standing there looking back at me with my own black eyes.

Mama wore her hair cut short, curled, and bleached. Every other month she and Aunt Alma would get together and do each other's hair, rinsing Aunt Alma's in beer or lemon juice to lighten it just a little, trimming Mama's back and bleaching it that dark blond she liked. Then they'd set pin curls for each other, and while those dried they would coax Reese into sitting still long enough that her baby-fine red locks could be tied up in rags. I would tear up the rags, rinse pins, strain the juice through a cloth happily enough, but I refused the perm Mama was always insisting she wanted to give me.

"Stinks and hurts," I complained. "Do it to Reese."

"Oh, Reese don't need it. Look at this." And Aunt Alma tugged a few of Reese's springy long curls free from the rags. Like soft corkscrews, the curls bounced and swung as if they were magical. "This child has the best hair in the world, just like yours, Anney, when you were a baby. Yours had a little red to it too, seems to me."

"No." Mama shook her head while she pulled more rags out of Reese's curls. "You know my hair was just blond. You had the red touch, you and Ruth. Remember how you used to fight over whose was darker?"

"Oh, but you had the prettiest hair!" Aunt Alma turned to me. "Your mama had the prettiest hair you ever saw. Soft? Why, it would make Reese's feel like steel wire. It was the softest hair in Greenville County, and gold as sunlight on sheets. It didn't go dark till she had you girls, a little bit with you and all dark with Reese. Hair will do that, you know, darken in pregnancy. An't nothing that will stop it once it starts."

Mama laughed. "Remember when Carr first got pregnant and swore she'd shave her head if it looked like it was gonna go dark?"

Aunt Alma nodded, her dark brown pin curls bobbing. "Rinsed it in piss, she did, every Sunday evening, Tommy Lee's baby piss that she begged off Ruth. All 'cause Granny swore baby-piss rinses would keep her blond."

"Didn't she stink?" I bit at the rubber tip of a hairpin, peeling the coating off the metal so I could taste the sweet iron tang underneath.

"Baby piss don't stink," Aunt Alma told me, "unless the baby's sick, and Tommy Lee wasn't never sick a day in his life. Carr didn't smell no different than she ever did, but her hair went dark anyway. It's the price of babies."

"Oh, it an't that." Mama pulled me up onto her lap and started the arduous process of brushing out my hair. "All us Boatwrights go dark as we get older. It's just the way it goes. Blond goes red or brown, and darker and darker. An't none of us stays a blond once we're grown."

" 'Cept you, honey," Aunt Alma grinned.

"Yeah, but I got Clairol, don't I?" Mama laughed and hugged me. "What you think, Alma? Should I cut this mop or not? She can't keep it neat to save her life, hates me pulling on it when I try to brush it out."

"Hell yes, cut it. I'll get the bowl. We'll trim it right down to her neck."

"*Noooo!*" I howled, and wrapped my hands around my head. "I want my hair. I want my hair."

"But you won't let us do nothing with it, honey."

"No! No! No! It's my hair and I want it. I want it long and tangled and just the way it is."

Aunt Alma reached over and took the hairpin out of my mouth. "Lord, look at her," she said. "Stubborn as the day is long."

"Uh-huh." Mama put both hands on my shoulders and squeezed. She didn't sound angry. I raised my head to look at her. Her brown eyes were enormous close up, with little flecks of light in the pupils. I could almost see myself between the flashes of gold.

"Well, what you expect, huh?"

I looked back at Aunt Alma. Her eyes were the same warm brown, deep and shining with the same gold lights, and I realized suddenly that she had the same cheekbones as Mama, the same mouth.

"She's just like you."

My mouth wasn't like that, or my face either. Worse, my black eyes had no gold. I didn't look like anybody at all.

"You, you mean," said Mama.

She and Aunt Alma nodded together above me, grinning at each other in complete agreement. I loosened my hands from around my skull slowly, letting Mama start brushing out my hair. Reese put her pudgy little fingers in her mouth and stared at me solemnly. "B-Bone," she stammered.

"Yes," Aunt Alma agreed, hefting Reese up in her arms. "Our stubborn Bone is just like her mama, Reesecup. Just like her aunts, just like a Boatwright, and just like you."

"But I don't look like nobody," I wailed.

Aunt Alma laughed. "Why, you look like our Bone, girl."

"I don't look like Mama. I don't look like you. I don't look like nobody."

"You look like me," Mama said. "You look like my own baby girl." She put her fingers delicately on my cheeks, pressing under my eyes. "You got the look, all right. I can see it, see what it's gonna be like when you grow bigger, these bones here." Her fingers slipped smoothly down over my mouth and chin. "And here. You gonna look like our granddaddy, for sure. Those Cherokee cheekbones, huh, Alma?"

"Oh yes, for sure. She's gonna be another one, another beauty to worry about."

I smiled wide, not really believing them but wanting to. I held still then, trying not to flinch as Mama began to brush relentlessly at my knotted hair. If I got a permanent, I would lose those hours on Mama's lap sitting in the curve of her arm while she brushed and brushed and smoothed my hair and talked soft above me. She always seemed to smell of buttery flour, salt, and fingernail polish—a delicate insinuating aroma of the familiar and the astringent. I would breathe deep and bite my lips to keep from moaning while my scalp ached and burned. I would have cut off my head before I let them cut my hair and lost the unspeakable pleasure of being drawn up onto Mama's lap every evening.

"Do I look like my daddy?" I asked.

There was silence. Mama brushed steadily while Aunt Alma finished pulling the rags from Reese's hair.

"Do I? Like my daddy, Mama?"

Mama gathered all my hair up in one hand and picked at the ends with the side of the brush. "Alma, get me some of that sweet oil, honey, just a little for my palm. That's enough."

The brush started again in long sweeping strokes. Aunt Alma started to hum. I dropped my head. It wasn't even that I was so insistent on knowing anything about my missing father. I wouldn't have minded a lie. I just wanted the story Mama would have told. What was the thing she wouldn't tell me, the first thing, the place where she had made herself different from all her brothers and sisters and shut her mouth on her life?

Mama brushed so hard she pulled my head all the way back. "You just don't know how to sit still, Bone."

"No, Mama."

I closed my eyes and let her move my head, let her pull and jerk my hair until she relaxed a little. Aunt Alma was humming softly. The smell of sweet oil on Mama's fingers hung in the air. Reese's singsong joined Aunt Alma's hum. I opened my eyes and looked into Mama's. You could see Reese's baby smile in those eyes. In the pupils gold flecks gleamed and glittered, like pieces of something bright reflecting light.

3

Love, at least love for a man not already part of the family, was something I was a little unsure about. Aunt Alma said love had more to do with how pretty a body was than anyone would ever admit, and Glen was pretty enough, she swore, with his wide shoulders and long arms, his hair combed back and his collar buttoned up tight over his skinny neck.

Sometimes after Glen had been over to visit and gone, Mama would sit on the porch and smoke a cigarette, looking off into the distance. Sometimes I'd go slide quietly under her armpit and sit with her, saying nothing. I would wonder what she was thinking, but I didn't ask. If I had, she'd have said something about the road or the trees or the stars. She'd have talked about work or something one of my cousins had done, or one of the uncles, or she'd have swatted my butt and sent me off to bed, then gone back to sitting there with her face so serious, smoking her Pall Mall cigarette right down to the filter.

"You and Reese like Glen, don't you?" Mama would say now and then in a worried voice. I would nod every time. Of course we liked him, I'd tell her, and watch her face relax so her smile came back.

"I do too. He's a good man." She'd run her hands over her thighs slow, hug her knees up close to her breasts, and nod to herself more than me. "He's a good man."

The nights Mama worked at the diner, she'd leave us with Aunt Ruth or Aunt Alma. But sometimes, if she wasn't working too late, she would make up a bed of blankets and pillows in the backseat of her Pontiac and take us with her. She'd feed us dinner in a booth near the kitchen and let us listen to the jukebox for a while before she put us to bed in the car, telling me sternly not to unlock the door for anyone but her. While we sat in that booth, I'd watch her at work. She was mesmerizing, young and sweet-faced and too pretty for anyone to be mean to her. The truckers teased her and played her favorite songs on the jukebox. The younger ones would try to get her to go out with them, but she'd joke them out of it. The older ones who knew her well would compliment her on us, her pretty girls. I watched it all, admiring the men with their muscular forearms and broad shoulders as they sipped the coffee my mama served them, absorbing the music as it played continuously, keeping Reese from spilling her milk or sliding down under the table, and smiling at Mama when she looked over to me.

"You're Anney's girl, an't you?" one of them said to me. "Your little sister looks just like her, don't she? You must look like your daddy." I nodded carefully.

When Glen Waddell came, Mama would get him a beer and sit with him when she could. Sometimes, if she was busy, he would carry us out to her car when Reese got sleepy, holding us in his big strong arms with the same studied gentleness as when he touched Mama. I always wanted to wait till Mama could tuck us into our bed of blankets, but she seemed to like for Glen to carry us out with all the truckers watching. I'd see her look over as he went out with us, see her face soften and shine. Maybe that was love, that look. I couldn't tell.

My mama dated Glen Waddell for two years. People said it took her time to trust men again after Lyle Parsons died. Mama would occasionally take Reese and me with her to pick Glen up from his new job at the RC Cola plant. Sometimes he would still be working, lifting flats of soda bottles to stock his truck for the next morning's route. All those full cases had to be loaded and the empties pulled off and transferred to the conveyor belt for cleaning and shipment to the bottling plant. He would shift each case of twenty-four bottles above his head and onto the truck with a grunt, swinging from his hips with his whole weight, arms extended and mouth sucked in against his tongue with concentration. His collar was open, his pale blue short-sleeved uniform shirt was limp, and it stuck to his back in a dark stripe down his spine. Mama would still be in her waitress dress, smelling of salt and fried food, and just as sweaty and tired as he was, but Glen would smile at her like he knew she sweat sugar and cream. Mama would lean out the window of the car and call his name softly, and he would blush dark red and start moving a little faster, either to show off his strength or to get out of there sooner, we weren't sure.

Glen was a small man but so muscular and strong that it was hard to see the delicacy in him, though he was strangely graceful in his rough work clothes and heavy boots. There were bottle fragments on the pavement, crushed shards ground into the tarmac, and all the men wore heavy work boots with thick rubber soles. Glen Waddell's feet were so fine that his boots had to be bought in the boys' department of the Sears, Roebuck, while his gloves could only be found in the tall men's specialty stores. He would pivot on those boy-size feet, turning his narrow hips and grunting with his load, everything straining and forceful, while his hands cradled cases and flats as delicately as if they were soft-shelled eggs. His palms spread so wide he could easily span half a case's width, keeping every bottle level no matter how high he had to throw the flat.

People talked about Glen's temper and his hands. He didn't drink, didn't mess around, didn't even talk dirty, but the air around him seemed to hum with vibration and his hands were enormous. They hung like baseball mitts at the end of his short, tight-muscled arms. On his slender, small-boned frame, they were startling, incongruous, constantly in motion, and the only evidence of just how strong he was. When he reached for Reese and me, he would cup his palms around the back of our heads and drop down to look into our faces, his warm, damp fingers tangling gently in our hair. He was infinitely careful with us, gentle and slow with those hands, but he was always reaching for Mama with sudden, wide sweeps of his arms. When he hugged her, he would lay his hands on her back so that he covered it from neck to waist, pulling her as tight to him as he could.

Mama was always taking Glen's hands between hers, her fingers making his seem even bigger, harder, and longer. "He's a gentle man," she told her sisters. "You should see how tender he gets, the way he picks Reese up when she falls asleep in the back of the car, like she was so delicate, so fine—like that glass that chimes when you click it against your teeth." My aunts would nod, but not with much conviction.

But I could tell that Mama had begun to love Glen. I saw how she blushed when he looked at her or touched her, even in passing. A flush would appear on her neck, and her cheeks would brighten until her whole face glowed pink and hot. Glen Waddell turned Mama from a harried, worried mother into a giggling, hopeful girl.

One afternoon Glen dropped the last case onto the truck and turned to look at Mama, Reese, and me waiting in Mama's old Pontiac. The sun caught his sweat, shiny beads and rivulets, so that he seemed to glitter in the light. He wiped his face, but the sweat kept coming down in tracks, and he looked as if he were weeping. He walked toward us slowly, dropped by the door in a crouch, and reached through the window to take Mama into a tight embrace.

"Oh Anney," he whispered. "Anney, Anney." His voice was a husky tremolo. "You know. You know, I love you so. I can't wait no more, Anney. I can't. I love you with all my heart, girl."

His arms stretched over the seat and pulled Reese and me forward, pressing us into Mama's neck and back. "And your girls, Anney. Oh, God! I love them. Our girls, Anney. Our girls." He sobbed then, pulling us in tighter so that Reese's bird bones crunched into my shoulder and the haze of his sweat drifted all around us. His face slid past Mama's hair, pressed into mine, his mouth and teeth touched my cheek. "Call me Daddy," he whispered. "Call me Daddy 'cause I love your mama, 'cause I love you. I'm gonna treat you right. You'll see. You're mine, all of you, mine."

His shoulders shook, his body reaching through the window seemed to rock the whole car. "Oh, Anney." He shuddered. "Don't say no. Please, Anney, don't do that to me!"

"Glen," Mama breathed. "Oh, Glen. I don't know." She trembled and slowly stretched her own arms up and around his shoulders. "Oh, God. All right, I'll think about it. All right, honey. All right."

Glen jumped back. He slammed his hands down on the car top, once, twice, three times. The echoes were like shots. Mama was crying quietly, her shoulders heaving back against Reese and me.

"Goddam," he screamed. "Goddam, Anney!" He spun in a circle, whooping. "I knew you'd say yes. Oh, what I'm gonna do, Anney! I promise you. You an't never even imagined!" He spread his arms wide and whooped again. His face looked like someone was shining a hot pink light on it. He pulled the door open and reached for Mama, his hands still shaking as they wrapped around her back. He drew her in so close that she came off her feet, and then he swung her around in the air, laughing and shouting. Reese put her hands on my shoulders and held on. I could feel the vibration as she shook gently to the echo of Glen's shouts. We both smiled and held on to each other while Glen danced Mama around the parking lot in the shelter of his arms.

"You just don't like the Waddells," Mama told Granny. She was standing on Aunt Alma's porch, wearing a blue-and-white polka-dot blouse Glen had bought her. It showed off the color of her eyes, he'd said. From the look on her face anyone could see that she was making an effort to be patient with Granny.

"Glen loves me, loves my girls. Don't matter if his family is stuck-up and full of themselves. Glen's not like that."

"You don't know what that boy is like, Anney. You just don't know."

"I know he loves me." Mama spoke with conviction, certain that Glen Waddell loved her more than his soul and everything else would come from that. "I know enough," she told Granny.

"That boy's got something wrong with him." Granny turned to Aunt Alma for support. "He's always looking at me out the sides of his eyes like some old junkyard dog waiting to steal a bone. And you know Anney's the bone he wants."

"You just don't think anybody's good enough for Anney," Alma teased. "You want her to go on paying you to keep her girls every day till she's dried up and can't imagine marrying again."

It was a continuation of a fight that had been dragging on all week. Now it was Sunday, and Glen was coming over to take everyone out to the lake for a picnic. Granny was refusing to come along even though Mama had packed chicken hash and Jell-O with her in mind.

"Let it go, Anney, and help me with this camera." Aunt Alma had a new Brownie and was determined to document every family occasion she could. "You can't win a fight with

Mama no way. Just leave her alone and let her come to her senses in her own good time."

When Glen arrived, it was the camera that coaxed Granny out of the house and onto the porch with the rest of us. But then it was Glen who didn't want his picture taken. "I an't no movie star," he told Alma, and kept putting his hand up in front of his face when she pointed her camera at him.

"It's that new haircut," Earle joked. "Glen don't want people to know his ears stick out that far. I'm with you, Glen. We're too ugly for photographs. Let the women and kids line up for 'em and leave us alone."

Uncle Earle liked Glen Waddell well enough, but like Granny he didn't think much of the Waddell family. He'd even said so to Glen's face, but the boy had just grinned at him, and that didn't seem right. Even if he didn't get on with his people, Earle believed that Glen shouldn't let anybody bad-mouth them. If they had traded a few punches over it, bled on each other a little and made up after, the whole thing would have felt better to Earle all around. But Glen was a quiet sort who never fought in friendly style. He either gave you that slow grin or went all out and tried to kill you. The latter earned him a little respect, Earle admitted. The cops had had to be called on Glen once at the foundry before he left to take the job at the RC Cola plant. Glen was a grown man, a work-ing man, and he loved Anney Boatwright. Everybody knew that, even Granny.

"Now, Earle, don't you be making no trouble." Granny pushed her hair back behind her ears and smoothed down the wrinkles on her green print blouse. "I want Alma to get pic-tures of everybody. I want a book of family pictures for my cedar chest."

Earle laughed and sneaked around to poke Alma while she was focusing on Granny and Mama, then chased Reese and me out into the yard, catching Reese and throwing her up in the air so high she flapped her arms like she was going to fly. I dodged them and cut through the bushes, ignoring the brambles that caught in the skirt of the new dress Mama had made me wear. From the other side of Earle's truck, I stood and looked back at them, Granny up on the porch with her hesitant uncertain smile, and Mama down on the steps in her new blouse with Glen in that short brush haircut, while Alma posed on the walkway focusing up at them. Everybody looked nervous but determined, Mama stiff in Glen's awkward embrace and Glen almost stumbling off the steps as he tried to turn his face away from the camera. It made my neck go tight just to look at them.

Only Earle and Reese were relaxed, Reese shrieking and giggling, still up in Earle's arms, her legs outstretched as he spun the two of them around and around on the wet grass in the bright sunlight. "Bone, Bone," Reese screamed. "Oh, Bone, help me! Help me!"

"I'm gonna fly you to the stars, little girl," Uncle Earle teased through clenched teeth, making Reese scream all the louder. The words were barely our of his mouth when he slipped in the grass, coming down hard on his butt. His legs flew straight out in front of him, and Reese landed safely on his lap, her scream turning to a giggle as Earle started to curse.

"Goddam, I've ruined these britches now."

"Serve you right if you did," Granny yelled at him. "You could have killed that child. Reese, you get your little dimple ass up here with your mama."

"You come on too, Bone," Mama called to me. "You and Reese come on up here for Alma to get a picture of the four of us together."

"Yeah, come on, girls." Glen held on to Mama with both hands around her waist.

"Smile, now, everyone," called Alma as the shutter clicked.

The spring Mama married Glen Waddell, there were thunderstorms every afternoon and rolling clouds that hung around the foothills north and west to the Smokies. The moon came up with a ghostly halo almost every night, and there was a blue shimmer on the horizon at sunset.

"An't no time to be marrying," Granny announced. "Or planting or building nothing."

"You sure, now, Anney?" Earle must have asked Mama twice before he drove her down to the courthouse in his pickup truck to meet Glen and get the license. It seemed he just couldn't take her ready smile for an answer, even though he agreed to be best man after Glen's brother had refused the honor. He asked her one more time before he let her out of the truck. "You're worse than Granny," Anney told him. "Don't you want to see me settled down and happy?" He gave it up and kissed her out the door.

Granny wasn't surprised when she heard that Great-Grandma Shirley had turned down her invitation to the wedding dinner Aunt Alma organized. The Eustis aunts, Marvella and Maybelle, the ones who insisted they could tell the future from their beans, also skipped the dinner, though Marvella was polite about it. "I know he loves Anney," Marvella told Alma when she came by to collect flowers from their garden. "And sometimes love can change everything."

Maybelle was not so generous. "Yeah, Glen loves Anney. He loves her like a gambler loves a fast racehorse or a desperate man loves whiskey. That kind of love eats a man up. I don't trust that boy, don't want our Anney marrying him."

"But Anney loves Glen," Alma told Maybelle impatiently. "That's the thing you ought to be thinking about. She needs him, needs him like a starving woman needs meat between her teeth, and I an't gonna let nobody take this away from her. Come on, Maybelle, you know there an't no way to say what's gonna happen between a man and a woman. That an't our business anyway, that's theirs."

Alma took Maybelle's hands between her own. "We just got to stand behind our girl, do everything we can to make sure she don't get hurt again."

"Oh, Lord." Maybelle shook her head. "I don't want to fight you, Alma. And maybe you're right. I know how lonely Anney's been. I know." She pulled her hands free, tucked some loose gray hairs up in the bun at the back of her neck, and turned to her sister. "We got to think about this, Marvella. We got to think hard about our girl."

They did what they could. The sisters sent Mama a wedding present, a love knot Marvella had made using some of her own hair, after Maybelle had cut little notches in their rabbits' ears under a new moon, adding the blood to the knot. She set the rabbits loose, and then the two of them tore up half a dozen rows of their beans and buried honeycomb in a piece of lace tablecloth where the beans had flourished. The note with the love knot told Mama that she should keep it under the mattress of the new bed Glen had bought, but Mama sniffed the blood and dried hair, and shook her head over the thing. She couldn't quite bring herself to throw it away, but she put it in one of her flower pots out in the utility room where Glen wouldn't find it stinking up their house.

Reese and I hated the honeymoon. We both thought we would get to go. For weeks before the wedding Mama kept telling us that this was a marriage of all of us, that we were taking Glen as our daddy at the same time she was taking him as a husband. She and Alma had even sewed us up little lace veils to wear as we walked ahead of her at the wedding, Reese carrying flowers while I carried the rings. But Mama and Glen left halfway through Aunt Alma's dinner, with only one quick kiss goodbye.

"Why don't we get to go?" Reese kept demanding while everybody laughed at her. I got so mad I hid in Alma's sewing room and cried myself to sleep in her rocker. When I woke up I was on her daybed with a quilt across me and the house quiet. I got Alma's picture album out and climbed into the rocker. The new pictures from the picnic were at the back. There were half a dozen snapshots of Reese and me, alone, together, and with Granny or Earle. There was only one good one of Glen and Mama, only one in which you could see her smile and his eyes. In most of them, Mama's head was bent so that only her chin showed, or Glen's face was turned away so that you saw only the pale line of his neck and ear under his new haircut. Because of that, perhaps, the good picture was even more startling.

Everything in that picture was clear, sharp, in focus, the contrast so strong you could trace the lines where sunlight sheared off and shade began. There was a blush on Mama's cheek like the shadow of a bird, polka dots on her seersucker blouse, a raised nap on her dark calf-length skirt, and a fine part in her brushed-back blond hair. Mama was beautiful in it, no question, though there was a puffiness under her eyes and a tightness in the muscles of her neck that made her chin stick out. But her smile was full, her eyes clear, and you could see right into her, see how gentle she was in the way her neck angled as she looked past Glen to Reese and me, the way her hands lay open on her lap, the fingers slightly bent as if they were ready to catch the sunlight.

Beside Mama, Glen was half in shadow with his head turned to the side, but the light shone on his smile, his cheek, his strong hands and slender frame. The smile was determined, tight, forceful, the eyes brilliant in the camera lens, gleaming in the sun's glare, the shoulders tense and hunched forward a little, one arm extended to hold Mama close, reaching around her from where he sat to her left. You could not tell a thing about Glen from that picture, except that he was a good-looking man, strong and happy to be holding his woman. Mama's eyes were soft with old hurt and new hope; Glen's eyes told nothing. The man's image was as flat and empty as a sheet of tin in the sun, throwing back heat and light, but no details—not one clear line of who he really was behind those eyes.

I tried to imagine what it would be like to live with him once the honeymoon was past. I looked at the picture again and remembered the day of the picnic, the way he kept pulling Mama back against him, his hands cupped over her belly possessively. I had heard Alma tease Mama the day before the wedding that she better hurry up and get married before she started showing. Mama had gotten all upset, demanding to know how Alma had found out she was pregnant. I wondered if she had told Glen yet.

"Come on, girls." Glen's voice when he called Reese and me for the picture had had a loud impatient note I had never heard before. I'd come back around Earle's truck at a walk and looked into his face carefully. Yes, he knew. He was so pleased with himself, he looked swollen with satisfaction under that terrible haircut. Mama had said he wanted her to have his son, and it looked to me like he was sure he had it on the way.

I sat in that rocker with those pictures until morning

woke the house and Aunt Alma came to check on me. I ran my fingers over Reese's baby smile on one, traced Earle's dark hair on another, examined just how far Granny's chin pushed out under her lower lip, and looked back to my own face in each to see how the camera had seen me—my eyes like Mama's eyes, darker but open as hers, my smile fiercer and wider than Reese's, and my body in motion across Alma's yard like an animal leaping into the air.

Glen was like a boy about the baby, grinning and boasting and putting his palms flat on Mama's stomach every chance he could to feel his son kick. His son—he never even entertained the notion Mama might deliver a girl. No, this would be his boy, Glen was sure. He bought a crib and a new layette set on time payments, put them in their bedroom, and filled the crib with toys a boy baby would love. "My boy's gonna look like the best of me and Anney," he told everyone insistently, as if by saying it often enough he could make it so. He even went out to Aunt Maybelle and Aunt Marvella's house with a gift of sweet corn for the rabbits, just so he could look into their eyes when he said "a boy" and hear them say it back to him when they took the corn.

"They said it was a boy," he told Earle later over pinto beans and cornbread at Aunt Ruth's house—the first evidence he'd ever given that he believed in the Eustis aunts' claim to women's magic. He was bursting with pride.

"Well, goddam, Glen. Congratulations." Earle kept his face carefully neutral.

"Never come between a man and his ambitions," he told Uncle Beau after Glen had gone. "Glen ever gets the notion that anybody messed up his chance of getting a boy child out of Anney, and he's gonna go plumb crazy."

"A man should never put his ambition in a woman's belly." Beau didn't like Glen much at all, couldn't, he admitted, since he never trusted a man who didn't drink, and Glen was as close to a teetotaler as the family had ever seen. Beau spit out the side of his mouth. "Serve him right if she gave him another girl."

Uncle Nevil harrumphed, pouring them each a short glass of his home stock. Nevil never wasted words when he could grunt, or a grunt when he could move his hands. He was supposed to be the quietest man in Greenville County, and his wife, Fay, was said to be the fattest woman. "The two of them are more like furniture than anything," Granny had once said. "Just taking up space and shedding dust like a chifforobe or a couch." Nevil and Fay had heard her and in their quiet way refused to be in the same room with her ever again. It complicated family gatherings, but not too much. As Aunt Alma told everybody, Nevil wasn't any great loss to conversation anyway.

It was a surprise, then, when Nevil sipped his whiskey, lifted his head, and spoke so clearly he could be heard out on the porch. "Me, I'm hoping Anney does give him a son, half a dozen sons while she's at it. That Glen's got something about him. I almost like him, but the boy could turn like whiskey in a bad barrel, and I'm hoping he don't. Anney's had enough trouble in her life." He sipped again and shut his mouth back to its usual flat line.

Earle and Beau stared at him, unsure whether to laugh or curse, but finally they dropped their glances into their cups. It was true enough, they both agreed. Anney deserved an end to trouble in her life.

The night Mama went into labor, Glen packed the Pontiac with blankets and Cokes for Reese and me, and parked out in the hospital lot to wait. He'd been warned it was going to take a while for the baby to come, and when he couldn't stand pacing the halls anymore, he came down to smoke cigarettes and listen to music on the car radio while Reese and I napped in the backseat. At some point well before dawn, when it was still dark and cold, he reached across the seat to tug my shoulder and pull me up front with him. He gave me some Coke and half a Baby Ruth and told me he'd been in to check a little earlier and Mama was doing fine.

"Fine." I blinked at him and nodded, unsure what I was supposed to do or say. He smoked fiercely, exhaling out the top of the window where he'd opened it just a few inches, and talking to me like I was a grown-up. "I know she's worried," he said. "She thinks if it's a girl, I won't love it. But it will be our baby, and if it's a girl, we can make another soon enough. I'll have my son. Anney and I will have our boy. I know it. I know."

He talked on, whispering quietly, sometimes so softly I could not understand him. I pulled my blanket around me and watched the sprinkling of stars visible just over the tall fir trees at the edge of the lot. The song playing low on the radio was a Kitty Wells tune that Mama liked. I rocked my head to the music and watched the night. I was thinking about the baby Mama was having, wondering what it might be like, if maybe it wouldn't be a girl. What were they going to name it? Glen Junior, if it was a boy? They had never said. Mama thought it was unlucky to choose a name for a baby till it was born.

Glen put his hand on my neck, and the stars seemed to wink at me. I wasn't used to him touching me, so I hugged my blanket and held still. He slid out from behind the steering wheel a little and pulled me up on his lap. He started humming to the music, shifting me a little on his thighs. I turned my face up to look into his eyes. There were only a few lights on in the parking lot, but the red and yellow dials on the radio shone on his face. He smiled, and for the first time I saw the smile in his eyes as plain as the one on his mouth. He pushed my skirt to the side and slid his left hand down between my legs, up against my cotton panties. He began to rock me then, between his stomach and his wrist, his fingers fumbling at his britches.

It made me afraid, his big hand between my legs and his eyes glittering in the dim light. He started talking again, telling me Mama was going to be all right, that he loved me, that we were all going to be so happy. Happy. His hand was

46

hard, the ridge of his wristbone pushing in and hurting me. I looked straight ahead through the windshield, too afraid to cry, or shake, or wiggle, too afraid to move at all.

He kept saying, "It's gonna be all right." He kept rocking me, breathing through his mouth and staring straight ahead. I could see his reflection in the windshield. Dawn began to filter through the trees, making everything bright and cold. His hand dug in further. He was holding himself in his fingers. I knew what it was under his hand. I'd seen my cousins naked, laughing, shaking their things and joking, but this was a mystery, scary and hard. His sweat running down his arms to my skin smelled strong and nasty. He grunted, squeezed my thighs between his arm and his legs. His chin pressed down on my head and his hips pushed up at the same time. He was hurting me, hurting me!

I sobbed once, and he dropped back down and let go of me. I bit my lips and held still. He brought his hand up to wipe it on the blanket, and I could smell something strange and bitter on his fingers. I pulled away, and that made him laugh. He kept laughing as he scrubbed his fingers against the blanket. Then he lifted me slightly, turning me so he could look into my face. The light was gray and pearly, the air wet and marble-cold, Glen's face the only thing pink and warm in sight. He smiled at me again, but this time the smile was not in his eyes. His eyes had gone dark and empty again, and my insides started to shake with fear.

He wrapped the blanket around me tight and put me back with Reese in the nest of blankets and pillows he'd built up so many hours ago. I hunched my shoulders against the seat and watched Glen's head in the gray light, his short hairs bristly and stiff. He lit another cigarette and started humming again. He looked back once and I quickly closed my eyes, then was too afraid to open them again. His hum went on in time to the soft radio music, and the smell of Pall Malls began to soothe me. I didn't know I was falling asleep until I woke up in the bright gray light of full morning.

Glen was gone, the car still and cold. There was an ache between my legs, but I wasn't afraid in the daylight. I sat up and looked out on gray clouds and dew-drenched fir branches. The asphalt looked wet and dark. There were a few nurses going in and out the emergency-room doors, talking in low mumbly tones. I breathed through my mouth and watched as more and more people drove into the lot, wondering if I had dreamed that whole early-morning scene. I kept squeezing my thighs together, feeling the soreness, and trying to imagine how I could have bruised myself if it had been a dream.

When Glen came out of the emergency room, the doors swung back like a shot in the morning air. His face was rigid, his legs stiff, his hands clamped together in front of him, twisting and twisting. I looked into that face and knew it had not been a dream. I pulled Reese up against me, ignoring her soft protesting cry. Glen climbed in the car and slammed the door so hard Reese woke up with a jerk. She twisted her head like a baby bird, looking from me to Glen's neck and back again. We sat still, waiting.

He said, "Your mama's gonna be all right." He paused.

"But she an't gonna have no more babies." He put his hands on the steering wheel, leaned forward, pushed his mouth against his fingers.

He said, "My baby's dead. My boy. My boy."

I wrapped my arms around Reese and held on, while in the front seat, Glen just sobbed and cried.

After Mama got home from the hospital, her sisters came around to see us every day. Aunt Ruth had been in the hospital with what Granny called female trouble only a few weeks before, and still wasn't well enough to do much but sit with Mama for an hour or two and hold her hand, but she called every morning. Aunt Alma practically moved in and took over, making Mama stay in bed, doing all the cooking, and fixing beef and bean stew. "To put some iron back in your blood, honey," she said.

Aunt Raylene showed up in her overalls and low boots to clean the house from one end to the other, going so far as to make Reese and me help her move furniture out in the yard for the sun to warm it. When she went in to change the sheets on Mama's bed, she lifted Mama easily and carried her out to sit on the couch in the fresh air. Everyone stepped around Glen like he was another chair or table, occasionally giving him a quick hug or squeeze on the shoulder. He didn't respond, just shifted from the table to the porch when Raylene started sweeping. When Nevil and Earle came over, he stood out in the yard with them and drank until his shoulders started to go up and down in fierce suppressed sobs and they looked away to spare him being embarrassed.

I watched him closely, staying out in the yard as much as I could, squatting down in the bushes where I hoped no one could see me. I put my chin on my knees and hugged myself into a tight curled ball. Mama's face had been so pale when they brought her home, her eyes enormous and unblinking. She had barely looked at me when I tried to climb up in her lap, just bit her lips and let Aunt Alma pull me away. I cried until Aunt Raylene took me out in her truck and rocked me to sleep with a damp washcloth on my eyes.

"Your mama's gonna need a little time," she told me. "Then she's gonna need you more than she ever has. When a woman loses a baby, she needs to know that her other babies are well and happy. You be happy for her, Bone. You let your mama know you are happy so she can heal her heart."

They did name him Glen Junior, Reese told me. She had heard Aunt Ruth and Aunt Alma talking. They had buried the baby in the big Boatwright plot Great-grandma Shirley owned, with the four boys Granny had lost and Ruth's stillborn girls and Alma's first boy. Glen had wanted a plot of his own but had no money to buy one, and that seemed to be the thing that finally broke his grief and turned it to rage. His face was swollen with crying and gray with no sleep. He found a house over by the JC Penney mill near the railroad tracks and came home to announce we were moving. Aunt Alma was outraged he'd take us so far away, but Mama just nodded and asked Raylene to help her pack.

"It'll be all right," she told Reese and me.

Glen put his arms around Mama and glared at Aunt Alma. "We don't need nobody else," he whispered. "We'll do just fine on our own."

I n the rented house, well away from the rest of the family, Daddy Glen promised Mama that when they had enough money put by, he was going to adopt Reese and me. We were a family, and he was our daddy now, he kept saying. Mama held on to his hands and nodded wordlessly. "These are my girls," he told her. "I'm going to make sure they grow up to be something special. Whatever I have to do." She smiled and kissed him, her open mouth pressing his lips hungrily.

Reese put her fat little hands on his arm and said, "Daddy," and the two of them lifted her up between them.

"Daddy," I tried to say, but it sounded funny in my head. I remembered those moments in the hospital parking lot like a bad dream, hazy and shadowed. When Daddy Glen looked at me, I saw no sign that he ever thought about it at all. Maybe it had not happened. Maybe he really did love us. I wanted him to love us. I wanted to be able to love him. I wanted him to pick me up gently and tell Mama again how much he loved us all. I wanted to be locked with Reese in the safe circle of their arms.

I stood still and felt my eyes fill with tears. Mama pulled away from Daddy Glen and gathered me up. Over her shoulder I saw Daddy Glen's icy blue eyes watching us, his mouth a set straight line. He shook himself and looked away. I held on to Mama with fingers as hard and cold as iron.

Daddy Glen didn't like us listening to all those stories Granny and Aunt Alma were always telling over and over again. "I'll tell you who you are," he said. "You're mine now, an't just Boatwrights." He told us about his daddy, Mr. Bodine Waddell, who owned the Sunshine Dairy, and about his brothers. His oldest brother, Daryl, had lost his bid for district attorney, but his law firm was building a reputation as the one to hire if you wanted a city contract. His older brother, James, was about to open up his dental office, and starting next year we'd go to him to get our teeth fixed.

"Granny says we got good teeth," I told Daddy Glen. "She says the one thing God gave the Boatwrights is hard, sharp teeth."

"And you believe everything she says, don't you?" His eyes sank into the wrinkles of his squint, shiny as mica in sunlight, while his mouth twisted so that one side of his grin was drawn up. He looked as if he was about to laugh, but instead he just pursed his lips and spat.

"Your granny is the worst kind of liar. That old woman wouldn't tell the truth if she knew it." He put his hand under my chin, his big, blunt fingers pressing once lightly and then pulling away. "You stay clear of that old woman. I'll tell you what's true. You're mine now. You and Reese just keep your distance from her."

I didn't trust Daddy Glen, didn't believe him when he said all

Granny's stories were lies, but I never could be sure which of the things she told me were true and which she just wished were true, stories good enough to keep even if they were three-quarters false. All the Boatwrights told stories, it was one of the things we were known for, and what one cousin swore was gospel, another swore just as fiercely was an unqualified lie. Raylene was always telling people that we had a little of the tarbrush on us, but the way she grinned when she said it could have meant she was lying to make somebody mad, or maybe she just talked that way because she was crazy angry to start out.

"What's it mean?" I asked Ruth's youngest boy, Butch.

"Means we got some colored people somewhere back up the line." He grinned at me. "Means Raylene's a pisser. She'll say anything, and everybody knows it."

I thought about that a while, and then asked anyway. "Do we?" I watched his smile widen slowly into a smirk.

Butch was just one year older than me, and I knew I could ask him anything—not like Garvey or Grey or Aunt Ruth's other boys. They were always trying to pretend they were more grown-up than they were, and I could never tell what might start them acting weird. Butch was different—a little soft, not put together too tightly, some people said.

"The boy don't act like a Boatwright," was the way Uncle Earle put it. "Don't seem to have a temper in him at all. And he's got a right strange sense of humor. Don't know what's serious."

But I loved Butch the best of all my cousins. I could talk to Butch, ask him things, and most of the time he'd purse his lips, squint, and drawl me an answer that was sure to be trustworthy—that is, if he wasn't in one of his teasing funny moods. Sometimes his answers would sound strange if plausible, and it wasn't till much later that I'd figure the joke in what he'd said.

So when Butch said, "Colored, oh yes, we got colored," I wasn't sure if he was kidding or not. He pushed his white-blond hair back behind his ears and squinted and grinned right into my face. "Boatwrights got everything—all colors, all types, all persuasions. But the thing is"—he sucked his lower lip up between his teeth and looked around to make sure we were alone—"Boatwright women got caustic pussy. Kills off or messes up everything goes in or out their legs, except purebred Boatwright babies and rock-hard Boatwright men. And even with us, it burns off anything looks the least bit unusual, polishes babies up so they all pretty much look alike, like we been rinsed in bleach as we're born.

" 'Cept you, of course, all black-headed and strange." His face became expressionless, serious, intent. "But that's because you got a man-type part of you. Rock-hard and nasty and immune to harm. But hell, Boatwright women come out that way sometimes." I stared at him, open-mouthed and fascinated, pretty sure he was shitting me but taken with it all anyway. His tongue slipped out between his lips, and there might have been the beginning of a grin in his eyes.

"Naaaa," I hissed at Butch. "Naaaa!"

People were crazy on the subject of color, I knew, and it was true that one or two of the cousins had kinky hair and took some teasing for it, enough that everyone was a little tender about it. Except for Granny, people didn't even want to talk about our Cherokee side. Michael Yarboro swore to me that Cherokees were niggers anyway, said Indians didn't take care who they married like white folks did.

"Oh, lots of care they take," Aunt Alma hooted. "The Yarboros been drowning girls and newborns for surely two hundred years." Butch didn't have to tell me about that one. The Yarboro boys were talked about worse than my uncles, and everybody knew they were all crazy. When I started school, one of the Yarboro cousins, a skinny rat-faced girl from the Methodist district, had called me a nigger after I pushed her away from the chair I'd taken for mine. She'd sworn I was as dark and wild as any child "born on the wrong side of the porch," which I took to be another way of calling me a bastard, so I poked her in the eye. It had gotten me in trouble but persuaded her to stay away from me. I didn't worry too much about what people thought of my temper. A reputation for quick rages wasn't necessarily a disadvantage. It could do you some good. Daddy Glen's reputation for a hot temper made people very careful how they talked to him.

Reese's daddy's people lived back up in the hills above Greenville. Her grandmother had a farm off the Ashley Highway, but we rarely went there to visit. Mrs. Parsons didn't seem to like Mama, though she was always pulling out some present for Reese and never failed to give me a nod of welcome. I was jealous of Reese for having Mrs. Parsons as a grandmother, since Mrs. Parsons looked like one in a way my granny never did. She looked like a granny you'd read about or see in a movie. I loved her thick gray-and-white braids, pinned together at the back of her neck, loved the stinky old cow that lived in a shed behind her four-room shotgun house, and the sweet red tomatoes and pulpy green peas she grew over near her creek. Mrs. Parsons wore blue gingham aprons and faded black dresses with long sleeves she would roll back to her elbows. My granny wore sleeveless print dresses that showed the sides of her loose white breasts and hitched up on her hips. She kept her thin gray hair curled tight in a permanent wave, tying it back with string when it went limp in the heat. She wore dark red lipstick that invariably smeared down onto her knobby chin, and she was always spitting snuff and cursing. Mrs. Parsons would talk sadly about her lost boys and her distant daughter while shelling peas into a galvanized bucket. My granny would get so mad she'd start throwing furniture out the screen door. She was always moving out of Aunt Ruth's or Aunt Alma's house to go stay with one of her sisters, and threatening to burn down whichever place she had left behind. I loved Granny, but I imagined Mrs. Parsons might be a better choice for a grandmother, and sometimes when we went to visit I'd pretend she was mine.

Every time we went to see Mrs. Parsons, Daddy Glen would whine that Mama shouldn't be running up there to that hateful old woman. "I don't like that old biddy telling stories on you," he kept saying, imagining that Grandma Parsons damned him and Mama as soon as Mama was out of the sound of her voice. I didn't bother to tell him that she never spoke about them at all, that she talked about everyday stuff, how the garden was going or the weather or the cow's disposition. The only grown-up she ever mentioned was Reese's daddy, Lyle, and then only to say Reese had his smile—the soft, slow baby grin she told us had made Lyle the best-loved boy in the county. It was Mama who told us Lyle had been the youngest of three boys, and that the two others had died within a year of Grandma Parsons's favorite. She told us to be kind to Mrs. Parsons, who was left with only one daughter she never saw and a couple of brothers who were waiting to sell off her land when she died.

"Reese should get a share of that land," Daddy Glen told Mama one autumn afternoon when we came back from visiting up in the hills. "Not that she'll ever need anything from those stuck-up mountain people." He rubbed at the back of his neck and looked out through the kitchen window as if he were looking into the future. "Still, it's only right she gets what her daddy would have wanted her to have. You let me deal with them. I'll take care of our girl."

When Grandma Parsons's brother, Matthew, came by with some papers for Mama to sign, Daddy Glen met him at the door and took the papers in hand. "We'll just look at these," he said loudly, and then walked him out to the edge of the property, lowering his voice so we couldn't hear what he said. Mama bit her lips and watched as the stiff-backed Matthew glared at Daddy Glen and then climbed into his truck. She went out as the truck drove off.

"Honey, you didn't say nothing rude to him, did you?"

Daddy Glen turned to her with a sweet little smile. He put his arm around her and kissed her on the temple. "Don't you worry," he said, and gave her a quick pat on the behind. "I know what I'm doing. You got to be clear with these people, real clear." He looked so pleased with himself that he couldn't stop grinning. "I know their type. I sure do."

Mama frowned, and he gave her a little shake. "Now, don't you go signing none of those papers when I'm not here. I'm telling you, you don't know what they might be stealing from you. Let me handle it." She nodded nervously, shooing us back in the house for dinner.

Grandma Parsons called that night, but Daddy Glen took the phone and talked to her in a quiet husky voice that reminded me of the way Uncle Nevil would sometimes whisper from behind his cupped hand. "Uh-huh," he said. "That's right."

Mama watched for a moment and then stepped outside to smoke in the shelter of the side porch. I followed her out and leaned into her hip. Her hand stroked down the back of my head, smoothing out my hair. Her face was lit by the reflection from the streetlight, her mouth turned down and her eyes sad. I could tell she was worried.

"It'll be okay," I whispered up at her, and she smiled back down at me.

"Yeah, probably," she said. "And if it won't, it just won't. Sometimes, Bone, you got to do things you wish you didn't have to, and I don't want to hurt that old woman. I really don't. But Glen needs to take care of this, you understand? He needs to do it, and I've got to let him." She ground out the cigarette under her heel but didn't go back inside until Daddy Glen got off the phone.

"Now they understand." He tapped his forefinger on Reese's nose happily and made her giggle. "They know how it's gonna be now, for sure."

Two weeks later Grandma Parsons showed up late Sunday afternoon while Daddy Glen was over at his brother James's new office helping the painting crew put up shelves. "Two hundred and fifty dollars," she told Mama quickly when she got out of Matthew's truck. He'd driven her down to see us but wouldn't get out himself. "It's due you since Lyle was in the army for six months before they found out he had bad feet. Like I told your husband, they sent it over to me and wouldn't make it out to you unless you filed those papers. But I've brought it down to you in cash. I never should have got it, but Lyle still had me listed as his only family, just never got around to changing it, I suppose. I told them it should rightly go to you and Reese. I did, but they never paid me no mind." She looked up once at Mama and then down at Reese, who had run up to grab her around the hips. Her face was tense, and her fingers shook as she raked them through Reese's curls.

"You gonna get a lot of money then, Grandma?" Reese asked her.

"No, child. And I don't care."

"You come on in, Mrs. Parsons." Mama looked embarrassed, her fingers pulling at the belt loops of her shirtwaist dress. "Let me get you some ice tea, and you can sit with your grandchild a while."

Mrs. Parsons looked like she was going to cry. "I thought maybe you weren't gonna let me see her no more."

"Oh God!" Mama took Mrs. Parsons by the shoulders and pulled her into a quick embrace. "I wouldn't do that. I wouldn't let nobody else do that either. You can see Reese anytime you want. You know how much she loves you."

The two of them swayed slightly, Mrs. Parsons stiffly as if she was still unsure of her welcome and Mama as if she could barely hold in all the other things she wanted to say. Grandma Parsons's brother kept his face turned away, smoking out the window of his truck. I kept close to Mama and watched the muscles in his neck jump as the two women sniffed and cleared their throats.

"Well." Mrs. Parsons licked her lips. "Maybe I'll just come in a minute, have a little water before we start back."

"You could stay for dinner." Mama's face was flushed red and getting darker as I watched.

"Well, no, we couldn't do that." Mrs. Parsons glanced over at her brother's shoulder, but he didn't turn to look at her. "We do have to get back. I'll just stay a minute or two."

It wasn't until she was sitting on Mama's Sears sofa, with Reese drawn up between her legs and the envelope with the money "from the insurance" passed over to Mama, that Grandma Parsons relaxed a little. She got her brush out so she could pull the tangles out of Reese's white-blond hair and keep her hands busy. "Your hair was red as fire when you were born," she told Reese. "Now it's as white as your daddy's was."

Reese liked being told she looked like her daddy, and she kept his picture hidden in her underwear drawer where Daddy Glen wouldn't see it and get his feelings hurt. Now and then, I'd go get it out myself, look into that grinning boy's face that had nothing to do with me, and get all hot and tight with jealousy. Lyle had been as pretty as a girl and so white-blond he could have been a model in magazines. Reese had hair as fine as Lyle's and a smile that came easy and fast, but she had too the Boatwrights' narrow face and long skinny neck. Still, I envied the way she could look from that picture to Mama's face to Grandma Parsons's bent shoulders and guess how she might still change before she grew up. She had another family, another side of herself to think about, something more than Mama and me and the Boatwrights. Reese could choose something different for herself and be someone else altogether.

"Oh, Reese'll likely go dark." Mama spoke hesitantly, as if she didn't want to argue but didn't want to chance any misunderstanding. "Might even go red again."

"She might, but she might not. Among our people hair stays blond sometimes." Mrs. Parsons tried to smile at Mama, but her face didn't soften until she looked down at Reese. I was sitting on the arm of the sofa next to Mama, where I could look out the window to see the waiting truck and the empty road all the way up to the next intersection. I kept listening for the sound of the Pontiac, hoping not to hear it. Daddy Glen might come home while Mrs. Parsons was still here, and

I knew Mama was worried about that, her hands pulling again at her belt loops nervously.

Mrs. Parsons looked over at Mama's hands and then spoke carefully. "That money's all there's gonna be, I'm afraid. My property an't worth much, and truth is I signed it over to Matthew just after my boys died. Matthew's promised to take care of me, and I trust that he will. Thing is, Lyle didn't have no title to the land and no other insurance as far as we know."

Mama shook her head once and looked up directly into Mrs. Parsons's face. "I know he didn't have nothing," she said. "I knew that when he died, and it's never mattered to me. Didn't expect his death benefit, to tell you the truth. Thought he wasn't entitled to nothing from the army." Her face looked sad but not so stiff as it had. Mrs. Parsons's face was a match for hers.

"I wish you would get lots and lots of money from the insurance." Reese wiggled happily in Grandma Parsons's arms and beamed at all of us.

"Oh, I don't need no money, child." Grandma Parsons laughed and pushed herself up off the couch. "I'm afraid I've got to get going, Anney. It's a long trip for me to get home." I looked closely at Mama to see if she had heard the old woman say her name, but Mama was already up and reaching for Mrs. Parsons's glass.

"Don't you want more?" Mama was saying as she headed for the kitchen. Mrs. Parsons shook her head and said no while hanging on to Reese. I saw Mama's shoulders relax a little as she turned to come back to us. The road outside was still quiet.

Grandma Parsons bent over to hug Reese tightly one more time. "You just remember, honey, I got the best of Lyle when I got you," she told her. That sounded strange to me, as if she'd hatched my baby sister herself off her boy's dead frame. But Reese grinned like a princess and wiggled her toes into the nap of the rug. She followed Grandma Parsons out to the truck begging her to stay over.

"Reese, be good," Mama told her. "You can see your grandma next month when we go up to her place."

"You will come?" Mrs. Parsons looked sad and nervous all over again.

"We'll come." Mama's voice was emphatic, but I saw her eyes flick once up the road as she spoke. Mrs. Parsons nodded brusquely and climbed in the truck. Her brother never said a word, just started the engine and put it in gear. Reese was waving fiercely even before Matthew gunned the engine. I saw Mrs. Parsons wipe her eyes as the truck pulled away, and then I saw the Pontiac come around the corner of the intersection up the road. Mama's hands curled into fists and pulled up in front of her belly. I leaned in close to her and watched the Pontiac as it edged slowly past the truck. When it reached us, Daddy Glen leaned out the window. He looked back up the road and then over at Mama.

"You didn't sign nothing?" he demanded.

"No, Glen." I felt Mama's hips shift awkwardly as she spoke. I looked up to watch her face as her mouth shifted into an equally awkward stubborn smile. "You know I wouldn't sign anything that you hadn't looked at first."

Daddy Glen smiled as if that satisfied him. I let my air out carefully. Reese went on waving though the truck was long gone. I hooked my thumbs in the belt loops of my jeans and stood by her until Mama and Daddy Glen went back into the house.

"He's quiet, but you make Glen mad and he'll knock you down," Uncle Earle said good-naturedly. "Boy uses those hands of his like pickaxes." If they thought we weren't near enough to hear, Earle and Beau would go on about Daddy Glen's other parts.

"He gets crazy when he's angry," they laughed. "Use his dick if he can't reach you with his arms, and that'll cripple you fast enough." I was too young to understand what they meant, why they laughed so mean and joked that no woman would ever leave Daddy Glen, or roared and spat comparing the size of his nose to his toes to his fingers.

"Man's got a horse dick," Butch boasted to other boys, and that I understood. But it wasn't Daddy Glen's sex that made me nervous. It was those hands, the restless way the fingers would flex and curl while he watched me lean close to Mama. He was always watching me, it seemed, calling me to him whenever Mama and I would start talking, sending me to get him a glass of ice tea or a fresh pack of cigarettes out of the freezer, where he kept his cartons so they wouldn't go stale in the summer heat. Mama told me I should show him that I loved him, but no matter how hard I tried, I never moved fast enough for him.

"That child an't never gonna love me," he complained tearfully to Mama one afternoon.

"Oh, Glen, don't say that." Mama's voice was thin and shaky, as if she were afraid he was right. "Bone loves you, honey." She kissed his cheek, put her hands on either side of his face, and kissed his lips. "She loves you. We all love you." Daddy Glen pulled her down to him and sighed softly as she kissed his eyelids and then rubbed her cheeks against his.

I ran outside. Dinner would be late, or we'd wind up going out for hamburgers. Whenever they started kissing on the couch, they'd go in the bedroom and shut the door for an hour at least. When they came out Daddy Glen would be smiling and easy in his body. Mama would be sleepy-eyed and soft all over, the pink in her face fresh and delicate.

"They sure like to do it a lot," Reese told Alma disgustedly. But Alma just laughed.

"Everybody does, girl, everybody does." She swatted lightly at the seat of Reese's jeans and hugged me to her side. "Don't make no mistake about that. Love is just about the best thing we've got that don't cost money or make you sick to your stomach. You'll see. Wait till you get a little bigger. You'll see."

Reese grimaced and wiggled uncomfortably. "Mushy stuff," she yelled as she ran off. "All that mushy stuff. I an't gonna have none of it."

Aunt Alma laughed carelessly. I pulled away from her and went after Reese. It *was* mushy. Mama and Daddy Glen always hugging and rubbing on each other, but it was powerful too. Sex. Was that what Daddy Glen had been doing to me in the parking lot? Was it what I had started doing to myself whenever I was alone in the afternoons? I would imagine being tied up and put in a haystack while someone set the dry stale straw ablaze. I would picture it perfectly while rocking on my hand. The daydream was about struggling to get free while the fire burned hotter and closer. I am not sure if I came when the fire reached me or after I had imagined escaping it. But I came. I orgasmed on my hand to the dream of fire.

Daddy Glen didn't do too well at RC Cola. He kept getting transferred to different routes or having to pay for breakage, and no matter how hard he and Mama worked, there never seemed to be enough money to pay the bills. He kept telling Mama that sooner or later his brother would pay him for all the work he'd done, but even after the offices of James Waddell, D.D.S., were open and busy, James never mentioned it.

"Maybe you better ask James for that money he was gonna give you," Mama finally suggested the day Daddy Glen came home to say he'd been laid off.

"I can't do that." Glen's face seemed to squeeze in on itself as he ran his hands down from his hairline to his neck, wiping sweat off the shadowy stubble on his cheeks and then resting his chin on his fingertips as if he were praying. "Oh, Lord God, no, I can't do that. I'd rather starve." His eyes looked shrunken and his chin stuck out. He looked everywhere but over at Mama where she sat. Instinctively I put down the glass I'd been rinsing and stepped out of the kitchen into the hall where he couldn't see me without turning around.

"Glen, honey." Mama leaned forward. "I know it's hard,

but James is your brother, and baby, we're just about broke. We're not gonna have the rent if you don't get it from him."

"Anney, you don't understand." Daddy Glen brought his hands up to cover his face completely. "James never said nothing about paying me at all. Hell, he never even asked my help. I just went over there, just did it. I never talked to him about money. I couldn't. Hell, I don't even think he wanted my help nohow."

Glen brought both his fists down hard on his thighs, pounding them half a dozen times before he lifted his hands and held them in front of him, open and extended. "I'm sorry, Anney. God, I'm so sorry." Tears pooled in his eyes and slid down his cheeks. His hands began to shake. "But it an't just hard. It's impossible. I can't ask James for nothing. I can't ask none of them for shit. It would kill me."

Mama sighed and looked away. "Well . . ." She hesitated and then reached out to take the hands that still hung in the air. "Well, we'll just see, then. There's other jobs, other things we can do. We can get Earle's help to move, maybe stay with Alma. Something." She looked into Glen's face, but whatever she hoped to see there didn't come, her eyes kept shifting away, then back.

"Oh, Glen. Baby, it'll be all right. We'll do what we have to do. Don't you worry."

After that things seemed to move irreversibly forward. We moved and then moved again. We lived in no one house more than eight months. Rented houses; houses leased with an option to buy; shared houses on the city limits; brick and stucco and a promise to buy; friends of friends who knew somebody had a place standing empty; houses where the owner lived downstairs, next door, next block over, or was a friend of a man had an eye on Mama, or knew somebody who knew Daddy Glen's daddy, or had hired one of the uncles for a short piece of work; or twice—Jesus, *twice*—brand-new houses clean and bought on time we didn't have.

Moving had no season, was all seasons, crossed time like

a train with no schedule. We moved so often our mail never caught up with us, moved sometimes before we'd even gotten properly unpacked or I'd learned the names of all the teachers at my new school. Moving gave me a sense of time passing and everything sliding, as if nothing could be held on to anyway. It made me feel ghostly, unreal and unimportant, like a box that goes missing and then turns up but you realize you never needed anything in it anyway. We moved so often Mama learned to keep the newspapers in the cardboard dish barrels, the pads and cords and sturdy boxes.

"Don't throw that away. I'll need that again before long."

The lines in Mama's face sank deeper with every move, every failed chance, every "make do" and "try again." It got to where I hated moving worse than anything, and one hot summer day I took a butcher knife and chopped holes in Mama's dish barrels, though all that came of it was a swat across the seat and the same old line.

"Don't you know how much that cost?"

I knew to the penny what everything cost. Late on Sunday afternoons, Mama always sat at the kitchen table counting change out of her pocketbook and juggling bills, deciding which could not be paid, not yet, anyway. Rent was eighty dollars a month, too much by far when Daddy Glen had been bringing home only sixty dollars a week. Groceries ran as much as the rent, and that was only because we got vegetables from my aunts' gardens and discount meat from the man who sold ground beef and chicken to the diner. Then there were the clothes Reese and I were always needing, uniforms for Mama and Daddy Glen, and shoes. Shoes were the worst. Dresses could be passed on from cousins or picked up now and then at church rummage sales. But shoes wore out or were outgrown at a frightening rate. Until the ringworm got so dangerous, we went barefoot all summer long.

Though I had never complained before, suddenly I wanted new shoes, patent-leather Mary Janes—not the cheap blue canvas sneakers I was always getting at $1.98 every seven months or so. I wasn't a baby anymore, I was eight, then nine years old, growing up. In one year I went from compliant and quiet to loud and insistent, demanding shoes like the kids at school wore. I wanted the ones with little tassels behind the toes but was willing to settle for saddle oxfords. I knew there was no chance of getting a pair of those classy little-girl patent-leathers with the short pointy heels, but I looked at them longingly anyway. Mama just laughed and bought me penny loafers.

"Who do you think we are, girl?" she said. "We an't the people who buy things for show."

I couldn't help it. Just for a change, I wished we could have things like other people, wished we could complain for no reason but the pleasure of bitching and act like the trash we were supposed to be, instead of watching how we behaved all the time. But Mama's laughter shamed me. I wore the penny loafers with only token protest.

"Don't worry about it," Mama's friend Mab told her. "Children are happier with dirt between their toes." But I noticed that her girls turned up for school in saddle oxfords, and at church in patent-leather pumps, and sniffed at Reese and me in our discount loafers. I wasn't sure what Mama noticed, what she could afford to notice, but when I sat with her on Sunday afternoon and watched her run down her columns of figures, I suspected that she saw everything and hated it all. She'd look out at my flushed and sweating stepfather muscling the lawnmower around the edges of the yard and sigh into her coffee cup.

"We an't gonna be able to stay here," she'd say, and I knew it was about time to move again.

One winter we spent three months staying over with Aunt Alma, who had bought a new house on no money down. None of us expected her to keep it, and the bank filed papers on it almost as soon as we'd arrived. Something happened to me, something I had never felt before and did not know how to fight. Anger hit me like a baseball coming hard and fast off a new bat. The first day at the district school the teacher pursed her lips and asked me my name, and that anger came around and stomped on my belly and throat. I saw tired patience in her eyes, a little shine of pity, and a contempt as old as the red dust hills I could see through the windows of her classroom. I opened my lips but could not speak.

"What's your name, now, honey?" the woman asked me again, speaking slowly, as if she suspected I was not quite bright. The anger lifted in me and became rage.

"Roseanne," I answered as blithely as if I'd never been called anything else. I smiled at her like a Roseanne. "Roseanne Carter. My family's from Atlanta, just moved up here." I went on lightly, talking about the school I'd gone to in Atlanta, making it up as I went along, and smiling wider as she kept nodding at me.

It scared me that it was so easy—my records, after all, had not caught up with me—that people thought I could be a Roseanne Carter from Atlanta, a city I had never visited. Everyone believed me, and I enjoyed a brief popularity as someone from a big city who could tell big-city stories. It was astonishing, but no one in my family found out I had told such a lie. Still, it was a relief when we moved that time and I went off to a new school under my real name. For months after, though, I dreamed that someone came up to me and called me Roseanne, that the school records finally exposed me or one of those teachers turned up at my new school. "Why'd you tell such a lie?" they asked me in the dream, and I could not answer them. I didn't know. I really didn't know.

One month, Earle announced that he had finally sold that old wallhanger Beau had foisted off on him to some fool from Greenwood who couldn't tell the difference between a decent shotgun and a piece of corroded junk. He insisted on loaning Mama a little money, telling her that she was better than a bank for him. "You know how I am, Anney," he said. "If I keep cash, I'll just throw it away on nothing at all. If I give it to you, then come the time when I really need it, I know you'll give it to me if you got it, and if you don't, well then, at least you'll feed me. Won't you, little sister?"

Daddy Glen got mad at Mama for taking the money, as if she had done it just to prove he couldn't support us. He screamed at her that she had shamed him. "I'm a grown man," he yelled. "I don't need your damn brother to pay my way." He spent a week not speaking to any of us, and when Earle dropped by to visit, Daddy Glen grumbled that he didn't have time to shoot the shit, and drove off like he had work to do.

"Too much pride in that boy," Earle told Mama mildly. "If he don't lighten up a little he's gonna rupture something. Hell, we all know we got to help each other in this life." He winked at me, hugged Reese, and teased Mama till she giggled like a girl and made him a fried-tomato sandwich. When he got ready to leave, he gave Reese a quarter and me a half-dollar.

"You're growing up, honey," Uncle Earle told me. "You're gonna be as pretty as your mama one of these days." I smiled and rolled that half-dollar in my palms. Earle had lived alone since his wife left him, and he spent most of his evenings either out drinking or over at one of his sisters' houses. Before Mama had decided she was going to marry Daddy Glen, Uncle Earle was always around, but we saw less and less of him all the time. For a moment then, I wished we lived with him so Mama could take proper care of him and he could give us coins and make Mama laugh.

When Daddy Glen came home late that night, he refused to go to bed even though he had to work the next day. He sat out in the living room with the radio on, his expression fixed and angry. Mama sat up with him and tried to get him to talk, but he still wouldn't speak to her. When we got up the next morning, his face looked thin and white, and his blue eyes were so dark they looked black.

The strained silence lasted for weeks, and even after it seemed to ease, Daddy Glen was different. His face took on a brooding sullen look. At dinner one night I watched him shove his plate away angrily. "Nothing I do goes right," he complained. "I put my hand in a honey jar and it comes out shit!"

"Oh, Glen," Mama said. "Everybody has trouble now and again. Things will get better. Just give it time."

"Shut up!" he screamed at her. "Don't give me that mama shit. Just shut up. Shut up!"

Mama froze, one hand still lifted to reach toward the bread basket. Her face was like a photograph, black-and-white, her eyes enormous dark shadows and her skin bleached in that instant to a paper gloss, her open mouth stunned and gaping.

Reese dropped her head down into her hands and gave a soft thin cry that turned immediately to sobs. Without even thinking about it, I locked my fingers tight to the edge of the table and pushed myself up to a standing position. Daddy Glen's face was red, swollen, tears running down his cheeks. Mama's eyes swept over to me like searchlights, and his followed.

"Oh, God," he moaned, and Mama shuddered. Daddy Glen stumbled around the table, his hip thudding against the edge, shaking the bowls and glasses. "Oh, Anney. I'm sorry. Oh, God! I don't want to be yelling at you." He kissed her forehead, cheekbones, chin, his hands pressed to the sides of her face. "Oh, Anney, I'm sorry!"

"It's all right," she whispered, stroking his arms, and trying to push him away. "It's all right, honey. I understand."

Reese went on sobbing while I stood gripping the edge of the table with no idea what I had been about to do. I looked down at my hands, my fingertips flattened and white, my nails bitten off in ragged edges. My hands were still, but my arms were shaking. What had I been going to do? What had I been going to do?

Daddy Glen looked at me standing there. "I know how

much your mama loves you," he said, putting his hand on my arm, squeezing tight. When he let me go, there was a bruise, and Mama saw it right away.

"Glen, you don't know your own strength!"

"No." He was calmer now. "Guess I don't. But Bone knows I'd never mean to hurt her. Bone knows I love her. Goddammit. You know how I love you all, Anney."

I stared up at him, Mama's hands on my shoulders, knowing my mouth was hanging open and my face was blank. What did I know? What did I believe? I looked at his hands. No, he never meant to hurt me, not really, I told myself, but more and more those hands seemed to move before he could think. His hands were big, impersonal, and fast. I could not avoid them. Reese and I made jokes about them when he wasn't around—gorilla hands, monkey paws, paddlefish, beaver tails. Sometimes I worried if he knew the things we said. My dreams were full of long fingers, hands that reached around doorframes and crept over the edge of the mattress, fear in me like a river, like the ice-dark blue of his eyes.

6

Hunger makes you restless. You dream about food—not just any food, but perfect food, the best food, magical meals, famous and awe-inspiring, the one piece of meat, the exact taste of buttery corn, tomatoes so ripe they split and sweeten the air, beans so crisp they snap between the teeth, gravy like mother's milk singing to your bloodstream. When I got hungry my hands would not stay still. I would pick at the edges of scabs, scratch at chigger bites and old scars, and tug at loose strands of my black hair. I'd rock a penny in my palm, trying to learn to roll it one-handed up and around each finger without dropping it, the way my cousin Grey could. I'd chew my fingernails or suck on toothpicks and read everything I hadn't read more than twice already. But when Reese got hungry and there was nothing to eat, she would just sob, shiny fat tears running down her pink cheeks. Nothing would distract her.

We weren't hungry too often. There was always something that could be done. Reese and I walked the side of the highway, picking up return deposit bottles to cash in and buy Mama's cigarettes while she gave home permanents to the old ladies she knew from the lunch counter. Reese would wrinkle her nose and giggle as she slipped the pack of Pall Malls into Mama's pocket, while I ran to get us a couple of biscuits out of the towel-wrapped dish on the stove.

"Such fine little ladies," the women would tell her, and Mama would pat her pocket and agree.

Mama knew how to make a meal of biscuits and gravy, flour-and-water biscuits with bacon-fat gravy to pour over them. By the time I started the fourth grade, we were eating biscuit dinners more often than not. Sometimes with the biscuits Mama would serve a bowl of tomato soup or cold pork and beans. We joked about liking it right out of the can, but it was cold because the power company had turned the house off—no money in the mail, no electricity. That was hunger wrapped around a starch belly.

One afternoon there was not even flour to make up the pretense of a meal. We sat at the kitchen table, Reese and I grumbling over our rumbling bellies. Mama laughed but kept her face turned away from us. "Making so much noise over so little. You'd think you girls hadn't been fed in a week."

She got out soda crackers and began to spread them with a layer of dark red ketchup spotted with salt and pepper. She poured us glasses of cold tea and told us stories about real hunger, hunger of days with no expectation that there would ever be biscuits again, how when she was a kid she'd wrestled her sisters for the last bacon rind.

"We used to pass the plates around the table, eight plates for eight kids, pretending there was food gonna come off the stove to fill those plates, talking about food we'd never seen, just heard about or imagined, making up stories about what we'd cook if we could. Earle liked the idea of parboiled puppies. Your aunt Ruth always talked about frogs' tongues with dewberries. Beau wanted fried rutabagas, and Nevil cried for steamed daffodils. But Raylene won the prize with her recipe for sugar-glazed turtle meat with poison greens and hot piss dressing."

After a while Reese and I started making up our own pretend meals. "Peanut butter and Jell-O. Mashed bug meat with pickles." Mama made us laugh with her imitations of her brothers and sisters fighting over the most disgusting meals they could dream up. She filled our stomachs with soda crackers and ketchup, soda crackers and mayonnaise, and more big glasses of tea, all the time laughing and teasing and tickling our shoulders with her long nails as she walked back and forth. Reese finally went outside to chase the dogs from next door and yell insults at the boys who ran them. But I stayed back to watch Mama through the kitchen window, to see her fingers ridge up into fists and her chin stand out in anger. When Daddy Glen came back from fishing with my uncles, she was just like a big angry mama hen, feathers up and eyes yellow.

"Soda crackers and ketchup," she hissed at him. "You so casual about finding another job, but I had to feed my girls that shit while you sat on your butt all afternoon, smoking and telling lies." She shoved her hands under her arms and sucked her lips in tight so that her mouth looked flat and hard.

"Now, Anney . . ." Daddy Glen reached out to touch her arm. She slapped his hand down and jumped back like a snake that's caught a rat. I backed away from the window and ran around to the side of the house to watch from the open door to the driveway. I had never seen Mama like that. It was scary but wonderful too. She didn't seem to be afraid of anything.

"Not my kids," she told Daddy Glen, her voice carrying like a shout, though she was speaking in a hoarse whisper. "I was never gonna have my kids know what it was like. Never was gonna have them hungry or cold or scared. Never, you hear me? Never!"

She went in the bathroom and washed her face, her under-arms, and her neck. Mama was pulling her hose carefully up her legs when I ran in to stand beside her, too scared and excited not to stay close. She paused to hug me briefly. "Go call and have your uncle Earle come by here to pick you up when he gets off. You and Reese better stay at your aunt Alma's place till I get back." I ran out to the kitchen, where the phone was, but didn't call. Instead I hung back in the doorway and watched her reflection in the mirror down the hall.

Mama put on a clean bra and one of the sleeveless red pullover sweaters she'd gotten from her friend Mab down at the diner—the one Mab joked was made to show just how high her tits could point. Daddy Glen came to the doorway and stood watching her with his throat working but no sound coming out. Mama outlined her mouth in bold red lipstick, combed back her dark blond hair, and hung her big old purse on one arm. She glanced up the hall and saw me leaning against the kitchen doorway.

"Did you call Earle?"

I nodded, uneasy at lying, but not wanting to upset her. It would be hours before Earle would be free to come get us, and I'd already decided not to wait for him.

Mama paused, shook her head, walked back to the bedroom, and reached under the bedframe to pull out the box where she stored her shiny black patent-leather high heels. When she stood up in those, she looked like a different person, older and harder, her mouth set in a grim little smile. Her blond hair looked even brighter, her eyes darker, her complexion paler. She was coldly beautiful. Daddy Glen was still standing in the hall, but Mama stepped around him as if there wasn't really anyone there, as if cocking her hip and swinging to one side were just a normal part of walking down the hall. Daddy Glen swayed a bit as she passed but did not move to stop her. His hands hung along his pockets while he breathed through his mouth like he was going to be sick. Her heels clicking on the floor were almost as loud as the cracking of his knuckles where he stood. I followed closely behind Mama, afraid to look back at Daddy Glen, afraid my glance might break the spell that seemed to be holding him in the hallway. Mama said nothing, just gave me a hug and a kiss, and slid behind the wheel of her Pontiac.

When the car engine roared, the spell broke. Daddy Glen ran out and stood on the tarmac watching Mama drive away. His face was rigid. He didn't even look in my direction, but my belly crawled up tight against my backbone. I felt as if the grass had turned to ammonia and was burning in my throat, as if Daddy Glen's skin was radiating red heat and waves of steamy sweat. Around the narrow straps of his sleeveless T-shirt I watched the muscles in his shoulders roll and bunch. I knew he could easily break my arms as methodically as he was cracking his knuckles, wring my neck as hard as he was wringing his hands. I backed up carefully, then ran around the house, climbing the fence between our yard and the neighbor's so I couldn't be seen.

Reese was jumping rope with the MacCauley twins and didn't want to go with me, but she cheered up when I told her we would walk to the highway and hitchhike instead of calling for a lift. Reese loved flagging down strangers on the highway and begging a ride the four miles over to where Aunt Alma lived. She had promised me she would never do it without me, but I worried that as soon as she was a little older she would be hitchhiking all over the county. So every time we hitched a ride, I made up a new horror story. The habit was so strong in me that nervous as I was, I automatically started another one, this time about the phantom driver who went around picking up girls and skinned them like young deer, eating the meat and tanning their hides to make coin purses and pocketbooks.

"He'll never get us," Reese laughed. "We just have to be careful never to take a ride with a man alone." I thought about that for a moment.

"Well, it an't so easy to know who the phantom is," I told Reese. "Sometimes he catches a married couple first, hiding in the back of their car while they're in the gas-station bathroom.

When they drive off, first he murders them and then he props them up so you'd think they were the only people in the car. That way he catches lots of people who would never get in a car with a man alone."

Reese chewed her lower lip and stared up the highway. I could see she was thinking this new information over carefully. She examined the people in the truck that stopped for us, an elderly woman in a dark blue shirtwaist dress, and a younger man in khaki work clothes. Before climbing in back she slapped the side of the cab hard enough to see both of them jump in their seats. I bit my tongue to keep from laughing.

The old lady scolded us for catching a ride on the highway. "You could get killed or worse," she told us through the back window. "Young girls on the roads are an invitation to the wicked. Anything could happen to you." We both nodded solemnly and thanked her politely when we jumped off just down the road from Aunt Alma's place.

It was past midnight when Mama came for us. Reese was asleep in Aunt Alma's bed, but I was sitting up with Uncle Wade, nodding over the picture puzzle he worked at when he couldn't sleep.

"Girl, your mama," he said, giving me a little push. I jerked fully awake when Mama touched my shoulder. Her hands were heavy and smelled faintly of Jergens Lotion.

"Come on, Bone," she whispered. "We're going home." She thanked Uncle Wade in a tired voice. Her hair was limp and her face scrubbed clean. She was still wearing that pullover sweater, but she'd added a loose white shirt and changed back to her waitress flats.

"Don't talk," she told me. "Just get Reese's shoes and come on." She lifted Reese without disturbing Aunt Alma and carried her out to the car. I followed her, holding on to her right side while Reese leaned into her left shoulder. At the car, she paused and looked up into the dark night sky. In the light from the house, her face was all hollows and angles, her eyes sunken and glittery.

"Damn!" she whispered softly, and leaned her forehead against the cool metal above the car door. "Damn, damn."

"Mama," Reese whimpered. I pressed my cheek against Mama's side and kept still. There was a long cold moment while we waited, and then Mama pushed herself back up straight and opened the door.

"All right," she said, as if she were wrapping up some long conversation with herself. "All right."

I looked back to Aunt Alma's house. Uncle Wade was standing in the kitchen looking out at us, his face stern and his mouth hard. Why was he angry? I wondered. What could have made him look so terribly angry?

"Cook you some eggs," Mama said as she steered us into the kitchen and sat us at the table. There was flour in a can, a jar of jelly, butter in a dish, a bag of tomatoes, fatback in a sealed package, and a carton of fresh eggs all speckled brown. She put most of it away and then whipped the eggs up with sweet milk, laying slices of green tomato to fry around the sides of the pan before she poured the eggs in.

"My mama used to cook this late at night," she announced, blinking in the too-bright light. Daddy Glen was sitting in the living room in front of the television set with the sound turned down low, not looking at us and not speaking. I watched Reese's eyes flicker toward him and then back to Mama and over to me. Daddy Glen's hands kept moving on his thighs, the fingers working into knots, tightening on his trousers and then shaking against the dark fabric like the legs of dying june bugs turned belly up in the night. Mama pulled a tray of biscuits out of the oven and grinned at us.

"You got to get the tomatoes almost done before you put the eggs in, 'cause you don't cook the eggs much at all. Want them soft. Want them to melt like butter between your teeth and your tongue." She spooned me out a scoop of eggs and put two biscuits on the plate next to the soft browned tomatoes. Reese spread butter on her biscuits and poured a big dollop of jelly next to her eggs. My stomach was so tight I didn't see how I could eat, but Mama sat right across from me and smiled so wide I knew I had to eat it all. I did, slowly, while Daddy Glen sat silent in the next room and Mama went on talking like he wasn't there at all. My eyes kept sliding over to where his hands gripped his thighs. I curled mine under the table, rubbed my leg muscles.

The biscuits stuffed me but didn't satisfy. Once I started eating I could not get full. Reese seemed to feel the same way. She ate until her eyes looked swollen shut from too much food. Then she lay her face down on the table as if she were going to nap right there. Mama smiled at her and reached over to tuck her lank blond hair behind her ears where it couldn't fall in her eyes. She buttered all the biscuits that were left and wrapped them in a towel to keep for morning. All the time she went on talking about nothing in particular, about her mama and meals she had watched her aunts cook up late at night, about a noise the Pontiac had started to make, and how she really needed to clean out the trap on the washing machine.

I listened to Mama with my mouth open. It felt like there was a wind blowing from my neck down to my belly, hot and chill at the same time, dropping little sparks into my nervous system. Finally Mama put Reese and me to bed together, sitting up beside us as if she were going to spend all night there. I could hear the television set still playing softly in the front room, and I tried to stay awake, but the food was like a drug in my system. I slid off into the dark and a dream of great soft strangling clouds lying like fogbanks on a field of blackberries. I woke up to Reese's swollen frightened face and the low angry sound of Daddy Glen's voice down the hall. I linked my fingers with Reese's and prayed for silence, closing my eyes so tight my ears buzzed.

• • •

We had to move again that next week, but Mama said the new place would be better now that Daddy Glen was going to be working out at the Pepsi plant. But the new house wasn't new. It looked just like the last three—small and close and damp-smelling no matter how many times Mama aired it out. It was just like all the houses Daddy Glen had found for us—tract houses with white slatted walls and tin-roofed carports. The lawns were dry, with coarse straggly grass and scattered patches of rocky ground. There were never any trees or bushes. Mama would sometimes put in flowers or spade up a patch in the back for vegetables that somehow never got planted before we would move again, but the houses always looked naked and abandoned.

"Unloved," Temple, Aunt Alma's oldest girl, told me while helping us unpack in the new bedroom. "Your daddy's always finding you houses where it looks like nobody ever really wanted to live. This place looks like people just stopped in and left as fast as they could." I didn't argue. She was right.

My aunts were always moving too—all of them but Aunt Raylene, who had rented the same house for most of her adult life. No one else seemed to stay any one place very long, but the houses they chose were older ones that tended to resemble each other, not like the ones Daddy Glen wanted, with the jalousie windows, carports, and garbage disposals that never worked. Alma always lived in big old rickety houses with wide porches and dogs lying out flat in the sun. Aunt Ruth liked the ones that had black walnut trees to spread shade over my uncles' pickup trucks.

Daddy Glen sneered at my aunts' houses with their coal-grate fireplaces and chicken coops in the backyard. "I wouldn't live in your place if you paid me," he swore to Travis one Sunday. But Travis just grinned and gave him a shove. "The problem is, Glen boy, you got to pay them landlords, and hell, they don't care what we think about nothing, what kind of place we think we want to rent. Shit! We all do what we can, you know?"

I loved it when Alma and Wade moved out to the country next to wide flat fields of peanuts and strawberries. It was just past the edge of town, near the West Greenville truck routes, where everything was run-down and cheap and nobody minded if you parked your car on the grass. There were always kids on the porch, cousins going in and out of screen doors, laundry hanging out back, and chickens running around, and no matter which aunt we visited there was always something to do.

"Catch me that hen," Aunt Alma would tell me. "Then pick over these beans and wash those tomatoes." Reese would help, we would sit out on the porch together, blending in with the cousins and their friends so completely that sometimes Aunt Alma or Aunt Ruth would forget we were there until Mama called looking for us. It didn't matter where we were living so long as we could go stay with one of our aunts.

Over at Aunt Alma's we could listen to Garvey and Grey fight, to Little Earle giggle and squeak, to Uncle Wade drink and cuss, to the radio playing and the chickens clucking outside the windows. Over there we got to slide around on a big tarp with the sprinkler shooting cold water up in a shower. At Aunt Ruth's we could watch Uncle Travis cut up potatoes for her, a beer at his side and a cigarette dangling from one side of his mouth, ashes occasionally dropping into the peels. Aunt Ruth even let us play in just our panties, though after Reese got ringworm Mama insisted we keep our clothes on, and after we got chiggers she made us scrub down as soon as we came home. Reese and I didn't mind. We still wanted to go visiting at every chance. It was alive over at the aunts' houses, warm, always humming with voices and laughter and children running around. The quiet in our own house was cold, no matter that we had a better furnace and didn't leave our doors open for the wind to blow through. There was something icy in Daddy Glen's houses that melted out of us when we were over at our aunts'.

Daddy Glen's brothers lived in big houses they owned, with fenced-in yards and flowering bushes. "This is how people ought to live," he told us when he drove us over to visit his brothers. More than anything Daddy Glen wanted a house like Daryl and James had—a new house with a nice lawn and picture windows framed in lined curtains. The houses he chose for us were always shabby imitations. Mama sewed curtains, washed windows, and polished floors. Daddy Glen mowed the grass and sent us out with scissors to dig up the weeds along the driveway. He yelled at Earle and Beau if they drove up on the grass, and he chased the dogs that came and knocked over our garbage cans in the night.

"Nobody wants me to have nothing nice," he'd complain, and then get in one of his dangerously quiet moods and refuse to talk to anybody. He brooded so much Reese and I patrolled the yard, picking up windblown trash and dog turds—anything that would make him mad. Every new house made him happy for a little while, and we tried to extend that period of relative calm as much as possible, keeping everything sparkling clean and neat.

"Things are gonna be different here," he'd tell Mama. Reese and I would keep our faces expressionless and stay out of his way. Neither of us believed things would ever change, but we knew better than to say so. Sometimes it seemed Daddy Glen could almost read the thoughts we were trying to hide, catch us with his eyes thinking that nothing he did was going to make any difference.

"It eats a man's heart out," he told Mama one time, "knowing no one trusts him." It seemed our unbelief was what made him fail. Our lack of faith made him the man he was, made him go out to work unable to avoid getting in a fight, made him sarcastic to his bosses and nasty to the shop owners he was supposed to be persuading to take his accounts. Money would get tighter and Daddy Glen would stare at us like we cost him cash with every breath we took.

The rent would be late one month, impossible the next, and late again after that. Daddy Glen started going for long drives in the evening, and people started coming to the door during the day. They'd bang on the jamb after ringing the bell. If Mama was home, she would sit at the kitchen table with a cigarette between her fingers, staring off into space and saying nothing.

Reese or I would go to the door and yell out, "Mama's not to home. I can't let you in, my mama's not to home."

The men and women who came to our door would wheedle and threaten, cajole and rage. They'd call Mama's name so loud all the neighbors could hear. Mama would push her hair straight back from her face, light another cigarette, and hug us. Reese and I would grin and look carefully out from under the curtains to be sure the landlord or the bill collector had gone, and then run back to tell her.

"My smart girls," Mama would praise us. "My strong, smart girls." Her face would relax then, the sharp lines of her eyebrows would soften, and she would pull us up close to her one more time, every time.

"We're not bad people," Mama told us. "We're not even really poor. Anybody says something to you, you keep that in mind. We're not bad people. And we pay our way. We just can't always pay when people want."

Reese and I nodded earnestly, agreeing wordlessly, but we didn't believe her. We knew what the neighbors called us, what Mama wanted to protect us from. We knew who we were.

Uncle Nevil and Aunt Fay got a place on such a steep hill that we could play in the dirt under the front porch with the dogs. When we stood on tiptoe, we could barely reach the floorboards above us. The house was set so deep in the hill that the dogs could not dig out from under it, and the back rooms were always cool and shadowy. I loved that house, the cool dimness under the porch ripe with the smell of dogs and red dirt, but Daddy Glen hated it.

"It's a goddam nigger shanty! Don't they care how they're living?" He wouldn't put us in such a house, he insisted. He moved us instead to a cinder-block house where the tile floors were always peeling up in the damp and where we didn't stay very long anyway. "But a decent neighborhood," he told Mama, who said nothing, just unpacked the dishes one more time.

My aunt Alma earned Daddy Glen's undying contempt the year I was nine and she moved out on my uncle Wade. Uncle Earle joked that Alma had finally caught Wade doing just what he'd been doing for years.

"Messing around," Cousin Deedee said. "If he was my husband, I'd shoot his dick off."

"Might be a factor in why you don't have one—a husband, that is," Aunt Alma told her, and then laughed at the idea of shooting Uncle Wade in his private parts. "It'd get his attention anyway," she told Mama. "But hell, the man's a dog. Don't care where he sticks it. Don't know the value of what he had. Might as well take myself out of reach of his dirty ways."

She moved her brood of kids into an apartment building downtown, a second-floor frame walk-up with a shaky wide porch hanging off one side. No matter where she lived, Alma always had a porch.

Nobody else we knew had ever lived in an apartment. Mama took us over to visit with a paper sack of towels and cotton diapers for the new baby from the Salvation Army thrift store. Aunt Alma smiled to see her, pulled a pitcher of cold tea out of the icebox, and shooed us out on the porch.

A long flight of steps ran off the porch and looped back past the lower apartment extending down to the yard. Grey and Little Earle were sitting on the top steps, leaning over to watch the kids from downstairs, who were looking out their windows up to where we all stood. Shiny brown faces kept pressing against the glass and then withdrawing, stern blank faces that we could barely tell one from the other.

"Niggers," Grey whispered proudly. "Scared of us."

I wrapped my fingers around the banister rail, working

splinters loose from the dry wood, and leaned over to look for myself. I had never seen colored people up close, and I was curious about these. They did look scared.

"Their mama won't let them come out." Little Earle was chewing a splinter off the railing and picking at another. "We heard her this morning, telling 'em she'd beat their asses if they even opened that door. She sure an't happy we moved in here."

"Well, neither is Daddy," Grey laughed.

"Must be hot cooped up in there," Patsy Ruth whispered.

I nodded, still watching the window. It looked like there were three of them down there, taking turns looking out, fully fascinated with us as we were with them. Reese came up behind me and pulled at my arm. I didn't turn; it seemed as if the face in the window was looking at me.

"Can't we go down in the yard?"

"It's hotter down there, no breeze at all, and dusty. Better up here." Grey spat over the rail to the parched bare ground far below. "Besides, we'd have to go past them." He nodded at the window.

I slit my eyes against the bright light. The face in the window narrowed its eyes. I couldn't tell if it was a boy or a girl—a very pretty boy or a very fierce girl for sure. The cheekbones were as high as mine, the eyes large and delicate with long lashes, while the mouth was small, the lips puffy as if bee-stung, but not wide. The chocolate skin was so smooth, so polished, the pores invisible. I put my fingers up to my cheeks, looked over at Grey and then back down. Grey's cheeks were pitted with blackheads and flushed with sunburn. I'd never thought about it before, but he was almost ugly.

"What you staring at, Bone?" Grey poked me.

I couldn't say what I was thinking, couldn't say, "That child is prettier than you." I pulled myself back from the railing and tore off a splinter of my own before turning to look into Grey's face.

"I like it here. Like it a lot better than that rickety old

place where you were living before," I lied. "How many bedrooms you got?"

Grey's face relaxed, and I realized he had been afraid I was going to say something nasty. "More room here than it looks like. Got a room just for Little Earle and Tadpole and me. Patsy Ruth and Temple got their own, and Mama even said I could keep a tank on the dresser and get my turtles back from Garvey." Little Earle nodded enthusiastically. It was the first time anyone had mentioned Garvey, who had stayed with Uncle Wade, but I said nothing. Mama had told me it caused a terrible fight when Wade kept Garvey and let his twin go on with Aunt Alma.

"Don't call the baby Tadpole," Patsy Ruth interrupted. "Call her Annie. You know Mama hates it when you call her Tadpole."

The door opened and Aunt Alma looked out. "You kids playing good?" She squinted against the sun.

"No problem, Mama," Grey told her. I looked down to the window below us again. It was a girl, I was almost sure, a fierce girl watching us distrustfully. Grey pulled himself up from the steps with one big hand. The girl's eyes followed his fist and then looked back to me. I tried to smile but my face felt stiff, nervous. The girl's face remained expressionless and pulled back into the darkness of the apartment.

"Don't you be mean to those kids downstairs," Aunt Alma told Grey. "I don't want no trouble with these people."

"Yes, Mama," Grey and Little Earle echoed. The window below stayed dark.

The next time we went over to visit, Grey told me there were five of them downstairs, same as upstairs, with the daddy off working up north and none of the kids as old as he was. The woman kept to herself, wouldn't do more than nod to Aunt Alma, but the kids started hanging out on the steps again after the first week, running inside whenever one of the uncles' trucks pulled up but otherwise ignoring the white children.

Sometime in the second week they held a spitting contest, upstairs against down, and Grey won. After that things got a little easier. Grey showed his pocketknife to the boys downstairs and in turn admired a set of tools the oldest boy had from his father. It was only the girl who kept herself aloof, staying with her mama while the boys played out in the yard.

"She's pretty, if niggers can be pretty," Grey told me, "but not friendly. Looks like she expects me to bite her neck or something."

"You call her that and she might bite you. I would." I was remembering the girl's intent, determined face. I had heard all the hateful jokes and nasty things people said about "niggers," but on my own, I had never before spoken to a colored person in anything more than the brief, careful "sir" and "ma'am" that Mama had taught us. I was as shy with those kids as they seemed to be with us. As nervous as the idea made me, I wished that girl would come out so I could try to talk to her, but she never did more than look out the windows at us. Her mama had probably told her all about what to expect from trash like us.

"Boy howdy, you should have heard what Daddy and Uncle Beau said when they came over, the things they called them." Grey frowned and kicked one foot against the other. "Daddy's awful mad we moved in here."

I knew what he meant. Uncle Wade and Aunt Alma had been over at our place the week before, Wade looking worn-down and shabby and cursing Alma to her face.

"Running off with a man's children, living in that dirty place with niggers all around. My little girls having to go up those stairs past those nigger boys. My wife walking the street past those peckerwoods!" Uncle Wade's sunburned face was thinner than usual and dark with outrage.

Aunt Alma just laughed at him. She looked better than ever. She was a little thinner too, but that was good on her. Her face was smooth and relaxed, her skirt loose on her soft hips. She didn't look like she was missing Uncle Wade too much. "That man's worse than a boy," she'd told Mama, "wears you out wanting stuff done for him all the time, running after his meals, washing his clothes, hell, washing him and his greasy hair!" Now she just laughed and pushed her bangs back casually with one small hand.

"I'm paying my own rent, thank you, Mr. Wade Yarnall." She looped a curl around one ear and grinned over at Mama proudly. "I don't need to listen to your complaints about my life, your nonsense about my children. They're clean and fed and happy where they are. Nobody's messing with them. Nobody's messing with me, and nobody's gonna."

"But it's a scandal! She can't stay there." Aunt Carr was on Uncle Wade's side, but she always had been, Mama told me. Carr had come down from Baltimore to stay with us on her yearly summer visit. "Your aunt Carr was always sweet on Wade," Mama confided to me one afternoon when we were hanging out laundry. "Back when we were still girls, she thought she'd marry Wade. Never got over him picking Alma."

"Hellfire, Anney. Carr an't never gotten over anything. Girl remembers every wrong anybody ever done her or thought of doing her. Bet you she recites them out loud each night before she goes to sleep, just to keep them straight in her mind." Uncle Earle was standing at the end of the clothesline with a big paper sack in his arms and a wide grin on his dark tanned face. He put the bag down and hugged me when I ran to him, laughing at Mama's annoyed expression.

"Come on, Anney. You know what I say is true. Don't you be giving me that old angry look." He nudged his sack. "I got enough papershell pecans to make two dozen pies. Why don't you let me and your baby here pick them out for you while you roll out a bunch of pie crusts?"

Mama put the last pin on a pair of Daddy Glen's worn jockey shorts and gave a shake to one of his shirts so that the sleeves hung down straight. "Some days, I don't know how anybody stands you, Earle Boatwright, always saying the worst about everybody. I think the one who sits up nights is you, just thinking of evil-hearted things to say about people."

Earle laughed again. "Oh, you're right, baby sister. I spend all my spare time making notes on things people have done that they don't want no one to talk about, and I make sure I talk about just those things." He hefted his bag on one hip and me on the other. "Tell me, Bone, has your mama told you yet how your aunt Carr come to live so far away in Baltimore City and come home so rarely we barely recognize her when she does?"

"Oh, Earle!" Mama put one hand over her mouth and grabbed the pecans with the other. "Don't talk bad about Carr. Come on in and I'll get out my Karo syrup and pie pans."

Earle swung me up high so that I straddled his shoulders, my legs hanging down on either side of his neck. "Yes, ma'am. I got a taste for pecan pie the way you make it when you're mad." He tickled my bare foot till I grabbed his ears to make him stop.

"When your mama's pissed at me, Bone, she chops the nuts up fine the way I like them. Otherwise she don't bother, and if the nuts an't chopped small they don't sweeten up right for my taste."

At the screen door he paused, and I pulled his ears again. "But what about Aunt Carr? An't you gonna tell me how she moved to Baltimore?" He turned his head to look up at me and gave his famous slow grin. "You know your mama don't want me to tell you that story."

I kicked my feet against his chest. "But an't you gonna tell me anyway?"

Earle laughed and swung me down. He pushed the screen door with his hip and took a quick look inside to see that Mama had gone on to the kitchen. "Well." He lit a cigarette, striking the match one-handed.

"Your aunt Carr was a sensitive girl, tender on the subject of how pretty your mama and Alma were when she wasn't much to look at herself. Carr wanted to be beautiful so much it made her mean. She used to talk so awful about Raylene it was a shame, insisting Raylene had to learn to use makeup and fix her hair, start working on getting herself a man. But I always thought she just went on at Raylene so she could boast about how hard she worked at looking good. Raylene and Alma and your mama used to just laugh at her about it, make her so mad. I an't saying Carr didn't love her sisters, but sometimes you could tell she didn't much like them. And oh! She did have a thing for the young Mr. Wade. The girl just plain wanted him, and maybe she could see that he wasn't giving a minute's notice to her when Alma was around. It wore on her bad.

"Then one Thanksgiving Wade joked where everyone could hear that Alma was the younger, sweeter version of Carr—the blossom next to the windfall, I think he said. Carr's face was a study right then. You could see every thought running across it, none of them pretty. And by Christmas, I swear that girl had snapped up old Baltimore Benny like he was new bait in a cold spring. Had her first baby by the next fall, and got Benny to move back up with his people right after that. It took Wade and Alma another five years to marry themselves, though Alma's twins waited barely long enough for the preacher to stop talking before they pushed their way out of her belly."

Earle rolled his cigarette between his thumb and forefinger. "Seems like after that we were all grown up and everything was different. It's the way of things. One day you're all family together, fighting and hugging from one moment to the next, and then it's all gone. You're off making your own family, scared of what's coming next, and Lord, things have a way of running faster and faster all the time." He looked off across the yard as if he were seeing a lot more than his oil-green Chevy parked on the street.

"Well, where are you?" Mama called to us from the kitchen. "I an't gonna make no pies all by myself when you two can help." I ran inside while Earle followed slowly behind, dropping his lanky form into a kitchen chair turned around so he could rest his chin on the back of it.

"You just don't want me telling stories where you can't hear, little sister."

"Lies, you mean." Mama passed me the sifter and a bowl of flour, then poured out a mound of pecans between her and Earle. She took her big butcher knife and started rocking it back and forth across the nuts, chopping them fine. "You know, Bone, Earle's hair was a dull brown when he was a boy and started school. It just got darker and blacker every year." She looked over at her brother with a crooked smile. "What you think, Earle, was it school or sin that made your hair so black?"

Earle palmed a mouthful of pecans, tugged on the lock that hung down over his forehead, and sighed a long mournful moan. "Oh, school, little sister. That's why I had to quit, you know. I had to stop the process before it went too far. If I'd gone on, my hair would have turned so black it would have started to absorb all the sunlight in Greenville County. Crops would have failed and children gone hungry just because of my selfish need to learn algebra and geography. I had to quit and take that job building the new runway out at the air base. It was the only thing to do to save us from starvation and the cold cold night."

"Oh, you!" Mama slapped Earle's shoulder lightly. "I can't say nothing without you telling your awful lies." She pulled in her rolling pin and leaned on it as she crushed a couple of cups of pecans down to mealy bits. "God's keeping track, Earle Boatwright. One of these days your stories are gonna come back on you. You an't gonna know what to say then, I swear."

Uncle Wade and Aunt Alma fought for weeks, with Aunt Carr and Mama stepping in now and then, until Aunt Carr had to go home to Baltimore and Daddy Glen got laid off from his new job at the Pepsi plant and Mama started working too hard to go visiting Aunt Alma much. It didn't look like they would ever make up, but then again, nobody acted like it was any big deal. Aunt Alma had sworn she wouldn't have Wade back in her life till he crawled the length of Main Street singing what a dog he was, but when the baby got sick and the boys started running around at night, she gave it up and moved back in with him.

"I knew what he was like when I married him," Alma told Mama. "I guess he an't no worse than any other man." But she was still mad enough not to move back into their bedroom for a few months. She treated Wade as if he were a tenant in his own house, barely speaking to him until he apologized to her. At first Uncle Wade was indignant, swearing that Aunt Alma would go to hell for treating him like a stranger. He did apologize eventually, though he wouldn't admit he had done anything wrong.

"A man has needs," he kept telling everybody from Daddy Glen to the gas-station attendants on White Horse Road. "A man has needs, and she was pregnant. Was I gonna take the risk of hurting my own baby in her womb?"

Wade's woeful complaint was a joke to all the aunts. "A man has needs," they'd laugh each time they got together. "So what you suppose a woman has?"

"Men!" one of them would always answer in a giggling roar. Then they would all laugh till the tears started running down. I wasn't at all sure what was so funny, but I laughed anyway. I liked being one of the women with my aunts, liked feeling a part of something nasty and strong and separate from my big rough boy-cousins and the whole world of spitting, growling, overbearing males.

"**D**on't you ever let me catch you stealing," Mama commanded in one of her rare lectures, after Cousin Grey got caught running out of the White Horse Winn Dixie with a bargain quart of RC Cola. "You want something, you tell me, and if it's worth the trouble we'll find a way. But I an't gonna have no child of mine caught stealing."

I took Mama at her word and hung around with my cousins Garvey and Grey, planning not to get caught and not to tell Mama. But one afternoon after I produced Tootsie Rolls for Reese and me, Mama took my hands in hers like she was going to cry.

"Where'd you get them?"

"Uncle Earle," I suggested.

"No." Mama dropped down a little so her face was close to mine.

"Aunt Alma." Carefully, I made my face a mask.

"Don't lie too." The lines in her face looked as deep as the rivers that flowed south toward Charleston. "Tell me the truth."

I started to cry. "Downtown with Grey and Garvey this morning, at the Woolworth's counter."

Mama used her forefinger to wipe the tears off my cheeks. She wiped her own. "Is this all of it? How many did you take?"

"Two others, Mama. I ate one, gave Reese one."

Mama leaned back in her chair, dropping my hands. She shook a cigarette out of the pack and lit it carefully. I sat still, watching her, waiting. Tears kept collecting in the corners of my eyes, and I had to turn to wipe them away on my shoulder, but I kept watching Mama's face as she sat and smoked without looking at me. The fingers of her right hand rubbed together steadily like the legs of grasshoppers I had seen climbing up the long grass at Aunt Raylene's place. Her lips moved steadily too, as if she were sucking on her teeth or about to speak, but she was quiet a long time, just sitting there looking off through the open window smoking her cigarette.

"You know your cousin Tommy Lee? Aunt Ruth's oldest boy?"

I frowned, trying to remember their names. There was Dwight, I knew, Lucius, D.W., Graham, yeah, Tommy Lee, and Butch. Aunt Ruth had only two daughters and six boys, most of them married with boys of their own. All of them were so alike that I never could keep track of anyone but Butch, and I rarely saw him anymore since he had gone to live with Ruth's oldest girl, Mollie, in Oklahoma. The younger boys turned up occasionally to wrestle Reese and me, give us candy, or tell us stories. The older ones had the sunken eyes and planed faces of men, and they never gave us anything except nasty looks. I couldn't have said which of the older ones was Tommy Lee, though I'd heard people talk about him enough— about what a hardass he was, about his girlfriends and his dirty mouth, his stints in the county jail and the fights he got into.

"He's bad," Mama said, her eyes still looking out the

window. "He's just bad all the way through. He steals from his mama. He's stolen from me. Don't dare leave your pocket-book around him, or any of your stuff that he could sell. He even took Deedee's green stamp books one time and traded them off for some useless thing." Her eyes drifted back to my face, the stunned brown of the pupils shining like mossy rocks under water.

"I remember when we were just kids and he was always stealing candy to give away. Thought people would like him if he gave them stuff, I suppose. Now he's always saying how he's been robbed, and he's got a story to account for everything he does. Beats his girlfriends up 'cause they cheat on him. Can't keep a job 'cause people tell lies about him. Steals 'cause the world's been so cruel to him. So much nonsense. He's just bad, that's all, just bad. Steals from his mama and sisters, steals from his own."

I dropped my head. I remembered Grey telling me how he learned to break locks from Tommy Lee, that Tommy Lee was the slickest piece of goods in Greenville. "Boy knows how to take care of himself for sure. Never owes nobody nothing." Grey's face had flushed with respect and envy when he said it, and I had felt a little of the same—wishing I too knew how to take care of myself and could break locks or start cars without a key or palm stuff off a counter so smoothly that no one would know I had done it. But to steal from your mama! My face felt stiff with shame and anger. I wasn't like that. I would never steal from Mama.

Mama's hand touched my chin, trailed along my cheek, and stroked my hair. "You're my pride. Do you know? You and your sister are all I really have, all I ever will have. You think I could let you grow up to be like that?"

I shook my head. The tears started again, and with them hiccups. Mama went and got a cool washcloth to wet my face. "Don't cry, honey. It'll be all right. We'll take care of it, it'll be all right." She put the Tootsie Rolls in a paper bag and gave me a handful of pennies to carry. She kept talking while she brushed my hair and then hers, called Reese in and told her to stay on the porch, turned the heat down on the beans that were cooking on the stove, and walked me out to the car. She told me about when she and Aunt Raylene were girls, how they had worked for this man out past Old Henderson Road, picking strawberries for pennies every day for weeks, going through the rows and pulling loose the red ripe ones for him to sell in his stand by the side of the road.

"Only the ripe ones, he kept telling us, but it was so hot and the dust was so thick, sometimes we'd pull up the ones that weren't quite ripe, you know—green ones, or half-green anyway. We'd hide them under the ripe ones when we set them up for him. People would buy a box and then get home to find those half-ripe ones, call him up to complain. He'd get so mad, but we were just kids, and his yelling didn't bother us so long as he kept paying us for the work."

"What'd he pay you?"

Mama waved her hand as if that didn't matter. "Not enough, you know, not enough. Strawberry picking is terrible work, hurts your back, your eyes. You get that juice all over you, get those little prickers in your hands. An't enough money in it even for children, even if you eat as many as you can. After a while you don't want any anyway." She laughed.

"Though Raylene sure could eat a lot. Faster than you could see, she'd swallow handfuls of berries. Only proof she'd been eating them was her red red tongue."

She stopped the car in front of the Woolworth's, cut the engine, and sat for a moment, her hands resting on the wheel. I looked out at the big display windows, where stacks of plastic picnic baskets, little tin office waste cans, and sleeveless cotton sundresses on hangers were squeezed behind ratty stuffed animals and tricycles with multicolored plastic streamers on the handlebars. The thought of going back in there with Mama made me feel sick to my stomach and almost angry at her. Why couldn't she just let me promise never to do it again?

Her hand on my shoulder made me jump. "Your granny

found out what we'd been doing, 'cause we got lazy, you know, and started putting more and more green ones in the bottom of the boxes. Grandpa laughed about it, but your granny didn't laugh. She came over there one afternoon and turned half a dozen boxes upside down. Collected a bucket of green strawberries and paid the man for them. Took us home, sat us at the kitchen table, and made us eat every one of them. Raylene and I puked strawberries all night long."

"You must have hated her!"

Mama was quiet, and I got scared. I didn't want her to think I hated her. I didn't even want to be angry at her. I clamped my teeth tight and tried not to start crying again.

"There an't no other way to do it," she said quietly. "I hate it. You hate it. You might hate me for it. I don't know, and I can't say what might happen now. But I just don't know no other way to do it. We're gonna go in there and give the man back his candy, pay for what you ate, and that will be all there is to it. It will be over, and you'll be glad it's settled. We won't ever have to mention it again."

Mama opened the door briskly, and I followed her numbly. There was a flush on her cheeks as she walked me back to the candy counter, waited for the salesgirl to come over, and stood me right in front of her. "My daughter has something to tell you," she said, and gave me a little push. But I couldn't speak. I held out the bag and the pennies, and started to cry again, this time sobbing loud. The girl looked confused, but Mama wouldn't say anything else, just gave me another little push. I thought I'd strangle on my tongue when the manager walked over to us.

"What's this?" he said in a booming voice. "What's this? You got something for us, little girl?" He was a big man with a wide face and a swollen belly poking out from under a buttoned-up vest. He stooped down so that his face was right in front of me, so close I could smell the sharp alcohol scent of after-shave.

"You do, don'tcha, honey?" He looked like he was swallowing an urge to laugh at us. I was suddenly so angry at him my stomach seemed to curl up inside me. I shoved the bag at him, the pennies.

"I stole it. I'm sorry. I stole it."

Mama's hand squeezed my shoulder, and I heard the breath come out of her in a sigh. I closed my eyes for a moment, trying hard not to get as mad at her as I was at that man.

"Uh-huh," he said. "I see." I looked up at him again. He was rummaging in the bag, counting the Tootsie Rolls and nodding. "It's a good thing, ma'am," he said, still talking loudly, "that you caught this when you did." He nodded at me. "You're a fortunate little girl, truly fortunate. Your mama loves you. She doesn't want you to grow up to be a thief."

He stood back up and passed the pennies to the salesgirl. He stretched a hand out like he was going to put it on my head, but I stepped back so that he would have had to bend forward to reach me. "Son of a bitch," Grey would have called him, "slimy son of a bitch probably eats Tootsie Rolls all day long." If he reached for me again, I decided, I'd bite him, but he just looked at me long and carefully. I knew I was supposed to feel ashamed, but I didn't anymore. I felt outraged. I wanted to kick him or throw up on him or scream his name on the street. The longer he looked at me, the more I hated him. If I could have killed him with my stare, I would have. The look in his eyes told me that he knew what I was thinking.

"I'm gonna do your mama a favor." He smiled. "Help her to teach you the seriousness of what you've done." Mama's hand tightened on my shoulder, but she didn't speak.

"What we're gonna do," he announced, "is say you can't come back in here for a while. We'll say that when your mama thinks you've learned your lesson, she can come back and talk to me. But till then, we're gonna remember your name, what you look like." He leaned down again. "You understand me, honey?"

I understood. I understood that I was barred from the

Woolworth's counters. I could feel the heat from my mama's hand through my blouse, and I knew she was never going to come near this place again, was never going to let herself stand in the same room with that honey-greased bastard. I looked around at the bright hairbrushes, ribbons, trays of panties and socks, notebooks, dolls, and balloons. It was hunger I felt then, raw and terrible, a shaking deep down inside me, as if my rage had used up everything I had ever eaten.

After that, when I passed the Woolworth's windows, it would come back—that dizzy desperate hunger edged with hatred and an aching lust to hurt somebody back. I wondered if that kind of hunger and rage was what Tommy Lee felt when he went through his mama's pocketbook. It was a hunger in the back of the throat, not the belly, an echoing emptiness that ached for the release of screaming. Whenever we went to visit Daddy Glen's people, that hunger would throb and swell behind my tongue until I found myself standing silent and hungry in the middle of a family gathering full of noise and food.

It was not only Daddy Glen's brothers being lawyers and dentists instead of mechanics and roofers that made them so different from Boatwrights. In Daddy Glen's family the women stayed at home. His own mama had never held a job in her life, and Daryl and James both spoke badly of women who would leave their children to "work outside the home." His father, Bodine Waddell, owned the Sunshine Dairy and regularly hired and fired men like my mother's brothers, something he never let us forget.

"Awful proud for a man runs cows," Beau said of him once, and Glen was immediately indignant.

"Daddy don't have to handle the cows," he told Earle. "Farmers all over the county bring him their milk, or he has it picked up. Daddy just processes the milk, bottles it under the Sunshine label, and his trucks deliver it."

"Oh, yeah," Earle nodded solemnly. "That's a big difference, that is. Man don't run cows, he just leases the rights to their titties."

Glen looked like he was going to spit or cry but controlled himself. "Just don't say nothing about my daddy." He almost growled. "Just don't."

Earle and Beau let it go at that. Glen couldn't help what a shit his daddy was, and it was never smart to talk bad about a man's people to his face. With the passage of time, Glen had gotten more and more peculiar about his family, one moment complaining of how badly they treated him and the next explaining it away. Worst of all, he insisted that we all had to go over to his brothers' or daddy's places whenever there was any kind of family occasion, though it was clear to me that they were never happy to see us. We wound up going over to Daddy Waddell's place at least once every other month. In the Pontiac with the top down and paper scraps blowing around on the floor, Reese and I would lean over the front seat to watch Mama try to keep her hair neat in the whistling wind and listen to Daddy Glen lie.

"We won't stay long," he would always promise, and Mama would smile like she didn't care at all. We gritted our teeth. We knew that he would not have the nerve to leave before his father had delivered his lecture on all the things Glen had done wrong in his long life of failure and disappointment.

"Your daddy wants his daddy to be proud of him," Mama once said. "It about breaks my heart. He should just as soon whistle for the moon."

It was true. Around his father, Glen became unsure of himself and too careful. He broke out in a sweat, and his eyes kept flickering back to his daddy's face as if he had to keep watching or miss the thing he needed most to see. He would pull at his pants like a little boy and drop his head if anyone asked him a question. It was hard to put that image of him next to the way he was all the rest of the time—the swaggering bantam rooster man who called himself my daddy.

"Old Glen's a cock and a half," my uncle Earle would

99

tease. "An't nobody better take a bite out of his ass. Boy'll get you down if it takes bare bone to do it." Which was true enough. Half a dozen times I came home from school to find Mama and Glen sitting at the kitchen table with that white-eyed scared look that meant he'd jumped somebody who'd said something to him and lost yet another job.

"Man can't keep his temper," Granny complained, but grinned in spite of herself. Everybody did. It was the one thing that saved Daddy Glen from the Boatwrights' absolute contempt. The berserker rage that would come on him was just a shade off the power of the Boatwrights' famous binges. "You mess with one of those boys and you reap the whirlwind," people said of my uncles, and after a while of Daddy Glen. Tire irons and pastry racks, pitchforks and mop handles, things got bent or broken around Daddy Glen. His face would pink up and his hands would shake; his neck would start to work, the muscles ridging up and throbbing; then his mouth would swell and he would spit. Words came out that were not meant to be understood: *Goddam motherfucker son of a bitch shitass!* Magic words that made other men back off, put their hands up, palms out, and whisper back, "Now, Glen, now, now, Glen, now, hold on, boy . . ."

"Your daddy's a son of a bitch himself, a purely crazy pigfucker," Grey was always telling me with a little awe in his voice, a hunger to be half again as dangerous. I'd smile and nod and bite the inside of my lips, replaying in my head two separate movie images: Daddy Glen screaming at me, his neck bright red with rage, and the other, impossible vision just by it, Daddy Glen at *his* daddy's house with his head hanging down and his mouth so soft spit shone on the lower lip.

"I hate to go over there," Mama said, "hate standing around waiting for his daddy to notice us." She was brushing our hair out fine and loose and putting little barrettes up on the peak where she wanted it to stay back. Reese and I stood still and said nothing. We knew we were not supposed to pay attention when Mama talked about Daddy Glen's people.

"Whose birthday is it?" was about the only safe thing to ask, since it was always somebody's birthday, or a wedding or christening. The Waddells didn't have as many cousins and aunts and uncles as we did, but the women still made babies— somebody was always celebrating something.

One Sunday it was a double, a birthday for James and one of his kids. "One of the children," Daddy Glen's sister-in-law Madeline corrected me. "Kids are billygoats."

Goddam right, I thought, staring over at my puffy cousin in creased pants, an eight-year-old copy of his fat ugly father. They served us tea in the backyard, just us—Anney's girls, they called us. Their kids went in and out of the house, loud, raucous, scratching their nails on the polished furniture, kicking their feet on the hardwood floors, tracking mud in on the braided rugs.

"Those little brats need their asses slapped." Mama was sitting with us at the picnic table in the garden, out where no one could hear her. She'd come to check on us where we sat in our starched dresses, our faces as stiff as the sleeves. Reese and I were sweaty and miserable trying not to wiggle around on the benches, to look well-behaved for Mama's sake and stay out of the way of those kids who hated us as much as we did them.

"When are we going?" we kept asking Mama, knowing she couldn't tell us but asking just the same.

"Soon," she'd say, and light another cigarette with shaking hands. Mama didn't smoke in Daddy Waddell's house, though no one ever told her she couldn't. They just didn't leave ashtrays out. But I once saw Madeline smoking over the kitchen sink, dropping her ashes down the drain. It made me wonder if all of them went off in the kitchen or bathroom to smoke, pretending the rest of the time that they didn't have any such dirty habits.

"Can't we go home now?"

"No, James wants to show Daddy his new lawnmower."

"I thought he got a new one last year."

"This one's the kind that you can ride on while you cut the grass."

"Don't seem the yard's big enough to need that."

"Well"—Mama gave a short laugh—"I don't think James buys anything just 'cause he needs it." She brushed herself down carefully before going back in, though there wasn't a speck of ash on her. "You girls play nice, now."

We sat still, wonderfully behaved, almost afraid to move. "Yes, ma'am. No, ma'am." We kept our backs straight and never spoke out of turn, trying to imagine that Daddy Glen would look out and see us and be proud. His people watched us out the windows. Behind them, shelves of books and framed pictures mocked me. How could Reese and I be worthy of all that, the roses in their garden, the sunlight on those polished windows and flowered drapes, the china plates gleaming behind glass cabinets? I stared in at the spines of those books, wanting it all, wanting the furniture, the garden, the big open kitchen with its dishes for everyday and others for special, the freezer in the utility room and the plushy seats on all the dining-room chairs. Reese tugged at my arm, wanting me to talk to her, but I couldn't speak around the hunger in my throat.

From behind the rosebushes, I heard Daryl and James talking. "Look at that car. Just like any nigger trash, getting something like that."

"What'd you expect? Look what he married."

"Her and her kids sure go with that car. . . ."

I pushed my black hair out of my eyes and looked in at one of my wide-mouthed cousins in a white dress with eyelet sleeves looking back at me, scratching her nose and staring like I was some elephant in a zoo—something dumb and ugly and impervious to hurt. What do they tell her about us? I wondered. That we're not really family, just her crazy uncle's wife's nasty kids? You're no relative of mine, you're not my people, I whispered to myself. New and terrible words rolled around in my head while the air turned cool on my neck.

To Reese's surprise, I got up, shook out my skirt, and

strolled off for a walk through Madeline's rosebushes. I put my hands out and trailed them lightly along the thorny stalks and plush blossoms, scooping buds off as I passed. I pulled the buds apart, tearing the petals and dropping them down inside my dress. I even pulled up my skirt and tucked some in my panties, walking more slowly then to feel the damp silky flowers moving against my skin.

Trash steals, I thought, echoing Aunt Madeline's cold accent, her husband's bitter words. "Trash for sure," I muttered, but I only took the roses. No hunger would make me take anything else of theirs. I could feel a kind of heat behind my eyes that lit up everything I glanced at. It was dangerous, that heat. It wanted to pour out and burn everything up, everything they had that we couldn't have, everything that made them think they were better than us. I stood in the garden and spun myself around and around, pouring out heat and rage and the sweet stink of broken flowers.

I was ten, a long-boned restless ten, when we moved to West Greenville so Daddy Glen could be closer to the new uniform plant where he'd gotten a job as an account salesman. Boxing up dishes and pots in the utility shed, Mama found the remains of the love knot Aunt Maybelle and Aunt Marvella had given her. It had been reduced to scraps held together by dust and seemed to have survived only because it had fallen between the bottom of one flower pot and the bowl of another. Mice had picked the ribbon apart from the hair, and bugs had carried off most of the herbs and blood. Even so, the knotted core of the old lace scrap had somehow held all that time. Mama recognized the thing from the color of the ribbon.

"That was a wedding present from your Eustis aunts," Mama told me, but I already knew what it was from Granny's stories. As Mama carefully tried to gather it up, the whole thing fell to dust. My stomach cramped, and I wrapped my arms tight around my middle. Impatiently, Mama swept out the shed and packed up her laundry baskets. "Root magic," she muttered to me.

That week Marvella woke up in the night after dreaming her hair had turned to barbed wire, and Maybelle woke up in the morning sure the rabbits had eaten all their beans. They found instead that a dog had dug up the honeycomb and torn right through the lace. Neither of them told the other what they thought it meant.

The new house in West Greenville was so far from any of the aunts' houses that there was rarely time to stop by and see them. Granny was still keeping Reese for Mama when she could, but it was out of the way to take her to Alma's and pick her up, and Mama decided maybe it was time to start trusting me to keep us both alive while she was at work. After that we only saw Granny on the Sundays when Mama would let Daddy Glen sleep and take us over to visit with Aunt Ruth or Aunt Alma. "Hate you being so far away," her sisters would complain, but Mama would just smile and tell them how nice our new house was, how hard Daddy Glen was working. And it was a nice house, with a big wide yard, but it also cost more, which meant Mama had to take on a few extra hours to bring in a little more money. It didn't seem as if Daddy Glen's route was working out as well as they had hoped.

"Your daddy's having to work awfully hard these days," Mama told us. "You girls be quiet when he gets home. Stay out of his way and let him get his rest."

"He loves you," Mama was always saying, and she meant it, but it seemed like Daddy Glen's hands were always reaching for me, trembling on the surface of my skin, as if something pulled him to me and pushed him away at the same time. I would look up at him, carefully, watchfully, and see his eyes staring at me like I was something unimaginable and strange. "You don't look like your mama," he said once, "except when you're asleep." Sometimes when I ran by him, his hands would suddenly catch me, half-lift me, and pull me back to him. He would look into my face, shake me once, and let me go.

"Don't run like that," he'd say. "You're a girl, not a racehorse."

Reese and I joked about that and played racehorses when we got home from school every day, running through the empty house and jumping on the big hassock that sat in front of his chair. One day we chased each other into the house as always, not noticing the car out back, not seeing Daddy Glen until he caught my shoulder in one big hand.

"What did I tell you?" he shouted, and lifted me high, shaking me back and forth till my head rocked on my neck. "You bitch. You little bitch." My body slammed the wall, my heels knocking hollowly a foot above the floor. I saw Reese run away through a shimmering wave of dizziness, and then I was under his arm being carried down the hall to the bathroom. He kicked the door shut behind us and dropped me.

"I'm sorry, I'm sorry." I was so frightened I stuttered.

"Not as sorry as you're gonna be." He pulled his belt free from the loops and wrapped the buckle end around his palm. "I've waited a long time to do this, too long."

His face was pale, his jaw rigid, his eyes almost red in the glare of the fluorescent light over the mirror. I stumbled back against the tub, terrified, praying Mama would come home fast. Mama would stop him. His left hand reached for me, caught my shoulder, pulled me over his left leg. He flipped my skirt up over my head and jammed it into that hand. I heard the sound of the belt swinging up, a song in the air, a high-pitched terrible sound. It hit me and I screamed. Daddy Glen swung his belt again. I screamed at its passage through the air, screamed before it hit me. I screamed for Mama. He was screaming with me, his great hoarse shouts as loud as my high thin squeals, and behind us outside the locked door, Reese was screaming too, and then Mama. All of us were screaming, and no one could help.

When Daddy Glen unlocked the door, Mama slapped him and grabbed me up in her arms. He held one hand to his cheek and watched as I hiccuped and cried into her neck. "You son of a bitch," she cursed him, and ran water to wash my face.

"She's my girl too," he said. "Someone's got to love her enough to care how she turns out." His face was sullen, swollen and empty, like he had woken up from a long, long sleep.

"I don't want to hear it," Mama yelled, pushing him out the door. She put me on her lap and washed my face, my neck, the backs of my swollen thighs.

"Oh, my baby," she kept saying. I lay still against her, grateful to be safe in her arms. The air felt funny on my skin, and I had screamed so hard I had no voice left. I said nothing, let Mama talk, only half hearing what she was whispering. "Baby," she called me. "Oh, girl. Oh, honey. Baby, what did you do? What did you do?"

What had I done? I had run in the house. What was she asking? I wanted her to go on talking and understand without me saying anything. I wanted her to love me enough to leave him, to pack us up and take us away from him, to kill him if need be. I held on to her until she put me to bed, held on to her and whimpered then. I held on to her until I fell into a drugged, miserable sleep.

I woke up to the sound of them talking, their words echoing through the closed door of the bedroom. I heard everything he said, heard Mama crying in his arms. Daddy Glen told her I had called him a bastard, that I had come running through the house knocking things over and called him that name. He cried and swore he hadn't meant to beat me so bad, he didn't know what had made him do it. He sobbed and then beat his fists against the mattress so hard the springs squeaked.

"She told me she hated me," he said, "told me I would never be her daddy. And I went crazy, Anney. I just went crazy. Do you know? Do you understand how much I love you all, love her?

"And—oh, God, Anney! They laid me off today. Just put me out without a care. And what am I going to do to feed these girls now?"

Reese lay on the bed with me, her fingers in her mouth, her eyes enormous. She said nothing. I lay still, listening to Daddy Glen's lies, wondering if he thought he was telling the truth. I kept looking into Reese's face, her baby face, smooth and empty and scared. The sound of Mama crying grew softer, faded. In the stillness that followed I heard Daddy Glen whispering, heard a murmur as Mama replied. Then there was a sigh and the creak of their bed as he comforted Mama and she comforted him. Sex. They were making love, Mama sighing and sobbing and Daddy Glen repeating her name over and over. I looked into Reese's eyes, and we listened to the small sounds they were making.

"You made him mad," Reese whispered. "You better be careful."

I tried to be careful, but something had come apart. Something had gotten loose like the wild strands of Aunt Marvella's hair unraveling in the dust. There was no way I could be careful enough, no way to keep Daddy Glen from exploding into rage. Dr Pepper took him on as a route man, but at less pay than the uniform service. He had one of the short routes, not much money to be made on it, and not enough work to make it full-time. He came home at odd hours, early and late. Mama started working later and later, for whatever money she could get, and I stayed out of the house as much as I could. If I went home when he was there and Mama wasn't, he was always finding something I'd done, something I had to be told, something he just had to do because he loved me. And he did love me. He told me so over and over again, holding my body tight to his, his hands shaking as they moved restlessly, endlessly, over my belly, ass, and thighs.

"You're just like your mama," he'd say, and press his stubbly cheek to mine.

I would stand rigid, ashamed but unable to pull away, afraid of making him angry, afraid of what he might tell Mama, and at the same time, afraid of hurting his feelings. "Daddy," I would start to whisper, and he would whisper back, "Don't you know how I love you?" And I would recoil. No, I did not know.

He never said "Don't tell your mama." He never had to

say it. I did not know how to tell anyone what I felt, what scared me and shamed me and still made me stand, unmoving and desperate, while he rubbed against me and ground his face into my neck. I could not tell Mama. I would not have known how to explain why I stood there and let him touch me. It wasn't sex, not like a man and woman pushing their naked bodies into each other, but then, it was something like sex, something powerful and frightening that he wanted badly and I did not understand at all. Worse, when Daddy Glen held me that way, it was the only time his hands were gentle, and when he let me go, I would rock on uncertain feet.

Daddy Glen smelled of sweat and Coca-Cola, of after-shave and cigarettes, but mostly of something I could not name—something acid, bitter, and sharp. Fear. It might have been fear. But I could not have said if it was his fear or mine. I could not say anything. I only knew that there was something I was doing wrong, something terrible. He said, "You drive me crazy," in a strange distracted voice, and I shuddered but believed him.

I became even more afraid of Daddy Glen, the palms that slapped, the fingers that dug in and bruised, the knuckles he would sometimes press directly under my eyes, the hands that shook and gripped and lifted me up until his eyes would stare into mine. My own hands were so small, my fingers thin and weak. I wished they were bigger, wider, stronger. I wished I was a boy so I could run faster, stay away more, or even hit him back.

Grey gave me a rubber ball, hard rubber, black and small enough to hide in my hand. I cupped it in my palms so no one would see. I worked that ball with passion, rolled it between my fingers with determination, squeezed it stubbornly, clenching each finger against my thumbs. One day my hands would be as strong as Daddy Glen's were. No matter the size, I told myself, one day my hands would be a match for his. Some days I thought I was working that ball so that I could grow to be more like him; other days I knew that wasn't why.

That spring, Earle and Daddy Glen argued over some tools

Daddy Glen swore he had loaned Earle and never gotten back. Earle took offense and stopped coming over to visit. After that Daddy Glen started talking bad about the Boatwrights all the time, glaring at me if I asked Mama anything about what he now called "that trash." He made fun of how often the uncles would get blind drunk and shoot up each other's trucks, he talked dirty about Mama's nieces who were always sneaking off to the Rhythm Ranch to sip whiskey and dance with men older than their fathers. No matter what Daddy Glen said, Mama never said much at all. Her face was tired all the time.

"I don't want to hear it," she'd say when I tried to tell her something Granny or Aunt Alma had passed on to me. "Nothing to be proud of in shooting people for looking at you wrong."

I was ashamed of the way Daddy Glen talked, but Mama didn't seem ashamed. She just got quiet, more and more quiet all the time. I begged her to tell me stories like Granny did, but she said I was too young to hear such things. Maybe when I was grown and had my own family she would tell me what few things she thought I needed to know, but until then she expected me to ask no questions she didn't want to answer. Glen was right, Mama told me, she didn't want me to grow up as wild and mean as Earle or Beau or even Raylene.

When Daddy Glen beat me there was always a reason, and Mama would stand right outside the bathroom door. Afterward she would cry and wash my face and tell me not to be so stubborn, not to make him mad. I'd promise, but I had a talent for sassing back and making Daddy Glen mad, though it was hard to know how not to make him mad. Sometimes when I looked up into his red features and blazing eyes, I knew that it was nothing I had done that made him beat me. It was just me, the fact of my life, who I was in his eyes and mine. I was evil. Of course I was. I admitted it to myself, locked my fingers into fists, and shut my eyes to everything I did not understand.

"Bone." Cousin Deedee was the first to call me Bone, but everyone did by the time we were living in West Greenville. Dog bone, penny bone, suckle bone, milk tooth, goat head, horse head, tiger bone, collarbone, hipbone, neckbone, knees and toes.

"You are hard as bone, the stubbornest child on the planet!" Daddy Glen told me. "Cold as death, mean as a snake, and twice as twisty."

Daddy Glen was careful not to hit me when one of the aunts was visiting, and never much when Mama would see, except for those times he could justify as discipline, dragging me into the bathroom while she waited on the other side of the locked door. It was when Reese and I were alone with him that he was dangerous. If I ran from him, he would come after me. He shook me so hard my head wobbled loosely, and he'd joke that chickens and goats had more starch to them than a Boatwright, even a half-Boatwright like I was.

It was the bones in my head I thought about, the hard, porous edge of my skull cradling my brain, reassuring me that no matter what happened I could heal up from it eventually. It was the heat in my heart, my hard, gritty center. I linked my fingers behind my head, clenched my teeth, and rocked back and forth. The sturdy stock we were boasted to be came down in me to stubbornness and bone.

I was always getting hurt, it seemed, in ways Mama could not understand and I could not explain. Mama worried about how careless I was, how prone to accident I had become. "Maybe you're thin-boned," she guessed, and started buying me vitamins. I didn't know what to say to her. To say anything would mean trying to tell her everything, to describe those times when he held me tight to his belly and called me sweet names I did not want to hear. I remained silent, stubborn, resentful, and collected my bruises as if they were unavoidable. There were lumps at the back of my head, not swellings of flesh and tissue but a rumpled ridge of bone. My big toes went flat and wide, broken within a few months of each other when I smashed into doorjambs, running while looking back over my shoulder.

"How could you do that?" Mama asked me. It was my fault, I wasn't supposed to run in the house.

"She's always getting into something," Daddy Glen complained. "Lucky she's such a hardheaded brat."

I watched him from under lowered lashes, my head turned slightly to the side, careful not to grin out of my unmarked stubborn face.

"Bone, be more careful," Mama begged me.

I didn't daydream about fire anymore. Now I imagined people watching while Daddy Glen beat me, though only when it was not happening. When he beat me, I screamed and kicked and cried like the baby I was. But sometimes when I was safe and alone, I would imagine the ones who watched. Someone had to watch—some girl I admired who barely knew I existed, some girl from church or down the street, or one of my cousins, or even somebody I had seen on television. Sometimes a whole group of them would be trapped into watching. They couldn't help or get away. They had to watch. In my imagination I was proud and defiant. I'd stare back at him with my teeth set, making no sound at all, no shameful scream, no begging. Those who watched admired me and hated him. I pictured it that way and put my hands between my legs. It was scary, but it was thrilling too. Those who watched me, loved me. It was as if I was being beaten for them. I was wonderful in their eyes.

My fantasies got more violent and more complicated as Daddy Glen continued to beat me with the same two or three belts he'd set aside for me. Oiled, smooth and supple as the gristle under chicken fat, those belts hung behind the door of his closet where I could see them and smell them when I helped Mama put away his clothes. I would reach up and touch the leather, feel it warm under my palms. There was no magic in it, no mystery. Sometimes I would make myself go in that closet and wrap my fingers around those belts as if they were something animal that could be tamed.

I was ashamed of myself for the things I thought about

when I put my hands between my legs, more ashamed for masturbating to the fantasy of being beaten than for being beaten in the first place. I lived in a world of shame. I hid my bruises as if they were evidence of crimes I had committed. I knew I was a sick disgusting person. I couldn't stop my stepfather from beating me, but *I* was the one who masturbated. *I* did that, and how could I explain to anyone that I hated being beaten but still masturbated to the story I told myself about it?

Yet it was only in my fantasies with people watching me that I was able to defy Daddy Glen. Only there that I had any pride. I loved those fantasies, even though I was sure they were a terrible thing. They had to be; they were self-centered and they made me have shuddering orgasms. In them, I was very special. I was triumphant, important. I was not ashamed. There was no heroism possible in the real beatings. There was just being beaten until I was covered with snot and misery.

My collarbone fused with a lump the second time it was broken—an accident, Daddy Glen insisted, just like the first time when I had fallen off the porch. In the hospital the young intern glared and ordered lots of X-rays.

"How'd she break her coccyx?" he demanded of Mama over the sheaf of X-rays when we were ready to go home. He had a funny accent and a mass of black curly hair. He leaned over Mama like he was going to hit her.

"Her what?"

"Her tailbone, lady, her ass. What have you been hitting this child with? Or have you just been throwing her up against the wall?"

"What are you saying?" Mama's face was white and stiff; his was red and angry. "What are you saying?" This time Mama's voice went high and loud. A middle-aged nurse in a rumpled uniform was suddenly at my right side, one hand on the doctor's arm and the other reaching for Mama. There was a tag on her pocket that read "Myer."

"Let's not get excited," she said. "Let's calm down."

The doctor took hold of my chin. His fingers were warm, the skin rough and dry. "Tell us," he said. "You tell us."

I looked into his pupils and I could see myself there, my face tiny and strange above the bandage wrapping my shoulder and arm. He looked angry, and impatient, and disgusted. He glared at Mama with no pity at all. I could feel Mama's fingers gripping the palm of my free hand, hear her breathing like she was going to be sick. When I looked up into her face I saw her terror, and behind it her love for me. Daddy Glen was outside waiting in the car with Reese. The nurse started talking, but I didn't listen.

"Mama, take me home," I whispered. Mama's hand slipped around my waist. Her fingers felt icy through the thin cotton material of my blouse—icy but comforting.

"Let go of my girl," she told the doctor. His mouth twisted, and he gave my chin a little shake. I let my eyes move over his face. He didn't know us, didn't know my mama or me. "You can tell us," he said in his stranger's voice.

I held on to Mama and wouldn't say anything at all. The doctor slapped the bed beside me hard, then turned and slammed the door open with his fists. I looked at the nurse. Mrs. Myer was watching me carefully, her hand over her mouth, her eyes old and wise.

"I'm sorry," she said to Mama finally, dropping her hand. "He's young and he's not been here long."

We waited, Mama holding me, Mrs. Myer taking long, slow breaths and glancing back at the door. A black woman with a clipboard full of papers came in and passed them over.

"You'll need to sign this," Mrs. Myer told Mama. She didn't look at me again.

I knew exactly what she thought, but I didn't know about Mama. Her face was strange and hard, her hand where it held me was still cold, but now it was shaking too. For the few moments they left us alone, she looked into my face like it was a map of hell.

"Bone," she whispered.

I waited.

"Sweetheart."

Someone walked past in the hall. I put my head over against Mama's breast, listening to her heart, not wanting to hear anything else.

"Baby."

"Mama," I begged. "Mama, take me home."

"We're gonna go to Aunt Alma's house," she told me while lifting me into the backseat. The look she gave Daddy Glen when he tried to help her seemed to freeze his heart. His hands stretched before him, he kept reaching out but not touching her. In the front seat, Reese sat with her thumb in her mouth, her face blank and still. Propped up in the back with pillows, I leaned my cheek against the plastic seat cover and tried not to move too much. My shoulder felt hot and enormous, like a balloon full of pain waiting to blow through me. Daddy Glen followed Mama around the front of the car, plucking at her shoulders hesitantly, but she kept shaking him off. *"Don't!"* she shouted once. The car shook when she slammed the door, and I gritted my teeth. Daddy Glen leaned in the window, pleading, tears showing on his face in the lights of the emergency room entrance.

"Anney, oh, Anney, just talk to me. Don't do this. Anney, please, Anney!"

Mama started the car off slowly, letting him hang on to the side until she pulled out into the street. I didn't see the look she gave him then, but I heard his cry, hoarse and meaningless, as she gunned the engine, her foot holding down on the brake, the Pontiac jerking but holding. He let go of the door but didn't step back. His face was still close and then it was gone.

Mama's chin was sharp, shining now against other car lights, now against the lights from the dash. I watched the tears on her face when she looked back at me. I closed my eyes, opened them. Everything seemed spongy and strange, but

I couldn't care anymore. The cool air rushing in the window was damp and sweet. If there really was a God or even magic, that air would blow through me and out again. It would go back down that road to the hospital, sweep up the dirt, and throw it in Daddy Glen's eyes. It would make him see who he was, what he had done. That doctor would come out on his way home, see him there, and know who he was. The wind would tell him, the moon, or maybe even God. That doctor would know, and he would start his car, knowing. He would slam that car into gear and roar across that lot. The grille would stop just inches from Daddy Glen's terrified face.

"You son of a bitch," that doctor would scream. *"You ever touch that child again and I'll grind you into meat and blood!"*

Daddy Glen would weep tears of blood. Jesus, maybe, would come into his heart. He'd follow us out to Alma's and get on his knees before the whole family. "I have sinned," he'd say, and hold his hands out to me, beg my forgiveness and cry my name. Mama would say no. My aunts would say no. My uncles, Reese, the minister, everyone in the world would stand up and say no. But I would pull myself up from my sickbed. I would look right into his eyes, into the lamps of his soul.

Yes, I would say.

Yes. I forgive you.

Then probably I would die.

I almost laughed, my shoulders shook. The pain was hot and took the story away so fast I made a little sound. I swallowed hard, determined not to cry. Mama reached over for me. Her face looked old, very old and tired. It made my heart hurt to see her look that way. I couldn't hurt her, I couldn't.

"I'm sorry," I whispered.

"Don't, honey, don't. You didn't do anything wrong." Her lips were swollen where she had bitten them, and I felt my own lips swollen and cracked against my teeth.

"I love you." My voice was so soft I didn't think she heard me. But hers came back to me, quick and low.

"I love you too."

Two weeks later we were back home with Daddy Glen. Nothing had changed. Everything had changed. Daddy Glen had said he was sorry, begged, wept, and swore never to hurt me again. I had stood silent, stubborn, and numb. He had gotten down on his knees in front of Alma, Wade, their kids, and Mama, pulled Reese and me into his embrace, and vowed that he couldn't live without our love. Mama had knelt on the floor with him and made him swear an oath never to raise his hand to me again.

I had looked into his wet features and had known, without question, what was going to happen. Mama would forgive him, though she would watch him close and make him earn her trust again. He would be good, he would be careful. But after a while, Daddy Glen would begin to talk about the accident a little differently. He would remember things that had happened around that time, things I had said, looks I had given him.

One day, maybe months from now, there'd be something I'd done that would make it all seem justified. Then Daddy Glen would take me into the bathroom again, crying that it hurt him more than it could ever hurt me. But his face would tell the truth, his hands on my body. He would show me just how much he hurt when Mama left him in that parking lot, and then when he beat me, we would both know why. But Mama wouldn't know. More terrified of hurting her than of anything that might happen to me, I would work as hard as he did to make sure she never knew.

I set my teeth and tried to ignore everything but what was right in front of me. I talked to no one and kept my face buried in books. At night, I lay in bed with my clasped hands pushing up against the tender place between my legs, listening to the radio and trying not to think. My shoulder had healed quickly under Mama's patient, watchful care, but I felt as if something inside me would never be all right. I woke up so angry my throat hurt. My teeth felt ground down to the nerves. I would go look in the mirror, expecting to see blood in my mouth, but there was nothing, only my teeth small, white, and sharp. Mama kept me close to her. She even let me get up at dawn to sit with her during her most private moments, the hour when she sipped coffee and watched the sun rise.

"Never have been able to sleep past sunrise," she told me. "No matter how little sleep I've had, I just come awake." Her face was haggard. She hugged me to her hip and laid her chin on the top of my head. It was as if I was her mother now, holding her safe, and she was my child, happy to lean on my strong, straight back. I closed my eyes, wanting time to stop, wishing the moment would go on forever, the day never begin. But inevitably Daddy Glen would get up, or Reese, and Mama would rinse her coffee cup and go put on her uniform.

Afternoons after school, Mama insisted Reese and I go over to Aunt Alma's and stay until she came to get us. I'd help Aunt Alma with her garden or her canning, and while we worked I would make up stories in my head. My cousins loved my stories—especially the ones that featured bloodsuckers who consumed only the freshly butchered bodies of newborn babies, green-faced dwarfs promising untold riches to children who would bring them the hearts of four and forty grown men. Grey told me that I had "a very interesting mind for a girl." But Aunt Alma came to the porch one day when I was telling one of the boys' favorites and got so upset she looked like she would piss herself. If she had heard it all she would probably have beaten me harder than Daddy Glen. My stories were full of boys and girls gruesomely raped and murdered, babies cooked in pots of boiling beans, vampires and soldiers and long razor-sharp knives. Witches cut off the heads of children and grown-ups. Gangs of women rode in on motorcycles and set fire to people's houses. The ground opened and green-black lizard tongues shot up to pull people down. I got to be very popular as a baby-sitter; everyone was quiet and well-behaved while I told stories, their eyes fixed on my face in a way that made me feel like one of my own witches casting a spell.

"Girl," Cousin Grey told me, "sometimes your face is just scary!"

"Bone's gotten almost mean-hearted," Aunt Alma told Mama. "Something's got to be done."

Mama started taking me with her to the diner. There I could earn my own money washing dishes, money Mama didn't make me save for clothes but let me spend as I pleased, mostly on secondhand books from racks at the thrift store that I could then trade in at the paperback exchange. Reese complained that I never played with her anymore, that I was always working or reading or sleeping. When school let out for the summer, I found a hiding place in the woods near Aunt Alma's where I could camp for hours with a bag of Hershey Kisses and a book. The librarian gave me *Black Beauty*, *Robinson Crusoe*, and *Tom Sawyer*. On my own I found copies of *Not as a Stranger*, *The Naked and the Dead*, *This Gun for Hire*, and *Marjorie Morningstar*. I climbed up a tree to read the sexy parts over, drank water out of the creek, and only went home at dark.

Mama was still worried about me, I could tell. "Honey, are you all right?" she asked me one morning. I just shrugged and went back to the paperback copy of *The Secret Garden* I'd never returned to the school library. She pushed the book down and took it away, making me look at her. Her face was thinner, her skin rougher, and there were shadows under her eyes that never went away. People no longer talked about how beautiful she was, but about how beautiful she had been.

"I want you to do something for me." She looked down at the book in her hands, at her fingers tracing the cracked spine and tape-wrapped cover. I gritted my teeth, afraid of what she might ask.

"Your aunt Ruth isn't doing well, you know. She's gotten a lot weaker this summer, Travis says."

That surprised me. I had thought Mama would want to talk about how withdrawn I had become, how I never watched television with them now, or played with Reese or talked to anybody. Besides, Aunt Ruth had been sick so long everybody took it for granted. Could she really be that much worse?

"Now that Deedee and Butch are gone, Travis worries about Ruth when she's home alone. He asked me if you might not be willing to stay out there for a while, at least until she's better."

Mama opened *The Secret Garden* to the place where I had slipped my bookmark, a piece of ribbon embossed with the Piggly Wiggly logo. "What do you think?" she asked.

"I don't know," I said automatically. I hadn't seen Aunt Ruth in a while, not since the day after Christmas, when Mama had taken us over to Aunt Alma's for dinner with all her sisters. Even then Aunt Ruth had been thin and weak, her fingers blue and swollen where they lay in her lap. What would I do if she got worse while I was with her? What if she were to die?

"Well . . ." Mama closed the book and passed it back to me. "I want you to go out there for a while, at least a week or so, while Travis gets a little time for himself."

I nodded.

"Good." Mama sighed as if something difficult had been settled. She reached over and pushed my hair back behind my ears. "Oh, Bone, why are you always letting your hair hang down in your eyes like that? You've got such a pretty face. If you'd let me give you a permanent, people could see your eyes and your smile."

I grinned at her and shook my head. Her face relaxed a little, and she smiled back at me. "You are so stubborn." Her fingers trailed lightly across my brow, smoothing back a few loose strands of hair. "Even more stubborn than your mama, I think."

Aunt Ruth had changed in ways I had not imagined possible. Her hair, once thick and dark red, was almost all gone. What remained had paled to orange straw that she covered with a green-checked cotton scarf when she went out. She had grown so thin that I probably could have lifted her all by myself, though she would never allow me to try. But the greatest change was in how she moved and talked. She had always been the slow, soft-spoken aunt, the quiet one who thought a lot and said little. Now she talked continuously, moving her fingers in constant little jerking motions and shifting her eyes around all the time as if she were afraid she might miss something. Bird-like, she lifted her head and craned to see out the windows while her fingers picked at the afghan she kept across her lap no matter how hot it was. She lived on the couch now, with occasional forays to her rocker on the porch, and had made Travis take down the curtains so that nothing blocked her view. She watched the sunrise and the sunset and napped whenever she chose, and between naps she talked. After the first few days of refilling her juice glass and watching her make her slow, careful way to the bathroom, I began to suspect that my main purpose was to provide Aunt Ruth with an audience, someone who would nod at appropriate moments and not interrupt.

"When we were kids, we pretty much never saw our daddy," she told me one afternoon. "He was always off working or drinking or traveling somewhere. I got the idea that men weren't expected to hang around much. Now, when Travis is too much with me, he gets on my nerves, even when I'd almost like to have him here to help. It's good I've got you to stay with me, Bone. You don't get on my nerves at all."

Aunt Ruth lay back on the couch, hugging her belly with both arms, her eyes narrowing as her cheekbones caught the light pouring in the open door. The bones in her face stood out sharp and high. Propped on the couch with her legs drawn up so that her bare feet were against my thigh, she looked almost like a girl, a witch girl with a narrow gray face. Nobody should be that thin, so thin the pulse in her throat made the skin over her collarbones vibrate. She shaded her eyes for a moment, looking down the couch at me.

"You know, when you close your eyes, you look just like your mama when she was a girl."

I nodded. I wasn't paying much attention. Aunt Ruth had been talking a lot about Travis for the two weeks I'd been staying with her—about Travis and her daddy, about Uncle Earle and her brothers and sisters, about things that had happened long before I was born and she imagined no one had told me yet. I should have been glad to hear it all, finally, and to ask all the questions I had saved up for years. But for the first time in my life, I couldn't think about all those old stories. All I could think about was going home. When was Mama going to take me home? Did I want to go home?

I bit my lips, took a careful breath before I let what I had been thinking come out of me. Aunt Ruth looked over at me expectantly.

"Daddy Glen hates me." There, it was said. I drew my knees up and wrapped my arms around them, just waiting for her to say it wasn't so. She was looking directly at me, her face still, calm, open. I knotted my hands into fists.

"Tell me, Bone." Her voice was almost a whisper. "You think I'm dying?"

My stomach lurched. I looked out the door. Of course she

was dying. I looked back at her and then away again. "Naah, you're just awful damn sick."

"Bone."

I shook my head. The light coming in the screen door was too bright. Tears began to run down my face.

"Bone?"

"Auntie, don't ask me." I looked up. Lord, she was so thin!

"Well, can we talk to each other or not?" Her voice sounded tired. She closed her eyes and brought one hand up to rub the soft skin at her right temple. It looked slightly bruised, a blue shadow on the parchment gray.

"I don't know." I took the skin of my forearm between my teeth and sucked at it. I didn't know what to say to her at all.

"Well." She was quiet for a moment, then dropped her hand and kind of pushed herself up a little.

"I think we can. I think we have to. There's a lot of things I can't do anymore, but hell. . . ." She reached out to me, her fingers beckoning. "You slide over here."

I hesitated and then moved down until I could fit my hip between her legs. My back was against one thigh, and I draped my knees over the other. She put her arm around me and pulled me to her breast. "Honey," she whispered, and just held me for a moment.

"You're right, girl. Glen don't like you much. He's jealous, I think." She ran her fingers over my face, flicking away the tears and stroking my cheeks. "There's a way he's just a little boy himself, wanting more of your mama than you, wanting to be her baby more than her husband. And that an't so rare, I'll tell you."

I looked up at her. Her mouth was drawn into an awkward grin.

"Men," she said solemnly, "are just little boys climbing up on titty whenever they can. Your mama knows it as well as I do. We all do. And Glen . . ."

She was still for a minute, her eyes moving around the room as if she were looking for something. They came back to me. She pulled me tighter.

"Bone, has Daddy Glen ever . . . well . . . touched you?" Her gray cheeks developed matching streaks of pink. "Has he ever hurt you, messed with you?" Her hand dropped down, patted between my legs.

"Down here, honey. Has he ever hurt you down there?"

I searched Aunt Ruth's face carefully. I knew what she meant, the thing men did to women. I knew what the act was supposed to be, I'd read about it, heard the joke. "What's a South Carolina virgin? 'At's a ten-year-old can run fast." He hadn't done that. Had he? I felt my tongue pushing against the back of my teeth. Aunt Ruth's cheeks got a brighter pink, almost red. I dropped my head.

"No," I whispered. I remembered his hands sliding over my body, under my blouse, down my shorts, across my backside, the calluses scratching my skin, his breath fast and hard above me as he pulled me tighter and tighter against him, the sound of his belt pulling through the loops of his pants in the damp stillness of the bathroom. I shuddered.

"No." I said it louder. "He just looks at me hard. Grabs me sometimes. Shakes me." I hesitated, looking up at her flushed, sunken cheeks. "You know, when I'm bad." Tell her, I thought. Tell her all of it. Tell her. "But the way he looks at me, the way he twists his hands when he looks at me, it scares me, Auntie. He scares me."

Aunt Ruth rocked me against her breast.

"Oh, honey," she breathed. "What we gonna do with you?"

Afternoons, while Aunt Ruth slept in snatches, I scraped at the old paint on her front porch, keeping an eye on her through the screen door in case she needed me. Uncle Earle had promised to repaint the porch and the front of the house, and said he'd pay for my school clothes in the fall if I would get the wood all clean and scraped down for him. Every few days he'd stop by at lunchtime to talk quietly with Aunt Ruth and check on my progress. Half the time, Aunt Ruth would be asleep when he came, and he would sit out on the porch with me, smoking Uncle Travis's tobacco and telling me stories while I worked. It seemed to me that Aunt Ruth's illness was making him remember her when she was young and well, when they had all been kids together living out in the country north of Greenville, and when the two of them had first married and started their families—Aunt Ruth with Uncle Travis, and Earle with Teresa. He talked like Aunt Ruth did, as if he were continuing a conversation that was going on in his head all the time, musing, reminiscing, talking on and on.

"Your mama ever tell you about our daddy?" he began one afternoon, rolling a cigarette. "Man was something, all right. People called him 'that Boatwright boy' till the day he died. Took better care of his dogs than his wife or children—not that Mama needed much taking care of. Your granny is tougher than all her sons put together; she sure never seemed to expect much out of Daddy. Thing is, I think all of us, we're just like him. Your uncle Beau is a drunk. You know that, but so is your uncle Nevil, and so am I, I suppose. But an't none of us as shiftless as our daddy was, or as pretty, so we don't get away with it the way he did. It's why Teresa left me. She always said she wanted a man like a long, cool drink of water. Go on about it like women do when they're laying in your arms all soft and wanting to talk, talking about that crystal spring, that pure essential liquid."

He laughed a short, abrupt laugh, though I could see in his eyes no humor, just a gleam that seemed hard and angry. His fingers pressed down, inching the paper tight around the packed tobacco, then drawing the cigarette up so he could lick it closed.

"Teresa sure could talk. Lord God!" He looked off to the side as if remembering things he could not stand to face directly. I dropped my head. I didn't want him to stop talking.

"Teresa used to tell me how I filled her up, satisfied her

very soul. And every time, I'd think about our daddy—how Mama had to catch a drink of him now and then, so the man never filled her up, never actually eased her thirst. The woman always looked pinched and dry. I didn't want to do that to Teresa. Didn't want to be like that. I wanted to pour over that woman like a river of love. But shitfire! When she left me she told me I wasn't even a full mouth of spit. Me, her long, cool drink of water! Damn!"

Uncle Earle brushed tobacco flakes off his lap. "I just don't understand sometimes, Bone, how things got so messed up, the simplest things—me and Teresa, Mama and Daddy, your mama and Glen. Hell, even Ruth and Travis. You know, Travis left Ruth once when their kids were little, just took off for two months and never said a thing. And anybody can see how he loves her. Sometimes I just don't understand."

He tried to light the cigarette, but it fell apart in his hands. Looking down at the mess of damp tobacco all over his jeans, he swore and pushed himself up off the step. "Sad, an't it," he said, "a man who can't even keep a cigarette together? Sad as hell." He walked away, brushing his jeans as he went.

Aunt Ruth wanted to make sure I understood who our people were and what they had done. She devoted two whole days to the story of Great-Uncle Haslam Boatwright, who had driven a truck over at the JC Penney mill until he shot his wife and her lover on a weekend visit to Atlanta. He'd been locked away in the Georgia State Penitentiary ever since. She told me more about my real daddy and Lyle Parsons, and the whole story of how Daddy Glen had courted Mama through a solid year of lunches at the diner before she would ever date him. Best of all, she told me how Uncle Beau and Uncle Earle had tried to enlist in the army during the Korean War and had been thrown out of the recruiting office into the muddy street after the sergeant got their arrest records. Drunk and determined, they had made so much noise that the army boys called the county sheriff to lock them up.

"Oh, come on, son," Beau was supposed to have told that sergeant after punching out the deputy and chewing on the ear of some innocent fool who'd made the mistake of trying to help. "You an't gonna find better soldier material anywhere in the county. Hell, you can see we already know how to fight!"

Telling the story, Aunt Ruth snarled and twanged like Uncle Beau did when he'd been drinking, sounding so like him that I giggled to hear her.

"Bet they didn't really want to be in no army," I told her. "Bet they went down there on a dare or something."

"Well, they an't the type to play soldier," she agreed, "but they'd love the chance to shoot strangers, drive trucks, and work on engines. No different really from what they do now, except for the uniform. They love that story, though, never seem to pay no mind to the fact that the army didn't want no trash that has spent so much time in jail and hasn't even finished high school."

"They're drunks," I said, and Aunt Ruth just nodded.

"Kind of. No different from Travis, I suppose. But you know, they don't think about it. It's like going to jail. They think that a working man just naturally turns up in jail now and then, just like they believe they got a right to stay drunk from sunset on Friday to dawn on Monday morning. Beau himself swears that he was fine until he started drinking on weekdays." She shook her head, pushing her thin hair back with one trembling hand.

"You can't tell them nothing."

"Beau got his taste for beer as a boy," Aunt Ruth told us one Saturday morning. She was sitting out on her porch while I scraped at the railing and Earle cleaned the gunk out of the works of the old wringer washer she'd decided to sell.

"He used to go off with Raylene to that roadhouse over at the Greer city limits after she quit school and he'd just turned thirteen. They earned a little money by sweeping up and cleaning and stocking the coolers full of beer and Coca-

127

Cola. They'd always take themselves a few bottles as a bonus. Never hurt Raylene none, but she didn't have the taste. Liked cola better, matter of fact, and only took beer to sell back to Beau. Boy liked bottle beer better than mother's milk, and that's most of what he's always drunk, no matter what that wife of his swears. Beer can rot you out too, destroy your liver and turn your brains to bleached oatmeal. It's a fact. He didn't need that white liquor they sell over at the franchise."

"Oh, hell!" Earle slapped his palm against the oily metal of the wringer. He never liked to hear anything bad said about his brother Beau. He didn't even like to hear people repeat things he said himself. "Beau's got worse stuff than beer in his life. Beer's nothing. Keeps you regular, beer and pinto beans. If Beau was to stop drinking his beer, he'd probably swell up and explode." His restless black eyes dared Aunt Ruth to contradict him.

"That wife of his, that Maggie, is the trouble in Beau's life. Little white-faced thing, white eyes, white-headed, bruises soon as the wind blows hard. Woman makes babies the way you make biscuits. All the time pregnant with some little whey-faced empty-eyed child of God. Hellfire, Beau couldn't get ahead of himself if he gave up everything but black coffee and hard work. Seven children! Bad enough Alma's got so many, but at least she knows how to keep hers fed and clean. That little Maggie can't even change a diaper without coming on a dizzy spell. Woman has eaten Beau alive. Like some vampire sucking the juice out of him. You cut that girl open and you'd find Beau's blood pumping her heart."

"Magdaline's not the reason Beau's gonna bleed himself to death," Aunt Ruth snorted. "She don't make him drink that poison."

"Don't she?" Earle slammed the wringer down on the rags he'd spread out to spare the porch boards. "Tell the truth, Ruth. Don't you think she's got even a little to do with Beau keeping himself blind drunk all the time?"

Aunt Ruth pulled herself around to look Earle right in

the face. "You making out like you think that's what's wrong with your life, Earle Boatwright? Your woman eat the heart out of you? The mother of your daughters drive you to drink and day jobs and cursing on my porch in the broad daylight?"

I hugged my knees up close and watched Earle's face. He was always arguing with Aunt Ruth, but it rarely got so mean. I bit my lips and saw him hang his head. When Earle looked up, his face was red and his eyes all shiny.

"Yes, Ruth," he whispered. "The bitch of it is, I do."

Aunt Ruth harrumphed out her nose and then pulled herself out of her rocking chair to stalk over and grab him around the neck. "I'm sorry, baby." She looked a little wet-eyed herself. "That was a low thing for me to say. I know. I know how you miss your girls. Know how you ache for what is gone. Don't think I don't hurt for you, baby. Don't think I don't know how you hurt."

"Oh, Ruth!" Earle tried to jerk away, but Aunt Ruth was holding him too tight. I bit down harder, tasting metallic blood in my mouth, feeling my eyes swell up with hot tears, but almost choking on a crazy need to laugh. Aunt Ruth looked so funny, all spindly and frail hanging on to her big tall red-faced brother so hard she was nearly choking him. But he had always been her baby, like Beau and Alma and Raylene and Mama. Ruth had half-raised them and still acted more like their mother than Granny ever did. I watched Aunt Ruth's bluish fingers clutch at Earle's arms while he tried to keep his greasy black hands off her yellow chenille robe.

"Oh, Ruth," he groaned and gave it up. He hugged her back, picking her up in his arms. "Don't cry on me. We'll both be sick if you get to crying all over me." He stumbled across the porch and went down on one knee to put her back in her rocker. "It an't fair. I an't never been able to argue with a woman when she starts crying."

I hung on to the porch railing, watching the two of them hug each other tight. I couldn't imagine hugging Reese like that, telling her how I really felt, crying with her. It made me

jealous, made me wish I was part of that embrace, that genera-
tion, as quick to yell and curse as to cry and make up. Daddy
Glen said I was a cold-hearted bitch, and maybe I was. Maybe
I was.

The morning Mama drove up in Beau's truck, I was on the
porch with four little earthenware pots and Aunt Ruth's big
bucket of wandering Jew. She'd had the idea the day before
that she'd like to hang those pots just under the eaves of the
porch, and swore that I could leave half the plant in the bucket
and break up the rest of the red-and-blue-green tangle into the
little pots.

"What you think, sister?" Aunt Ruth called to Mama.
"An't they gonna look fine up there under the eaves? Stuff's so
sturdy it might even grow up over the roof."

"Might," Mama agreed, coming up to give me a fast hug.
"Grows quick enough anyway."

"People say it's a weed but I've always liked it, specially
since it don't take any effort to keep it going." Aunt Ruth
patted the seat of the cane-back chair beside her rocker. "Come
sit with me. An't seen you in weeks." She leaned forward to
look directly into Mama's face as she sat down. "You look
different, almost rested. What you been doing, napping a
lot?"

Mama laughed and shook her head. "Just sleeping better
since it cooled off a little." She pointed at the pile of wet moss
and clay I was mixing with black dirt. "Everything looks
fresher now that the heat's broke. I'd swear, Bone, you've
grown a full inch this month."

I just grinned and went on gently separating the tightly
meshed roots of the old plant. Aunt Ruth had said some of it
would die back but if I could avoid bruising the fine hairs on
the roots, most of it would live. So I had to go slow as I
unraveled the long, pale shoots.

"Oh, Bone's gonna be a tall thing." Aunt Ruth took a
sip of tea and shook the glass. "You want something to drink,

Anney? Bone made me up a fresh pitcher this morning, got lots of sugar and lemon in it."

"Lord, yes. It might have cooled down a bit, but it's still hot enough." I jumped up, slapping my hands against my jeans to loosen the dirt. "But don't put too much ice in it," she called.

She didn't have to say that. I knew how Mama liked her ice tea. I took a lemon and cut six paper-thin slices from the middle, dropped them in a glass, and squeezed the rest of the juice over them. Three cubes of ice on that, then I poured the sweet tea up to the rim of the glass. I sipped it as I carried it to the porch. I heard them before I stepped through the door.

"You think it's gonna last?" Aunt Ruth's voice was soft, Mama's reply even softer.

"I sure hope. You know what his daddy's like, but Glen's like a new man since he started this job. He's sure this shows how much his daddy cares about him, hiring him on and giving him his own route. Doesn't even seem to matter that he's getting less money than the other routemen, says that's just to prove he an't getting no special treatment."

"Sounds special to me, sounds nasty. The whole bunch of them make my bones hurt."

"Oh, Ruth. I don't know."

I put my head against the screen and waited.

"Glen's had so much trouble, been through so many jobs. An't many people would take him on at all at this point, and God knows, he's trying so hard. He's out of the house at dawn, don't get home till after sundown, goes in on weekends to do maintenance on his truck. He wants to do good, he wants to prove himself. He acts like a different man."

"Well." Aunt Ruth sounded less sure of herself than Mama did. "He ask about Bone?" There was a pause. I put my teeth on the rim of Mama's glass.

"He an't mentioned her once since she came over here." Mama's voice had dropped even more. Now it was a whisper.

"He's good as gold with Reese. But it's like he don't even remember Bone, like she was run off or dead, somebody we're not supposed to mention at all. I tell you, Ruth, I don't know what to do some days."

"Doesn't sound like you have a lot of choice, honey." Aunt Ruth's voice was kind but firm. "You knew when you went back what the problem was. I can't say whether he's a good or a bad man. I know you love him, like I know I don't much care for him myself . . ."

"Ruth . . ."

"No, listen to me. I an't gonna tell you to leave him. He's your husband, and it's clear he thinks the sun rises and sets in your smile. I an't sure whether he's crazy jealous of Bone like Granny thinks, or if it's something else. But he an't never gonna be easy with her, and she an't never gonna be safe with him."

"He does love her. I know he does." Mama's whisper was fierce.

"Maybe. Still, I look at Glen and I can see he an't never been loved like he needed to be. But the boy's deeper and darker than I can figure out. It's you I worry about. I know the kind of love you got in you. I know how you feel about Glen. You'd give your life to save him, and maybe that'll make it come out right, and maybe it won't. That's for God to fix. Not me."

"Ruth, think about what you said about him. Anybody can see how Glen got bent, what his daddy's done to him. I an't never seen a boy wanted his daddy's love so much and had so little of it. All Glen really needs is to know himself loved, to get out from under his daddy's meanness."

My teeth ached with the cold from the ice in Mama's glass. I knew I should push through the door, let them know I could hear them, but I stood unmoving, listening to Mama.

"You never saw him when he used to come down and wait for me to get off work at the diner. That was when I started to love him, when I saw him look at Bone and Reese with his face so open I could see right into his soul. You could see the kind of man he wanted to be so plain. It was like looking at a little boy, a desperate hurt little boy. That's when I knew I loved him."

"Oh, Anney."

I pushed the door open with my foot and stepped through. Their heads turned to me, Mama leaning forward on her chair close to Ruth's bent neck, Ruth looking paler and more worn than when I had gone into the kitchen.

"Took you long enough." Aunt Ruth's glance was too intent.

"I sliced the lemon the way Mama likes. You can see right through those slices." My face felt frozen. I gave Mama her glass and went back to the overturned bucket and the broken mass of roots. I tore one half free and dumped it back in the bucket and then just as roughly started breaking out four equal sections of roots and top growth. As I worked I kept my face down, my eyes on the plant.

"I was telling your aunt Ruth that Daddy Glen's started a new job over at the Sunshine Dairy. He's real pleased about going to work for his daddy, and it looks like this job is going to work out pretty good."

"That's good." I shook dried dirt free from one clump of roots and then set the mass down in the damp mix in the earthenware pot. "You want me to use that braided cord to hang these up, Aunt Ruth?"

"Yeah, the brown cord Travis brought home from the dime store. It should hold up pretty good."

I nodded without looking at her.

"You get that done, Bone, and we can talk about when you're gonna come home. Reese's been missing you pretty bad."

"I thought I was gonna stay till school started again." I kept my voice neutral, my head still down. "Aunt Ruth can't possibly get along without me. She needs me."

There was a long silence, and then Aunt Ruth cleared her throat. "Bone's right, Anney. I don't know how I'd drag my sorry butt out of bed without Bone to wake me up. She gets up in the morning singing along to the radio. Sounds just like Kitty Wells sometimes." She might have been starting to laugh, but coughed instead.

I looked up then, carefully, trying to keep my face in the shade. Mama was leaning forward into the sun, her fingers laced together on her knees, her eyes squinted against the light but intent on me. Aunt Ruth was leaning back in her rocker, her hand up, almost covering her mouth. Mama pulled her fingers free and dropped her hands down so that her palms cupped her knees.

"Well, I can see how you might not be able to stand the loss of that. But maybe I'll just bring Reese out on Saturday. Wouldn't want her to forget what her big sister looks like."

I spooned loose dirt into the little pot, sprinkled water on the dusty leaves. The cutting drooped already, getting ready to lose half its growth. But the stem was moist and flexible under my fingers. Strong. It would come back strong.

In August the revival tent went up about half a mile from Aunt Ruth's house on the other side of White Horse Road. Some evenings while Travis and Ruth sat and talked quietly, I would walk up there on my own to sit outside and listen. The preacher was a shouter. He'd rave and threaten, and it didn't seem he was ever going to get to the invocation. I sat in the dark, trying not to think about anything, especially not about Daddy Glen or Mama or how much of an exile I was beginning to feel. I kept thinking I saw my uncle Earle in the men who stood near the highway sharing a bottle in a paper sack, black-headed men with blasted, rough-hewn faces. Was it hatred or sorrow that made them look like that, their necks so stiff and their eyes so cold?

Did I look like that?

Would I look like that when I grew up?

I remembered Aunt Alma putting her big hands over my ears and turning my face to catch the light, saying, "Just as well you smart; you an't never gonna be a beauty."

At least I wasn't as ugly as Cousin Mary-May, I had told Reese, and been immediately ashamed. Mary-May was the most famous ugly woman in Greenville County, with a wide, flat face, a bent nose, tiny eyes, almost no hair, and just three teeth left in her mouth. Still, she was good-natured and always volunteered to be the witch in the Salvation Army's Halloween Horror House. Her face hadn't made her soul ugly. If I kept worrying about not being a beauty, I'd probably ruin myself. Mama was always saying people could see your soul in your face, could see your hatefulness and lack of charity. With all the hatefulness I was trying to hide, it was a wonder I wasn't uglier than a toad in mud season.

The singing started. I leaned forward on the balls of my feet and hugged my knees, humming. Revivals are funny. People get pretty enthusiastic, but they sometimes forget just which hymn it is they're singing. I grinned at the sound of mumbled unintelligible song, watching the men near the road punch each other lightly and curse in a friendly fashion.

You bastard.

You son of a bitch.

The preacher said something I didn't understand. There was a moment of silence, and then a pure tenor voice rose up into the night sky. The spit soured in my mouth. They had a real singer in there, a real gospel choir.

Swing low, sweet chariot . . . coming for to carry me home . . . swing low, sweet chariot . . . coming for to carry me home.

The night seemed to wrap all around me like a blanket. My insides felt as if they had melted, and I could taste the wind in my mouth. The sweet gospel music poured through me in a piercing young boy's voice, and made all my nastiness, all my jealousy and hatred, swell in my heart. I remembered Aunt Ruth's fingers fluttering birdlike in front of her face, Uncle Earle's flushed cheeks and lank black hair as they'd cried together on the porch, Mama's pinched, worried face and Daddy Glen's cold, angry eyes. The world was too big for me, the music too strong. I knew, I knew I was the most disgusting person on earth. I didn't deserve to live another day. I started hiccuping and crying.

"I'm sorry. Jesus, I'm sorry."

How could I live with myself? How could God stand me? Was this why Jesus wouldn't speak to my heart? The music washed over me. . . . *Softly and tenderly, Jesus is calling.* The music was a river trying to wash me clean. I sobbed and dug my heels into the dirt, drunk on grief and that pure, pure voice soaring above the choir. Aunt Alma swore all gospel singers were drunks, but right then it didn't matter to me. If it was whiskey backstage or tongue-kissing in the dressing room, whatever it took to make that juice was necessary, was fine. I wiped my eyes and swore out loud. Get that boy another bottle, I wanted to yell. Find that girl a hardheaded husband. But goddam, keep them singing that music. Lord, make me drunk on that music.

I rocked back and forth, grinding my heels into the red dirt, my fists into my stomach, crooning into the dark night and the reflected glow from the tent. I cried until I was dry, and then I laughed. I put my head back and laughed until my voice was hoarse and the damp fog came in to cover the lights from the revival. If Aunt Ruth had come out to me then, I would have apologized for everything, for living and not loving her enough to save her from the cancer that was eating her alive. I didn't know. For something, surely, I would have had something to apologize for, for being young and healthy and sitting there full of music. That was what gospel was meant to do—make you hate and love yourself at the same time, make you ashamed and glorified. It worked on me. It absolutely worked on me.

10

The gospel revival tent had been a revelation, but the "Sunrise Gospel Hour" became an obsession. Every morning, before Aunt Ruth and Uncle Travis were up, I'd go sit close to the radio in their parlor to listen to the "Sunrise Gospel Hour." In the stillness of the early dawn, I would lean into the speaker and practice my secret ambition, cupping my fingers next to my chin and tilting my head back to whisper-sing so no one could hear me. I sang quietly along with everything, not just the gospel shows but the country hits that followed—Marty Robbins, Kitty Wells, Johnny Cash, Ruth Brown, Stonewall Jackson, June Carter, Johnny Horton. I sang so quietly I could barely hear my own voice, but in my imagination my song soared out strong and beautiful.

Aunt Ruth would always smile when she saw me with my head pressed close to the radio. "Turn it up," she'd say. "You an't the only one likes a little music." Sometimes she'd even start humming along. One weekend she got Earle to bring his record player over and we spent two days listening to her favorite songs. It turned out Aunt Ruth had a bunch of her own records in a box under her bed, an original Carter Family set, Patsy Montana singing "I Want to Be a Cowboy's Sweetheart," the Clinch Mountain Clan doing Hank Williams's "Are You Walking and a-Talking for the Lord," Roy Acuff's "Wabash Cannonball," and Roy Acuff singing "The Wreck on the Highway." Her prize was a copy of Al Dexter and the Troopers singing "Pistol Packing Mama." Every time the chorus came on, she'd pound her hand on the couch and sing along, waving at me to join in with her. We'd yell it out, "Pistol packing mama, lay that pistol down," until we drove Uncle Travis out to sit on the bumper of his car with a bottle of Jack Daniel's.

He came in once to get a hunk of cheese for a meal and stopped in to complain. "You're scaring off the dogs. Give it a break."

"Leave us alone, old man." Aunt Ruth's face was pink and happy. "We're full of the spirit."

"But you sound terrible," he told us sadly. "You just can't sing."

"Oh, hell, Travis, we know." Aunt Ruth looked too pleased with herself to take offense, but I was shocked. I thought we'd been sounding pretty good. "We know and we don't care. It's just so much fun. Why don't you join us? Come on. Bone, put on that one Earle loaned us. You like Stonewall Jackson, don't you, Travis?"

"Oh, no. You an't gonna get me started. I an't no singing fool." He backed out the door like he was afraid something was gonna jump on him. I shrugged and put on the Jackson song. If I squeezed my neck down tight I could almost mimic Stonewall's deep sad sound. My voice came out rusty and dark as his, like a man singing up from the bottom of a coal mine.

Aunt Ruth beamed at my attempt, laughing until she almost strangled. "Oh, God, Bone! Good God, you are something. You are just about more than I can stand." She fell back weakly, her fingers still keeping time to the music. "Lord God, you are. You are. Lord God, play it again."

The weekend before school was supposed to start, Mama said I had to move back home and leave Aunt Ruth to the care of her daughter Deedee. Deedee had agreed to come home only after Travis promised to make the payments on her prized Chevy sedan, and she delayed her arrival until the night before I was to leave and showed up irritable and complaining of having to come back at all. She acted like her mama's illness was her personal cross to bear. I was appalled.

"She could die any time," I told Deedee the next morning. "Don't you ever think about that?"

We were out on Aunt Ruth's porch waiting for Mama to come for me, Deedee sitting in the rocker while I leaned against the rail. Deedee just smirked, lit another of the Chesterfield cigarettes that Aunt Ruth hated, and tossed the dead match back at me. "She an't gonna die, not yet anyway, not till I'm out of my mind with boredom and ready to kill her myself. You don't know, Bonehead. You don't know how long Mama's been dragging around. I been picking up after her and my lazy-assed brothers all my life. People always whining at me what a tragedy it is, Mama so sick and likely to die. Uh-huh, right, I say. First it was female trouble and she couldn't lift nothing, then it was bad lungs and nobody supposed to smoke in the house. Never could play the radio or make no noise after sunset so she could get her rest. Never no boyfriends could come by and honk to take me out. No new dresses 'cause her medicine cost so much. Nothing but wheezing and whining and telling me what to do."

Deedee's face was hateful, her eyes flinty and piercing. She reached up and grabbed my forearm, pulling me down close to her. "You don't know what it's like, Bone. Getting out on your own and then being dragged back home. Wait a few years, get yourself a sweetheart, a job that pays you your own money, stuff you like to do that your mama thinks is silly or sinful." She let go of my arm and kicked the rocker into motion. "Hell, just about everything I like in this world is silly or sinful. Silly sinful Deedee, that's what they call me. Well, damn them, I don't care. I got my car and my own plans, and when that car's paid for, you can bet your ass I'll be gone again. Next time I get out of here, the devil himself an't gonna be able to drag me back."

The hair on the nape of my neck stood up. I didn't know what to say, what to think. Earle had finished painting the porch last weekend, and now the white boards shone in the sun, throwing the noon light up into Deedee's dark eyes. I remembered Earle leaning against the porch rail shaking his head, his voice hoarse and sad as he complained that he just didn't understand how things could get so messed up. The simplest things, I thought. I went down the stairs and squatted on the bottom step with my fingers templed on my knees as if I were praying. Deedee sounded like she hated her mama, wanted her to die. I couldn't understand that, couldn't stand to think about it. I watched for Mama's car and sang over and over in my head, "Sun's gonna shine, sun's gonna shine, in my back door, someday." Song was prayer, prayer was song. What could I sing that would touch Deedee's heart or my own, comfort either one of us?

Every afternoon after school I was supposed to go stay with Reese at Aunt Alma's, but instead I started going over to the West Greenville Cafe on the Eustis Highway. The jukebox had as many old songs as new—Loretta Lynn, Teresa Brewer, Patsy Cline, and Mama's favorite, Kitty Wells. The truckers loved that music as much as I did. I'd sit out under the cafe windows and hum along with those twangy girl voices, imagining myself crooning those raw and desperate notes. Everybody knew that Opry stars started as gospel singers. All those women singing about their unfaithful men sang first about the certain love of God. Half asleep in the sun, reassured by the familiar smell of frying fat, I'd make promises to God. If only He'd let me be a singer! I knew I'd probably turn to whiskey and rock 'n' roll like they all did, but not for years, I promised. Not for years, Lord. Not till I had glorified His name and bought Mama a yellow Cadillac and a house on Old Henderson Road.

More than anything in the world, I decided, I wanted to be one of the little girls in white fringed vests with silver and gold embroidered crosses—the ones who sang on the revival circuit and taped shows for early-morning television. I wanted gray-headed ladies to cry when they saw my pink cheeks. I wanted people to moan when they heard the throb in my voice as I sang of the miracle in my life. I wanted a miracle in my life. I wanted to be a gospel singer and be loved by the whole wide world.

Jesus, make me a gospel singer, I prayed, while Teresa sang of what might have been God and then again might have been some black-eyed man. But Jesus must have been busy with Teresa, because my voice went high and shrill every time I got excited, and cracked hoarsely if I tried to croon. The preacher at Bushy Creek Baptist wouldn't even let me stand near the choir to turn the pages of the hymnal, and without a voice like Teresa's or June Carter's, I couldn't sing gospel. I could just listen and watch the gray-headed ladies cry. It was an injustice I could not understand or forgive. There had to be a way to stretch my voice, to sing the way I dreamed I could. I prayed and practiced and stubbornly hoped.

Driving from Greenville to the Sunshine lot on Highway 85 past the Sears, Roebuck warehouse, the air base, the rolling green and red-mud hills—a trip we made almost every other week now that Daddy Glen was working for his father—we would sometimes get to singing like some traveling gospel family. *While I was sleeping somebody touched me, while I was sleeping, Oh! Somebody touched me . . . musta been the hand of the Lord . . .*

Full-voice, all-out, our singing filled the car and shocked the passing traffic. Reese howled and screeched, Mama's voice broke like she too dreamed of Teresa Brewer, and Daddy Glen made sounds that would have scared cows. None of them cared, and I tried to pretend I wasn't that bad. I put my head out the window and wailed for all I was worth. The wind filled my mouth and the roar obscured the fact that I sang as badly as any of them.

Once I got so carried away that I went and sang into the electric fan when we got home. It made my voice buzz and waver like a slide guitar, an effect I particularly liked. Mama complained it gave her a headache and would give me an earache if I didn't cut it out.

"What the hell is she doing?" Daddy Glen acted like I was singing just to make him mad. "She trying to take the paint off the walls or just sour the milk?" He reached past the fan for me with one of his big hands.

"Glen." Mama's voice was soft, but it stopped him. He looked at her like she had stuck a needle in his heart.

"You shouldn't encourage her," he told Mama. "Gonna have her thinking she can do any damn thing she pleases, and then where will we be? Hell, she's out running the county every afternoon as it is."

Mama put her arm around Daddy Glen's waist. "I know you worry, but trust me, honey. I know where Bone is every minute. I wouldn't let nothing happen to my little girl." Daddy Glen relaxed under Mama's touch until he was almost smiling.

"Bone, get your daddy some ice tea," she told me. "And put some extra sugar in it like he likes."

I got the tea and then a washcloth so Mama could cool Daddy Glen's neck while they sat together. Mama didn't look at me once the whole time, but Daddy Glen did, his eyes sliding over me like I was a new creature, something he hadn't figured out yet how to tame. It had been a long time since he had caught me alone, and sometimes I could almost convince myself that he had never held me tight to his hips, never put his hands down inside my clothes. I pretended it had all been a bad dream that would never come back, but I was careful to stay away from him.

I ran off before Daddy Glen could ask for anything more and took the fan out on the back porch. I sang to myself as softly as I could, humming into the motor, thinking about how gospel singers were always on the road. Even if I didn't get to be the star, I might wind up singing background in a "family"—all of us dressed alike in electric-blue fringed blouses with silver embroidery, traveling in a big bus, and calling home from different cities. But it would be better to be a soloist and be in demand all the time. All I needed was a chance to turn my soulful black eyes on a tent full of believers, sing out the little break in my mournful voice. I knew I could make them love me. There was a secret to it, but I would find it out. If they could do it to me, I would find a way to do it to the world.

"Bullshit and apple butter," Granny laughed cruelly when I finally told her about watching the morning gospel singers and wanting to be like them. "You got to be joking, Bone! You can't sing, girl. You can't sing at all."

"Not now," I admitted grudgingly. "But I'm working on it. I'm gonna get better. And think about it, Granny. Think about what it would be like."

"Oh, I know." Granny's expression became gentle, her voice careful. "I know the power of gospel singers. Some of these Christian women will believe anything for the sake of a gospel singer."

"Anything." I loved the way she said that. Granny's "Christian women" came out like new spit on a dusty morning, pure and precious and deeply satisfying.

"Anything," I echoed, and she gave me her toothless, twisted grin. We were sitting close together in Mama's lawn chairs in the backyard. Granny always complained about Mama not living in houses with porches and rocking chairs, but she liked Mama's reclining lawn chair. Now she reached out, put her hand on the back of my neck, squeezed, and laughed.

"You got a look like your granddaddy sometimes." She pinched me and laughed again. "Bastard was meaner than a snake, but he had his ways. And didn't I love his ways? Lord Christ!" She leaned back and rolled the snuff around in her mouth.

"Man had only two faults I couldn't abide. Wouldn't work to save his life and couldn't stay away from gospel singers. Used to stand out back of revival tents offering 'em the best homemade whiskey in Greenville County. Then he'd bring me that slush they cleaned out of the taps. Bastard!" She stiffened and looked back over her shoulder, afraid Mama might be listening. Mama didn't allow anybody to use that word in her house.

"Well, shit." She spit to the side. "You got a little of that too, don't you? A little of that silliness, that revival crap?"

"Cousin Temple says you a heathen."

"Oh, Temple, huh. Temple's a pure damn fool."

I said nothing. Granny wiped her chin.

"Don't you go telling your mama everything you hear."

"No ma'am."

"And don't go taking that gospel stuff seriously. It's nice to clean you out now and then, but it an't for real. It's like bad whiskey. Run through you fast and leave you with a pain." She wiped her chin again and sighed like she'd taken to doing lately. I hated that sigh. I liked her better when she was being mean. When she started sighing, she was likely to start crying. Then her face would squeeze down on itself in a way that scared me.

"I an't no fool." I rocked back and forth in my chair, pushing off hard with my bare feet. Granny's face twitched, and I saw the light come back into her eyes.

"You know how your mama feels about that word." It was true. Mama had given me one of her rare scoldings for calling Reese a fool. She hated it almost as much as "bastard."

"An't no fool and an't no bastard." I rocked steadily, watching Granny's face.

Granny laughed and looked back over her shoulder nervously. "Oh, you gonna be the death of your mama, and won't I be sorry then."

She didn't look sorry. She looked better. I said it again. "An't no fool and an't no bastard."

Granny started laughing so hard she choked on her snuff. "You're both, and you just silly 'bout that music just like

144

your granddaddy." She sounded like she might strangle from laughing. "And goddam, he was both too."

My gospel thing did get on Mama's nerves after a while, but Aunt Alma reassured her. "It's obnoxious but normal, Anney, and you know it. Every girl in the family gets religion sooner or later." Mama nodded absently. She wasn't so sure it was that simple. Mama almost never went to church, but she took God and most issues of faith absolutely seriously.

"Oh, Anney's a Christian woman," Uncle Earle told Aunt Alma the morning after the night Mama threw him out for puking liquor on her kitchen table. "But she wears me down being so stubborn all the time. You'd think she never took a drink of whiskey or chased no good-looking man in her life."

"She's just as stiff-necked as she can be," Cousin Deedee agreed. She was supposed to be with Aunt Ruth but seemed to be over at Alma's or Raylene's more than she was home. "You know, Bone, your mama's the kind gets us all in trouble to begin with. Like something out of one of them stories they tell in Sunday school, supposed to be a lesson to the rest of us." She smirked at me. "Ask for nothing, trust in God. Do the right thing. Right! And he'll send you bastards and rabies before he's through.

"I hate," Deedee swore, "the very notion of a Christian woman with her hard-scrubbed, starved-thin, stiff and scrawny neck!"

"She hates herself," Mama told us when Reese repeated what Deedee had said. "And I don't know that God has much of anything to do with it." She gave me one of those sharp, almost frightening looks she seemed to have developed over the summer. "People don't do right because of the fear of God or love of him. You do the right thing because the world doesn't make sense if you don't."

I no longer accepted everything Mama told me as gospel, but I knew what she meant. Doing the right thing shouldn't have anything to do with like or love or goodness or Jesus, though most people swore Jesus had something to do with everything. I knew Mama believed in Jesus well enough, even though she wouldn't talk about it, and I decided that deep in her heart she understood exactly what I was doing. I gave myself over to the mystery of Jesus' blood, reading the Bible at the kitchen table after dinner and going to the Wednesday-night services for young people. Mama said nothing, Reese teased me, and Daddy Glen sneered.

Aunt Alma thought the whole thing was funny. "Well, at least she an't copying Bible passages out and hiding them in your drawers like my Temple did. You just got to let her ride it out. When Temple got it, I teased her a little and the girl nearly took my head off. Almost had the preacher out to talk to me—as if I wasn't a good Baptist—just because I don't see no reason to go to church every Sunday of my life."

"But you should go to church," I told Aunt Alma imperviously. She made me mad talking like I wasn't serious about my faith. "You should witness your faith and get Uncle Earle to go with you. He thinks the world of you, and he'd listen to you if you talked to him right."

"If I started talking to Earle about Sunday-morning church services and witnessing for our faith, he'd think I'd lost my mind." Alma laughed and pinched my chin. "You go for us, girl. You witness. If the world really is gonna end tomorrow, I'd rather save you than any of those drunken uncles of yours. And don't you even try to talk Jesus to Earle. The man is impossible to talk to about God and religion."

I took Aunt Alma's warning as a challenge and started talking to Uncle Earle about faith and good works. I played him Mama's most tearful gospel country music and repeated all the most dramatic soul-saving stories I'd found in the pamphlets the Christian Ladies' Aid Society passed out. Earle loved the whole thing, my sincerity, the Bible verses, and the thinly veiled threats of perdition. But most of all he loved the argument. While I tried to prove to him that God was love and Jesus saved, he set out to prove to me that the world was irredeemably corrupt.

"Never mind the ninety and nine, let's talk about the poor lost sheep in this county," Uncle Earle would start off. One shot glass of whiskey and a tall glass of beer and he was ready to address the issue of Jesus, only occasionally reminding me of his wife, Teresa. He blamed the loss of Teresa on Jesus, naturally—Jesus who made Catholics, Catholics who were so particular on the subject of fornication and made it so hard for a decent Baptist man to get a divorce. He was funny about Catholics, damning them for making his life so difficult and admiring them at the same time.

"At least," he told me, "Catholics are interesting, got all that up-and-down stuff, chanting, velvet carpet on the pews and real watered wine for communion. What the hell Baptists got? Grape-juice communions, silly rules against dancing and movies, self-righteousness by the barrelful, damn-fool preachers in shiny suits, and simpleminded parishioners! Baptists could learn something from the Catholics."

Sometimes in his arguments, Uncle Earle would get Teresa, the Catholic Church, and the county marshals a little confused. Given enough whiskey, he'd start talking about the way they had all united to blight his life. If there was a God, Earle had decided, He was on the side of Teresa, the Catholics, and the marshals. But there was no God, Earle told me, no God and no hope in churches. People were better off learning to rely on themselves and each other, instead of running around praying for what they weren't going to get.

"I gave up churches—all churches—because I saw what they were," he told me. "Take a look at those oil color paintings on the wall of every Sunday school in South Carolina. Jesus in the mountains. Jesus in the desert. Jesus against the night sky. Jesus got the lost one in his arms. Jesus wants you, each and every one of you. He'll climb mountains, walk the hot sands, brave the night winds, search among the many for the one not found. And you are never so valuable as when you stand outside the fold, the one God wants. Oh, don't I know! Don't I know?

"They want you, oh yes, they want you. Till they get you. An't nothing in this world more useless than a hardworking religious fool. It an't that you get religion. Religion gets you and then milks you dry. Won't let you drink a little whiskey. Won't let you make no fat-assed girls grin and giggle. Won't let you do a damn thing except work for what you'll get in the hereafter. I live in the here and now, and I need my sleep on a Sunday morning. But I'll tell you, Bone, I like it that they want me, Catholics and Baptists and Church of Gods and Methodists and Seventh-Day Adventists, all of them hungry for my dirty white hide, my pitiful human soul. Hell! None of them would give two drops of piss for me if I was already part of their saggy-assed congregations."

Uncle Earle would drink and swing back his glossy black hair. The more he drank, the more he would talk. Perversely, the more he talked, the more I wanted to hear, though every word out of his mouth was blasphemy. What I really liked was how he talked about Jesus. He talked about Jesus in a way I understood even when I couldn't put it together with all he said. He talked about Jesus like a man dying for need of him, but too stubborn to sit down to the meal spread within reach. Earle talked the language of gospel music, with its rhythms and intensity. I heard in his drawled pronouncements the same thing I heard when I listened to the music, the desperation swelling rough raw voices, the red-faced men and pale sweating women moaning in the back pews. "Lord, Lord!" Moaning and waiting, waiting and praying, "to be washed, *Lord Jesus*! washed in the blood of the Lamb!" The hunger, the lust, and the yearning were palpable. I understood that hunger as I understood nothing else, though I could not tell if what I truly hungered for was God or love or absolution. Salvation was complicated.

I put my hand on Earle's forearm and felt with a dizzy

sensation how tight and hot the skin was, as if every muscle in his body was fighting off God. If I had not been so certain of his prospects of hellfire and damnation, it would have tickled my pride to see what a challenge to God's patience Earle managed to be. As it was, all I could think was how marvelous it would be when he finally heard God speaking through me and felt Jesus come into his life.

I tried to do all I could to save my poor uncles from their heathen ways, but when I tried to get them to go to Sunday services, Earle just laughed at me, Nevil grunted, and Uncle Beau worked himself into a coughing fit. "Goddam women and their goddam churchgoing ways," Uncle Beau yelled at Granny, as if she had put me up to it. "A man don't have to have God on his ass to know what he should do. A man don't need a woman preaching at him all the time."

"Stop cursing like that," Granny told him mildly enough. "You the biggest fool in Greenville County, and it an't the women made you who you are. You been after somebody to blame your life on since you was born." She spit snuff and told me to get out of the house and into the sunshine.

I didn't argue with her. If I got balky, she was sure to make me squeeze up a piece of her leg when she had to take her insulin shot. She always made me do it when she was angry at me, which was plenty of reason to keep her from getting mad.

"If God lived in a whiskey bottle," I heard Granny tell Uncle Beau as I headed out the door, "He'd of filled up your heart a long time ago. But He don't, and you an't never gonna be saved, so keep your nastiness to yourself."

Uncle Earle got work building a carport and took some of the money to get Mama a little electric record player and four records. "That's all I'm giving for free," he told her, scooping up gravy with one of her biscuits. "I even bought you some of those old June Carter songs you like. What's that funny one? 'Nickelodeon,' right?"

He scooped and sopped, and drank sweet tea down like it was whiskey. Mama said he'd eaten so many of her biscuits by now he was like a child of her own.

"A man belongs to the woman that feeds him."

"Bullshit," Aunt Alma insisted. "It's the other way around and you know it. It's the woman belongs to the ones she feeds."

"Maybe. Maybe."

Out of those four records, there was only one Mama liked, and she damn near wore it out. "The Sign on the Highway," it was called, and after a while I could sing it from memory. *"The sign on the highway, the scene of the crash . . . the people pulled over to let the hearse pass . . . their bodies were found 'neath the signboard that read—Beer, Wine and Whiskey for sale just ahead."*

What surprised me was that Mama, who wouldn't go to church and never even said Jesus' name, had the same response to that music I did. She cried every time she heard it, and she wanted to hear it all the time. It was a gospel song, of course, a kind of a gospel song. Mama would play it over and over, and I'd come in to sit with her while she listened, her with a glass of tea in one hand and the other over her eyes, and me as close to her as she'd let me, both of us crying quietly and then smiling at each other and playing it again. Uncle Earle would come in and laugh at us.

"Look at you two. You just as crazy as you can be. Look at you. Crying over some people didn't never really die. That's only a slide guitar and some stupid folks can't make a living no other way 'cept acting the fool in front of people like you." He stomped off out the screen door while Mama wiped her face and I sat still. He kicked each step as he went down.

"I swear this family's got shit for brains."

Since I was getting nowhere saving my uncles, I fell back on the only capital I had—my own soul. I became fascinated with the idea of being saved, not just welcoming Jesus into my heart but the seriousness of the struggle between salvation and damnation, between good and evil, life and death. God and the devil were the ultimate arbiters, and everyone knew what was being fought over. It was just like Uncle Earle had told me: if you were not saved, not part of the congregation, you were all anyone could see at the invocation. There was something heady and enthralling about being the object of all that attention. It was like singing gospel on the television with the audience following your every breath. I could not resist it.

I came close to being saved about fourteen times—fourteen Sundays in fourteen different Baptist churches. I didn't fake my indecision, the teary-eyed intensity and open-mouthed confusion that overtook me when the preacher turned his glance on me. There was something about the way his face looked when he cried out for all those who felt the "call" to come forward, something in the way the old women in the front pew turned around to look up and down the aisles. The music would come up and the choir would start half-humming, half-singing "Softly and Tenderly, Jesus Is Calling," and a pulse would start to throb in my temples. Tears would pearl up in the corners of my eyes, and my tongue would seem to swell in my mouth. I wanted, I wanted, I wanted something—Jesus or God or orange-blossom scent or dark chocolate terror in my throat. Something hurt me, ached in me. I couldn't tell if it was the music or the eyes or the waxed smell of the hardwood floors, but everything ran together and drew me down the aisle to the front pew, where the preacher put his hand on my head and some stiff-necked old woman came forward to hold my hand.

Once there, I would cry silently and hold on while a few other people came down too. Then we would all pray together. I could not have explained, but it was not actually baptism I wanted, or welcome to the congregation, or even the breathless concentration of the preacher. It was that moment of sitting on the line between salvation and damnation with the preacher and the old women pulling bodily at my poor darkened soul. I wanted that moment to go on forever, wanted the choir to go on with that low, slow music. I wanted the church to fill up with everyone I knew. I wanted the way I felt to mean something and for everything in my life to change because of it.

When the music stopped and the sweaty preacher sat down with his little notebook to talk to me, my face would go rigid and my voice sink to a whisper of shame and nervous terror. Every time that moment was the same. The smell of watery ammonia would blot out the orange blossoms and whatever old woman was hugging me would flake pancake makeup on my bare arms. I would start to gag and have to run off to the girls' room in the basement to wash my face. Then I would stare into my eyes in the mirror and know I wasn't ready. It wasn't right. The magic I knew was supposed to wash over me with Jesus' blood was absent, the moment cold and empty. I would stumble out into the sunshine guiltily, still unsaved, and go on to a new church the next Sunday.

I'd begun to think about trying out the Church of God or the Holy Church of Jesus' Disciples when Mama caught on to me. She took me to Aunt Ruth's church at Bushy Creek and had me baptized beneath the painting of Jesus at the Jordan. When my head went under, my throat closed up and my ears went deaf. With cloudy water soaking my dress and my eyes tight shut, I couldn't hear the choir or feel the preacher's bruising grip. Whatever magic Jesus' grace promised, I didn't feel it. I pushed up out of that dirty water, shivering, broke out in a sweat, and felt my fever rise.

I sneezed and coughed for a solid week, lying limp in my bed and crying to every gospel song that came over the radio. It was as if I were mourning the loss of something I had never really had. I sang along with the music and prayed for all I was worth. Jesus' blood and country music, there had to be something else, something more to hope for. I bit my lip and went back to reading the Book of Revelation, taking comfort in the hope of the apocalypse, God's retribution on the wicked. I liked Revelations, loved the Whore of Babylon and the promised rivers of blood and fire. It struck me like gospel music, it promised vindication.

I recognized Shannon Pearl immediately on the first Monday of the school year. I'd seen her with her family at the revival tent. Her daddy booked singers for the circuit, and her mama managed the Christian bookstore, a religious supply store downtown south of Main Street, a place where you could get embossed Bibles, bookmarks with the 23rd Psalm in blue relief, hot plates featuring the Sermon on the Mount, and Jesus and that damned lamb on everything imaginable—slipcovers, tablecloths, even plastic pants to go over baby diapers.

Shannon got on the bus two stops after Reese and me, walking stolidly past a dozen hooting boys and another dozen flushed and whispering girls. As she made her way up the aisle, I watched each boy slide to the end of his seat to block her sitting with him and every girl flinch away as if whatever Shannon had might be catching. In the seat ahead of us Danny

Yarboro leaned far over into the aisle and began to make retching noises.

"Cootie train! Cootie train!" somebody yelled as the bus lurched into motion and Shannon still hadn't found a seat.

I watched her face—impassive, self-sufficient, and stubborn; she reminded me of myself, or at least the way I had come to think of myself. Sweat was showing through her dress, but nothing showed in her face except for the eyes. There was fire in those pink eyes, a deep fire I recognized, banked and raging. Before I knew what I'd done, I was on my feet and leaning forward to catch her arm. I pulled her into our row without a word. Reese stared at me like I was crazy, but Shannon settled herself and started cleaning her bottleglass lenses as if nothing at all was happening.

I glared at Danny Yarboro's open mouth until he turned away from us. Reese pulled a strand of her lank blond hair into her mouth and pretended she was sitting alone. Slowly, the boys sitting near us turned their heads and began to mutter to each other. There was one soft "cootie bitch" hissed in my direction, but no yelling. Nobody knew exactly why I had taken a shine to Shannon, but Reese and I were back at Greenville Elementary and everyone there knew me and my family— particularly my cousins Grey and Garvey, who would toss you against a wall if they heard you'd insulted any of us.

Shannon Pearl spent a good five minutes cleaning her glasses and then sat silent for the rest of the ride to school. I understood intuitively that she would not say anything, would in fact generously pretend to have fallen into our seat. I sat there beside her watching the pinched faces of my classmates as they kept looking back toward us. Just the way they stared made me forget all my newly made vows to behave like a good Christian; their contemptuous, angry faces made me want to start a conversation with Shannon and shock them all. I almost grinned, imagining Shannon and me discussing all the enemies we had in common while half the bus craned their necks to hear. But I couldn't bring myself to do that, couldn't even think what I would say to her. Not till the bus crossed the railroad tracks at the south corner of Greenville Elementary did I manage to force my mouth open enough to say my name and then Reese's.

She nodded impartially and whispered "Shannon Pearl" before taking off her glasses to begin cleaning them all over again. With her glasses off she half-shut her eyes and hunched her shoulders. Much later, I would realize that she cleaned her glasses whenever she needed a quiet moment to regain her composure, or more often, just to put everything around her at a distance. Without glasses, the world became a soft blur, but she also behaved as if the glasses were all that made it possible for her to hear. Commotion or insults never seemed to register at all when she was cleaning her glasses. It was a valuable trick when you were the object of as much ridicule as she was.

Six inches shorter than me, Shannon had the white skin, white hair, and pale pink eyes of an albino, though her mama insisted Shannon was no such thing. "My own precious angel is just a miracle child," Mrs. Pearl declared. "Born too soon, you know. Why, she was so frail at birth we never thought the Lord would let her stay with us. But now look at her. In my Shannon, you can just see how God touches us all."

Shannon's fine blue blood vessels shone against the ivory of her scalp. Blue threads under the linen, her mama was always saying. Sometimes, Shannon seemed strangely beautiful to me, as she surely was to her mother. Sometimes, but not often. Not often at all. Every chance she could get, Mrs. Pearl would sit her daughter between her knees and purr over that gossamer hair and puffy pale skin. "My little angel," she would croon, and my stomach would push up against my heart.

It was a lesson in the power of love. Looking back at me from between her mother's legs, Shannon was wholly monstrous, a lurching hunched creature shining with sweat and smug satisfaction. There had to be something wrong with me, I was sure, the way I went from awe to disgust where Shannon was concerned. When Shannon sat between her mama's legs or chewed licorice strings her daddy held out for her, I purely hated her. But when other people would look at her scornfully or the boys up at Lee Highway would call her Lard Eyes, I felt a fierce and protective love, as if she were more my sister than Reese. I felt as if I belonged to her in a funny kind of way, as if her "affliction" put me deeply in her debt. It was a mystery, I guessed, a sign of grace like Aunt Maybelle was always talking about. Magic.

Christian charity, I knew, would have had me smile at Shannon but avoid her like everyone else. It wasn't Christian charity that made me give her a seat on the bus, trade my fifth-grade picture for hers, sit at her kitchen table while her mama tried another experiment on her wispy hair—"Egg and cornmeal, that'll do the trick. We gonna put curls in this hair, darling, or my name an't Roseanne Pearl"—or follow her to the Bushy Creek Highway store and share the blue popsicle she bought us. My fascination with her felt more like the restlessness that made me worry the scabs on my ankles. As disgusting as it seemed, I couldn't put away the need to scratch my ankles or hang around what Granny called "that strange and ugly child."

Other people had no such confusion about Shannon. Besides her mother and me, no one could stand her. No amount of Jesus' grace would make her even marginally acceptable, and people had been known to suddenly lose their lunch from the sight of the clammy sheen of her skin, her skull showing blue-white through the thin, colorless hair, and those watery pink eyes flicking back and forth, drifting in and out of focus.

"Lord! But that child is ugly!"

"It's a trial, Jesus knows, a trial for her poor parents."

"They should keep her home."

"Now, honey. That's not like you. Remember, the Lord loves a charitable heart."

"I don't care. The Lord didn't intend me to get nauseous in the middle of Sunday services. That child is a shock to the disgestion."

I had the idea that because she was so ugly on the outside, it was only reasonable that Shannon would turn out to be saintlike when you got to know her. That was the way it would have been in any storybook the local ladies' society would let me borrow. I thought of *Little Women*, *The Bobbsey Twins*, and all those novels about poor British families at Christmas. Tiny Tim, for Christ's sake! Shannon, I was sure, would be like that. A patient and gentle soul had to be hidden behind those pale, sweaty features. She would be generous, insightful, understanding, and wise beyond her years. She would be the friend I had always needed.

That she was none of these was something I could never quite accept. Once she relaxed with me, Shannon invariably told horrible stories, most of which were about the gruesome deaths of innocent children. *". . . And then the tractor backed up over him, cutting his body in three pieces, but nobody seen it or heard it, you see, 'cause of the noise the thresher made. So then his mama come out with ice tea for everybody. And she put her foot down right in his little torn-open stomach. And oh Lord! don't you know . . ."*

I couldn't help myself. I kept going over to Shannon's house to sit and listen, openmouthed and fascinated, while this shining creature went on and on about decapitations, mutilations, murder, and mayhem. Her stories were remarkable, not fantasies like the ones I made up. Shannon's stories had the aura of the real—newspaper headlines and autopsy reports— and she loved best little children who had fallen in the way of large machines. It was something none of the grown-ups knew a thing about, though once in a while I'd hear a much shorter, much tamer version of one of Shannon's stories from her mama. At those moments, Shannon would give me a grin of smug pride. Can't I tell it better? she seemed to be saying. Gradually I admitted to myself what hid behind Shannon's impassive pink-and-white features. Shannon Pearl simply and completely hated everyone who had ever hurt her, and spent most of her time brooding on punishments either she or God would visit on them. The fire that burned in her eyes was the fire of outrage. Had she been stronger or smarter, Shannon Pearl would have been dangerous. But half-blind, sickly, and ostracized, she was not much of a threat to anyone.

Mr. and Mrs. Pearl were as short as Shannon was, and almost as pale. Neither of them trusted their fine complexions to the sun's glare. Mr. Pearl always wore a dark worsted fedora and a suit to match. Mrs. Pearl stayed in the store out of the sun and wore both hat and gloves whenever she went out. They always looked secretive and self-contained, their prim mouths shut tight. It was impossible to imagine them naked, stepping out of their baths or pressing their pulpy bodies close together in the privacy of their bedroom. They looked like children dressed in their parents' clothes, and their various enterprises seemed to me no way for grown people to make a living. Mrs. Pearl admitted they never quite covered Shannon's medical expenses, so they took up collections from sympathetic congregations.

I couldn't imagine asking strangers to pay your bills, but I didn't say anything. I was so careful with the Pearls, so quiet and restrained and politely attentive, I might have been a cousin of theirs. It was worth it to me to play at being one of them. With Shannon and her family I finally got to meet the people I'd dreamed about—the Blue Ridge Mountain Boys, the Tuckerton Family, the Carter Family, Little Pammie Gleason (blessed by God), the Smoky Mountain Boys, and now and then—every time he'd get saved—Johnny Cash. Sunday morning, Sunday evening, Wednesday prayer service, revival weeks; Mr. Pearl would book a hall, a church, or a local TV program. Because I was Shannon's friend I got to go on the tours, to meet the stars of both the country western and gospel circuits. That was enough to stop me worrying about my fascination with Shannon. I could easily credit the whole enterprise to my odd but acceptable lust for gospel music.

Shannon knew the words to every song in the Baptist hymnal and spoke familiarly of every gospel group that toured the Opry circuit. Gospel was her family's life, and she knew all there was to know about it, though she didn't seem to feel the music's impact the way I did. Shannon made fun of preachers and choir singers, telling her most devastating jokes about the hallelujah jumpers, who completely lost consciousness of themselves when they sang and began to spring up on the balls of their feet, swinging their arms in the air. I could never have told her my secret ambition, never have told her that I cried when I listened to tent shows on the radio late at night.

"Those eyes of yours could break the heart of God," Mrs. Pearl told me as she patted my black hair fiercely. I blinked and tried to tear up for her. "Lashes, oh! Bob, look at the lashes on this child. You grow up you can do Maybelline commercials on the television, honey. 'Course, not that you're going to want to. You don't ever let anybody talk you into putting any of that junk on you. Your eyes are a gift from *God*!" She leaned close to my shoulder and put one hand on the top of my head, turning me so that I looked directly into her eyes. Her caramel-brown pupils were enormous flat surfaces that reflected nothing; her voice was honey-coated and sincere. I could not tell if she was making fun of me or speaking from her heart.

"Mama has more ways of saying 'God' and 'Jesus' than any preacher I've ever heard." Shannon blinked her pink eyelids at me. "She's got a talent for it, talking real soft and low one minute, saying 'Gawd' so that you see him in your mind like some kind of old family relation, all quiet and well-mannered like an old man. Or she can drag it out long and loud, *'Gaaaaad*,' and just shock you senseless. When she really gets going she's got this hollow-sounding moan that just about rocks you off your feet.

"Her 'Jesus' is even better. Everybody says 'Jesus' so much round here, you forget sometimes who he was supposed to be, but Mama rations her Jesuses. You hear her say 'Jesus' the way she does and you know for sure that Jesus was a real person, that little boy used to bring doves back to life, that quiet young man never known to curse or fornicate. You can just see him—a man, like your daddy maybe, aged by the sins of the world, a life sacrificed for you personally." Shannon cackled her raspy laugh.

"I'll tell you. I couldn't stand it when I was little, but I got used to it as I got older. Now I love it, people getting all pale and nervous when Mama starts talking about 'Gaaaaad.' "

The bookstore never made any money. It was Mrs. Pearl's specialty sewing that was the backbone of the Pearl family income. Not surprisingly, she was famous for gilt-rendered scenes on the costumed sleeves and jackets of gospel performers. I got to where I could spot a Mrs. Pearl creation on the "Sunrise Gospel Hour" without even trying. She had a way of putting little curlicues at the base of the cross that was supposed to suggest grass, but for everyone who knew her, it was an artist's signature.

There was no doubt that Mrs. Pearl loved her work. "I feel like my whole life is a joy to the Lord," she told me one day, surrounded by her sewing machines and racks of embroidery thread. She was knotting tassels on a red silk blouse for one of the younger Carter girls. "My sewing, Mr. Pearl's work, the store, my precious daughter." She glanced over at Shannon with a look that mirrored the close-up of Mary and the Baby in the center of the *Illustrated Christian Bible* that was always on special down at the store.

"Everything that comes to us is a blessing or a test. That's all you need to know in this life . . . just the certainty that God's got His eye on you, that He knows what you are made of, what you need to grow on. Why, questioning's a sin, it's pointless. He will show you your path in His own good time. And long as I remember that, I'm fine. It's like that song Mr. Pearl likes so much—'Jesus is the engineer, trust his hand on the throttle . . .' "

Shannon giggled and waved me out on the porch. "Sometimes Mama needs a little hand on her throttle. You know what I mean?" She laughed and rolled her eyes like a broken kewpie doll. "Daddy has to throttle her back down to a human level or she'd take off like a helium angel."

I couldn't help myself. I laughed back, remembering what Aunt Raylene had said about Mrs. Pearl—"If she'd been fucked right just once, she'd have never birthed that weird child." I poked Shannon on one swollen arm, just in case she could read behind my eyes.

"Your mama's an ayn-gel," I whispered hoarsely, mocking the way Mrs. Pearl would say it, "just an ayn-gel of Gaaaaad."

"Gaaaaad damn right," Shannon whispered back, and I saw her hatred burning pink and hot in those eyes. It scared and fascinated me. Was it possible she could see the same thing in my eyes? Did I have that much hate in me? I looked back at Mrs. Pearl, humming around the pins in her mouth. A kind of chill went through me. Did I hate Mrs. Pearl? I looked at their porch, the baby's breath hanging in baskets and the two rocking chairs with hand-sewn cushions. Shannon's teeth flashed sunlight into my eyes.

"You look like the devil's walking on your grave."

I shivered and then spit like Granny. "The grave I'll lie in an't been dug yet." It was something I'd heard Granny say. Shannon grabbed my arm and gave it a jerk.

"Don't say that. It's bad luck to mention your own grave. They say my grandmother McCray joked about her burying place on Easter morning and fell down dead at evening service." She jerked my arm again, hard. "Think about something else quick." I looked down at her hand on my arm, puffy white fingers gripping my thin brown wrist.

"That child will rot fast when she goes," Aunt Raylene had said once. I felt sick.

"I got to go home." I pulled air in fast as I could. "Mama wants me to help her hang out the laundry this afternoon."

"Your mama's always making you work."

And yours never does, I thought.

"I like your family," Shannon sometimes said, though I knew that was a polite lie. "Your mama's a fine woman," Roseanne Pearl would agree, eying my too-tight raggedy dresses. She reminded me of the way James Waddell looked at us, of his daughters' smug, superior faces, laughing at my mama's loose teeth and Reese's curls done up in paper scraps. Daddy Glen was still working for the Sunshine Dairy and continued to take us over to his father's or one of his brothers' every few weeks, though they never seemed any happier to see us. Their contempt had worn my skin thin, and I had no patience for it. Whenever the Pearls talked about my people, I'd take off and not go back for weeks.

Now I took a deep breath, trying to get my stomach under control. Sometimes I really couldn't stand Shannon.

"We're gonna go to the diner for supper tonight. They have peach cobbler this time of year."

"My daddy's gonna make fresh ice cream tonight." Shannon smiled a smile full of the pride of family position. "We got black walnuts to put on it."

I didn't say anything. She would. She would rot very fast.

The gospel circuit ran from North Carolina to South Carolina, Tennessee, Georgia, Alabama. The singers moved back and forth on it, a tide of gilt and fringed jackets that paralleled and intersected the country western circuit. Sometimes you couldn't tell the difference, and as times got harder certainly Mr. Pearl stopped making distinctions, booking any act that would get him a little cash up front. More and more, Mama sent me off with the Pearls in their old yellow DeSoto, the trunk stuffed with boxes of religious supplies and Mrs. Pearl's sewing machine, the backseat crowded with Shannon and me and piles of sewing. We would pull into small towns in the afternoon so Mr. Pearl could do the setup and Mrs. Pearl could repair tears and frayed embroidery while Shannon and I went off to picnic alone on cold chicken and chow-chow. Mrs. Pearl always brought tea in a mason jar, but Shannon would rub her eyes and complain of a headache until her mama gave in and bought us RC Colas.

Most of the singers arrived late.

It was a wonder to me that the truth never seemed to register with Mr. and Mrs. Pearl. No matter who fell over the boxes backstage, they never caught on that the whole Tuckerton Family had to be pointed in the direction of the microphones, nor that Little Pammie Gleason—"Lord, just thirteen!"— had to wear her frilly blouse long-sleeved because she had bruises all up and down her arms from that redheaded boy her daddy wouldn't let her marry. They never seemed to see all the "boys" passing bourbon in paper cups backstage or their angel daughter begging for "just a sip." Maybe Jesus shielded their eyes the way he kept old Shadrach, Meshach, and Abednego safe in the fiery furnace. Certainly sin didn't touch them the way it did Shannon and me. Both of us had learned to walk carefully backstage, with all those hands reaching out to stroke our thighs and pinch the nipples we barely had.

"Playful boys," Mrs. Pearl would laugh, stitching the sleeves back on their jackets, mending the rips in their pants. I was amazed that she couldn't smell the whiskey breath set deep in her fine embroidery, but I wasn't about to commit the sin of telling her what God surely didn't intend her to know.

"Sometimes you'd think Mama's simple," Shannon said one night, giggling oddly. I wished she would shut up and the music would start. I was still hungry. Mrs. Pearl had packed less food than usual, and Mama had told me I was always to leave something on my plate when I ate with Shannon. I wasn't supposed to make the Pearls think they had to feed me. Not that that particular tactic worked. I'd left half a biscuit, and damned if Shannon hadn't popped it in her mouth.

"Maybe it's all that tugging at her throttle." Shannon giggled again, and I knew somebody had finally given her a pull at a paper cup. Now, I thought, now her mama will have to see. But when Shannon fell over her sewing machine, Mrs. Pearl just laid her down with a wet rag on her forehead.

"It's the weather," she whispered to me over Shannon's sodden brow. It was so hot that Jesus and the lamb were wilting off the paper fans provided by the local funeral home. But I knew if there had been snow up to the hubcaps, Mrs. Pearl would have said it was the chill in the air. An hour later, one of the Tuckerton cousins spilled a paper cup on Mrs. Pearl's sleeve, and I saw her take a deep, painful breath. Catching my eye, she just said, "Can't expect that frail soul to cope without a little help."

I didn't tell her that it seemed to me all those "boys" and "girls" were getting a hell of a lot of "help." I just muttered an almost inaudible "yeah" and cut my sinful eyes at them all. If they'd let me sing I'd never shame myself like that.

"We could go sit under the stage," Shannon suggested. "It's real nice under there."

It was nice, close and dark and full of the sound of people stomping on the stage. I put my head back and let the dust drift down on my face, enjoying the feeling of being safe and hidden, away from the crowd. The music seemed to be vibrating in my bones. *Taking your measure, taking your measure, Jesus and the Holy Ghost are taking your measure . . .*

I didn't like the new music they were singing. It was a little too gimmicky. *Two cups, three cups, a teaspoon of righteous. How will you measure when they call out your name?* Shannon started laughing. She put her arms around me and rocked her head back and forth. The music was too loud, and I could smell whiskey all around us. Suddenly my head hurt terribly; the smell of Shannon's hair was making me sick.

"Uh uh uh." Desperately I pushed Shannon away and crawled for the side of the stage as fast as I could, gagging. Air, I had to have air.

"Uh uh uh." I rolled out from under the stage and hit the side of the tent. Retching now, I jerked up the tarp and wiggled through. Out in the damp evening air, I let my head hang down and vomited between my spread hands. Behind me Shannon was gasping and giggling.

"You're sick, you poor baby." I felt her patting the small of my back comfortingly.

"Lord God!"

I looked up. A very tall man in a purple shirt was standing in front of me. I dropped my head and puked again. He had silver boots with cracked heels. I watched him step back out of range.

"Lord God!"

"It's all right." Shannon got to her feet beside me, keeping her hand on my back. "She's just a little sick." She paused. "If you got her a Co-Cola, it might settle her stomach."

I wiped my mouth, then wiped my hand on the grass. I looked up again. Shannon was standing still, sweat running down into her eyes and making her blink. I could see she was hoping for two Cokes. The man was still standing there with his mouth hanging open, a look of shock on his face.

"Lord God," he said again, and I knew before he spoke what he was going to say. It wasn't me who'd surprised him.

"Child, you are the ugliest thing I have ever seen."

Shannon froze. Her mouth fell open, and her whole face seemed to cave in as I watched. Her eyes shrank to little dots, and her mouth became a cup of sorrow. I pushed myself up.

"You bastard!" I staggered forward, and he backed up, rocking on his little silver heels. "You goddam gutless son of a bitch!" His eyes kept moving from my face to Shannon's wilting figure. "You think you so pretty? You ugly sack of shit! You shit-faced turd-eating—"

"*Shannon Pearl!*"

Mrs. Pearl was coming around the tent.

"You girls . . ." She gathered Shannon up in her arms. "Where have you been?" The man backed further away. I was breathing through my mouth, though I no longer felt so sick. I felt angry and helpless, and I was trying hard not to cry. Mrs. Pearl clucked between her teeth and stroked Shannon's limp hair. "What have you been doing?"

Shannon moaned and buried her face in her mama's dress.

Mrs. Pearl turned to me. "What were you saying?" Her eyes glittered in the arc lights from the front of the tent. I wiped my mouth again and said nothing. Mrs. Pearl looked to the man in the purple shirt. The confusion on her face seemed to melt and quickly became a blur of excitement and interest.

"I hope they weren't bothering you," she told him. "Don't you go on next?"

"Uh, yeah." He looked like he wasn't sure. He couldn't take his eyes off Shannon. He shook himself. "You Mrs. Pearl?"

"Why, that's right." Mrs. Pearl's face was glowing.

"I've heard about you. I just never met your daughter before."

Mrs. Pearl seemed to shiver all over, then catch herself. Pressed to her mama's stomach, Shannon began to wail.

"Shannon, what *are* you going on for?" She pushed her daughter away from her side and pulled out a blue embroidered handkerchief to wipe her face.

"I think we all kind of surprised each other." The man stepped forward and gave Mrs. Pearl a slow smile, but his eyes kept wandering back to Shannon. I wiped my mouth again and stopped myself from spitting. Mrs. Pearl went on stroking her daughter's face but looking up into the man's eyes.

"I love it when you sing," she said, and half giggled. Shannon pulled away from her and stared up at them both. The hate in her face was terrible. For a moment I loved her with all my heart.

"Well," the man said. He rocked from one boot to the other. "Well . . ."

I reached for Shannon's hand. She slapped mine away. Her face was blazing. I felt as if a great fire was burning close to me, using up all the oxygen, making me pant to catch my breath. I laced the fingers of my hands together and tilted my head back to look up at the stars. If there was a God, then there would be justice. If there was justice, then Shannon and I would make them all burn. We walked away from the tent toward Mr. Pearl's battered DeSoto.

"Someday," Shannon whispered.

"Yeah," I whispered back. "Someday."

Driving backcountry with Mr. Pearl when he went on his pros-
pecting trips meant stopping in at little rural churches with
gospel choirs, shabby tents with a soloist or two, and occasional
living-room prayer meetings that might shelter an extraordinary
young singer. Following up Mr. Pearl's tips was extended,
tedious work requiring great patience and tact. All too many
of the singers couldn't sing at all, and hadn't an ear good
enough to know when they went off tune. A few were enthusiastic enough that Mr. Pearl cautiously encouraged them to try
out for one of the existing gospel groups. But mostly all he
found was an echo of the real stuff, a diluted blend of harmony
and aspiration.

"Pitiful, an't it?" Shannon sounded like her father's daughter. "That sad old organ music just can't stand against a slide
guitar."

I nodded reluctantly. I still wanted to believe that spirit,
determination, and hard work could lift even the most pedes-
trian voice into the rarefied atmosphere of heartfelt gospel
music.

There was no predicting who the hand of God might
touch, where the clarion would sound. Sometimes one pure
voice would stand out, one little girl, one set of brothers whose
eyes would lift when they sang. Those were the ones who could
make you want to scream low against all the darkness in the
world. "That one," Shannon would whisper smugly, but I
didn't need her to tell me. I always knew who Mr. Pearl would
take aside and invite over to Gaston for revival week.

"Child!" he'd say. "You got a gift from God."

Uh huh, yeah.

Sometimes I couldn't stand it. I couldn't go in one more
church, hear one more choir. Never mind loving the music,
why hadn't God given me a voice? I hadn't asked for thick
eyelashes. I had asked for, begged for, gospel. Didn't God give

a good goddam what I wanted? If He'd take bastards into heaven, how come He couldn't put me in front of those hot lights and all that dispensation? Gospel singers always had money in their pockets, another bottle under their seats. Gospel singers had love and safety and the whole wide world to fall back on—women and church and red clay solid under their feet. All I wanted, I whispered, all I wanted, was a piece, a piece, a little piece of it.

Shannon overheard and looked at me sympathetically.

She knows, I thought, she knows what it is to want what you are never going to have. I'd underestimated her.

That July we went over to the other side of Lake Greenwood, a part of the county I knew from visiting one of the cousins who worked at the air base. Off the highway we stopped at a service station to give Mrs. Pearl a little relief from the heat.

"You ever think God maybe didn't intend us to travel on Sunday afternoon? I swear He makes it hotter than Saturday or Friday."

Mrs. Pearl sat in the shade while Mr. Pearl went off to lecture the man who rented out the Rhythm Ranch. Shannon and I cut off across a field to check out the headstones near a stand of cottonwood. We loved to read the mottoes and take back the good ones for Mrs. Pearl to stitch up on samplers and sell in the store. My favorites were the weird ones, like "Now He Knows" or "Too Pure." Shannon loved the ones they put up for babies, little curly-headed dolls with angel wings and heartbreaking lines like "Gone to Mama" or "Gone Home."

"Silly stuff." I kicked at the pieces of clay pot that were lying everywhere. Shannon turned to me, and I saw tears on her cheeks.

"No, no, it just tears me up. Think about it, losing your own little baby girl, your own little angel. Oh, I can't stand it. I just can't stand it." She gave big satisfied sobs and wiped her hands on her blue gingham pockets.

"I wish I could take me one of these home. Wouldn't you

like to have one you could keep up? You could tell stories to the babies."

"You crazy."

Shannon sniffed. "You just don't understand. Mama says I've got a very tender heart."

"Uh huh." I walked away. It was too hot to fight. It was certainly too hot to cry. I kicked over some plastic flowers and a tattered green cardboard cross. This was one of the most boring trips I'd ever taken with the Pearls. I tried to remember why I'd even wanted to come. At home Mama would be making fresh ice tea, boiling up sugar water to mix in it. Reese would be slicing peaches. Daddy Glen would be out of the way, off working on the lawn mower. I swatted at mosquitoes and hoped my face wasn't sunburning. I was tired of Shannon, tired of her mama's endless simpering endearments, tired of her daddy's smug contempt, and even more tired of my own jealousy.

I stopped. The music coming through the cottonwoods was gospel.

Gut-shaking, deep-bellied, powerful voices rolled through the dried leaves and hot air. This was the real stuff. I could feel the whiskey edge, the grief and holding on, the dark night terror and determination of real gospel.

"My God," I breathed, and it was the best "My God" I'd ever put out, a long, scared whisper that meant I just might start to believe He hid in cottonwoods.

There was a church there, clapboard walls standing on cement blocks and no pretense of stained-glass windows. Just yellow glass reflecting back sunlight, all the windows open to let in the breeze and let out that music.

Amazing grace . . . how sweet the sound . . . that saved a wretch like me . . . A woman's voice rose and rolled over the deeper men's voices, rolled out so strong it seemed to rustle the leaves on the cottonwood trees.

Amen.

Lord.

"Sweet Jesus, she can sing."

Shannon ignored me and kept pulling up wildflowers.

"You hear that? We got to tell your daddy."

Shannon turned and stared at me with a peculiar angry expression. "He don't handle colored. An't no money in handling colored."

At that I froze, realizing that such a church off such a dirt road had to be just that—a colored church. And I knew what that meant. Of course I did. Still I heard myself whisper, "That an't one good voice. That's a churchful."

"It's colored. It's niggers." Shannon's voice was as loud as I'd ever heard it, and shrill with indignation. "My daddy don't handle niggers." She threw wildflowers at me and stamped her foot. "And you made me say that. Mama always said a good Christian don't use the word 'nigger.' Jesus be my witness, I wouldn't have said it if you hadn't made me."

"You crazy. You just plain crazy." My voice was shaking. The way Shannon said "nigger" tore at me, the tone pitched exactly like the echoing sound of Aunt Madeline sneering "trash" when she thought I wasn't close enough to hear. I wondered what Shannon heard in my voice that made her as angry as I was. Maybe it was the heat, maybe it was the shame we both were feeling, or maybe it was simply that Shannon Pearl and I were righteously tired of each other.

Shannon threw another handful of flowers at me. "I'm crazy? Me? What do you think you are? You and your mama and your whole family. Everybody knows you're all a bunch of drunks and thieves and bastards. Everybody knows you just come round so you can eat off my mama's table and beg scraps we don't want no more. Everybody knows who you are . . ."

I was moving before I could stop myself, my hands flying up to slap together right in front of her face—a last-minute attempt not to hit her. "You bitch, you white-assed bitch." I wrung my hands, trying to keep myself from slapping her pasty face. "Don't you never hit anybody in the face," Mama always said.

"You little shit, you fuck off." I put the words out as slick and fast as any of my uncles. Shannon's mouth fell open. "You just fuck off!" I kicked red dirt up onto her gingham skirt.

Shannon's face twisted. "You an't never gonna go to another gospel show with us again! I'm gonna tell my mama what you called me, and she an't ever gonna let you come near me again."

"Your mama, your mama. You'd piss in a Pepsi bottle if your mama told you to."

"Listen to you. You . . . you trash. You nothing but trash. Your mama's trash, and your grandma, and your whole dirty family . . ."

I swung at her then with my hand wide open, right at her face, but I was too angry. I was crazy angry and I tripped, falling onto the red dirt on my spread hands. My right hand came down on a broken clay pot, hurting me so bad I could barely see Shannon's dripping, flushed cheeks.

"Oh . . . shit. You . . . shit." If I could have jumped up and caught her, I would have ripped out handfuls of that cotton-candy hair.

Shannon stood still and watched as I pushed myself up and grabbed my right hand with my left. I was crying, I realized, the tears running down my face while behind us the choir had never stopped singing. That woman's voice still rolled over the cottonwoods. *Was blind but now I see . . .*

"You're ugly." I swallowed my tears and made myself speak very quietly. "You're God's own ugly child and you're gonna be an ugly woman. A lonely, ugly old woman."

Shannon's lips started to tremble, poking out of her face so that she was uglier than I'd ever seen her, a doll carved out of cold grease melting in the heat.

"You ugly thing," I went on. "You monster, you greasy

cross-eyed stinking sweaty-faced ugly thing!" I pointed all my fingers at her and spit at her patent-leather shoes. "You so ugly your own mama don't even love you." Shannon backed off, turned around, and started running.

"Mamaaaaa!" she wailed as she ran. I kept yelling after her, more to keep myself from crying now than to hurt her.

"Ugly . . . ugly . . . ugly."

12

There was no way on God's green earth that I was ever going to speak to Shannon Pearl again. I didn't even want to go to church. "Damn Bushy Creek anyway," I told Reese. "An't nobody there can sing worth a damn, and that preacher's so full of himself he crowds out all the air—what air there is, all those old biddies sweating talcum powder and perfume."

"Listen to you!" Reese rapped my belt buckle with her knuckles and then reached past me for the little bit of Coke left in the bottle I'd just set down. "Sounds like you done lost your religion."

Reese and I had turned from absolute allies into competitors overnight, arguing all the time and fighting over everything from who got the chicken gizzard to who was the toughest. After years of wearing finger curls and ruffled dresses, Reese had turned tomboy with a vengeance, wrestling and spit-

173

ting with the boys and refusing to wear anything Mama bought her. She'd begged a couple of pairs of Butch's old coveralls from Deedee and wore them all the time, but what she really wanted was a pair of blue jeans like the ones I'd bought myself with my dishwashing money. She was also fiercely jealous of the braided leather belt Uncle Earle had sent me, with its brightly polished buckle shaped like a horseshoe, and was constantly trying to get her hands on it. I had to keep my eye on her or she would have "borrowed" it every chance she got.

"You should talk," I snapped, wishing she would just go away and leave me alone. "You just go to church so you can beg Kool-Aid and cookies after Sunday school."

"I an't ashamed of that. I don't see you turning down nothing people are giving away for free. Besides, you're just jealous 'cause everybody's always petting on me at Sunday school, and it used to be you getting all the attention."

I snorted contemptuously but said nothing. You couldn't argue with Reese, she liked it too much. I hooked my thumbs behind my belt buckle and leaned back to stare at her, refusing to speak. Silence was the only way to get to Reese. She couldn't stand it if you wouldn't talk to her.

"Oh, don't you start that, you mean old thing." Reese stamped her bare feet in the dirt and pointed the Coke bottle at me. "I'm on to you, Bone. I know all your tricks, and I an't gonna play no more. You just sit on your damn old belt. I hope it strangles you. I an't gonna be there to see it."

It was around then that I discovered that Reese was masturbating almost as often as I was. In the middle of the night, I woke up to feel the bed shaking slightly. Instead of sprawling across the bottom of the bed as she usually did, her legs and arms thrown wide, Reese was at the far edge of the mattress, her body taut and curved away from me. I could hear the sound of her breathing, fast and shallow. I knew immediately what she was doing. I kept still, my own breathing quiet and steady. After a while there was a moment when she held her breath, and then the shaking stopped. Very quietly then I slipped my right hand down between my legs and held myself. I wanted to do it too, but I couldn't stand the thought that she might hear. But what if she did? I felt Reese relax and sprawl wide again. I held my breath, I moved my hand, I almost did not shake the bed at all.

Reese would go back to our bedroom alone every day when we got home from school. When she came out, I would go in. Sometimes I even imagined I could smell what she had been doing, but that could not have been so. She was a little girl and smelled like a little girl. Neither of us smelled like Mama, the ripe fleshy scent of a woman grown. I pulled my shorts down and made sure of it, carefully washing between my legs with warm soap and water every time I did that thing I knew my sister was doing too.

One afternoon, I went outside and stood listening for the sound of Reese alone in the bedroom. She was quiet, very quiet, but I could hear the rhythm of her breathing as it gradually picked up speed, and the soft little grunts she made before it began to slow down again. I liked those grunts. When Reese did it in the middle of the night, she never made any sound at all. But then, I was just as careful myself even when I was safely alone. I wondered if Reese did it differently in the daytime. I wondered if she lay on her back with her legs wide, the way I liked to when I was alone, rather than on her stomach with both hands under her the way she did at night. There was no way to spy on her, no way to know. But I imagined Reese sometimes while I did it myself, seeing her sprawled across our big Hollywood bed, rocking only slightly, showing by nothing but her breathing that she was committing a sin.

I walked in on Reese one afternoon while she was lying on the bed with a pair of mama's panties over her face. All her features were outlined under the sheer material, but her breath puffed the silk out over her lips. Frantically, she snatched them off and shoved them behind her on the bed. I grabbed a book I had been reading off the dresser and pretended I hadn't seen anything.

Reese played out her own stories in the woods behind the house. I watched her one afternoon from the top of the tree Mama hung her birdfeeder on. She hadn't seen me climb up there and didn't know I had a clear view of her as she ran around in an old sheet tied to her neck like a cape. She seemed to be pretending to fight off imaginary attackers. Then she dropped to the ground and pretended to be wrestling. Rolling around in the grass and wet leaves she kept shouting "No! No!" The haughty expression on her face was replaced by mock terror as she threw her head back and forth wildly like the heroine in an adventure movie.

I hugged myself tightly to the tree and rocked my hips against the indifferent trunk. I imagined I was tied to the branches above and below me. Someone had beaten me with dry sticks and put their hands in my clothes. Someone, someone, I imagined. Someone had tied me high up in the tree, gagged me and left me to starve to death while the blackbirds pecked at my ears. I rocked and rocked, pushing my thighs into the rough bark. Below me, Reese pushed her hips into the leaves and made grunting noises. Someone, someone, she imagined, was doing terrible exciting things to her.

Reese and I never talked about our private games, our separate hours alone in the bedroom. These days we barely talked at all. But we made sure no one else ever went in the bedroom when one of us was there alone.

It was the worst time for Reese and me to be fighting. Neither of us was ever supposed to be home in the afternoon without the other, but I couldn't tell when she might blow up at me and run off somewhere. Daddy Glen had gotten his dairy routes changed and no longer had a full schedule. He'd been coming home a lot in the afternoons and had gone back to looking worried all the time. He'd yell at me one day that I was getting too big to run around in a T-shirt with no bra, and the next accuse me of pretending to be grown-up. Mama said he was fighting with his daddy and we were to stay out of his way until things settled down. But Aunt Alma and Uncle Wade were fighting again too, so I couldn't hang around over there, and Aunt Ruth was really sick now.

"You go out to Raylene's," she told me finally.

"You never sent me to Raylene's before," I complained. "I thought you didn't want me going out to her place." I was hoping she'd let me come to the diner again and work in the kitchen. I liked it down there. I liked listening to the waitresses tell jokes and watching the truckers flirt with Mama like she was still the prettiest woman in the county.

"I never said that. I an't never said nothing to you about Raylene." I could tell Mama was angry from the high pitch of her voice. "Did somebody say something to you about Raylene?"

"No, Mama."

"You sure?" Mama took hold of my wrist so hard my skin burned. "You sure?"

"What would anyone say about Raylene?"

Mama let go of my arm.

"Never mind asking questions. Just don't you go making things up, little girl. You're not too big to have your britches warmed."

"I'm sorry. But you never sent me out to Raylene's before."

"Well, maybe I didn't think you were old enough to be staying out on the river before." Mama was exasperated and impatient. She pushed her hair back with both hands and wiped her lips. "Garvey's doing some work for Mr. Berdforth's service station these afternoons after he gets out of school. He can give you a ride, and I should hope I can trust you not to get in any trouble while you're there."

Garvey was happy to give me a lift to Aunt Raylene's place, particularly after Mama gave him a dollar for gas money. "I an't making no real money cleaning up for Mr. Berdforth," he told me. "Man's as cheap as they come. But at least I'm learning something. Daddy says a mechanic can always find a job."

"Yeah."

I was restless and uninterested in Garvey's troubles. Aunt Alma joked that the twins were too lazy to fart on their own, and sometimes I thought she was right. They were certainly dumb enough. Neither of them ever read a book or talked about anything but how rich they were gonna be "someday." Mama said you could tell they were starting to grow up by how silly they had become, that teenagers always got stupid before they got smart. I wondered if that was what was happening to me, if I had already started to get stupid and just didn't know it. Not that it mattered. Stupid or smart, there wasn't much choice about what was going to happen to me, or to Grey and Garvey, or to any of us. Growing up was like falling into a hole. The boys would quit school and sooner or later go to jail for something silly. I might not quit school, not while Mama had any say in the matter, but what difference would that make? What was I going to do in five years? Work in the textile mill? Join Mama at the diner? It all looked bleak to me. No wonder people got crazy as they grew up.

No matter what Mama said, I knew that it wasn't just because of where she lived that I had never spent much time with Aunt Raylene. For all she was a Boatwright woman, there were ways Raylene had always been different from her sisters. She was quieter, more private, living alone with her dogs and fishing lines, and seemingly happy that way. She had always lived out past the city limits, and her house was where the older boy cousins tended to go. Out at Raylene's they could smoke and curse and roughhouse without interference. She let kids do pretty much anything they wanted. With none of her own, Raylene was convinced that the best way to raise children was to give them their head.

"There's no evil in them," she'd always say. "They're just like puppies. They need to wear themselves out now and then."

Raylene's place was easy to get to on the Eustis Highway but set off by itself on a little rise of land. The Greenville River curved around the outcropping where her weathered old shotgun house stood, and from the porch that went around three sides, you could watch the river and the highway that skirted it. Raylene kept the trees cut back and the shrubs low to the ground. "I don't like surprises," she always said. "I like to see who's coming up on me."

When Raylene was young, Uncle Earle told me, she had been kind of wild. At seventeen she had run off with a guy who drove for the carnival, but she never married him. She came home two years later to take a job in the textile mill and rent the house where she still lived. Before he went off to Oklahoma, Butch told me that Raylene had worked for the carnival like a man, cutting off her hair and dressing in overalls. She'd called herself Ray, and with her short, stocky build, big shoulders, and small breasts, I could easily see how no one had questioned her. It was astonishing to imagine running off like that, and I would think about it with wistful longing. Grey or Garvey would talk about how they intended to go traveling once they got out of school, but a girl couldn't go roaming so easily. But Raylene had done it, and I loved to think how I might too. If I cut my hair real short, learned to smoke and talk rough, maybe I could. Still, Aunt Raylene had a couple of ugly scars behind one ear that she wouldn't talk about, and a way of looking sad and thoughtful that made me think her travels hadn't been the romantic adventures the boys described. If I followed her lead I might come back with worse scars, or not come back at all.

She'd come home to live her life alone, quit the mill after twenty years, still kept her gray hair cut short, and wore trousers as often as skirts. She had only a few friends, all equally quiet private people. Her only social activity seemed to be a weekly card game with the widowed choir director and two of the local schoolteachers. Deedee had called her a lonely old woman once, but Ruth had shushed her, saying a woman was only lonely who wasn't happy with herself, and Raylene was probably the only person any of us would ever meet who was completely satisfied with her own company. Not that anyone left her alone. The uncles were always dropping by around dinnertime, and Grey and Garvey seemed to be out there as often as they were home.

Raylene was said to be the best cook in the family and earned steady money by selling her home-canned vegetables and fruit. "Woman makes the best chow-chow in the state," Uncle Beau boasted. "And the second-best home brew." I had never tasted her whiskey, but Mama took as much of her chow-chow as Raylene would let her have. It had a smoky peppery taste like nothing else, sweet and spicy at the same time. When I started going out to her place I figured I would make Mama happy by talking Raylene out of a few extra jars. I never imagined that out on the river I would suddenly find myself as fascinated with my reclusive old aunt as I had ever been with gospel music.

"Trash rises," Aunt Raylene joked the first afternoon I spent with her. "Out here where no one can mess with it, trash rises all the time." She laughed loud, with great enthusiasm, and spit to the side in a way I had never seen a grown woman do before.

On summer nights Raylene kept old truck tires from the county dump smoldering in the yard to drive the mosquitoes away. The smoke rose in a thick stinking brown fog, drifting toward the river, where the men came to fish in the cool of the evening, and where Aunt Raylene kept the weeds cut back to discourage bugs and give her a clear view of the banks.

"I like to watch things pass," she told me in her lazy whiskery drawl. "Time and men and trash out on the river. I just like to watch it all go around the bend." She spoke softly, smelling a little of alcohol and pepper, chow-chow and home brew, and the woodsmoke tang that clung to her skin all the time. I watched her shift her hips in her overalls. She was as big around as Aunt Alma but moved as easily and gracefully as a young boy, squatting on her heels to pull weeds and swinging her arms as she walked around her yard. Uncle Earle had said she'd loved to dance when she was young, and she looked as if she still could.

Aunt Raylene's house was scrubbed clean, but her walls were lined with shelves full of oddities, old tools and bird nests, rare dishes and peculiarly shaped rocks. An amazing collection of things accumulated on the river bank below her house. People from Greenville tossed their garbage off the highway a few miles up the river. There it would sink out of sight in the mud and eventually work its way down to Aunt Raylene's, where the river turned, then rise to get caught in the roots of the big trees along the bank. Aunt Raylene said the garbage drew the fish in, and it was true that the fishing at her place was the best in the county. The uncles went to Aunt Raylene's to catch carp and catfish and big brown unnamed fish with rotting eyes and gilded fins that people were afraid to eat. Uncle Earle and Uncle Beau would put out their poles with little bells on the lines and stand in the tire smoke to drink whiskey and tell dirty stories. The bells would tinkle now and then, but they didn't always stop to go get their catch. Sometimes the whiskey and the stories were too good.

Raylene offered me a glass of lemon tea when I showed up, and then quickly put me to work. She had me pick the fresh vegetables out of her side garden so she wouldn't have to do all that bending over. "I just about ruined my back at that damn mill," she said with a grin and a sigh. "Always leaning forward and reaching. Now I'd rather run than bend. You be careful of your back, Bone, or it'll be damn stiff when you get old." She told me to go down to the river to pull in whatever trash had accumulated in the tree roots. I came home with fresh tomatoes, okra, two jars of chow-chow, and the head off a Betsy Wetsy doll, the one with the silly rubber curl on her forehead. Raylene told Mama I was the kind of girl she liked, quiet and hardworking, and said she'd pay in kind for my help a couple of days a week. So I started spending all my time with Raylene while Reese went off to afternoon Bible classes at the Jesus Love Academy.

Every day I dragged stuff up from the river—baby-carriage covers, tricycle wheels, shoes, plastic dishes, jump-rope handles, ragged clothes, and once the headlight off a Harley-Davidson motorcycle.

"This is good stuff," Aunt Raylene usually said. "You got an eye for things, girl. I can clean and patch those clothes up. We'll just soak the dishes in bleach and give the rest of it a scrubbing. Saturday morning we'll put out blankets and sell it off the side of the road. You get your mama to send you over on the weekend and I'll give you a tenth of everything we earn."

I loved her praise more than the money, loved being good at something, loved hearing Aunt Raylene tell Uncle Beau what a worker I was. Sometimes she'd come down to the river and watch me climb around the tree roots. "You're pretty sure on your feet," she told me. "Looks like you an't scared of falling in."

"Why should I be?" I watched her light a cigarette the same way Uncle Earle did, striking the match against her thumbnail. "A little river water an't gonna hurt me."

"No, it won't. It won't. But you'd be surprised how silly some people get about the notion of falling in, or getting their pants wet, or bumping themselves on an old river rock. I had Alma's girl Temple out here once after she quit school, and it turned out she was scared of snapping turtles. Girl was convinced they were waiting for her just under the surface of the water, waiting to snap her little toes off and eat them up! Can you imagine?" She took a drag on her cigarette, cupping it in her hand away from the river breeze.

"Oh, Lord." She arched her back and then sank down in a squat on the bank, her black serge skirt bunching up under her. "I am so tired of people whining about what might happen to them, never taking no chances or doing anything new. I'm glad you an't gonna be like that, Bone. I'm counting on you to get out there and do things, girl. Make people nervous and make your old aunt glad."

She wrapped her arms around her knees and looked off down the river. I saw her do that a lot, sit out there and stare into the distance. She always seemed completely comfortable with herself, elbows locked around her knees and one hand drawn up to smoke. Sometimes she'd hum softly, no music I'd ever heard. Aunt Raylene hated most everything that played on the radio, saved her greatest contempt for the kind of country ballads that bemoaned the faithless lover and always included a little spoken part during the chorus. "Terrible maudlin shit," she'd declare. "You don't like that, do you, Bone?"

I'd promised her that no, I didn't, 'course I didn't, not mentioning that I had liked it before. I would have hated for her to think I didn't have good sense. For my own protection, I never talked to her about gospel music. I couldn't bear it if Raylene laughed at the music I dreamed of singing.

Aunt Alma's girl Patsy Ruth came out to Aunt Raylene's to get out of caring for Tadpole. The baby had finally been diagnosed with a heart condition, though she didn't look sick, just very small and slightly blue. At four she still fit in Alma's laundry basket and had to be watched all the time. "Tadpole falls asleep and it looks like she an't breathing. Mama gets all crazy, thinks she's died or something, and goes shaking her till she cries. Gets on my nerves," Patsy Ruth complained. "I'd rather pull weeds for Aunt Raylene any day."

Patsy Ruth wanted to help me pull stuff out of the river but hated getting mud on herself. She stayed up on the exposed roots of the trees and rarely retrieved anything worth the trouble. Still, she was the one who saw the hooks—two of them, linked together with a rusted chain, big four-pronged things still dragging little shreds of rope.

"Lookit the shine!" she yelled, almost sliding down in the mud. "Lookit there. It's something, I bet you. Something."

I climbed out on one of the roots until I could reach down to the curved metal edge that was showing through the brown water. It was hard to untangle the hooks from the muddy trash. By the time I worked them free, I'd slid down and had one leg thigh-deep in the mud.

"You get your ass down here and help me," I yelled at Patsy Ruth, but she had no intention of risking the river. Instead she ran back to find Grey and Garvey.

"My sweet Jesus, look at the size of them." Grey pulled the hooks out of my hands even before I got them up the bank. "That sucker's longer than my arm."

"What is it?"

"It's a hook, a set of hooks."

"Any fool can see that. What's it for?" Garvey had come up too, and was just as eager to get his hands on the hooks as Grey was. He was always fighting with his brother, always challenging anything Grey said.

"Mountain climbing, it's for mountain climbing," Grey told us.

I didn't believe that any more than Garvey, but Grey was so insistent we kept quiet while we ran our fingers along the rusty points of the hooks.

"Look at the edge on them points. They'd sink into rock with no trouble at all."

"You don't need nothing like that to climb the mountains around here." Garvey pulled at the chain dangling down. "You don't need nothing."

"Oh hell, probably some Yankee brought them down, didn't know what our mountains were like." Grey was adamant. Nothing would serve but that we agree that the hooks were for climbing, no matter how silly it was to imagine Yankees coming down to climb our mountains with those hooks. But Garvey wasn't going to give in so easily.

"You an't got the sense you was born with," he spat. "Even Yankees an't that dumb."

"You calling me stupid?"

"Aw, for Jesus' sake."

I grabbed the hooks then, before somebody got himself stabbed with one. They were heavy, but not so heavy that I couldn't swing one around and throw it if I had to. Grey was right about one thing. Those barbs were sharp under the rust, and not only at the points but all along the edges that curled back on themselves. Gray-green algae hid most of the metal shine, but it came off easy with a little scraping. The rust was harder, but it too came off when I ran my pocket knife up and down the prongs. In the center of each hook where the four points came together, there was a packed mass of gluey river mud, weeds, and fish pieces. I set to scraping it all clean and got the boys interested enough to stop fighting for a while. They used a tire iron to pop the chain and separate the two hooks, each taking one as if they intended to keep them.

"Once we get them cleaned up, I'll show you how mountain climbers use them." Grey was still determined to convince us that he knew what the hooks were all about.

Garvey laughed at him. "You try throwing that son of a bitch up in a tree and you gonna put somebody's eye out when the chain catches on a branch."

"I an't gonna throw it up no tree." Grey looked disgusted. "I'm gonna use it to pull myself right up the side of the house. I'm gonna wave at you from the roof, and then you can tell me I'm crazy."

He did it too, tied a good long rope to the chain dangling off his hook and swung it around and around until he got it high enough, and launched it at the house. The barbs dug right into the wood below the roofline and gouged deep enough to support Grey's weight, though once he climbed up there, he couldn't swing around to get a leg over the roof's edge after all. Garvey tried it next, forgetting that they had been arguing, but he had the same problem. He did manage to hang on to the ridgepole while he worked the hook loose and tossed it down. Then he slid down after it, by some miracle not breaking any bones. Neither of them saw me grab Garvey's abandoned hook and start edging toward the side of the house.

"We'll aim it at the roof this time," Garvey told us. "Get it on the roof itself. Then we'll be able to climb over the top by pulling up on the rope."

"You'll do no such thing!" Aunt Raylene had come up

behind me while we were all looking at Garvey. She grabbed one hook out of my hands and the other from Grey. "You trying to kill one of these children?" She looked up then and saw the holes the hook had gouged in her wall.

"*Oh my Jesus!*" Her left hand snaked out and slapped first Grey, then Garvey. "You digging holes in my house! You planning to just walk off and leave it like that, I suppose. No matter that it's gonna let the rain in and rot my wall." The chain dangling from one fist knocked against the skirt of the print dress she'd worn to go into town. "I'm surprised you an't killed each other already. No." She shook her head and spat snuff juice to the side. "No. What's surprising is that I an't killed you already."

"It an't that deep a hole," Grey tried to tell her. "It an't gonna let the rain in."

The color rushed into Aunt Raylene's face, and her eyes went glassy. I thought for a moment how Uncle Beau said Aunt Raylene moved out to the river after she got in trouble on the carnival circuit and cut a man up for trying to mess with her. Now she looked like she was going to swing one of those hooks at Grey's belly. The other kids took off at a run, and Grey stumbled back out of her reach.

"Aunt Raylene," he pleaded, sweat breaking out on his face, "Aunt Raylene, now, Aunt Raylene, wait . . ."

"You crazy little bastard," she hissed at him. She caught his arm in one hand and shook him back and forth like a fish on a pole. "All of you. Don't you know what this is?" She waved the tines up close to Grey's face. "You think this is a big old fishhook? Well, it an't. It's for trawling, for dragging. You go down in the river and they'll use something like this to pull you up in chunks. Pull you loose from the junk in that deep mud. Pull you up in pieces, you hear me? Nasty slices of you, little boy, for your mama to cry over."

Aunt Raylene's tale didn't really scare us. When I tried to imagine my flesh in pieces it was like a cartoon, completely unreal, but in the night stringy terrible pieces of meat loomed in my dreams. The hooks got in my dreams too, dripping blood and river mud. Maybe it hadn't been fish parts I'd cleaned out of them. It could have been anything. I made up stories about where those hooks had come from, who had lost them, until Patsy Ruth got nightmares. She dreamed that she had drowned in the river and the morticians had to sew pieces of her back together to look like somebody. Only they had to sew different people's pieces together just to make up one reasonable body to bury to show her mama. When she told Aunt Alma, Alma told me to stop making up such gruesome stories.

Aunt Raylene put a lock on her cellar door to keep all of us away from the hooks, and everyone seemed to forget them. But a few weeks later, I started to dream about them again. This time their razor points whistled when the wind blew, and the steel edges reflected light where there was none. I would wake up from those dreams with my teeth aching, my ears throbbing as if there were a wind blowing on me, stinking, cold, and constant. I wanted one of those hooks, wanted it for my own, that cold sharp metal where I could put out my hand and touch it at any time.

I started going over to Aunt Raylene's place every chance I got, hanging out and being helpful. I pulled weeds and picked tomatoes, corn, and peppers. When canning started, I was there to boil the mason jars and melt the wax while Raylene cut and chopped at her kitchen table. I brought the fruit jars up from the cellar. I brought up the wax, the rubber seals, and the metal racks, and when Aunt Raylene went out to put her neck under the old water pump on the far side of the house, I brought up one of the hooks. I hid it under the porch before anyone could see, laughing because it was so easy to do, but when I got back to the kitchen, Mama was standing there over the bubbling vats.

"You want these peaches to boil over?" she asked me. "You got to watch this stuff close. You can't be running off in the yard with a fire under these pots." She planted me on a stool by the stove. "You sit here and keep your eyes open, little girl."

Aunt Raylene came in laughing, and pinched my shoulder. "Ah, Anney, Bone's the best you got, works like a dog, she does, just like you and me." I dropped my shoulders and stared into the simmering pot of peaches.

For three days running then, I sat at that stove while Aunt Raylene and Mama gossiped and cooked.

"How's Glen doing?" Raylene's voice was polite, as if she didn't care much whether Mama answered or not.

"Oh, he's fine. His dairy routes don't seem to have worked out the way he hoped, and I think he and his daddy were fighting for a while there. But lately he's been working more in the processing plant itself. He don't talk about it. Don't think he wants me to hear him complaining about his daddy, but at least it's full-time again. Just wish he made more money."

"I know what you mean."

"You do, don't you? When you first worked at the mill, you didn't make enough money to spit at."

"Oh, they never wanted to have me do what I knew how to do best. Wanted me to work on the line rather than fix their machines. Never could accept that I was a better mechanic than a mill worker. After a while I just gave up fighting them about it. Couldn't stand being that poor anymore, specially since my creditors couldn't hardly stand what I wasn't paying them." Raylene's grin was wicked. She poured herself some hot coffee and leaned over closer to Mama.

"Remember that time Alma wouldn't let the sheriff take her furniture?" she asked. "That time she started screaming for the neighbors how they were trying to rob her?"

"God, yes," Mama laughed. "And that sheriff like to peed in his pants when he saw her throwing clothes out the window and yelling, 'Take it all, why don't you? Take the kids too, take it all.' Oh, my sweet Jesus, yes."

"Wade always said she threw her housedress at him, and then just stood there in her underwear, and he wasn't gonna go near her after that."

"Oh no, girl. That's just what people tell. She didn't really do that. She just threatened to do that."

"It's a better story if she had done it, which is probably why they say she stripped down to her panties, huh?"

"Just like her, too. Alma an't scared of hell or high water."

"Not like her girls."

"No."

Mama looked over at me. "Give that rack a jiggle," she told me. "You don't want them jars to settle too much." She stretched her neck to look over without getting up. "I don't think those jars are setting deep enough in that pot."

Aunt Raylene poured mama some more ice tea. "Oh Anney. Bone's doing a good job. When she grows up, she's gonna know all she'll need about canning and cooking and gossiping in the kitchen."

Mama spooned a little more sugar into her tea. "Raylene, you're spoiling her. You should have had some of your own, and then you'd watch them all a little more sharply."

"Well, for not birthing any, it sure feels like I've raised a crowd. Seems like I've had somebody's kids under my feet for years now. An't nobody in this family ever been selfish with their children. Why, I've got up many a morning to find a porch full of young'uns somebody's dropped off in the night."

"Most often Alma's."

"Oh, don't go on about Alma. She's got a good heart, for all that temper of hers, and maybe because of it. And damn, but she's had a hard time, especially with her girls. It don't surprise me that this sick baby of hers is a girl. She's had no luck with her girls. Ever since Temple left home she's gone as sour as bad whiskey."

"Everybody says Temple takes after Alma, but I can't see it," Mama said. "I'd swear the girl was never easy in her body. Never gave a hoot about nobody or nothing, except her pride."

Aunt Raylene started giggling over the lip of her tea glass. "You know, she was standing in the yard that time the sheriff came and all the yelling started. Stood out there and tried to pretend wasn't nothing going on, wasn't no sheriffs in the yard with a warrant, no beating on the door, nobody throwing clothes out the window. The girl's purely amazing."

"What'd she do, offer him a glass of water?"

"Hell no, she tried to get Alma out of the house so she could give up the furniture quietly. She didn't care what happened, didn't care that the furniture-store man really was trying to rob her mama, just didn't want the neighbors to think they couldn't keep up the payments."

"As if everybody didn't know it already. You can't keep secrets like that."

"Well, you and I don't even try. And certainly Alma don't. She knows who she is. But it's different for the kids. Seems like they're all the time wanting just what they can't have, and they've got such a funny dose of pride."

"No pride at all or too much, I can't tell sometimes."

"Different from us is all, maybe." Aunt Raylene's face went slack and her voice dropped. "Look at your girls too, Anney. I've seen it in them. Not like Temple. No. But something. Something hard and angry that only shows now and again."

They went quiet and looked over at me. I tried to pretend I hadn't been listening, concentrating on waving the steam away so that I could see down into the pot. But if I slanted my eyes sideways, I could still see them clear. Through the steam they both looked older—two worn, tired women repeating old stories to each other and trying not to worry too much about things they couldn't change anyway. It struck me then how young they both were to be looking so old, neither of them as old as Madeline, Mama not yet twenty-six and Aunt Raylene less than ten years older. Still, they seemed so different from me, almost as if they had come out of another century. I wished then that I could be more like them, easier in my body and not so angry all the time. Too much pride or too little? What was wrong with me? I wondered.

■   ■   ■

190

After all the peaches had been canned, the tomatoes and the snap peas, Aunt Raylene did the rest of the fruit, the plums and the apples and the blackberries. The days were full of sweat and steam and boiling pots. I spent every minute I was not in school planted on a stool in her kitchen, peeling or scrubbing or watching pots while Aunt Raylene told me stories and my neck cramped with worry. I was afraid somebody would find my hook under her porch, but I couldn't get it out of there until the canning was done. If one of the uncles found that hook, I knew Aunt Raylene would figure out that it was me who had brought it up out of the cellar.

One early evening when we were almost finished putting up the canned fruit racks, Grey came into the kitchen, his face so bright it jumped out at me. His grin was spread so wide I gave him a shove before Aunt Raylene could see.

"You found it!" I hissed at him.

He stared at me for a long minute and then grinned wider. "You, huh, Bone? You the one been going in and out the cellar all this time, huh? Slick, girl, slick."

"Just keep your mouth shut or Aunt Raylene will hide it where we'll never find it."

"I an't gonna tell nobody."

"You looking like that, she'll know something is going on."

Grey laughed and twirled a finger in a smear of blackberry juice I hadn't had time to clean up. "You talk any louder and she'll hear it from you."

I looked down the center hall into the room at the end. Aunt Raylene was folding towels and humming to herself. I pushed Grey back out onto the porch and looped my arm around his neck. I knew that if I got bossy, he'd just run off with the hook and I'd never see it again. I thought about the way Mama was always gentling Daddy Glen, and I deliberately made my voice soft and slow.

"I got an idea," I whispered into Grey's ear. "Got a plan to use that hook for something nobody else would have ever thought of."

Grey grinned at me like I'd grown an extra set of teeth. "Something good, huh?"

"Something amazing, and I want you to help me." I tried to rub his neck, but he shook my hand off.

"Tell me."

I hesitated, looking back toward the door where Aunt Raylene might appear any minute. Grey's face was bland, showing nothing but patience. He wasn't like his brother. Of the two of them, he was the one who did things, who rarely told secrets even when he was trying to impress someone. I gritted my teeth and then shook my head. I might as well tell him and find out what he would do. I stepped away from him and shoved my hands down in my shorts.

"I want to get up on the roof of the Woolworth's one night. I got an idea how to get in there without anybody knowing."

Now Grey turned his head, looked back at. the door. "You're serious, an't you," he whispered. It was not a question. I stood still, waiting.

"Well, hellfire, Bone! You got past Aunt Raylene's suspicious mind, but grand theft's a different matter. What makes you think you can get away with it?"

I rocked back on my bare feet, trying to look confident. "There are things I've done you don't know nothing about, cousin. Stuff I an't never gonna tell you. Just like I won't never tell nobody what you and me are gonna do." I tried to narrow my eyes the way Uncle Earle's would shrink down when he played poker.

Grey pursed his lips, whistled, and leaned over the side rail of the porch. "All right, Bone, all right. But if we get caught, I'm gonna tell 'em it was your idea. You just better know that now."

I couldn't help myself. I laughed out loud. Grey grinned back at me, looking only a little puzzled. "Don't worry, cousin," I told him, "we get caught and I'll tell 'em. I promise." I didn't mention that there wasn't a chance in hell anyone would believe such a tale—not with Grey older than me and a boy besides. If we did get caught, I'd be in trouble, he'd be in more, but I had no intention of getting caught. I let him get the hook out from under the porch while I stayed up in the kitchen and kept Aunt Raylene busy.

"Just don't you tell nobody," I insisted.

"Won't tell a soul, Bone," he promised. "Not a soul." He grinned so wide I had to believe him.

That night I slept over at Aunt Raylene's place. After she was asleep, I snuck out to get the hook. I took it back to my room, pried the chain off, and cleaned and polished it. When it was shiny and smooth, I got in bed and put it between my legs, pulling it back and forth. It made me shiver and go hot at the same time. I had read in one of the paperbacks Daddy Glen hid in the garage about women who pushed stuff up inside them. I held the chain and thought about that, rubbed it against my skin and hummed to myself. I wasn't like the women in those books, but it felt good to hold that metal, to let those links slip back and forth until they were slippery. I used the lock I had found on the river bank to fasten the chain around my hips. It felt sun-warmed and tingly against my skin, as shiny as the sweat on Uncle Earle's freckled shoulders, as exciting as the burning light behind my eyes. It was mine. It was safe. Every link on that chain was magic in my hand.

I put my head back and smiled. The chain moved under the sheet. I was locked away and safe. What I really was could not be touched. What I really wanted was not yet imagined. Somewhere far away a child was screaming, but right then, it was not me.

13

I carried my hook home in a croker sack with the last of the zucchini and cucumbers from Aunt Raylene's garden. I didn't trust Reese enough to risk taking it in the house, so I hid it in one of Mama's packing boxes tucked up in the rafters over the washing machine. Up there it was safe and out of sight, a talisman against the dark and anything that waited in the dark. It made me stand taller just to know it was there, made me feel as if I had suddenly become magically older, stronger, almost dangerous. I would look up every time I helped Mama with the laundry, look up as if I were lost in thought or dreaming of the future.

"You've changed, Bone." Mama pulled towels and sheets out of the washing machine and dropped them into the basket I was holding.

"No ma'am, not really." I dropped my head down.

"Yes, you have. I'd say you were even a little taller. You

hold your head up more. I can even see your eyes now and then." Mama grinned at me and dropped the last of the towels in my basket. She had to reach over the machine for her bag of clothespins, an old T-shirt she had sewed closed at the bottom and hung on a coat hanger. While her face was turned, I looked up and made sure my box was still securely in place.

"Reese tell you that Shannon Pearl called?"

I was already going out the door toward the clothesline, but Mama's words stopped me. "She did?"

"Uh huh. I didn't talk to her, but Reese said she just asked if you were around. You might think about calling her back."

"I don't know, Mama. I don't know if I should."

"Well, I an't telling you that you have to, but you should think about it, Bone. An't no sense in being hardhearted, and talking to her won't kill you. She might want to apologize, you know."

"Yes ma'am." I started shaking out a sheet to hang it on the line. I didn't want Mama to see my face. I had no intention of calling Shannon Pearl.

Mama never asked why Shannon Pearl and I had quarreled. The only time she mentioned it was when she agreed with Aunt Raylene that it was probably better to stay out of kids' arguments. I'd walked in on them talking together and knew immediately what they had been discussing, so I turned right around and went back out. Mama had gotten angry when Mrs. Pearl called to tell her that I'd never apologized for taking a swing at Shannon, though not because she thought I should have been made to apologize. Her anger was at my careless stupidity.

"Don't you know you can put somebody's eye out, hitting them in the face?"

"Yes, Mama."

"No reason to be hitting people anyway."

"No ma'am."

"Well . . ." She looked at me closely. I knew she was waiting for me to say something, but I just kept my eyes on the table. "I don't know about the Pearls. They should have brought you home right away, 'stead of making you sit in the car while they went all over everywhere." She started rummaging through her purse for her cigarettes. "And I don't know why she's calling after all this time."

"No ma'am." I didn't want to discuss Shannon Pearl. By now, I was sure, she was lonely for someone to talk to and had gotten her mama to call us.

Mama sighed tiredly. "Well, you just stay out of trouble. I don't want to be explaining your behavior to other people all the time."

"No ma'am."

It was just before Thanksgiving that Shannon Pearl called our house and got me on the phone. "I'm not gonna apologize," she said right away, as if no time at all had passed. Her voice sounded strange after not hearing it for so long.

"I don't care what you do," I told her. I held the phone with my shoulder and picked my cuticles.

"Stop that," Mama said as she went by on her way to the kitchen.

"Yes ma'am," I said automatically.

"What's that?" Shannon sounded hopeful.

"I was talking to my mama. Why'd you call me?"

There was a sigh, and then Shannon cleared her throat a couple of times. "Well, I thought I should. No sense us fighting over something so silly, anyway. I bet you can't even remember what it was about."

"I remember," I told her, and my voice sounded cold even to me. For a moment I was ashamed, then angry. Why should I care if I hurt her feelings? Who was she to me?

"My mama said I could call you," Shannon whispered. "She said I could ask you over this Sunday. We're gonna have a barbecue for some of Daddy's people from Mississippi. They're bringing us some Georgia peaches and some eggshell pecans."

I bit at my thumbnail and said nothing.

"You could ask your mama if you could come." Shannon's voice sounded breathless and desperate, almost squeaky. "If you wanted to," she added. I wondered what she had said in order to get her mama to agree I could come over. Out on the porch Reese had started shouting at Patsy Ruth.

"You don't even know how to play this game!"

Why should I go to the Pearls' house and watch her fat relatives eat themselves sick?

"Mama gave me a record player," Shannon said suddenly. "I got a bunch of records for it."

"Yeah?"

"Lots of 'em." I heard her mother saying something in the background. "I got to go. Are you gonna come?"

"Maybe. I don't know. I'll think about it." I hung up the phone and saw Mama was watching me from the kitchen. "Shannon wants me to come over to her house this Sunday. They're having a barbecue."

"You want to go?"

"Maybe. I don't know."

Mama nodded and handed me a towel. "Well, come help me. And you be sure and tell me if you're going before Sunday. I an't gonna want no surprises on Sunday morning. I might want to spend the whole day in bed, you never can tell." She smiled, and I hugged her. I loved it when she looked like that. It made the whole house feel warm and safe.

"I might want to go on a trip myself." Mama slapped my behind lightly. "But I an't going nowhere till we get these dishes done, girl, and it's your turn to dry."

"Yes ma'am."

I didn't plan to go. I really didn't. I certainly didn't call Shannon back, and I didn't say anything to Mama either. But Sunday afternoon I started walking toward Shannon's house, carrying Reese's tin bucket as if I was going hunting for late muscadines. Along the way I shook the wilting gray-green vines that would die off as soon as the first good freeze came. In the movies, people were always swinging from vines like those, but every time Reese or I tried it, we wound up falling on our behinds. Maybe they had a different kind of vines in the forests where they made movies, but then they probably didn't grow muscadines there.

I hummed as I walked, snatches of Mama's favorite hymns and mine, alternating between "Somebody Touched Me" and "Oh Sinner Man." Reese always sang it as "Whoa Sinner Man," which made Uncle Earle bark out his donkey's-bray laugh. I missed Earle. We weren't going to see him until spring. He'd been sent to the county farm for busting a man's jaw and breaking a window down at the Cracker Blue Cafe. Aunt Alma said he'd gotten into more fights at the farm and a bunch of men had held him down and shaved off all his black hair. I tried to imagine him baldheaded.

"That'll slow down his womanizing." Aunt Alma had sounded almost pleased.

"What's womanizing?" Reese hadn't learned yet that asking questions when the aunts were talking just got you pushed outside. I'd tried to tell her that if she ever wanted to learn anything, she should just shut up and listen and try to figure it out later.

"What are you doing listening to other people's business?" Mama had been really angry. "You get out of here, all of you."

"See what you did." I'd been righteously indignant. I wasn't used to being put out with the little kids. "Now we'll never know why they shaved his head."

"Oh, I know that already." Reese smirked and put her arm around Patsy Ruth. "Granny said he tried to cut some fellow's dick off."

I'd never come up to the Pearls' house from the back before. I usually came down the road from the Sears Tire Center, but that Sunday I cut through the backyards of the big houses on Tyson Circle and through the parking lot of the Roberts Dairy Drive-In. There were magnolia and flowers all along the back of their property so no one could see that parking lot, and I had to wiggle past the mums that were planted close to their fence.

There were a lot of people there, and they all looked like Pearls. Short, puffy, overdressed men stood around holding massive glasses of tea and grinning at skinny, pale women with pink lipstick and flyaway hair. Little kids were running around over near the driveway, where some big boys were taking turns cranking an ice-cream maker. Two card tables had been set up in addition to the big redwood picnic table Mrs. Pearl was so proud of getting last year. It looked like people had already been eating, but the charcoal grill was still smoldering, and Shannon Pearl was standing beside it looking as miserable as any human being could.

I stood still and watched her. She was fiddling with a long-handled fork, looking over every now and then at the other children. Her face was flushed pink and sweaty, and she looked swollen in her orange-and-white organdy dress. I remembered Mama saying Mrs. Pearl just didn't know how to dress her daughter.

"She shouldn't put her in all that embroidery. As fat as that child is, it just makes her look bigger."

I agreed. Shannon looked like a sausage stuffed in a too-small casing. She also looked like she had been crying. Past the tables, Mrs. Pearl was sitting with half a dozen wispy thin women, two of whom were holding babies.

"Precious. Precious," I heard someone exclaim in a reedy voice.

"You fat old thing." One of Shannon's cousins ran past her and stage-whispered loud in her ear. "You musta eat nothing but pork since you was born. Turned you into the hog you are." He laughed and ran on. Shannon pulled off her glasses and started cleaning them on her skirt.

"Jesus shit," I muttered to myself.

I had always suspected that I was the only friend Shannon Pearl had in the world. That was part of what made me feel so mean and evil around her, knowing that I didn't really care enough about her to be her best friend. But hearing her cousin talk to her that way brought back the first time I'd met her, the way I'd loved her stubborn pride, the righteous rage she turned on her tormentors. She didn't look righteous at that moment. She looked tired and hurt and ashamed. Her face made me feel sick and angry, and guilty about her all over again.

I kicked at the short wooden fence for a moment and then swung one leg up to climb over. All right, she was a little monster, but she was my friend, and the kind of monster I could understand. Twenty feet away from me, Shannon sniffed and reached for the can of lighter fluid by the grill. She hadn't even seen me.

Afterward, people kept asking me what happened.

"Where were you," Sheriff Cole said for the third or fourth time. "And what exactly did you see?" He never gave me a chance to tell him. Maybe because it was hard to hear over Mrs. Pearl's screaming.

"Uh huh, and where were you?" He kept looking over his shoulder toward the grill and the sputtering fat fire.

I knew he hadn't heard a word I said. But Mrs. Pearl had. She had heard me clear, and she flailed at the people holding her, trying to get her hands on me. She kept screaming *"You!"* over and over like I had done something, but all I had done was watch. I was sure of that. I had never gotten two steps past the fence.

Shannon had put her glasses back on. She had the lighter-fluid can in one hand and she took up that long-handled fork in the other. She poked the coals with the fork and sprayed them with the fluid. The can made a popping noise as she squeezed it. She was trying to get more of the coals burning, it seemed. Or maybe she just liked the way the flames leaped up. She sprayed and sprayed, pulled back and sprayed again.

Shannon shook her hand. I heard the lighter-fluid can sputter and suck air. I saw the flame run right up to it and go out. Then it came back with a boom. The can exploded, and fire ballooned out in a great rolling ball.

Shannon didn't even scream. Her mouth was wide open, and she just breathed the flames in. Her glasses went opaque, her eyes vanished, and all around her skull her fine hair stood up in a crown of burning glory. Her dress whooshed and billowed into orange-yellow smoky flames. I saw the fork fall, the wooden handle on fire. I saw Mrs. Pearl come to her feet and start to run toward her daughter. I saw all the men drop their ice-tea glasses. I saw Shannon stagger and stumble from side to side, then fall in a heap. Her dress was gone. I saw the smoke turn black and oily. I saw Shannon Pearl disappear from this world.

They held the funeral at Bushy Creek Baptist. Mrs. Pearl insisted on laying an intricately embroidered baby blanket over the coffin. I gave it one glance and then kept my head down. Mrs. Pearl had put a cherub with pink cheeks and yellow hair on the spot that was probably covering Shannon's blackened features. I kept my hand in Mama's and my mouth shut tight. Reese had wanted to come, but Mama had refused to let her and sent her off to Raylene's for the day. Mama wasn't too happy that I wanted to go to the funeral either, but she agreed to bring me after I started crying. Daddy Glen had gotten angry at Mama for giving in to my "nonsense," as he'd called it, and gone off fishing with Beau and Nevil. Over the last few months, he'd started drinking, matching them beer for beer at family gatherings and coming home to fall asleep on the couch.

"Boy can't drink," Beau joked, taking great amusement in Glen's red-faced confusion after a few shots. "Just don't have the constitution for it."

"The belly," Uncle Nevil corrected.

"Right, the belly." They all laughed at that. Glen suddenly taking up drinking seemed to please them in some odd way.

"Damn fools," Raylene had complained.

"It don't matter," Mama had told her. "Glen an't gonna be a drinker no matter how hard he tries." It was true. Where

Beau and Nevil could drink for hours and only get noisy and mean, Daddy Glen would invariably fall asleep while they were still sipping away. He'd wake up with an aching head and a sour stomach when Beau and Nevil were starting to sip coffee to get ready for a day of work, both of them still half drunk from the night before but going on anyway. It all made me nervous, but like Mama I couldn't see anything that could be done about it.

"Did you ever see her?" Mrs. Pearl said to the preacher they'd brought in from their family church in Mississippi. "She was just an angel of the Lord."

The preacher nodded and laid his hands over Mrs. Pearl's as she hugged close a great bunch of yellow mums. Beyond them, the choir director had one hand on Mr. Pearl's elbow. Mr. Pearl was as gray as a dead man. I watched from under lowered lashes while the choir director pressed a paper cup into Mr. Pearl's hand and whispered in his ear. Mr. Pearl nodded and sipped steadily. He kept looking over at his wife and the flowers she was gripping so tightly.

"She loved babies, you know. She was always a friend to the less fortunate. All her little friends are here today. And she could sing. Oh! You should have heard her sing."

I remembered Shannon's hoarse wavering voice humming in the backseat of her daddy's car after she had told me a particularly horrible story. Was it possible Mrs. Pearl had never heard her daughter sing? I looked over to Mr. Pearl and saw his head dip again. If it had been me in that ball of flame, would they have come to my funeral?

Mrs. Pearl lifted her face from the flowers. Her watery eyes flickered back and forth across the pews. She doesn't understand anything, I thought. Mrs. Pearl's eyes moved over me sightlessly, her hands crushing the flowers pressed against her neck. She started to moan suddenly, like a bird caught in a blackberry bush, softly, tonelessly, while the preacher carefully pushed her down into the front pew. The choir director's wife ran over and put her arm around Mrs. Pearl as the preacher desperately signaled the choir to start a hymn. Their voices rose smoothly, but Mrs. Pearl's moan went on and on, rising into the close sweaty air, a song with no meter, no rhythm—but gospel, the purest gospel, a song of absolute hopeless grief.

I turned and pushed my face into Mama's dress. All my hardheaded anger was gone. As if she understood completely, Mama's hand stroked my neck and down my back while she crooned under her breath her own song—muted, toneless, the same hum I'd been hearing all my life.

Shannon's death haunted me. Suddenly I didn't feel so grown-up anymore. I tried to make up with Reese, but she had decided that Patsy Ruth was the only person she trusted in the world, and had her sleeping over all the time. The two of them whispered together, giggling and pointing at me and then running off. Even Mama was mad at me. Exhausted with the effort of trying to come up with something new to wear five days out of every week, I'd worn jeans to school one day and been sent home with a stern note.

"Your clothes are clean. You got nothing to be ashamed of," Mama had snapped. Any other time she might have been sympathetic about the girls at school laughing at me for wearing the same few A-line skirts and shirtwaist dresses over and over, but there was no money for new clothes, and no one to loan us any. Uncle Earle was still at the county farm, Aunt Alma had been laid off from her part-time job at the laundry, and Aunt Ruth was so sick Travis was paying a nurse to help Deedee care for her. Everyone was worried and irritable.

The back of my throat was tight all the time. Out in the utility room that hook no longer sang to me. The thought of its sharp pointy edges made me want to touch it again, but I could not bring myself to climb up and take it down. Even the river out at Raylene's made me scared and sad, the rolling dirty water reminding me of the rainy mud at Shannon's funeral. I kept thinking of how she had been standing there with her head down, all her life still open and unknown, what might have happened, who she might have become. I did not think of the fire but of the dull thudding sound of her life shutting off, everything stopping.

Everything in my life was just as uncertain. I too could be standing somewhere and find myself running into the wall of my own death. I began to tremble whenever Daddy Glen turned his dark blue eyes to me, a deep hidden shaking I prayed he couldn't see. No, I whispered in the night. No, I will not die. No. I clamped my teeth. No.

I took to watching myself in mirrors to see what other people saw, to puzzle out just what showed them who I really was. What did Daddy Glen see? Aunt Raylene? Uncle Earle? My hair had started to lighten, taking on red highlights instead of blue, but my eyes had stayed black as night. I looked at my cheekbones in the bathroom mirror. Not like Reese's smooth, soft face, my cheeks were high and strong. Maybe ugly. Probably ugly. I turned my head. My teeth were white and hard, sharp and gleaming. I was strong all over. Turned sunshine into muscle, Mama swore. She was proud of how sturdy I was, what I could lift and how fast I could run, but I was suddenly self-conscious and awkward. I had shot up in the last year, so much so that my bones seemed to ache all the time.

"Growing pains," Aunt Raylene told me. "Keep this up and you gonna be tall, girl."

I didn't want to be tall. I wanted to be beautiful. When I was alone, I would look down at my obstinate body, long legs, no hips, and only the slightest swell where Deedee and Temple had big round breasts. I had nothing to be proud of, and I hated Aunt Raylene's jokes that we were all peasant stock, descendants of women who used to deliver babies in the fields and stagger up to work just after. Gawky, strong, ugly— why couldn't I be pretty? I wanted to be more like the girls in storybooks, princesses with pale skin and tender hearts. I hated my short fingers, wide face, bony knees, hated being nothing like the pretty girls with their delicate features and slender, trembling frames. I was stubborn-faced, unremarkable, straight up and down, and as dark as walnut bark. This body, like my aunts' bodies, was born to be worked to death, used up, and thrown away. I had read these things in books and passed right over it. The ones who died like that, worked to death or carried off by senseless accidents, they were almost never the heroines. Aunt Alma had given me a big paperback edition of *Gone with the Wind,* with tinted pictures from the movie, and told me I'd love it. I had at first, but one evening I looked up from Vivien Leigh's pink cheeks to see Mama coming in from work with her hair darkened from sweat and her uniform stained. A sharp flash went through me. Emma Slattery, I thought. That's who I'd be, that's who we were. Not Scarlett with her baking-powder cheeks. I was part of the trash down in the mud-stained cabins, fighting with the darkies and stealing ungratefully from our betters, stupid, coarse, born to shame and death. I shook with fear and indignation.

"What the hell is that girl doing in the bathroom so long?" Daddy Glen was irritable as only a man who'd been drinking the night before can be. I turned the lock against him and tried not to listen when he yelled through the door.

"Bone, you get out of there and come help me with these potatoes." I washed my face and went out to Mama, still in her waitress uniform and flat white shoes. She smiled and passed me a pot. "Cut the eyes out but leave the skins on. We'll make mashed potatoes like your daddy likes them."

From the living room came Daddy Glen's grunt and then

the sound of the side door opening and closing. Mama put her hands on my shoulders and hugged me close. "I want you to go over to Alma's after school for a few days. I'll pick you and Reese up when I get off. I want you to keep those kids for Alma so she can get some time to spend with Ruth." Mama paused, and when she spoke again her voice was quieter.

"Daddy Glen's worried about Christmas and money. He'd like to do something special. Last night he was talking about how we've never had his brothers to dinner in all these years."

I looked down into the pot of potatoes, remembering the last time we had gone out to the Waddells', the way Daddy Glen had stuttered when his father spoke to him. That old man was horrible, and working for him must be hell, even I knew that. Mama leaned in so that her mouth was close to my cheek.

"I don't know. I just don't understand why his daddy treats Glen so bad. Glen's always trying to please him, and that old man takes every chance he gets to make Glen look like a fool. It just eats Glen up, eats him up." She sighed.

"Let's be careful for a while, Bone. Be real careful, baby." She hesitated as if there were something more she would say, but instead gave my shoulders another squeeze and went to change out of her uniform. I watched her walk away, her head bent forward. How long had it been since I had seen Mama not tired, not sad, not scared? Forever. It seemed like forever.

I kept looking for something special in me, something magical. I was growing up, wasn't I? But the only thing different about me was my anger, that raw boiling rage in my stomach. Cherokee maybe, wild Indian anger maybe, like Shannon's anger, bottomless and horrible. I pulled my lips back so my teeth showed. Every third family in Greenville might have a little Cherokee, but I had been born with a full head of black hair. I've got my great-granddaddy's blood in me, I told myself. I am night's own daughter, my great-grandfather's warrior child. I pushed my hair up high on my head and searched my pupils for the red highlights that sparked in the depths, dark shiny red like rubies or fresh bright blood. Dangerous, I told myself. I could be dangerous, oh yes, I could be dangerous. Let Daddy Glen yell at Mama again, let him hurt her, let him hurt me, just let him. He'd better be careful. He's got no idea what I might not do. If I had a razor, I would surely cut his throat in the dead of night, then run away to live naked and alone in the western hills like someone in a Zane Grey novel. All I had to do was grow a little, grow into myself.

Daddy Glen yelled at me at dinner. "That bathroom's a sty. Way your mama has to work, least you could do is clean up now and then, help out some around here." Mama sighed and pushed her plate away. Reese ate with her head down, and I said nothing. Mama had said to be careful. Carefully, I kept my head turned, watching lights from the highway reflect off the kitchen curtains, not looking at Daddy Glen.

After dinner, I scrubbed the tub and took a long, hot bath. I looked for black hairs in my navel and felt for fuzz between my legs. I was smooth and clean. I took up Mama's hand mirror and propped it at an angle between my legs. My chin was pink and dimpled, my neck pale underneath, so that I could see the blue lines of veins threading up to my ears. I put my palms flat on my cheeks, pushed back and slanted my eyes. My face remained unreadable, my eyes blank and silvery. My face told nothing. It was scary, stern and empty. I bent my head back, looking down to my reddish-brown nipples, my puckered belly button, long thighs, and bruised knees. My neck ached, my teeth, my lower spine and ass. All of me was ugly, pasty, and numb—nothing like Uncle James's girls in their white nylon crinolines and blue satin hair ribbons. They were the kind of little girls people really wanted. No part of me was that worshipful, dreamy-eyed storybook girlchild, no part of me was beautiful. I could see why Daddy Glen was hateful to me. At dinner when Mama had gone back to the bedroom to get her sweater, he had made a point of telling me that I didn't have anything to be so proud of.

"You think you're so special," he'd jeered. "Act like you piss rose water and honey. Think you're too good to be straightened out. Your mama has spoiled you. She don't know what a lazy, stubborn girl you are, but I do. I know you. I know you, and I an't gonna have you turning out like your useless cousins, not growing up under my roof."

"Hateful man," I whispered. "I don't care if his daddy does treat him bad. I don't care why he's so mean. He's hateful."

I rolled over and pushed my face underwater. I was no Cherokee. I was no warrior. I was nobody special. I was just a girl, scared and angry. When I saw myself in Daddy Glen's eyes, I wanted to die. No, I wanted to be already dead, cold and gone. Everything felt hopeless. He looked at me and I was ashamed of myself. It was like sliding down an endless hole, seeing myself at the bottom, dirty, ragged, poor, stupid. But at the bottom, at the darkest point, my anger would come and I would know that he had no idea who I was, that he never saw me as the girl who worked hard for Aunt Raylene, who got good grades no matter how often I changed schools, who ran errands for Mama and took good care of Reese. I was not dirty, not stupid, and if I was poor, whose fault was that?

I would get so angry at Daddy Glen I would grind my teeth. I would dream of cutting his heart out, his evil raging pit-black heart. In the dream it felt good to hate him. But the horrible thing was how I felt when I was awake and wasn't burning with anger. The worst thing in the world was the way I felt when I wanted us to be like the families in the books in the library, when I just wanted Daddy Glen to love me like the father in *Robinson Crusoe*. It must have been like what he felt when he stood around his daddy's house, his head hanging down.

Love would make me beautiful; a father's love would purify my heart, turn my bitter soul sweet, and lighten my Cherokee eyes. If he loved me, if he only loved me. Why didn't he love me? I drummed my fists on the porcelain walls of the tub, shook my head and howled underwater, came up to breathe and went under to whine again. If anyone had come in, they wouldn't have known I was crying, and I was sure even God couldn't hear me curse.

Over Christmas holidays at Alma's house, I spent my time organizing the cousins to act out complicated stories, half of them drawn from television programs. As long as everybody did what I told them, I was the best baby-sitter Aunt Alma had ever seen.

"You can be Francis Marion," I told Little Earle. "Reese and I will be Cherokee warriors, Patsy Ruth can be the British commander, Garvey will be the cowardly colonist, and Grey can be a colonist on our side."

"Swamp Fox, Swamp Fox, where have you been?" Little Earle began singing, but Patsy Ruth cut him off. "Why do I have to be the British commander? Why can't you be the bad guy and let me be a Cherokee?"

" 'Cause you don't climb trees worth a pig's ass. Everybody knows Indians can climb trees."

"Then I get to ride the horse, and I want to ride Grey's bike, not Little Earle's old one."

"If she gets to ride my bike, then I want to wear your cap."

"We don't use my cap in this one. We only use my cap when we play Johnny Yuma." I was losing patience, and I certainly didn't want to give up my rebel cap, the one Uncle Earle had brought back from the Fort Sumter general store. It was beautiful—gray, soft, with a slouched brim, and the Stars and Bars stitched in yellow thread.

"Johnny Yoo-ma," Little Earle started singing again, trying hard to imitate Johnny Cash's deep voice, "he roamed through the west . . . *Johnny Yoo-ma the rebel* . . . he wandered alone . . ."

"You always wear it." Grey swatted Little Earle's rear end and turned back to me with a look of sweet reason. "Don't matter if we're playing Frankenstein's monster, and you know didn't nobody wear no cap like that in the Frankenstein movie."

"Oh, for crying out loud." I let Grey wear my cap, but I lost interest in the Swamp Fox. Who'd ever heard of him before he showed up on Walt Disney?

Grey and Garvey would only play with us about half the time. They had taken up smoking and were busy practicing pitching pennies. When school started again, they planned to wipe out the lunch money of half the sixth grade. Meanwhile, they kept their distance unless I proposed a plot they really liked.

"Let's play Dalton Boys again," Grey kept suggesting. He'd perfected the trick of diving off his bicycle after pretending to be shot, and he loved to show it off.

"It's the Dalton *Girls*," I insisted. Reese and I had seen the movie and had told everybody the plot in such detail that the cousins would argue over just what did and did not happen even though they'd never seen it. All of us girls loved the idea of the gang of sisters who had robbed banks and avenged their dead brothers, but the boys preferred to play at Jesse James or the Younger Gang.

"In that movie maybe, but everybody remembers the real Dalton *Boys*." Garvey had seen the movie too, and hadn't gotten over how the Dalton brothers were killed off in the first scene so the women could learn to shoot guns and rob banks. "I don't think that movie was real anyway. I bet you their sisters never robbed no banks."

"What you want to bet?" Reese challenged. She'd loved that movie. "You think a girl can't beat your ass? You think I can't beat your ass?" She snatched my cap off Grey's head.

"You couldn't scare a chicken off a nest of water moccasins!" Grey tried to get the cap back, but Reese kept running and twisting out of his reach, yelling at him over her shoulder. "You're the one scared of water moccasins. Aunt Alma said you pissed your pants when she took you blackberrying, all 'count of you stepped near a little green snake thinking it was some old water moccasin."

"You shut your chicken-piss mouth." Grey jerked the cap back.

"You shut yours!" Reese kicked at his ankles.

"Girls!"

"Boys!"

"You give me my cap." I pulled it out of Grey's hands as he tried to hop out of the way of Reese's hard little feet. I was hoping she would really hurt him when Aunt Alma broke the fight up. She sent the boys to play in the backyard and told us girls we'd have to stay in front.

"If you can't play together, I'll keep you apart."

"I don't want to be around no stupid boys anyway." Reese spit in Grey's direction. Sometimes I agreed with every word out of my little sister's mouth.

"But what we gonna play now?" Patsy Ruth whined. "We can't ride the bikes in the front yard. We can't do much of nothing in the front yard."

I spun my rebel cap on my fist and had a sudden inspiration.

"We're gonna play mean sisters."

"What?" Patsy Ruth kept wiping snot off her lip. Mama swore Patsy Ruth had had a runny nose since she was born. "She'll be wiping snot the day she's married, wiping snot the day she dies." I gave Patsy Ruth the handkerchief I'd sneaked out of Daddy Glen's drawer for a bandanna.

"We're gonna play mean sisters," I told them all again, and I could see in my mind's eye Shannon Pearl's twisted mean face. "First we're gonna play Johnny Yuma's mean sisters, then Francis Marion's mean sisters, then Bat Masterson's. Then we'll think of somebody else."

Reese looked confused. "What do mean sisters do?"

"They do everything their brothers do. Only they do it first and fastest and meanest."

Reese still looked confused, but Patsy Ruth whooped.

"Yeah! I want to be the Rifleman's mean sister."

Patsy Ruth ran off to get Grey's old broken plastic rifle.

All afternoon she pretended it was a sawed-off shotgun like the one on "Wanted Dead or Alive." Reese finally got into it and started playing at being shot off the porch. I took Aunt Alma's butcher knife and announced that I was Jim Bowie's mean sister and no one was to mess with me.

I practiced sticking Aunt Alma's knife into the porch and listened to the boys cursing in the backyard. I was mean, I decided. I was mean and vicious, and all I really wanted to be doing was sticking that knife in Daddy Glen.

That evening, Patsy Ruth entertained Alma and Wade by running up and down yelling "Ten-four, ten-four" until she knocked over Aunt Alma's glass.

"What in God's name are you playing at, child?"

"I was being Broderick Crawford's mean sister," Patsy Ruth wailed, wiping her nose.

"His what?" Uncle Wade started laughing into his glass. "His what?" He rocked back on his cane-bottom chair and ground his cigarette out on the porch. Aunt Alma shook her head and looked at Patsy Ruth like she had gone crazy.

"Broderick Crawford's mean sister! My Lord, what they don't think up."

Patsy Ruth was humiliated and angry. She pointed at me. "She told me about it. She told me I could."

Wade reached out and slapped my fanny. "Girl, you got a mind that scares me." He swatted me again, but lightly, and he kept grinning. "Broderick Crawford's mean sister."

I didn't care. I played mean sisters for all I was worth.

Mama let Aunt Raylene take Reese and me along when she went to visit Uncle Earle at the county farm. Aunt Raylene said he would be there another three months and he was lonely to see his nieces and nephews.

"Why don't you take Grey and Garvey?" Mama asked her. "Show them what's gonna happen to them if they keep breaking into telephones."

"The hell with that." Aunt Raylene was sensitive about Grey and Garvey, who had been picked up by the highway patrol for drag-racing in Uncle Beau's truck when they were supposed to be staying the night at her place. Alma got mad at Raylene for not keeping a more watchful eye on them, and Raylene came close to slapping Garvey when he boasted that they were the youngest in the family ever to be arrested. Now Aunt Raylene folded some of Uncle Earle's clean underwear and put it in a paper sack while her face flushed red with anger.

"They get into any more trouble, the law won't have to send them away. I'll send them so far they'll never find their way home."

"Shit you will." Granny slammed a basket of food down on Aunt Raylene's kitchen table. "You'll visit them every month and take them sweet cornbread, just like you do Earle."

"You'll see what I'll do."

"I've seen it already."

I waited for them to really start fighting. Instead Granny leaned over and kissed Aunt Raylene right on the mouth, her lips pressing Raylene's with an audible smack. Aunt Raylene gaped in surprise, and Granny laughed until the tears came.

"Oh! Oh! Look at you. Raylene, I finally got you. Oh Lord! I enjoyed that." She dropped down on a kitchen chair and wiped her eyes. "Well, never mind, you just tell Earle that I love him. And then tell him if I'd beat his ass more when he was a boy, he wouldn't be where he is today."

"Nothing you could have done would have stopped Earle from his fighting." Raylene was trying to recover from the shock of Granny's kiss. "Earle had a spirit of meanness in him when he was born." I watched Aunt Raylene push her gray hair back up into her hairpins. Did I have a spirit of meanness in me? I wondered. It felt like it. It had felt like it for weeks. Maybe I hadn't been born with it, but I'd come to it, as Granny would say. I'd come to it soon enough.

Earle was a little skinnier and a little grayer around the eyes. His hair had grown back some, into a short black brush that stuck straight up all over his head. He kept running his hands over the top of his head as if he couldn't believe his thick wavy hair was gone. Still, when we settled down on the grass for our picnic, he had gifts for everybody—key tags and belts for all the boys and coin purses and hair barrettes for the girls, all of them hand-tooled and elaborately decorated. Aunt Raylene got a handbag as big as her lunch basket. For Mama he had a leather wallet stenciled with rose vines.

"You give her that, and tell her I think of her all the time." He laughed his black laugh. "I think of her biscuits. These cooks here can't make a biscuit a man can eat."

I played with the wallet and watched the other families on the grass. All the women had leather handbags with stenciled roses. Little tooled leather vines wrapped around the shoulder straps, the edges of the wallets. I ran my fingers over Mama's wallet and wondered how it was done.

How did they tool the leather?

I opened Mama's wallet and stroked the unfinished leather. Around us, women were feeding children and keeping close to their husbands. The glaring hot yard smelled of spoiling food, sweat, and sour baby diapers. I looked up at Uncle Earle and saw he was watching the women, sweat running down into his eyes.

"How do you do it?" I asked him, lifting the wallet to catch his glance. "Don't you have to cut all this stuff?"

He took the wallet from me and ran his fingers over the leather roses, the engraved vines. "We use punches. You hit them with a wooden mallet, pound out the design over and over again for hours. Just the thing for men in jail. Keeps 'em busy and off each other's necks." He grinned.

I stared up at him, not quite able to ask.

He laughed at me then, understanding perfectly.

"They count 'em—the punches, the blades. If the count don't match at the end of the afternoon, we don't get out for dinner. Of course, sometimes they count wrong, and sometimes the razors break." He wiped sweat on his jeans and brought his hand up, palm open. A slender metal blade glinted in the sunlight. He laughed again, that low growling laugh, while I stood with my mouth open.

"They think they so smart." He spit in the direction of the fence. He looked different without his long black hair, harder and older. Only his eyes were the same, dark and full of pain. Now those eyes burned in the direction of the guards walking the other side of the fence.

"They think they so damn smart."

My heart seemed to swell in my breast. His hand wiped again at his jeans, and I knew the blade was gone. He was my uncle. I was his favorite sister's favorite child. I knew absolutely that I was his and he was mine, and I was suddenly fiercely proud of him, and of myself.

"I love you," I whispered.

"Sure you do, sunshine." He laughed. "Sure you do."

Uncle Earle picked me up and hugged me tight to his shoulder. I looked toward the fence and narrowed my eyes. We're smart, I thought. We're smarter than you think we are. I felt mean and powerful and proud of all of us, all the Boatwrights who had ever gone to jail, fought back when they hadn't a chance, and still held on to their pride. When Aunt Raylene called my name, I took my time walking back to the car.

"Why does he have to be so stubborn?" Raylene was leaning forward with her hands on the wheel of the Pontiac. "Why does that man have to go looking for trouble all the time?"

"He don't look for trouble." I was still full of the magic of the hidden knife. "He just knows how to handle it when it finds him."

"He does, huh?" Aunt Raylene turned to look at me. "Well, if he knows how to handle it, how did he get his ass in jail? How come he couldn't handle himself well enough to stay out of jail? How come he couldn't handle his own temper enough not to break the jaw of the best friend he's got in this county?"

She shook her head and shoved her new pocketbook under the seat. "All you kids think your uncles are so smart. If they're so smart, why they all so goddam poor, huh? You tell me that."

I went looking for Grey when we got back from the county farm and told him it was time to use that hook. He gave me a slow grin of satisfaction and promised to meet me "anytime, anywhere." The look in his eyes was a match for the one I'd seen in Earle's, the one I imagined in my own. A small drum of excitement began to beat inside me, and the beat only sped up when I got the hook down. I gave it to Grey when he came over that night, even though it hurt me to let it go. It would be easier for him to get it down to Woolworth's without calling attention to himself. A boy with a sack could look perfectly innocent, while I would be asked what it was I was carrying. I ground my teeth in irritation but held on to the idea that I'd get it back soon enough. We would meet at Woolworth's Friday night, when Mama would be visiting Aunt Ruth and I was supposed to sleep over at Alma's.

Grey and Garvey seemed to fight all the time these days, boxing and wrestling as easily as some people spit, and it was clear to me that part of Grey's excitement about our plan was because his brother was not part of it. They were not identical twins—none of the twins in the family were identical—but Alma's boys looked more alike than either set of Aunt Carr's girls. They were both tall and rangy, with skin that tanned dark, and hair that went red-brown in the sun. Garvey was better-looking, with crystalline blue eyes and a sharp little cleft in his chin that was strangely endearing. Grey had a half-mean look about him. His eyes narrowed too easily, and he frowned all the time, even after Aunt Alma got him a pair of metal-frame glasses. Grey hated those lenses and wore them only when one of the uncles was around to slap him for wasting his mama's money.

"That Grey's getting bad habits," Uncle Beau said to Reese and me once. We said nothing, since of the two brothers, both of us liked Grey best. He might have looked meaner, but he had a sweetness about him that Garvey didn't. He'd always given us stolen candy and never pushed us around like Garvey did. But unlike his brother, Grey just didn't have any luck. When he turned thirteen, he suddenly began to grow thick red-brown hair on his chest and arms. He tried to shave it off with his daddy's straight razor, but that only made it grow back thicker. Garvey made fun of him for it, and in defense, Grey pretended stubbornly that he was proud of his "manly growth," of how he was "turning into a bear." It did make him look more different from Garvey—a lifelong ambition anyway. The only problem was that the hair didn't grow back thicker, just patchy, and it itched him. It ruined his tough-guy image, the way he was always standing around scratching at the reddish-brown hair on his forearms and the backs of his hands. Sometimes he'd seem to fall into a kind of trance, looking off into the distance, frowning and scratching.

I found him standing like that back of Woolworth's Friday night. It was late—well past midnight—and I'd had trouble sneaking out of Alma's house quietly enough not to wake Reese, so I was nervous and itchy myself. Grey scared me, standing out in the parking lot with the light pouring down from the Texaco sign across the street lighting up everything. A shadow hid the potato sack between his legs, and for a minute I thought he'd forgotten my hook.

"Don't sweat it," he laughed when I demanded the hook. "I got it right here." He squatted down and opened the sack, pulling out a four-pronged blackened object trailing a chain.

"You ruined it!" I hissed.

"I fixed it!" he almost yelled, and then looked over his shoulder and around the lot. "The paint will make it invisible when we throw it up the wall."

I grimaced and reached out to trace one paint-spattered point. It was still sharp, but the scary razor-and-steel feeling was gone. I swallowed hard. I had really loved the shine of it.

"Those suckers had too much gleam on them for safety." He sounded proud of himself for thinking of it. "Specially after I sharpened the points a little." He dropped one shoulder and leaned close to me. "I just toned down the light-catching side of the thing. Still kept it sharp. The hard part was painting the chain. Did each link separate so it wouldn't get all stiff and gummy. That's a heavy-gauge chain there. Soldered, I think." He grinned and scratched his hands happily.

I knew he was just trying to sound important, be the man and all, but it was hard for me to swallow my anger and nod back at him. "It's all right," I finally managed. He looked pissed, so I ran my hand along the chain and nodded again. "Good job."

"Damn right!"

Son of a bitch, I told myself, but said nothing more to him. It didn't matter what he thought he was doing. This whole thing was really about what I was doing. It was my plan, and the hook didn't matter as much as getting into the Woolworth's did, and I knew what he didn't. The way in was over the roof and through the fan vent. There wasn't any chance my tall, hairy, man-proud cousin would fit through the vent. He'd have to hold his pride and wait down below for me to open a door for him. And if he made me too mad, he could stand around and scratch his hands all night.

When it came down to it, there was a moment when I thought I wasn't going to make it. Grey had an easy time swinging the hook high enough to bite into the back roof of the Woolworth building, and I had only a little trouble shinnying up the rope with my feet braced against the wall. It was a little trickier at the top, where they'd stuck broken glass on the edge, probably to discourage people with ideas like mine. But the rope didn't fray, and I jumped the glass easily enough. I got a little cocky then, feeling good about myself. It was quiet and cool and clear up there on that roof. Greenville lay spread out to the east of me, the buildings gradually getting taller over toward the airport and the highway. I could see people standing under a streetlight two blocks away and cars speeding along the overpass above the Texaco station and the railroad siding. I spit off the roof and heard Grey cursing below me.

"You okay?" he whisper-yelled.

"Fine. Now shut up 'fore you get us in trouble." I walked toward the exhaust housing on loose crackly tar paper. At some point they'd covered the exhaust fan with chicken wire and a lattice of wooden slats. The chicken wire was rusty and pulled free pretty fast. I kicked at the slats until two broke off.

It was the fan blades that worried me. I could slip around them, I was sure, but the engine block was big and oily. That would be a tight piece. I sat back for a minute and looked around again. I felt strange and strong, like I had sipped some of Uncle Earle's whiskey or sucked on one of Uncle Beau's green pipes. The rooftop sparkled and shone in the glare of the streetlight.

It was the exhaust fan at the VFW that had given me the idea. There were no wood slats or chicken wire there, and the motor itself was small. I'd seen Uncle Beau's girls climb through it the weekend of the Baptist Mission Fish Fry. Myer Johnson had run the girls off and complained that he was always having to work on those fans—the only one he never had to mess with was the one on the Woolworth building. I'd known Myer was trying to sound important for my cousin Deedee's benefit, so I hadn't paid much attention. But later it came back to me so strong that I'd shaken suddenly in the middle of dinner and caught Mama's eye.

"You all right, honey?" I'd nodded and gone off to the bathroom by myself. Standing there wetting my neck and looking into my own eyes in the mirror, I'd worked it out. I hadn't actually been inside the Woolworth's in years, not since Mama had caught me stealing Tootsie Rolls, but I had a pristine memory of it—the long rows of counters and the lazy fans turning high up on the ceiling, with the big exhaust vent toward the back over the notions counter. Greenville summers were hot and sticky, and the Woolworth building was designed for them with its high ceiling and fans. The vent had a seal they put on for the winter and took off at the end of April, but I remembered seeing it come down once. It was nothing but a loosely fitting frame with cotton insulation in the top of it. The insulation had to be replaced pretty often, since the vent leaked when the rains came hard.

That vent would snap free with one good shove. It was as clear in my head as the face of the man who still managed the store—Tyler Highgarden. I knew his nervous, skinny-faced children from Greenville Elementary School. If they hadn't been such sorry miserable creatures, I'd have gotten the cousins to beat them up for their father's sins, but they'd never looked worth the trouble. Still, Tyler Highgarden and the Woolworth's humiliation had itched at me for years, always in the back of my mind. The revelation that there was something I could do about it was too exciting not to act on.

The fan blades weren't sharp, just greasy and covered with dust. I reached through and measured carefully, and then went back over to the water tower and pulled my hook free. I coiled the rope up and tied it around the prongs. I would push it ahead of me into the darkness. I didn't think it would get stuck, any more than I thought I would. I didn't even think of it as a weapon. All I knew climbing over the dirty blades and wiggling around the engine block was that I wanted those razor points with me. I was a little scared and half convinced I might get caught, but those points were sharp and certain and tangibly dangerous, the way I wanted to be. I couldn't leave them behind.

The exhaust pipe widened on the other side of the fan, and there was a filter there made of prickly stuff that bit my fingers. I unfastened it on my side, crawled through, then fastened it again, pushing the hook ahead of me in the dark. There was no warning at all when the hook suddenly banged against a sharp bend in the pipe and swung out of my hand. I fell after it, my shoulder hitting a thick cushion of cotton batting and the edge of the frame that held up the insulation and sealed the vent. The frame thudded and slipped sideways, dropping free on one side and swinging open. The hook fell ahead of me with a crash. I caught the edge of the vent cover, held myself an instant, then followed the hook. I bit my tongue as I fell, and it was a miracle I didn't scream. I hit the side of the rack that displayed pattern books and slammed into a glass countertop that broke with a dull snap under me. I gasped and registered immediately the points of the hook sticking up from another case just inches from my butt.

"Oh, my God," I whispered. "Sweet suffering Jesus." My hip ached where I'd hit, but nothing seemed broken.

I was suddenly soaking wet and shaking. I rolled off the counter, my sneakers breaking the rest of the glass as I tried to get to my feet. When I finally stood in the aisle, I saw that my hands were covered with a fine dust that glinted like diamonds in the slanting light. I took a deep slow breath and looked around. Above me the vent cover hung open, dirty cotton insulation still attached to the frame. Up near the front I thought I saw a shadow move. That was probably Grey waiting for me to let him in, but inside the store everything was perfectly still and musty, smelling of sweet toilet water and cheap starched clothes.

I pulled my hook free from the case and started toward the front doors. Broken glass from the notions case crunched under my feet. I stopped and looked down. Plastic thimbles, bobbins, and pins were scattered before me. Half a dozen pocket mirrors lay in an overlapping line. A shine reflected up into my eyes. I smiled and started forward. The candy counter had been moved further up front. I could see the double-stacked case of nuts right next to the popcorn machine. I swung the hook back and forth in my hand as I walked toward it, feeling the grin on my face widen and a looseness move down my back. How long was it since I had been in here? How long since I'd stood in front of the candy counter and smelled the peculiar Woolworth's smell of dust and cheap goods? I swung the hook back and forth, back and forth, letting the loose part of the rope slip through my fingers, back and forth—and let go, right into the nuts case. The glass shattered and the nuts poured out. I felt a shock of electricity shoot up my arm to

my shoulder; a river of nuts was flooding out of the case, a
tide of nuts, an avalanche. I started to giggle, a high-pitched
nasal laugh. When the sound stopped I saw that the case was
a sham. There hadn't been more than two inches of nuts pressed
against the glass front, propped up with cardboard.

"Cheap sons of bitches," I said out loud. There was a thin
layer of nuts lying there, some still rolling away. "Goddam
cheap."

I heard Grey pounding on the front door and hurried to
him. He was so impatient to get in I was afraid he was going
to break the glass. "Stop it," I yelled, and went for the jack
on display in the window. But Grey kept rapping on the glass
while I dragged it over to the door. "Stupid fool," I hissed at
him, but he just grinned. I got the brace fixed against one
door and the lever wedged in the crack against the other. Two
turns of the crank and the doors popped open with a snap.
Grey shot past me like a dog with his tail on fire while I
shoved the jack out of the way. I wanted to climb up and shut
that vent again, but looking back I saw there was no way I
could reach it. I had imagined Tyler Highgarden shaking his
head and wondering how we had done this to him. But with
that insulation hanging down everybody'd know how we had
gotten inside the store.

"Goddam!" Grey crowed, and I heard more glass break.
He'd cracked the front of the knife case and was happily
stuffing his pockets with jackknives of all sizes. I wrapped
my arms around myself, hugged my shoulders, and
shrugged. A breeze whistled in through the open door and
stirred the dust along the floor. I looked past Grey at all the
things on display. Junk everywhere: shoes that went to paper
in the rain, clothes that separated at the seams, stale candy,
makeup that made your skin break out. What was there here
that I could use? I remembered the rows of canned vegetables
and fruit at Aunt Raylene's place—rows of tomatoes and
okra, peaches and green beans, blackberries and plums that
stretched for shelf on shelf in her cellar. That was worth

something. All this stuff seemed tawdry and useless. I bit my lip and went back to get my hook.

Grey was running up and down the aisles, grabbing stuff and then dropping it. "Goddam, we're a team," he whispered at me, shook his head, and laughed. He snatched up a pillow case from the linens, took it up to the front, and started filling it with cigarettes.

"Yeah," I whispered. I kicked at the case in front of me. It was full of picture frames—wood, plastic, and metal gilt. The big ones were in the same style that James and Madeline had for their family pictures. For a moment I wanted to smash them, but these weren't theirs, even if they were the same cheap brand they wouldn't admit they had bought. I swung my hook back and forth, trying to think what it was that I really wanted, who I really wanted to hurt. My eyes ached, and my palms were raw and stinging. I felt like I was going to cry. Grey whooped "Goddam" again, and I felt something hard and mean push up the back of my throat.

I hugged that hook up tight to my midriff and ran back to the door, calling for Grey as I went. He was still grabbing things and throwing them down, the pillow case now looped into the waistband of his jeans. It took him twenty minutes to finally come up and join me. He was trembling, his dark-tan face streaked with sweat and dust. His mouth worked, opening and shutting, but no sounds came out. He had his shirttail tied tight around his middle to hold the stuff he couldn't carry. I put my hand on his arm.

"Come on. We an't gonna lock the door, you know." I squeezed my fingers and felt his excitement in the rigid band of muscles. "And your hands are full anyway."

He blinked at me, pushed his face close to mine. "I an't never gonna forget this, Bone," he told me. "Never in this life." I nodded solemnly back at him, and a smile broke out on his face. "Goddam!" he whispered once more as he went out the door, sounding this time like a happy child.

I pulled the double doors together so that they looked

shut and ran after Grey's shadow. We went up State Street past a little group of gray-faced men just down from the Texaco station, all of them looking so much like my uncles it made my throat hurt. I yelled at them as I ran, "The goddam Woolworth's doors are standing open. It's open. The whole store's wide open."

They looked at us, me hugging that hook to my belly, Grey stumbling with the weight of the bags he carried and stuff spilling out of his shirt. I saw one of them turn and look back up State Street toward the Woolworth's building. Another dropped a cigarette and started off at a run. I knew by morning there wouldn't be a case that hadn't been opened, a counter that hadn't been cleared. That was the thing that made me happy, the sound of those boots running down the street and the thought of what all those men would carry home. My ancient outrage at Tyler Highgarden seemed silly compared to that.

Under my sweaty fingers I felt the black paint flaking off the metal edge of one prong of that hook. I could scrape the rest of it down. My anger beat inside me. Maybe when the metal was clean and pure and shiny, I would take off one night. Maybe I would go all the way over to Uncle James's house and pull up my mama a rosebush or two.

16

I was sleepy the next day, and nervous. The exhilaration was gone. I kept expecting something to happen, someone to come in and confront me with what Grey and I had done. It had been so easy to get back to Aunt Alma's and into bed with Reese without anyone noticing—too easy. I kept waking up suddenly, all night long, until finally I jerked awake and the room was full of daylight. Reese was still heavily asleep near the edge of the bed, but I heard Temple talking in the next room. I got up and dressed, trying to look like I'd had all the sleep I needed.

Aunt Alma had stayed over at Aunt Ruth's with Mama. Patsy Ruth was complaining that she had been on her own and hadn't even known it. Garvey and Little Earle didn't care. They were too busy arguing over whether Little Earle had spit in Garvey's new harmonica. I kept looking at Grey's shining features, wondering why everybody else didn't see how smugly he was grinning, but there was too much confusion. No one even looked at him.

Temple had come by to make sure we all got some breakfast, her swollen belly showing how close she was to having her first child. She kept pushing herself up straight and putting her hand on her lower back as if it ached. She served us all bowls of grits with cheese and set a platter of fried fatback in the center of the table.

"Patsy Ruth and Little Earle." She called their names like they were stray puppies. "I promised Mama I'd make sure you got off to school, so move it along." She wiped grease off the edge of the platter and put a bowl of butter down beside it. "Bone, your mama said you were to stay over here till she comes to get you. But she might not get here till afternoon, so let Reese sleep as long as she wants."

"Why do we have to go to school if Bone and Reese don't?" Little Earle was offended.

"I don't know and I don't care." Temple sounded like she'd been married for twenty years. "All I know is you're going. If you want to argue with Mama about why, you can do it when she gets home tonight. Right now I've got to get Tadpole ready to come home with me."

I took a piece of fatback to chew and went into the living room with the book I'd gotten from Aunt Raylene, *The Lion, the Witch and the Wardrobe* by C. S. Lewis. I loved the story, but I was so tired I fell asleep, not waking up until Mama put her hand on my shoulder.

"Where's Reese, Bone?" Her voice sounded strange.

"I think she's still asleep, Mama." I pulled myself up off the couch and followed her into Alma's kitchen. She dropped her purse on the kitchen table and sank heavily into one of the metal chairs. Her mascara was smeared under bloodshot eyes. She sat quiet, looking at me. I couldn't read her expression.

"Mama, did I do something wrong?"

"No. No, baby." She shook her head, her eyes focusing on mine for just a moment before they looked past me.

"It's not you." She opened her bag, took out her Pall Malls, lit one, and began to rake her hair out with her other hand. I got her an ashtray.

"You want me to make coffee?"

"No, baby."

I sat down at the table.

"Is Alma still at Ruth's?"

She nodded, paused, and looked at me directly. "Bone, your aunt Ruth died early this morning." Her eyes glistened. I waited for her to start crying, but she didn't. She just sat there smoking. I looked at my hands. I couldn't believe what she had said. Aunt Ruth was dead? No. Mama cleared her throat.

"Alma is still with Travis and Raylene. I just came to get you and Reese. There's a lot to do. So much I can't even think yet."

"I'm sorry, Mama." My voice cracked. I swallowed hard, wanting to cry but feeling no tears come. Even after all this time, I had not really expected Aunt Ruth to die. Everybody kept saying she would beat this, the way she had before. Mama had talked as if this illness were just something that had to be gotten past, as if Ruth just needed time and quiet to get better. Everyone did. Then I remembered how thin she was when I stayed with her, how frail and weak, her whole body shaking when she laughed, the way she looked at me when she asked me if she was dying. I had known, of course I had known. It was death Aunt Ruth was thinking about all the time. Death was the reason she had talked so much, so intently, death was the fire burning her up. With every breath and laugh and wiped-away tear, she had been dying. I had known that, but I had still imagined Aunt Ruth would go on, her dying something always still to come. The fantasy had been helped along by not seeing her every day as I had all summer. All these months, I had known what was happening over at that house, known and denied it, because I could do nothing else.

"Ruth was never pretty, you know." Mama's voice surprised me. I looked up at the clock, but the light over the stove was off. There were half a dozen butts in the ashtray, and Mama's mascara had run even more. I licked my lips.

"Aunt Alma said she was striking."

"Oh." Mama shrugged. Her fingers wiped her cheek, smeared the mascara back toward her temple. "That's what they say when a girl's got a strong face and an't ugly, but an't pretty neither. When we were little I think Ruth would have given just about anything to be pretty. She used to stand in front of Granny's wardrobe mirror and stare at herself when she thought no one was looking, but I never teased her about it. She got enough teasing from the boys." Mama ground her cigarette out.

"Truth is, she just about raised me. Daddy was gone by then, and Granny was always running after the boys or your aunt Alma, who was always getting herself in some trouble or the other. Ruth was the one that was there for me, that I could talk to. Once she told me that she liked to pretend I was hers. I was the baby, had just started school when she married Travis and moved down the road from us. She was over at our place almost as much as hers, cooking for Granny and picking up after us. Travis used to get mad and come beating on the door yelling for her to get her ass home to him."

Mama pulled her lips in and bit the lower lip lightly. It was something I had seen Aunt Ruth do often, something I did myself when I was nervous. Now it almost made me cry. I wiped at my own eyes, watching Mama use the back of her hand to wipe her eyes again.

"For some reason, Ruth didn't think she could have babies. When she got pregnant, she was so happy. It was a mystery to me why she liked having children so much. Seemed like everybody else whined and complained about it, but Ruth just took on so, laughed and sang and made her own baby clothes. Then, one time, I asked her why she acted so happy, and she stared at me like I was just plain crazy. Told me it was proof. Being pregnant was proof that some man thought you were pretty sometime, and the more babies she got, the more she knew she was worth something. I just about cried, and at the same time I wanted to hit her for talking like that, talking like she wasn't worth something on her own. Talking like my love didn't make her worth something!"

I remembered all the times I had stared in the bathroom mirror, knowing I wasn't pretty and hating it. I felt a cold chill go up my back, as if Aunt Ruth had just touched my spine. Mama was shaking her head, reaching to open her bag, rummaging around and pulling out a napkin. Carefully she dabbed under her eyes. "Go get me some cold cream, Bone. Let me get some of this gunk off."

I ran into the bathroom and grabbed the Noxzema jar. Reese was there, her hair all tousled and her eyes gummy with too much sleep. "Why didn't you wake me up?" she complained. "Where is everybody?"

"Everybody's gone, but Mama's here. Get cleaned up and come out to the kitchen." I hurried away. Mama would have to tell her. I couldn't.

When I got back, Mama was still in the same position with the napkin under her eyes, but now she was truly crying. Big tears were spilling out and streaking down her face. I ran to her and threw my arms around her. For a moment we clung together, and then, awkwardly, she pulled her arms free and pushed me a little away.

"You loved her too, didn't you, Bone?" She looked hard into my face as if she could see inside me. "You know how much she loved you?"

I nodded. I couldn't talk. Mama hugged me to her, rocked me against her breasts. Her hands squeezed my shoulders and shook me a little.

"Oh, my little girl," Mama whispered. "I wish I could be sure Ruth knew how beautiful she was."

17

Reese had never been to a funeral before, and I was unsure how we were supposed to behave. Reese was just worried about what we were going to wear. "Don't we have to go buy black dresses?" she kept asking. "Mama, when we gonna go get our black dresses?" She sounded as if she was already thinking about going to school the day after the funeral in her new black dress. Not so long ago that was what I would have been thinking. Now all I could think about was Aunt Ruth and the way she had talked to me all last summer. When Mama shushed Reese and told her she could just wear her dark blue skirt and a white blouse, I went off to sit on the porch steps, hugging my knees to my chest.

There was a tight painful place inside me that squeezed me, not my heart, but just above my heart. I remembered the way Aunt Ruth had looked when she smiled at me, how thin she had been with her bird fingers and feverish eyes. But most of all I remembered the way she had laughed with Earle and then stared off into the distance all those long hours in the hot afternoons.

"Can we talk to each other or not?" she had asked me. I had tried, but in the end I had lied. I hadn't told her that she was dying, hadn't told her the truth about my fear of Daddy Glen. I hadn't told her that I knew what he was thinking when he looked at me, that I could see in his eyes not only confusion and anger but something hotter and meaner still. I hadn't told her about the way he had touched me. I had been too ashamed. Mama thought that keeping me out of the house and away from Daddy Glen was the answer, that being patient, loving him, and making him feel strong and important would fix everything in time. But nothing changed and nothing was really fixed, everything was only delayed. Every time his daddy spoke harshly to him, every time he couldn't pay the bills, every time Mama was too tired to flatter or tease him out of his moods, Daddy Glen's eyes would turn to me, and my blood would turn to ice. I had never said that to Aunt Ruth, never said it to anyone. I didn't know how.

My head ached so bad I didn't even hear Daddy Glen shout. I was still curled up on the porch when he stepped through the front door.

"I was calling you, girl." He grabbed me by the shoulder. He hadn't had time to shower yet, and his face was still sweaty, his uniform smelling of spilled milk. I looked up at him with hatred and saw the pupils of his eyes go small and hard.

"I didn't hear you," I said plainly, coldly.

"You damn well did." He pulled me up to my feet.

"I didn't," I yelled at him. My blood was pounding in my head. "I didn't hear you. You an't got no business calling me a liar." Through the open door I could see Mama come out of the kitchen, wiping her hands on a towel.

"Glen," she called. "Glen."

"You think 'cause your aunt died you can mouth off to

me?" Daddy Glen was almost spitting with rage. "You think you can say just anything you damn well please! You got another think coming."

He dragged me into the house. Reese jumped up off the couch and ran for the bedroom. "Glen," Mama called again, coming after us, but he didn't stop. My shoulder hit the door-jamb as he pushed me ahead of him into the bathroom. I stumbled and would have fallen on the floor, but he was still hanging on to my arm. The door slammed behind us.

"Glen! Don't do this, Glen!" Mama's hands beat on the bathroom door.

I stood, looking up at Daddy Glen, my back straight and my hands curled into fists at my sides. His features were rigid, his neck bright red. He kept one hand on me while he pulled his belt out of its loops with the other. "Don't you say a word," he hissed at me. "Don't you dare."

No, I thought. I won't. Not a word, not a scream, nothing this time.

He pinned me between his hip and the sink, lifting me slightly and bending me over. I reached out and caught hold of the porcelain, trying not to grab at him, not to touch him. No. No. No. He was raging, spitting, the blows hitting the wall as often as they hit me. Beyond the door, Mama was screaming. Daddy Glen was grunting. I hated him. I hated him. The belt went up and came down. Fire along my thighs. Pain. Had Aunt Ruth felt pain like this? Had she screamed? I would not scream. I would not, would not, would not scream.

Afterwards it was so quiet I could hear my own heartbeat. Sound came back slowly. There were speckles of blood on the washcloth when Mama rinsed it. I watched, numb and empty. I was lying against her hip, on their bed. The house was cold. From the radio came the low sound of Conway Twitty singing "But it's on—ly ma—ke be—lieve."

"Why, honey? Why did you have to act like that? The funeral's tomorrow, Raylene's expecting us to help clean up at

Ruth's before everybody goes back over there, Alma's baby's sick, and now . . ." She put the cool cloth on my neck.

"Bone. Is it because of Ruth? Is that why you started yelling at Glen? Honey, you know you can't do that."

Her skin was so pale, the shadows under her eyes so dark. She had wiped her lipstick off, but there was a little blotch still on her chin. Her lips trembled. She lit a cigarette with shaking fingers, keeping one hand on my shoulder. I could feel the bones in that hand. I heard her whisper as if she were talking to herself, "I just don't know what to do." I closed my eyes. There was only one thing that mattered. I had not screamed.

I spent the night before the funeral with Aunt Raylene over at Aunt Ruth's place, helping her clean things up a bit and cook a ham and two different casseroles, one with noodles and cheese and one big vegetable mix with a cornmeal crust. Deedee had spent the evening locked in her bedroom playing the radio, and Travis was still down at the funeral home when Aunt Raylene made me go to bed. I woke up late and had to hurry to get a bath while Aunt Raylene cooked some biscuits and a pan of bacon. I'd been careful the night before not to let Raylene see the bruises on my legs when she had put me to bed in Butch's old room. She had been so distracted she'd noticed nothing. This morning I had no appetite but ate a bacon biscuit dutifully and drank the rest of Aunt Raylene's coffee while she finished getting dressed. Then I went out on the porch to wait for her.

The radio was playing "Get a Job" by the Silhouettes, the chorus staccato and driven, echoing loud in the early morning. Deedee was sitting in the porch rocker in her nightgown with her hair still done up in pin curls.

"I hate that damn hillbilly music, always have," she told me conversationally while I stared at her.

"You got to get dressed. Aunt Raylene is just about ready to go." I looked around for somebody else, but Uncle Travis's truck was still gone and there was no one else there. Deedee looked like she hadn't slept. She was smoking an unfiltered Chesterfield, her hand trembling slightly as she sucked intently on it, and her eyes bloodshot and squinted against the sunlight.

"But that's all the music Mama would ever play," she went on as if I hadn't said a thing. "Howling, yodeling, whining music, trashy music. Get mad every time I played my stations, called it nigger music. Told me it would ruin me. Like she hadn't told me time and time again I was ruined already." Deedee had one leg drawn up so that her arm was propped on her knee, the cigarette poised just in front of her mouth. An almost empty pack was in her other hand, and there was a box of kitchen matches on the floor beside a saucer full of ashes.

The radio paused, pulsed, and the music changed. "Elvis Presley and the Jordanaires," the DJ announced, "at the fairgrounds in Spartanburg this Sunday afternoon. I'm gonna be there, you can bet on it. Now here's the man himself." The music that had been playing softly in the background came up loud now. "I got a woman mean as she can be . . ."

"I've seen Elvis now three times. What you think about that, Bonehead? You like Elvis?" Deedee looked at me almost hatefully.

I shrugged. "Well enough. I an't never seen him."

"You an't never seen anything."

"No."

Deedee threw the cigarette butt over the side of the porch and glared at me. "She loved you, you know, hell of a sight more than she did me."

I said nothing. Aunt Raylene stepped through the door, pulling on her gloves. "Deedee, you better take your hair down and get dressed. You should have been ready to go half an hour ago. Travis is already down at the funeral home."

"He's been down there all night." Deedee tucked her feet up under her on the rocker and put one hand over her eyes. "I sent Grey over with his good suit when I figured out he wasn't coming home."

"Well, I'm not surprised, I suppose." Aunt Raylene touched Deedee's cheek lightly, and for the first time I noticed the faint stain of tears. "It was good of you to make sure he had his suit. Now come on, girl. Get up and get dressed. We an't got no time for you to be moping on this porch."

Deedee's hand dropped into her lap, and she shook her head fiercely. "I an't going." She licked her lips and cleared her throat. "You understand, Raylene, I an't gonna do this. An't gonna go down there and let everybody mope all over me. Mama wouldn't care, and I can cry well enough here."

"Deedee, get up." Aunt Raylene gave the rocker a push, making Deedee overbalance so that she had to drop her feet to the floor to keep from falling. "I'm not kidding around with you. You got five minutes to put on your dress and shoes. You can take your hairpins out in the car."

"I told you, I an't going. And I an't!"

The slap startled me as much as it did Deedee. She put one hand to her face while Raylene raised her arm again. "I said get up." Aunt Raylene's voice was soft but perfectly clear. "I just an't gonna have this. Tonight or tomorrow, I'll talk to you about your mama. Then you can whine and bitch to your heart's content, curse and scream and do any damn thing you want. But right now, you're going to her funeral the way she would want. If you don't, ten years from now you're gonna hate yourself for missing it, and I damn sure am not gonna let that go by. So get your butt up out of that chair and wash your face before I slap you silly."

Deedee hesitated, her mouth hanging open, and Raylene drew her hand back. Immediately, Deedee was up and into the house. We heard the water running briefly and then her feet on the stairs. Aunt Raylene sighed and pushed a few stray hairs back behind her ears. She looked over at me carefully. "Go get in the car," she said. "We an't got time for no more nonsense."

· · ·

They had let Earle out of the county farm early so he could go to Aunt Ruth's funeral. He showed up at the funeral home drunk, wearing a brand-new dark suit with his old work boots, and hanging on to the arm of a ridiculously young and skinny girl no one had seen before. I was out front standing with Raylene and Alma when we saw him coming up the steps. He gave me one quick nod but kept his attention on his sisters. When Raylene snorted at him, he told the girl to go wait in his truck.

"Don't get snotty, Raylene," he said as the girl walked away. "That child is the only thing keeping me alive."

"And what are you doing for her?"

"Everything I can, sister, everything she wants."

"You marry her, then?" Aunt Alma looked tired and impatient.

"I'm going to. Hell yes. I am, I surely am."

"Goddam, Earle, you fool. One of your women gonna have you put in jail one of these days."

"An't no woman ever gonna put me in jail." Earle swayed a little on his old boots. "An't no woman would dare."

"Aww, Earle." Raylene shook her head at him and shrugged. She folded her big arms around his shoulders and pulled him to her breast. "I'm just glad you're here." When she let him go, she smiled for the first time since Ruth had died. "That child buy you that suit?"

"Why? Don't you like it?" Earle ran his hands down the sides of his suit coat. He was so thin that when he bent his arms the dark material flapped like a crow's wing. His hair was still bristly short and close to his head, but dark again, as if he'd dyed it. He only looked like himself when he grinned in embarrassment. "Don't you think she got me a good one?"

"It's good enough, especially since you didn't have to pay for it."

Beau was wearing his best dark suit, but it didn't fit him too well. He kept lifting one shoulder and then the other, trying to settle himself more comfortably. The smell of whiskey clung to him, but he looked more sober than he had in years—sober, irritable, and so nervous he was chewing on his lower lip. "Why the hell we just standing around here?" He turned to Raylene as if she were in charge. "This funeral should have been over two days ago, and now we're standing on these steps like we an't never gonna put Ruth in the ground."

"Beau!" Alma looked disgusted. "Don't talk like that. The kids will hear you."

Raylene's voice was soft and neutral. "We're waiting 'cause Travis asked us to wait. He's hoping Tommy Lee, Dwight, and D.W. will get here and go out to the grave with us."

"Hell! Those boys an't coming. Nobody's even seen Tommy Lee in two years, and last I heard D.W. was on his way to California." Beau cleared his throat and spit. "Travis isn't using his head."

"No, he an't," Raylene continued in that flat soft tone. "And you wouldn't either in his place. Ruth wanted all her children to come home, and Travis has just been trying to do everything the way she wanted. Give him a few more minutes and the funeral director will get him moving. I don't want you saying nothing to Travis."

"I wasn't gonna say nothing to Travis." Beau looked indignant. "I an't a fool."

"Come on, Beau." Earle put his hand on Beau's shoulder. "Come out to the truck with me a minute."

"Oh God!" Alma sounded like she was going to start yelling. "Now they're gonna both be drunk."

"I don't care." Raylene took her handkerchief out of her purse and wiped her mouth. "Beau has a drink, I know how he'll behave. I don't know that man at all when he's sober. Don't know what he'll do. But if Earle gives him a drink, he might even be able to cry. Let them take care of each other."

I saw Butch out at the gravesite, awkward in a dark suit that looked too big for him. He told me later that he had come there hours before and watched as the gravediggers finished rigging the canopy over the big hot-house sprays and ribbon-draped wreaths and pegged it down against the wind. It was cold and gray, with no sign of rain, just a steady harsh wind pushing at all the flowers. There was a big heart-shaped arrangement on a stand that read *Mother* in cursive script. He stood near it with his hands gripped tightly in front of him.

"Bone," he whispered when I came to stand beside him. "You better get a seat."

"I don't want to sit." The wind rocked the heart wreath, and we both put our hands out to steady it.

"I heard you spent the summer with her."

"Yeah."

"I got back once to see her just before Thanksgiving. Only got to stay a few days. Sorry I never got a chance to see you." His voice was low. We watched everyone come over and take their seats. Mama, Raylene, Alma, and Carr gathered around Granny. I hadn't seen Granny in a long time. She was gray-faced, empty-eyed, and slack-jawed.

"She looks like the doctor gave her something," I whispered to Butch.

"Looks bad," Butch agreed. His back stiffened, and he turned away for a moment to look out over the open field of low gravestones. When he turned back I saw his mouth was clamped shut and his eyes red-rimmed.

Nevil, Earle, and Beau remained at a distance, watching until the hearse pulled up and the men gathered to carry the casket to the grave. I saw that Dwight and D.W. were with the others, but there was no sign of Tommy Lee.

The wind was bitter. As they carried the coffin, the men struggled to keep the flowers on top of it. The preacher dropped his papers, and Little Earle ran to grab them. Patsy Ruth and Mollie were sitting with Reese, Grey and Garvey behind them. Temple was sitting with her husband, right behind Mama. Most of the other seats were filled with women from Bushy

Creek Baptist. When the preacher began with "Brothers and sisters," they all nodded together.

"Goddam," I heard Butch mutter. "Goddam."

"Goddam," I agreed.

"There should have been music," I told Butch when we were back at Aunt Ruth's. He was sitting with me in the cane-back chairs Uncle Travis had put out in the backyard, reaching into his pocket and sipping surreptitiously from an almost empty little bottle of Ancient Age whiskey. He also had a bottle of Pabst Blue Ribbon under his chair, Nevil's beer of choice, which he kept pouring into a metal coffee cup and drinking openly. I don't know how much he'd had, but he looked relaxed and comfortable despite the cold, wearing one of Uncle Travis's old army greatcoats and a plaid wool scarf wrapped around his neck. I had borrowed Uncle Nevil's fleece-lined jacket and leather gloves, and wasn't too chilled myself, but it wasn't surprising that no one else had joined us.

"What?" Butch muttered in my direction. "A little Carter Family caterwauling? Maybe that one about building your house for the Lord?" He snorted and began to sing a brief off-key chorus of "Will the Circle Be Unbroken." His breath came out in pale little clouds.

"You can't sing," I told him.

"Hell, none of us can." He passed me the whiskey. "You want a sip? Might warm you up."

I said nothing, just drank deeply. I liked the taste. It was strong, a little bitter, but warming.

Butch laughed gently, tipped the bottle back, and refilled his cup with Pabst. "Don't you tell your mama, now. She'd take my head off."

"Give me some." I took the cup before he could object and poured as much as I could of the beer down my throat. It tasted mild after the whiskey, but it hurt to swallow, whether because it was so cold or that I drank such a big gulp, I couldn't have said. For all I knew, beer was supposed to hurt going down.

Butch peered closely at me. "You trying to get drunk?" he asked.

"You think I can?"

"Oh, pretty surely. But I might have to go get another couple of bottles if you want to do it up right."

"Earle's in there too. Bet we could get some more whiskey from him or Beau."

"Whoa, Bone! Girl, you been growing up while I been gone? Drinking beer and stealing whiskey?"

I drained his cup and handed it back. "They still should have had music. Aunt Ruth loved music."

"Yeah." Butch knocked the cup against his knuckles, making a low hollow sound. "Yeah. She did. Used to love to play those scratchy old records. Kept them even after D.W. broke her record player. Always planned to buy her another one, but I never seemed to have any extra money. Couple of times I borrowed Earle's record player for her just so she could listen to it."

"Earle loaned it to her last summer while I was there. We played a bunch of her stuff."

Butch smiled. "Don't tell me. 'Gospel Train,' right? A little Hank Williams, the Monroe Brothers, Hazel Cole, and—who was that?—yeah, Blind Alfred Reed, right? Bet she even got out 'Wabash Cannonball,' and 'Where the Soul of Man Never Dies.' "

" 'Pistol Packin' Mama.' " I reached under Butch's seat for the Pabst bottle, took it up, and drained it. He stared at me, unbelieving. "She really loved that one. We sang it together all one afternoon." I set the empty bottle back under his chair.

His face crumpled slowly. "Goddam," he whispered. "I forgot that one. Shit." He dropped his head and covered his face with his hands. I watched his shoulders tighten, feeling far off and a little numb, the liquor like cotton batting all along my nervous system.

"Christ damn," Butch cursed, and stood up. "I hate this." He kicked his chair over, kicked it again and knocked it a couple of feet away, went after it, and gave it another kick. "I didn't think I'd feel like this. When I talked to Deedee, we both swore we weren't gonna act like this, and there she is up in Mama's bedroom now, crying like her heart's broke, like she lost her best friend in the world. And hell," he almost shouted, turning back to me, "she and Mama couldn't barely stand each other."

I nodded. "It don't make sense, does it? I always thought Deedee hated Aunt Ruth, she talked so bad about her. But this morning . . ." I paused to wipe my face. "It all looked different."

"Goddam, you're drunk." Butch walked over to me, tilted my face back, and put his down close to mine. His lips pressed my lips, his tongue slipped in and pushed at my tongue, I pulled my head away in surprise.

"How old are you now, Bone?" he asked.

"I'll be thirteen in May," I told him.

"Thirteen." Butch nodded. "I always liked you," he whispered. "Still do. You an't always a damn fool like everybody else." He straightened back up. "So don't go making more out of this than there is."

I got to my feet carefully. The back of my skirt was stuck to my legs. I pulled it free with one hand and felt one of the scabs tear loose. I winced, but Butch had bent down to retrieve the beer bottle and didn't see. I went back inside, walking slowly, placing one foot deliberately in front of the other. It was kind of interesting being drunk. I liked the numb part.

In the overheated house, there seemed to be no good air left. The kitchen was full of women standing around talking and watching over the stove. Mama and Alma were sitting at the table, Alma leaning on Mama's shoulder. Carr was over at the counter, slicing ham and laying it out on a platter. Temple and Mollie were with her, helping to put more food out. I didn't see Raylene anywhere. I checked the parlor, but it was full of smoke, the smell of whiskey, and men talking in husky voices. Travis was on the couch with his head fallen back, his cheeks all flushed, the veins on his nose showing blue-purple.

I went down the hall trailing my hands along each wall. This was not hard at all. As long as I moved slowly and kept my head up, there was no problem. I went into the bathroom and looked in the mirror. I was sweaty, flushed. Sure looked drunk to me. I grinned. It was too hot. The window over the toilet seemed to be painted closed. I straddled the toilet, pounded on the window frame until it loosened, and opened it. Cool air washed over my face. I bent down, pulled my panties off awkwardly, skirt up, and without turning around dropped down backwards on the toilet seat. Peeing had never felt so wonderful before. I laid my cheek on the cool porcelain back of the toilet and just enjoyed the release.

The door opened behind me. I pushed up, startled, and slipped, falling back down on the seat. Twisted around, I tried to push up again, but a loud abrupt hiccup plopped me right back on the seat again. Raylene laughed.

"Who slipped you a drink, Bone?" She didn't sound that angry. She pushed the door closed behind her and steadied me with one hand. "You're about falling-down drunk."

"No, I'm not. I only had a little."

"Uh huh. Yeah." She laughed and pulled some paper off the roll and handed it to me. "Come on. Let's get you up." Her hand was under my right elbow, helping me stand. I tried to back off the seat, but her grip held me.

"Aunt Raylene." I turned my head to look up at her again, ready to try and persuade her that I wasn't really drunk. Her expression stopped me. She was looking down at my panties where they draped my left shoe, the brown stains in the seat showing clearly in the bright light. She pulled me back a little, and her left hand lifted my skirt. I tried to push it back down with my numb fingers, but she had a good grip.

"Sweet suffering Jesus!"

A shock went right through me. Suddenly I was terrified, unreasonably, horribly terrified.

"No," I begged. "No, please." But the door was open. She was pulling me out. I hung back, but she was unstoppable. She pushed me into Deedee's empty bedroom.

"Earle," Aunt Raylene was yelling. "Earle, come here. You and Beau, you come here."

"No." I said it again. "Please, please."

"Be quiet, Bone. An't nobody gonna hurt you. I swear to you, an't nobody ever gonna hurt you again."

Earle pushed through the door. "Raylene, what you yelling about? The kids are asleep upstairs, and you're yelling loud enough to scare people in the next county."

Raylene whirled on him. "Shut up and look at this."

She turned me around and flipped my skirt up. I started to stutter. "No, no."

"Damn." Earle's voice was soft, and scarier than I could have ever imagined. I wrapped my fingers around the back of my neck, dropped my head, and shook all over.

"Leave me alone," I begged. My panties were still tangled on my left shoe.

"Hush, hush." Aunt Raylene's arms wrapped around me like a blanket. She sat on the bed and pulled me up on her lap. "Hush."

Earle was gone. The door opened again, and Nevil and Beau were there.

"It true?" Beau demanded. "That son of a bitch beat her bloody?"

"Like a dog," Raylene told him. "Child's striped all the way down to her knees." She pulled my panties free of my shoe and threw them at him. "I'd kill him." She said it in a very matter-of-fact tone that made me believe her.

"No," I moaned.

"Shit!" Nevil's voice was barely recognizable. There was a scream from down the hall, a loud crashing noise, and Earle's voice shouting, "I'll murder you, you son of a bitch!" Nevil and Beau turned together.

"*No*," I pleaded. "Aunt Raylene, please!" But she just held me tight. I turned, started punching her, trying to get free. Mama's arms came around me so suddenly I almost stopped breathing.

"Mama! I'm sorry. I'm sorry."

"Hush, Bone." Her voice sounded just like Raylene's had. "Just hush, baby. It's all right." Still terrified, I clung to her. Thudding, crashing sounds were coming from the front. They had gone out on the porch. Raylene stood with her back to the bedroom door, her arms crossed over her breasts, as if she expected us to try and fight her to get out. Mama just held me and whispered again, "It's all right."

After a few minutes, Raylene came over and sat beside us. "Anney." Her voice was husky. "Anney, did he beat you too? Tell me, did he hurt you?"

"Glen would never hurt me, Raylene. You know that." Mama pressed her mouth to the top of my head. "He'd never raise a hand to me." She sighed and hung her head.

"Oh, Anney." Raylene reached for Mama's hands, but Mama pulled away.

"Don't touch me. Don't." Mama almost spit. She drew me closer to her. I was shaking in her arms, and she was shaking too. "Oh God, Raylene. I'm so ashamed. I couldn't stop him, and then . . . I don't know." Her head bobbed up and down. When she spoke again her voice was fierce, desperate. "He loves her. He does. He loves us all. I don't know. I don't know. Oh God. Raylene, I love him. I know you'll hate me. Sometimes I hate myself, but I love him. I love him."

I looked up. Mama's eyes were deep and glittery. Her mouth was open, her lips drawn back from her teeth, her neck muscles high and rigid. Her chin went up and down as if she

246

wanted to cry but couldn't. "I've just wanted it to be all right," she whispered. "For so long, I've just hoped and prayed, dreamed and pretended. I've hung on, just hung on."

"Mama," I whimpered, and tried to push up to her. "I made him mad. I did."

"Bone." Raylene reached for me.

"No!" I jerked away and pressed my face against Mama's arm.

"Hush. Hush." Mama breathed. I held still and heard Raylene's hand drop.

We listened to the noises from the porch. Those thuds were Daddy Glen hitting the wall. Those grunts were his. Those curses were my uncles'. I put my fingers in my mouth and bit down. I looked up. Above me Mama's face and Raylene's were almost touching, both of them trembling and holding on as if their lives depended on each other.

18

Things come apart so easily when they have been held together with lies. It was that way with Mama and Daddy Glen. Aunt Raylene offered to let us all come stay with her, but Mama wouldn't consider it. The one day Daddy Glen spent in the hospital, she moved us into an apartment over the Fish Market just a few blocks from the boarded-up windows of Woolworth's. Every morning, I had to walk past those windows to get to the intersection where the bus picked us up for school. I saw the workmen replacing the shattered display windows with new plate glass panels, and one day I saw a very harassed-looking Tyler Highgarden supervising while box after box of dimestore notions was carried through the repaired doors. He never even looked in my direction, but I still felt the hair on the back of my neck rise up stiff and electrical. If everything hadn't been so confused, I might have told Mama what I'd done. But Mama and I did not talk at all.

It was a two-room apartment, one bedroom and a larger room that served for everything else. The kitchen was a stove, icebox, and sink in a little alcove to the side of the bedroom door. The bathroom smelled of damp, mildew, and fish, the latter seeping up from the shop below. It was dark, with dirty windows we had to scrub repeatedly to get clean. The only cheerful thing in the whole place was the blue-flowered wallpaper that set the kitchen area off from the rest of the front room. When I sat at the table to do my homework I always faced that wallpaper. I didn't want to look at Reese, camped out in the bedroom with her coloring books and angry scowls, or at Mama, sitting wordless over on the couch, smoking, wiping her eyes, and listening to the radio.

Mama had left the television set behind, left her washer, most of her furniture and dishes, and all of her knickknacks and good silverware. She had brought the sewing machine, the ironing board, our clothes, and most of hers. Since we hadn't been there to help her pack, it was hard to figure out how she had decided what to take and what to leave, and since she clearly didn't want to talk, it was impossible to ask. Reese complained about the television and her bicycle, but Mama just said she'd get us new ones in time. I didn't question her, didn't complain, barely spoke.

It was my fault, everything, Mama's silence and Reese's rage. I lay in the bed with my hands clutched under my chin and my knees drawn up to my breasts. I kept remembering those last few days like a hurried, confusing dream, not Daddy Glen beating me but the morning Mama told me about Aunt Ruth, not the Woolworth's robbery but talking to Butch, and not the noise and uproar when Benny, Aunt Fay, and Aunt Carr drove off to the hospital with Daddy Glen but those brief horrible moments when Aunt Raylene showed my thighs to Uncle Earle. I kept trying to figure out how I could have prevented it all from happening, not drunk that beer, not let anyone see, gone to Mama and made sure she knew that I had deserved that beating—kept everything smooth and quiet.

That night at Ruth's, Aunt Raylene had told me not to brood, that it would take time for Mama to forgive herself. For what? I wondered. Mama hadn't done anything wrong. I was the one who had made Daddy Glen mad. I was the one who made everybody crazy. No, Raylene told me. I wasn't to think that way. She had whispered in a rough, strained voice that Mama loved me, that she loved me, that Earle and my uncles loved me. She was insistent, holding me tight to her, but I didn't listen. I clamped my teeth together and sucked my tongue up so tight to the roof of my mouth that my throat ached. Mama was ashen and silent and wouldn't look at me. It was my fault, all my fault. I had ruined everything.

Daddy Glen showed up at the diner to try to talk to Mama, but she balled up her apron and hid in the washroom until the manager made him leave. She came home to sit on the couch, smoke a pack of cigarettes, and stare into space. When Reese tried to talk to her, she made us both go to bed early. The next morning, when Mama went over and applied for a job at JC Stevens, all I could think about were the times she had told us how much she hated the mills. When Reese and I got out of school, we found a note from Mama on the dish drain that said she'd be working until seven-thirty and to open a can of pork and beans for dinner. Reese ate hers spread between two layers of bread and refused to speak to me. I went down behind the Fish Market where big salt-stained flats were stacked in piles and empty washtubs lay tilted so they could drain and air out. I sat on an overturned washtub between the leaning piles of flats and cried into my elbow so that no one could hear me.

"It'll be all right," Mama kept telling Reese and me, but she didn't explain how. When Reese cried and said she wanted to go home, Mama held her and promised to let her stay with Patsy Ruth this summer. I sat at the table and watched them across the room, remembering the last time Mama had run away from Daddy Glen. It had only been a few days. This was now over a week. How much longer would she last? Another week? A month? I dug my nails into the soft skin inside my elbows and rocked a little on the chair. I wouldn't cry, not where Mama could see me. I wouldn't cry.

For Reese the whole thing had been an adventure until Mama refused to let her go over to sign her name on Uncle Wade's cast. Three days after the funeral Uncle Wade had shot himself in his right foot, and was stuck home limping around with his leg in a big cast the boys had plastered all over with oil and gas decals from the service station. We'd heard all about it from Little Earle at school, but Mama ignored Reese's begging and brought home a couple of paint-by-number sets for us instead.

"I don't want you going nowhere that I can't come keep an eye on you," she told Reese. When Aunt Raylene came over, Mama didn't even invite her inside, just spoke through the door.

"Let us be, Raylene. Just let me be for a while. I need some time to think."

"Anney, you can't hide away like you some criminal." Aunt Raylene sounded impatient. "You an't the one done nothing wrong. You an't the one at fault."

"I don't care who's at fault," Mama yelled. "I just need to be left alone!"

Aunt Raylene called Mama's name softly twice more but finally went slowly down the stairs and drove away.

We all shared one big bed, but most nights Mama would fall asleep on the couch, one arm thrown over her face so it covered her eyes. That night Mama lay on the couch, and cried so quietly I could just barely hear her through the closed door. I curled up on the far side of the bed and listened to the small sounds of her weeping until I fell asleep and dreamed that the walls of the apartment fell away and you could see all the way out to the house where Daddy Glen was sitting up staring through the open windows waiting for us to come back. When I woke up in the early dawn, I went to make sure Mama was all right. I tried to be quiet, but she was awake, lying there looking up at the dirty gray ceiling.

"Bone," she whispered. "It's too early. What are you doing up?"

I hesitated. I wanted her arms around me but I stood there rigidly, mouth shut tight, eyes dry.

"Oh, Bone," Mama sighed. She sat up and pulled me down beside her so that my head was on her shoulder. I began to shake with hard, mean sobs, a strange kind of crying without tears. Mama's hand moved automatically, stroking my head as if I were a wounded dog. I knew from the way she was touching me that if I had not come to her, pushed myself on her, she would never have taken me into her arms. I shuddered under that unfeeling palm, slapped her hand away, and ran for the bedroom. I crawled in beside Reese and pulled the pillow over my head. Reese woke up complaining, and when Mama came in I just scrunched down tighter, refusing to answer when she called my name.

"Bone, don't do this," she said, her voice angry and impatient. I burrowed deeper into the sheets. After a little while Mama said, "That's enough," and took Reese away. My head pounded with heat.

Lying alone on the big bed, I thought about Daddy Glen and the way he would come up behind me and gather me up in his arms to pull me close to his body. Remembering, I locked my hands between my legs and tightened every muscle in my body. When I was as hard and rigid as I could make myself, I tried to remember how it had started. What was it I had done? Why had he always hated me? Maybe I was a bad girl, evil, nasty, willful, stupid, ugly—everything he said. Maybe I was, but it didn't matter. I hated him, and these days I even hated Reese and Mama. I was a bowl of hatred, boiling black and thick behind my eyes.

I had been so proud of not crying that last time, so sure it was important. Why had it mattered? Whether I screamed or fought or held still, nothing changed. I curled up tighter still and thought about that, the way he beat me, the way I felt jammed against him and struggling, the smell of him and the feel of his sex against my belly. He had been pinning me against his thigh when he beat me. Had he come? Had he been beating me until he came in his trousers? The thought made me gag. I pushed my wrists harder and harder against my own sex until I was hurting myself. I could remember his smell, the sound of his breath above me, the hot sweat falling off his face onto my skin, the way he had grunted and shaken me. No, it did not matter whether I had screamed or not. It had all been the way he wanted it. It had nothing to do with me or anything I had done. It was an animal thing, just him using me. I rolled over and bit the pillow. I fell into shame like a suicide throws herself into a river.

After a while I cried myself back to sleep. I dreamed I was a baby again, five or younger, leaning against Mama's hip, her hands on my shoulders. She was talking, her voice above me like a whisper between stars. Everything was dim and safe. Everything was warm and quiet. She held me and I felt loved. She held me and I knew who I was. When I put my hand down between my legs, it was not a sin. It was like her murmur, like music, like a prayer in the dark. It was meant to be, and it was a good thing. I woke up with my face wet from tears I did not know I had cried, my hands still holding on between my legs.

"Mama," I whispered, but she had gone to work. I was alone in the quiet bedroom. It had been a long time since I had woken up like this, with that sweet good feeling between my legs, almost hurting me, but comforting too.

I brought my hands up and looked at them, spread the fingers and looked at the light reflected through the dingy shades. I rolled over and slowly loosened the muscles of my back and legs, keeping my hands in front of my face. The light shifted as the shades swung in the breeze. I thought about fire, purifying, raging, sweeping through Greenville and clearing the earth. I dropped my hands and closed my eyes.

"Fire," I whispered. "Burn it all." I rolled over, putting both my hands under me. I clamped my teeth and rocked, seeing the blaze in my head, haystacks burning and nowhere to run, people falling behind and the flames coming on, my own body pinned down and the fire roaring closer.

"Yes," I said. Yes. I rocked and rocked, and orgasmed on my hand to the dream of fire.

When I woke up it was afternoon, and the apartment was still and warm. I got up carefully. There was cold coffee on the stove, and biscuits in a towel-wrapped dish. I drank some coffee and chewed on a biscuit with a slice of cheese. A note in Mama's handwriting was on the table. "Don't go anywhere," it read. "I'll be home by dark and we'll talk."

My throat closed up. I didn't want to talk to her. I didn't know what I would say. I dressed myself quickly in jeans and a warm cotton shirt. When I left, I locked the door behind me. Once I was on the street, I thought about Reese coming home to an empty apartment and calling Mama at work. They'd be upset. Angrily I started walking. I didn't care anymore who got mad at me, what happened. Maybe I'd get killed out on the highway.

It had been Fay, Nevil's wife, who had driven Daddy Glen to the hospital after getting him up off the lawn and on his feet again. "He an't gonna die," she had said. "But a doctor should look at him. That cut over his eye might need a stitch or two."

Aunt Carr and Benny went with them. "You should always give a man a chance," she said before she got in the car. Earlier, she'd been the one who tried to stop the beating and gotten slapped for her trouble.

"My wife's getting ready to drive, an't she, and in my car." Nevil's voice was laconic and soft. "She wouldn't be if I wasn't giving that son of a bitch a chance." He was drinking black coffee out of a soup bowl, his knuckles all bloody and swollen, like Earle's and Beau's. Beau had managed to get kicked in the mouth and had lost a tooth. He was collapsed in a chair threatening to knock all Glen's teeth out as soon as he could stand to punch him again.

Through it all, Daddy Glen said nothing. His face was blood-streaked and bruised, and he could barely stand, but he didn't make a sound when Benny helped him into the car. He just put one hand over his eyes and lay back against the seat. Aunt Carr brought his coat. "You should be ashamed," she hissed at Earle as she went through Aunt Ruth's living room.

"Well, I'm not." Earle had a bottle of Jack Daniel's and was passing it over to Beau between sips. "I'm not ashamed of beating that asshole. I'm not ashamed of sitting here drinking. I'm not ashamed of a damn thing." He sat at the table with Beau and Nevil, all of them sweaty and bruised, drunk and indignant. None of them looked at me when I came through with Mama and Raylene, though Earle stumbled up and put his arms around first Mama then me. He smelled like blood, a copper-and-iron tang on top of the whiskey. I pushed at him, trying to get free, but he seemed not to notice, letting me go only when Mama pulled me out of his embrace.

"We're going," she told him.

Raylene and Nevil followed us out to the Pontiac, Raylene repeating, "You should come to my place," and Mama never stopping to acknowledge the suggestion. It was dark and cold, and Reese was shivering.

Aunt Alma brought out a couple of blankets. "We should talk," she said. "You're gonna need some help, Anney, and you shouldn't go back to that house alone." Nevil nodded.

Raylene said, "Anney, just listen to us." But Mama wrapped one blanket around Reese and handed the other to me. She kept putting one hand up, palm out, when either of her sisters got too close. "No," she said once. "Don't stop me. I know what I've got to do."

We'd slept the night in the car while Mama rummaged through our house, packing up the things she wanted and storing them in the trunk. She put boxes behind the front seat and piled sheets and quilts on them to make the backseat one big bed. Before dawn, she drove us down to the train station lot and parked the car under one of the big arc lights. She slept in the front seat, with pillows and blankets around her. When daylight came, she took us to a diner downtown and left us to eat our breakfast while she went to rent the apartment she had already picked out from the ads in the paper. She had been moving so fast, so steadily, it was impossible to talk to her, to ask her what was happening. But I could not have asked anyway. I knew.

It took me most of the day to walk to Aunt Raylene's. I walked with the same pace, the same deliberate energy, I had seen in Mama since Aunt Ruth's funeral. I sang to myself as I walked, sometimes out loud. Ruth Brown's "Mama, He Treats Your Daughter Mean." Patsy Cline's "Walking After Midnight." Out at the intersection of White Horse Road and the Eustis Highway, I even started on Elvis Presley. Singing kept me from crying. Singing kept me walking. The spirit of meanness that had come up in me broke out in song and movement. I felt hateful but strong, mean but powerful.

Aunt Raylene didn't seem that surprised to see me when I walked up her front steps. She was on the side porch, where she had set out flats to start seedlings. Her hands were covered in dirt, her hair tied back with a scarf, and she had a streak on one cheek. "Bone," she said briefly, and went on mixing black dirt and potash. "An't seen you in a while."

I wiped my face. Sweat was running down my neck. My feet hurt. I dropped onto a stool. "Get yourself a glass of something out of the kitchen," Aunt Raylene said, but I didn't move. After a while the dry tight feeling in my throat eased. I watched her spread the dirt out in her flats and layer fertilizer in each. She mixed again and again, turning the dirt over and not looking up at me.

"Spring's coming," she said finally.

I nodded.

"Your uncle Earle's staying here now." She wiped her hands on a rag and took a cigarette out of her overalls, leaned back against the table of flats, and lit it. "He took a room downtown with that little girl he brought to the funeral, but that looks like one of his shorter romances, 'cause she's still downtown. Man's living out of two suitcases and sleeping on the couch. Won't move into my spare room, keeps saying he an't gonna be here that long."

I loosened my jacket. When I spoke my voice was as flat and careless as hers. "Mama always said Earle lived from woman to woman. Told Daddy Glen that Earle had become a cradle robber, that there was nothing solid left in his life but whiskey and family." I paused, surprised to hear myself mention Daddy Glen. It felt suddenly hot on the porch.

"Well, I told him he should get himself a widow next time, some fat old girl to iron his shirts and wash his back. But Earle likes them young, likes them openmouthed and gawky. He's like all men, I suppose, loves a grateful woman, specially one that he don't have to do nothing to impress. And the girls he finds—my Lord, it about hurts my heart, these little strays he brings around. All Earle has to do is speak gently to them and they fall all over him. They're just like fruit in the sun, heavy and ripe for someone to pick."

I squirmed a little on my stool. "Uncle Earle told me he's sure there an't no woman ever regretted giving herself to him."

"Christ Lord, you love him just like one of them, don't you?" Aunt Raylene frowned at me. "You don't think it's cruel the way he takes up with these children? He's never divorced a one of them, never stays with any of them more than a few months. God knows how many babies he's planted."

"None." I bit my lip.

"You know that, do you?"

"He told me he took care not to make children anymore, said he didn't think he had no business making any more babies than he had already."

"Well, isn't he thoughtful!" Aunt Raylene ground out the stub of her cigarette on the side of one of the flats. She walked over near me and picked up one of the glass window frames leaning against the wall. Carrying it back, she set it down so that it covered two of her flats. Two more windows completed the task, leaving the mix to heat in the sun. She didn't look at me, and her lips were set in a thin straight line. I knew that meant she was mad at me.

"He only marries them 'cause they want it so bad." My eyes stung, as if the tears I had refused to shed on the long walk out were burning me now. My hands balled up into fists. "He loves them," I yelled. "He loves them more than they deserve."

"Bone." Aunt Raylene turned to me and shook her head. "Girl, you are seriously confused about love. Seriously."

"Oh?" I drawled at her sarcastically, and rocked to my feet. "And whose fault is that? Huh? How am I supposed to know anything about love, anyway? How am I supposed to know anything at all? I'm just another ignorant Boatwright, you know. Another piece of trash barely knows enough to wipe her ass or spit away from the wind. Just like you and Mama and Alma and everybody." I spit to the side deliberately. "Hell," I said softly to her face. "Hellfire. We an't like nobody else in the world."

Her dark eyes glittered at me, but I wasn't afraid. My insides were boiling, and my skin burned. My hatred and rage were so hot I felt like I could have spit fire. When she put her hand on my wrist, I felt the hairs on my forearm tingle and stand up. A cold electric current ran up to the back of my neck.

"People are the same," she said in a whisper. "Everybody just does the best they can."

I took a long breath and let it out in a rush of bitter words. "Other people don't go beating on each other all the time," I told her. "They don't get falling-down drunk, shoot each other, and then laugh about it. They don't pick up and leave their husbands in the middle of the night and then never explain. They don't move out alone to the edge of town without a husband or children or even a good friend, run around all the time in overalls, and sell junk by the side of the road!"

Aunt Raylene crossed her arms over her breasts and looked at me. "I don't like being yelled at, never have." Her hands gripped her upper arms so tightly I saw the fingers tremble.

"And I don't know about other people, but I've always

believed everybody does what they have to do in this life." She stopped and started again. "When you're thirty years old and supporting your own children and doing the best you can when you don't know where your next dollar is coming from, then you can yell at me. Maybe." She shook her head, and turned away, brushing loose dirt off her thighs.

"It's almost suppertime," she told me. "And you're filthy. You go get yourself cleaned up and I'll see whether I feel like feeding you or not."

"You don't have to feed me." I couldn't look at her and say it. My head dropped down and I wiped my nose on my sleeve.

"I know what I have to do and what I don't. You think about it, and you'll see that the biggest part of why I live the way I do is that out here I can do just about anything I damn well please."

I looked up at her hesitantly. Aunt Raylene's face was beet-red, and her eyes were not on me. They were looking out past the highway. She seemed like she wanted to cry almost as much as I did, but like me, wasn't going to let herself.

"I said, go wash yourself."

I went.

The stories I made up for myself changed. In the half-sleep that preceded full sleep I began to imagine the highway that went north. No real road, this highway was shadowed by tall grass and ancient trees. Moss hung low and tiny birds with gray-blue wings darted from the road's edge to the trees. Cars passed at a roar but did not stop, and the north star shone above their headlights like a beacon. I walked that road alone, my legs swinging easily as I covered the miles. No one stopped. No one called to me. Only the star guided me, and I was not sure where I would end.

I stayed at Raylene's for three days, and then Mama called to say I either had to come back or start school out there. I'd heard about the country school from Garvey years before, and knew I would hate it. They didn't even have a library. Reluctantly, I went back to the apartment over the Fish Market. Mama bought me a new pair of sneakers to replace the ones I had worn out, but said nothing about me running off in the first place. Several times I caught her watching me with a painful concentrated expression, but I didn't ask her what she was thinking. Reese told me that she had been crazy-angry when I turned up gone, and was ready to call the police when Aunt Raylene called.

"They talked about you a long time," she said. "Aunt Raylene told Mama to let you get it out of your system, and Mama told Aunt Raylene to mind her own business. I thought they were gonna yell at each other like they used to, but Mama just gave in. She said she didn't know what to do with you, didn't know what to do with nobody, and Raylene could keep you if you wanted to stay."

Reese grinned at me almost sweetly. "I didn't think you'd come back at all. I was all ready to take over your side of the bed for good." Reese's biggest complaint was that she was in the middle and Mama and I were both restless sleepers. "I wouldn't want Mama to be mad at me the way she's been mad at you," she added. "I don't see how you can stand it."

I didn't either.

It felt as if the world was falling apart in slow motion. Two days after I came back, Aunt Alma's baby girl finally died, her heart stopping the way everyone had been expecting since she was born. Fay called Mama to tell her, and Raylene came to stay with Reese and me while Mama went out to see Alma. "You've always been the one closest to her," Raylene told Mama, "and she's not handling this very well at all. You'd think we hadn't all known it was coming."

"You know how Alma loved Annie," Mama said. "Maybe she knew Annie was gonna die, and maybe she didn't, but she wanted her baby girl to live." I heard her from inside the apartment even though she was already out on the landing.

Her voice was pitched low, but the words sounded so intense I came to the door.

I watched Mama go down the stairs while Reese led Raylene inside to see how well she'd done her paint-by-numbers clown face. Once Granny had told me how Mama carried me down to the courthouse after I was born and fought with the man there about the way they had made out my birth certificate. Telling me that story, Granny's eyes had glittered and her mouth had turned up in a fierce smile. "You don't know how your mama loves you," she had said. "You can't even imagine."

Like Alma loved Annie, maybe, like Ruth loved her sons D.W. and Dwight and Tommy Lee, so much that she made Travis swear not to bury her until they got home. I chewed on a fingernail and watched Mama walk away, wondering if she still loved me and what I would do when we went back to Daddy Glen.

Raylene had brought some of her home-canned blackberries with her. She and Reese made a skillet cobbler the way Raylene said she had learned when she was with the carnival. She dropped lots of little butter slices on the bottom of the skillet, sprinkled brown sugar over that, then poured her blackberries, more butter, and a handful of white sugar over everything. Unsweetened biscuit dough made the top crust, and the cobbler was ready to eat in half an hour. It wasn't as good as Aunt Fay's pies, but Reese gorged on it, eating almost half the pan by herself. Afterwards, she leaned forward lazily on the table, almost asleep, her blue-stained lips slightly parted.

Aunt Raylene looked through the paintings and picked up the Japanese mountain scene I had not bothered to finish. She waved it at me. "Reese tells me you won't give this to her, even though you don't want to finish it."

"It's mine. I might finish it sometime."

"Uh-huh." Raylene put the cardboard drawing back. I waited for her to say something more, but she turned away and started cleaning up the kitchen.

It was still early. I went out on the landing to watch the cars pass by, people from the nearby housing development on their way out to the new discount grocery, a few trucks with men coming home late from work, a bus from Bushy Creek Baptist with flat-faced children pressed against the windows staring at me hatefully. I glared back at them. Anger was like a steady drip of poison into my soul, teaching me to hate the ones that hated me. Who do they think they are? I whispered to myself. They piss honey? Shit morning-glory blossoms? Sit on their porches every Sunday morning and look down on the world with contempt?

"I hate them," I told Aunt Raylene when she came up behind me, waving at the bus as it passed. "Looking at us like we're something nasty."

Aunt Raylene was picking blackberry seeds out of her teeth, looking off into the distance, and she surprised me when she reached over and slapped my shoulder. "They look at you the way you look at them," she told me bluntly. "You don't know who those children are. Maybe they're nasty and silly and hateful. Maybe not. You don't know what happens to them when they go home. You don't know their daddies or mamas, who their people are, why they do things, or what they're scared of. You think because they wear different clothes than you and go by so fast, they're rich and cruel and thinking terrible things about you. Could be they're looking at you sitting up here eating blackberries and looking at them like they're spit on a stove—could be they're jealous of you, hungry for what you got, afraid of what you would do if they ever stepped in the yard."

She reached down and pulled her string bag from her pocket and began to roll a cigarette. "You're making up stories about those people. Make up a story where you have to live in their house, be one of their family, and pass by this road. Look at it from the other side for a while. Maybe you won't be glaring at people so much."

I looked up at her sourly. "People say you ran off to the

carnival with a man, but you never say nothing about him. How come he didn't marry you?"

The paper in Aunt Raylene's hands shook. "People say? People will say anything. I ran off to the carnival, yeah, but not for no man. For myself. And I an't never wanted to marry nobody. I like my life the way it is, little girl. I made my life, the same way it looks like you're gonna make yours—out of pride and stubbornness and too much anger. You better think hard, Ruth Anne, about what you want and who you're mad at. You better think hard."

She licked the cigarette paper and smoothed it closed. She lit it and tucked the dead match back in her pocket. She smoked carefully, watching me as if she expected me to talk back to her, but I held still. When she finally spoke again, her voice shook a little. "It's not so cold tonight, not so cold. Smell of spring in the air."

I turned my face away and said nothing. After a minute Raylene shrugged and went back inside. I squatted down and hugged myself until I was as small as I could get, watching the cars pass and listening to Reese fuss as Aunt Raylene took her off to bed. I closed my eyes and tried to make up a story for myself. I pretended we were back in that house over in West Greenville that Mama had loved so, pretended that Daddy Glen had joined the Pentecostal Church and gotten a cross-country trucking job that would pay him lots of money but keep him away from home. I imagined Mama getting a job where she could sit down all she wanted, where the money was good and she never got any burns or had to pull her hair back so tight off her face that she got headaches. Maybe she could be a teacher? Or one of those women behind the makeup counter at the Jordan Marsh? I bit my lips and let it all play out under my eyelids—Reese in a new dress for Easter, me with all the books I wanted to read, Mama sitting in the sun with her feet up, Daddy Glen far away and coming home only often enough to make Mama smile. I fell asleep there dreaming, loving the dream.

That spring the storms were astonishing, torrents of water that sheeted down and flooded everything from the sagging old houses on Old Henderson Road to the warehouses and cafes out on White Horse Road, but the day Aunt Alma went crazy it was perfectly clear, hot and dry with the mud standing up in stiff peaks, and ruts off every driveway. It was Monday, the day Reese had gone over to Fay and Nevil's when she got out of school, to go shopping with their girls.

"She's almost nine," Fay had told Mama. "She's old enough. Can't be too protective, you know." After Reese drove her crazy begging, Mama agreed reluctantly.

I was walking home slowly, trying to keep my skirt from blowing up in the wind and thinking about the luxury of an hour or two before Reese would get home, a solid piece of time when I would be able to lie around on the couch, listen to the radio, drink Coca-Cola, and read the paperback of *The Group* I had finally managed to sneak out of the library. Walking up past Woolworth's in the fresh spring breeze, I was carrying my shoes and tugging at my hem when I saw Mama running down the stairs from the apartment. She was still wearing her hair net and flat white shoes, so she couldn't have been home very long. From the way she was moving, something had to be wrong, so I picked up and ran, reaching the car just as she did. Even so, she had the Pontiac engine roaring by the time I grabbed the door handle. I jumped in and threw my books in the backseat before she could stop me, but I was still surprised when she didn't tell me to get out, just gunned the engine so that the wheels spun as we pulled out onto the highway.

"It's your Aunt Alma," she said. "Little Earle called. Sounded terrible. Couldn't even get out what had happened, so don't ask." Mama looked stern—scared and angry at the same time. I wondered what was wrong, if it was something Uncle Wade had done, or maybe one of the cousins. It could be anything with the way Aunt Alma had been since Annie died.

"Don't we just lead charmed lives?" Aunt Alma had said the last time we saw her. "Bad things seem to be happening all the time."

I concentrated on gripping the door handle while Mama roared out toward the West Greenville Highway. She took the Old Henderson Road turnoff, past the gas station where Uncle Wade had been working before his accident, and turned onto the dirt road that cut through open country where the interstate was supposed to go in next year. Aunt Alma had gotten a deal on one of the condemned farmhouses out there, and had moved in after Ruth died.

Little Earle was waiting for us beside the cow grate down near the mailbox, his face white and his shirt streaked with muddy brown stains. There was snot all over his upper lip, and he kept wiping his hands down over his middle where the worst of the mud had smeared. Mama didn't get out of the car, just stopped for a minute and leaned out the window. "You all right?" she yelled, and he nodded. He sure didn't look all right to me.

"She's up at the house," he whispered, as if he were afraid to talk too loud. "I tried. I tried, but she wouldn't let me do nothing." He hugged his shoulders tightly. "She's up there by herself. I got the girls away and called you." There was a pause as he gulped air between every few words. "And then Uncle Earle. Uncle Earle said not to go back, and anyway, she scared me. Mama scared me." He stopped and looked back up the dirt drive that wound to the side and disappeared into the pines. "Oh God, Auntie, she's gone crazy as a milk cow, just like Daddy said she would!"

"Wipe your face and keep quiet," Mama told him fiercely. "I'll send Bone down for you in a little while, and I don't want you scaring your sisters. You wash your face and get some of that dirt off yourself." She sounded almost hateful—a way I had never heard her talk before to any child. I turned from watching Little Earle to look at her and almost rolled across the seat when she started the Pontiac racing up the drive again. Behind us I heard another engine, and looked over my shoulder to see Uncle Earle's flatbed truck trailing a cloud of red dust, a rattle of tools bouncing around. He yelled something, but Mama didn't stop, just sped into Aunt Alma's yard and nearly knocked over her garden barrels before killing the engine and jumping out of the car. I pushed over to the driver's side to follow right behind her, but Mama yelled at me to stay there without even turning around. I froze where I was while she ran toward the porch and Aunt Alma's hunched still figure.

Chickens were screeching and running away, dust was settling behind the Pontiac, but everything else was dead still. I could see a row of white faces watching from Aunt Alma's chicken-wire garden fence—Patsy Ruth, Reese, and Fay's girls, Grace and Mattie. The sun was pouring down, hot and steamy, and there were puddles under the black walnut tree that hadn't had a chance to dry up. There was no sign of Uncle Wade or his truck, and everything looked strangely peaceful. Then I saw that all Aunt Alma's flower baskets were lying in the yard, buds and herbs scattered. Near one of the baskets was the porcelain wringer off her old washing machine, and the lumps in the dust and mud seemed to be clothing. The sound of Mama's voice drifted over to me, a lulling murmur of softly accented phrases that reminded me of the way Aunt Alma had always talked to baby Annie. Aunt Alma was quiet, bent over, and didn't respond as Mama wrapped her arms around her and whispered reassuring nonsense.

I opened the car door on my side quietly and stepped out. There was a fork under my foot, the tines buried in the ground. Flatware was scattered everywhere, and an egg turner stuck up out of a broken flowerpot. I stepped over a smashed plate and saw dozens of spools of thread under the porch and a pair of pliers under the Pontiac's right front tire. Dust was on everything, making it hard to see what was what until I looked closely. Just past the fender, a little breeze lifted a tangle of red-brown curly hair from the hairbrush that lay near a shattered hand mirror. I bent over and saw a stack of faded pictures half buried under the crushed petals of black-eyed susans and a smear of baby's breath. The fan-shaped wedge beside them looked like the venetian blinds that Aunt Alma had always hung in her bathroom.

"Honey. Sweet girl. It's all right," Mama was saying. I looked over at them. Aunt Alma's feet were resting on a little pile of chopped black slats—45 rpm record fragments—and her pale stockings had slid down over her broken-at-the-heel brown shoes. There was mud on her calves and knees, plainly visible where her yellow flower-print dress was pulled up. A strip of the hem on her white cotton slip hung down behind her knees. The sleeves of her faded blue sweater were rolled back, and it was all covered with dried mud like the dress. Her hands were as dirty as the rest of her, stained dark, her nails broken and the cuticles torn.

Blood, I realized. That was blood among the mud stains all over Aunt Alma's hands, dress, sweater, calves, and face. Her hair was matted with it. A chill went through me, and the skin on top of my head went tingly and hot. Aunt Alma's fingers were knotted together in her lap. Her face pointed straight ahead, but her eyes were completely unfocused, looking inside not out. She opened her hands slowly and brought them up to her face, the torn, raw fingers sliding past her cheekbones to push her hair back, spreading fresh blood on her temples. There were cuts on her forearms, one on her left cheek, and another on her neck, below her chin. My mouth hung open. I turned my head. There was glass everywhere, shattered, scattered, gleaming in the sun. I was standing barefoot in a yard of broken glass.

"He'll be back soon," Aunt Alma was saying. "Back any minute now, I know. I'm ready for him." She turned and looked Mama full in the face. "I'm ready for him," she said again, her voice as calm and familiar as Mama's. "I'm ready for him."

"Yes," Mama said. "I see, honey. You are. We both are. We'll just sit here a while and wait for him." She kept her face pressed close, not looking away from Aunt Alma's eyes, as if only her presence was keeping Alma attached to the earth. One of the girls started whimpering over by the garden. I looked back, unable to resist the notion that everyone had gone crazy. Women all over Greenville County were going to smash stuff and then sit down to wait for Armageddon or sunrise or something. It sounded like a good idea to me.

"Bone, get away from there." It was Uncle Earle's whisper. He was standing well back over near the stand of pines where the drive turned, his black hair gleaming in the sunlight and an expression on his face of almost comical nervousness. "Come on, girl. Get back in the car and let your mama handle this." His hands were flat on his thighs, and his jaw was set. He looked scared, deathly scared.

"I'm gonna cut his throat," Aunt Alma said in the most reasonable voice imaginable. "I got the knife for it."

"Where is that?" Mama asked her.

"In my pocket." Aunt Alma's hands came down, patted the skirt of her dress. Her right hand slipped into a pocket I hadn't noticed before and came out with a razor, the straight edge closed into the handle. She flicked her wrist and it swung open, the blade shining in the sunlight. She brought her left hand up and laid the blade on her palm, looking down at it like it was beautiful.

"Oh, that'll do it," Mama said, her voice still soft and matter-of-fact. She looked back over at me. "Bone, girl, go inside and get your aunt a glass of tea, why don't you?" Her eyes tracked past me to Uncle Earle, and she shook her head slightly. He nodded and started backing away toward the pines. "We should get you cleaned up a little, Alma. You look like you got caught in a storm." She gave a soft little laugh and pulled gently at her sister's arms. Alma shuddered and hunched over the razor. Mama went still, her face carefully empty.

I stared at them. They seemed more alike than ever. Aunt Alma was a good ten years older than Mama and maybe twenty pounds heavier, but she had the same strong features, cheekbones standing out like hammer hooks under eyes sunken and shadowed. Their hair was the same texture, dry and fine, though Mama's was more blond for the rinse she used on it, and flattened out a little from the hair net she had to wear at work. Aunt Alma's hair had a reddish sheen peculiar to all the women on her side of the family. It was their necks, though, that were identical, rigid cords of tendons standing out so that the little hollow where the collarbones met looked even deeper and more pronounced. The skin was the same, work-roughened and red-tinged under the tan, though Aunt Alma wore no makeup and Mama's was streaked with sweat. Family they were, obviously related, clearly sisters. When I swallowed loud, they both turned to me with the same gesture and the same expression.

"An't you gonna do what I asked?" Mama prodded, just as if Aunt Alma wasn't sitting there covered in her own blood.

Aunt Alma stirred, lifted her head, and looked over at me. I couldn't see where to put my feet.

"Girl children," Aunt Alma sighed. "Dreamers always standing around sucking on their teeth."

"It's a fact," Mama agreed, and shook her head in resignation.

I wanted to laugh, but instead I flushed in embarrassment. How old was I going to have to be before they stopped talking about me like that? I took a breath and stepped over the shattered pieces of flower pots, past the broken records, and up the steps. There was more rubble in the doorway, propping the screen door half open. The kitchen chairs had been smashed and the table overturned, the cabinets emptied and everything all over the floor. I picked my way across to the refrigerator, surprised that it wasn't standing open, more surprised to find that the contents were intact and there was ice in the freezer. There was a gallon jug of tea ready-made. I turned back toward the porch, seeing Mama and Aunt Alma still sitting together on the steps.

"You want a glass of tea too, Mama?" I asked slowly.

"Yes, honey, that would be nice." She put her arm all the way across Aunt Alma's shoulders and hugged her close. "Your aunt and I just want to sit here a while before we start cleaning all this up."

"I want another baby," Aunt Alma was saying in a slurred tone. We had her in Patsy Ruth's bed, bundled in blankets, with bandages on her hands. Alma's big old bed was broken in half, though we couldn't figure out how she had managed to smash that oak headboard so completely. She lay there murmuring softly, groggy from the toddy Mama had made for her with whiskey, hot water, honey, and lemon. "I told him that. Told him I wanted another little girl. Told him it wasn't gonna be all right until I had another baby." She paused. She still had the razor in her hand, closed now but gripped too tight to get away from her. We'd cleaned up a good bit, got the kids off to Aunt Raylene's, and made sure Uncle Wade wouldn't be coming home until someone went to get him. We hadn't done anything with the yard, just picked most of the broken glass and ripped clothes off the floor, put the kitchen back together more or less, and cleaned and bandaged Aunt Alma. None of the kids had been hurt, just scared to death. The only casualty was one of the puppies, whose neck had been broken when something or someone fell on him. Grey and Garvey had showed up just before sundown to work on the yard a little and help round up the various animals. Mama wouldn't let them come in the house. I watched them for a while as they wandered around shaking their heads and exclaiming in awe over how much destruction Aunt Alma had managed to do.

Mama had stayed right beside Alma, keeping her hands on her, steadying and quieting her, and keeping between me and that razor that never left Aunt Alma's hand. She talked as if nothing had happened, and in fact most of it was about me, about how slow I answered, how daydreamy I was, how much I looked like my great-aunt Malvena. I'd been surprised to hear all that, more surprised when she said I would stay here with Alma, give her a hand now that spring was warming up. "You need some help around this place, Alma," Mama told her. "You'll like having Bone around. Maybe you can even get her to sing for you now and then."

My mouth had fallen open, and I'd stood transfixed, as close to the bed as I dared. Did she mean that? Did Mama think I was reliable? Did I look like my great-aunt Malvena? Did she really think I could sing?

Aunt Alma barely acknowledged what Mama said, just went on with her complaints about Uncle Wade. "I said, 'Give me a baby, Wade. Just give me a baby.' " She tried to sit up, and Mama leaned over to soothe her, climbing in bed with her.

"You know what he said to me? You know what he said to me?" Alma asked, hanging on to Mama with one desperate hand. She didn't wait for an answer. She took hold of the blanket in her fist, shook it and hissed the answer between her teeth. "Said, 'What you want an't what I want.' He said, 'You old and ugly and fat as a cow, crazy as a cow eaten too much weed, and you smell like a cow been lying in spoiled milk.' Said, 'I wouldn't touch you even if you took a bath in whiskey tonic and put a bag over your head.' He laughed at me. Then he walked right out of here."

She lay back limply. There were tears on her face, and her lips had flattened back against her teeth. She shook her head slowly back and forth. "All this time, taking care of him, loving him, giving him children and meals and clean clothes and loving him. Loving him, and him to talk to me that way." She cried deep, broken sobs.

"And Annie!" she wailed. Mama gathered Aunt Alma up like a little girl, rocked her back and forth while she cried. It didn't last long. In the silence that followed, the two of them murmured a little, something I couldn't hear clearly. It sounded like Mama said something about Uncle Wade being a loving man, that Aunt Alma loved him. Then Aunt Alma's voice came out loud and strong again.

"Oh, but that's why I got to cut his throat," she said plainly. "If I didn't love the son of a bitch, I'd let him live forever."

"Woman takes it in her head to go crazy, you just might as well stand back." Uncle Earle was joking to Grey and Garvey out on the porch in the dark, the three of them standing close together smoking and sharing a beer. They'd wanted to get in the house so bad Mama had finally let them move some of the broken furniture, insisting they do it quietly so that Alma could sleep.

"Oh, women," Garvey grunted. "They're not that hard to handle."

"You think!" Uncle Earle laughed. "I'm telling you, boy, you never can predict what a woman might not do. You remember that little girl from Nashville I brought around two summers ago, sweet little thing not any bigger than Bone and all pasty-faced, blond, and giggly?"

"Tiny, yeah," Grey almost laughed. He sounded like he remembered her well. "She was so shy nobody got to know her."

"Well, that little thing," Uncle Earle drawled, "that little thing just about cut my balls off with a pair of scissors one night. Got me by the short hairs and tried as hard as she could. If I hadn't been twice her weight and six times as scared, she'd have left me a eunuch." He laughed like the idea still made him nervous. "I'm telling you, women are dangerous. You need to keep it in mind."

I leaned my face against the screen door. It creaked slightly, and they all looked over toward me. I must have been silhouetted against the kitchen light like some ghostly night creature, because they all jumped. Earle's face went stiff.

"Bone," he said, "you better get back in there with your mama. She might need your help." Grey stood there quietly beside Earle, his hand still holding a beer can. I waited a minute, looking at him, remembering when he swore he would never forget what we had done. He lifted the beer can, drank deeply. He looked so proud to be standing on that porch drinking with Uncle Earle.

"Didn't you hear Earle?" Garvey's tone was harsh. I looked at him directly and snorted. Little boy pretending to be a man didn't scare me, but I backed into the kitchen anyway. I remembered that Nashville girl perfectly well. She had been so shy she stuttered whenever she tried to answer a question, and she was terrified of bugs of any kind. We'd teased her until she cried and went running to Earle like he was her father, not her supposed-to-be husband. She hadn't looked to me like the kind that could do any damage at all, or even think about it. Not like Aunt Alma, who was, after all, a Boatwright, and dangerous as any man even when she wasn't crazy.

But you can't tell with women, I thought. I looked down at my hands in the dim light of the lamp Mama had set up on the counter near the sink. My hands were small, the tendons blue and fine under pale skin, like Alma's and Mama's. We all had small hands. I looked back down the hall to the bedroom. I could just see the smashed and tumbled bed frame.

No, I thought, you just can't tell with women. Might be you can't even tell with girls.

"I never realized before how much you look like Alma." It was so late it was almost morning. Mama's voice came out of the darkness from the direction of the doorway. "But when we were sitting on those steps together and you were standing in the yard, I saw it so clear. I saw what you're gonna look like when you're full-grown. You're gonna be as pretty as Alma was when she was a girl, prettier than you can imagine."

I said nothing. I was wrapped in a blanket, sitting on Little Earle's mattress up against the wall where we had dragged it earlier in the evening. Aunt Alma had finally gone to sleep, and Mama had decided it was safe for us to try to get some rest. But for an hour she had been sitting propped up on her pillow, smoking, and I had been staring into the dark, listening to the cows move around in the pasture near the house.

Mama shifted restlessly, turning toward me. "Bone," she said softly. "What is it you think about all the time?"

"Nothing much." I looked at the cigarette's burning tip. My eyes had adjusted to the dark so that I could make out the shape of her body, her shoulders pushed up on the pile of old pillows, her arms lying on top of the blanket. "Nothing I could explain."

"You're always so quiet, always watching." Mama's voice was soft, and sounded more relaxed than I had heard in a long time. "I can tell when you're mad, you know. You get that storm-cloud look on your face, and you've had that enough lately." She shifted in her blanket, put the cigarette out in a saucer on the floor.

"The thing is, if you're not mad, I can't tell what's happening inside you. You never look happy. You look like you're waiting. What are you waiting for, Bone?"

For you to go back to Daddy Glen, I thought, and hugged my blanket tighter around my shoulders.

"Bone?"

I touched the backs of my fingers to my throat, felt the warmth there, the pulse in the hollow beneath my chin.

"Bone? You're not asleep?"

"No."

"You don't want to talk to me?"

My fingers were wet, my chin, the edge of the blanket. I remembered Aunt Alma's direct look this afternoon when she'd talked about loving Wade, about wanting to kill him. I didn't understand that kind of love. I didn't understand anything. I swallowed and tried not to make a sound.

"You're still mad at me, aren't you?" Mama sounded like she wanted to cry. I bent forward and pressed my mouth to the blanket edge. "Not gonna tell me anything?"

One of the cows moaned out in the dark pasture. I swallowed again. "I'm waiting for you to go home," I said. "I'm waiting for you to go back to Daddy Glen."

There was a long silence. "You think I'm going to?" Mama whispered finally.

"Uh-huh," I said.

"Oh, Bone." She sat up, took another cigarette out, and lit it with a match. In the glow I saw her cheeks pale and shiny. "You want to come over here and sit by me?"

"No." I didn't move. I felt as if I had become hypersensitive, as if I could hear everything, the cow's hooves in the damp grass, the dew slipping off the porch eaves, Mama's heart pounding with fear.

"Bone, I couldn't stand it if you hated me," she said.

"I couldn't hate you," I told her. "Mama, I couldn't hate you."

"But you're sure I'm gonna go back to him."

"Uh-huh." I coughed and cleared my throat.

"Oh God, Bone! I can't just go back. I can't have you hating me."

"I an't never gonna hate you." I took a deep breath, and made myself speak with no intonation at all. "I know you love him. I know you need him. And he's good to you. He's good to Reese. He just . . ." I thought a minute. "I don't know."

We were quiet for a while. When Mama spoke she sounded almost like a girl, unsure of herself and scared. "Maybe he needs to talk to somebody. Raylene said maybe he needed a doctor."

I wiped my face and shrugged. Now I felt tired, aching tired, so deeply tired it was hard to pull air all the way down into my lungs. "Maybe," I said.

"I won't go back until I know you're gonna be safe." Mama's voice was determined. "I promise you, Bone."

"I won't go back." The words were so quiet, so flat, they didn't seem to have come out of me. But once they were said, some energy seemed to come back to me.

"I wouldn't make you, honey."

"No. I know. It's not that, Mama. I know you wouldn't." I sat up, rocked my head forward, and heard my neck bones make an odd cracking sound as the muscles stopped straining. When I spoke this time, my voice was strong, the words clear. "I know you'll go back, Mama, and maybe you should. I don't know what's right for you, just what I have to do. I can't go back to live with Daddy Glen. I won't. I could go stay with Aunt Carr for a while or move in with Raylene. I think she'd be glad to keep me. But no matter what you decide, when you go back to Daddy Glen, I can't go with you."

"Bone." Mama got up from her mattress so fast I felt myself push back against the wall nervously. Her hands came down on my shoulders, squeezed gently. "What are you saying to me?" she asked.

I could see her face. The moon must have risen. In the dim reflected light from outside, her cheekbones and shadowy eyes were ghostly. She was afraid.

"I love you," I said, "but I can't think of anything else to do."

She gripped me hard. I could feel her fingernails biting in, the intensity of her fear. She shook her head and pulled me to her neck. "Oh God, what have I done?" she cried.

"Mama, don't," I said gently. "Please." She let go of me but still knelt there close. I wondered if she could see me as clearly as I could see her. If so, what was she seeing in my face?

A rain began to fall outside. With no wind, it came down in a sweet, sprinkling whisper, little drops flicking through the tender new growth on the trees and bushes. Mama put her palms flat against her eyes. "All right," she said. "All right."

I swallowed. I wanted to reach for her, to say I was sorry, to say that I hadn't meant it, that I would go back with her, but I didn't move. After a minute she got up and went back to her pallet. She didn't smoke anymore. She pulled her blanket up and lay still, so quiet she might have been asleep as soon as she lay down.

Much later, in the early dawn with the blanket pulled over my head, I heard Mama start crying, trying hard not to make a sound and almost succeeding. Only her breath catching every little while gave her away. My own eyes were dry. I didn't feel like I was going to cry. I didn't feel like I was ever going to cry again.

20

It was peaceful out at Aunt Alma's. The spring ripened until the yard and surrounding woods were lush green and full of singing birds. The three surviving puppies ran in stumbling leaps and falls, rolling over each other and digging between their mama's titties. The clothes scattered across the yard had to have the dirt shaken out before they could be washed. The washer itself worked pretty good, though Earle could not figure out how to fix the wringer. I hung the soggy clothes out on a line that Grey put up between the porch and the black walnut tree, though none of them came truly clean and some of them Mama set aside as garbage. I made a big pile off the porch of the things that were broken beyond repair, and Uncle Earle hauled it away.

Alma came back to herself slowly. She didn't want to talk much, but then neither did I. Mama came out every afternoon for a while, then every other day, and finally every few days.

She'd bring Alma some little treat, some sweet corn succotash, or chow-chow and biscuits, or once even a little blackberry cobbler. For me she brought books, paperbacks she traded for down at the book exchange, or magazines she got from the women she worked with over at the Stevens mill. One afternoon, Alma passed her the razor she'd been keeping in her apron pocket.

"You'll feel better if you take this away," she said to Mama. They both looked at the deadly thing.

"You sure you don't still need it?" Mama ran her fingers over the smooth polished handle and the dull outside edge. "If it makes you feel better, you should just keep it."

"No." Aunt Alma sighed and combed through her hair restlessly with her fingers. It had gone full gray in the weeks since she'd wrecked the house, and she had cut it off short with that razor the afternoon before. "I an't got the urge no more. I still don't want to see Wade yet, but I an't thinking about cutting his throat no more either."

"It's just as well," Mama told her. "Leave him alive to suffer. He's been staying over at Fay's, and Carr's been with him every minute. She says she don't dare go home again until she knows Wade's gonna be all right. But between his leg itching him and her nagging and whining at him, Wade looks like he's liable to shoot himself again any minute." They both smiled.

Nobody said anything about me having to go to school out in the country. Mama had brought me a list of books to read and a note from my teacher, saying that so long as I wasn't gone more than a month everything could be made up. I wondered what Mama had told her, but I didn't ask. It was such a relief not to have to sit in those boring classes, to be able to read as much as I wanted, sit up late with Alma, and get up when I felt like it. Mama and I were being a little easier with each other but still tender. I heard from Reese that Mama had seen Daddy Glen a couple of times and they were talking again. I tried not to worry about the future, not to think too much about anything. I worked in Alma's garden, saving what I could of her herbs and flowers, and put in some seedlings and cuttings Raylene brought by. The days were a gift, long and warm, the nights quiet and cool. I slept dreamlessly and woke up at peace.

The afternoon Daddy Glen showed up, Alma was out in the garden by herself, putting in the tomato seedlings Raylene had brought over the day before. I planned to go off on a picnic, had packed a cloth bag with a bottle of tea and lemons, and was spreading bread with peanut butter to go with it. The puppies had gotten in the kitchen and were tumbling over themselves to beg me for treats. I gave them each one teaspoon of peanut butter and dragged them out on the porch to watch them chew and yawn and try to lick the tops of their mouths.

I was giggling at them when a Ford pulled up into the yard and Daddy Glen climbed out. He looked the same, though there was a scar over his left eye and he seemed to limp slightly as he walked toward the porch. He wore his work clothes, khaki trousers and white shirt with the sleeves rolled up to his elbows. His brown shoes were scuffed and dusty. There was a little beard showing, as if he had shaved the night before and not this morning. I stood and watched as he came up the steps, not knowing what to do.

"Bone," he said. His voice was hoarse and deep. I wondered if Aunt Alma heard it out in the garden behind the house. His eyes looked bright and intent, his jaw tense. "Your mama an't here, is she?" he asked.

I shook my head no. I put my hands behind my back and clasped them tightly. He stepped up on the porch and looked me over, up and down, and back up to my face. His lips thinned out.

"You're getting bigger," he said. "Gonna be ready to start dating boys any day now. Getting married, maybe, starting your own family." He spat to the side. "Breaking some man's heart just 'cause you can."

I licked my lips, unclasped my hands. "I'll get you something to drink," I said. I pushed through the screen door as fast as I could, but he was right behind me, his hand pulling my fingers off the little latch.

"You do that," he said. He looked at the table, where the peanut butter jar still stood with the lid off. "Making yourself a sandwich? Make me one."

I didn't know what to do. Get him a glass of tea, make him a sandwich, keep my head down, and hope that Aunt Alma would come back in? I thought of her and her bandaged hands, her sore back and thin neck. I looked in Daddy Glen's eyes again and was too afraid to move.

"Don't act like that. You an't got no reason to be afraid of me." He moved toward me. "I talked to Anney, you know. She's gonna come back. She promised, just needs a little time, time to make it up to you." I saw his fingers curl up and loosen again. He flung his huge hands out to the side and shook his head, laughing.

"That woman loves you more than I can understand. Needs time to work things out with you." He sneered the words. "Time with you. My sweet Jesus." He shrugged his shoulders, put his hands on his hips, and put his face close to mine.

"You're gonna have to tell her it's all right," he said. "You're gonna have to tell her you want us all to be together again."

He paused, looking at me intently. My stomach hurt. I looked down. My sweaty fingers were rolled into fists.

"No," I whispered. "I don't want to live with you no more. Mama can go home to you. I told her she could, but I can't. I won't."

"Won't?" He touched my cheek. I looked up at him. "You won't live with me?" His eyes were hard blue rocks, his mouth an angry line. "You're not even thirteen years old, girl. You don't say what you do. I'm your daddy. I say what you do."

"No." I said it quietly. My throat was so tight it was hard to say anything. I saw him rock back away from me, close his eyes, push his hands together in front of his body as if he were about to pray. He shook his head.

"No," I said again.

"I'm trying to be reasonable with you, girl. I want you to talk to your mama. I want you to stop this nonsense before you make me really mad." His clasped hands shook. He opened his eyes.

"No." I said it louder. "I'd rather die than go back to living with you."

"You would?" His lips curled into a mean smile. "I bet you would," he said in a whisper.

There was a long quiet moment. I could hear my heartbeat.

"Make me that sandwich," he said, "and we'll talk."

I stood unmoving, watching his face and hands. "No. I don't want to talk. I want you to leave."

He shook his head and went on smiling.

"I'll tell Mama," I said desperately. "I'll tell her."

His hands came up and grabbed my shoulders, shook me. "You don't want to make your daddy a sandwich?" His voice grated with rage. "You don't want to do nothing for me?" Another shake. He lifted me so that my feet came off the floor. My mouth opened. I wanted to scream, but nothing came out. I remembered all the times he had lifted me like that before, lifted me, shaken me, then pulled me to his chest, held me against him and run his hands over me, moaned while his fingers gouged at me. I had always been afraid to scream, afraid to fight. I had always felt like it was my fault, but now it didn't matter. I didn't care anymore what might happen. I wouldn't hold still anymore.

I tried to wiggle free, and he laughed. He dropped me. I staggered back against the table.

"You're the one. You're the reason. She loves me, I know it. But it's you, you're the one gets in the way. You make me crazy and you make her ashamed, ashamed of you and ashamed of loving me. It an't right. It an't right her leaving me because of you. It an't right."

His voice got harder, hoarser but no louder, and it was the quiet that terrified me. It reminded me of Alma with the razor in her hand and madness in her eyes. Daddy Glen's eyes were just as crazy, more crazy. There was pain in them, deep pain, yes, but hate was the thing that made them burn. Suddenly his fist shot out like it was on a spring. His knuckles raked the side of my chin, and I fell back on the table.

"You can't destroy me so easy," he said. "Anney's gonna come back, she told me. She just needs a little time. I can understand that after everything that's happened." He leaned toward me, one hand extended. "But if she wasn't gonna come back to me, I'd kill you. You know that? I'd break your neck." His hand touched the side of my face, my ear, my neck, slid down my front, the slight swells of my breasts. His blue eyes trailed down my body.

"Ahhh," Daddy Glen moaned. He pulled me to his chest, holding me tight, breathing hard. There was blood in my mouth and a roar in my head. I went hard, stiff, metal-hard, as hard as the butter knife I found I had grabbed without thinking. He kissed me wetly, his teeth grinding into my mouth. I jerked that knife up and rammed it into his side hard as I could. It slid along his belt, smearing peanut butter on his shirt, not even tearing the material but hurting him anyway. I could tell.

"Damn you!" He threw me away from him so that my back hit the counter and I slipped down, falling as he came toward me, kicking at me. His boot hit me solidly in the shoulder. His arm came down, caught my right wrist, and jerked hard, pulling me up sharply, then dropped me. Something gave, crunching audibly, while a wave of sickening heat followed, and my arm flopped uselessly under my body.

"You little cunt!" He kicked again, and his boot slipped along the side of my head, cutting my ear so that blood gushed. Then that boot thudded into my belly and I rolled sideways, retching bile down my right arm.

"*You!*" he cursed, and it echoed in my head. "*You goddam little bastard!*"

"*You!*" I told him. "Mama's never gonna go back to you. I won't let her. I hate you."

"I've prayed for you to die," he hissed between set white teeth. His hand caught the front of my blouse and dug into the material. "Just die and leave us alone. If it hadn't been for you, I'd have been all right. Everything would have been all right." He sobbed and dragged me forward so that I was up on my knees swaying in his grip until my blouse tore, and I fell back under him. He grabbed for me again, and something hit me hard between the legs. I screamed. His boot or his leg? He dropped down on top of me.

"You're not going anywhere." He laughed. "You think you're so grown-up. You think you're so big and bad, saying no to me. Let's see how big you are, how grown!" His hands spread what was left of my blouse and ripped at the zipper on my pants, pulling them down my thighs as my left hand groped to hold them. I tried to kick, but I was pinned. Tears were streaming down my face, but I wasn't crying. I was cursing him.

"Damn you! Damn you! Damn you! *God will damn you!*"

He reached with one hand to shove my pants down almost to my ankles and with the other to open his britches. "You'll shut up. I'll shut you up. I'll teach you." He ripped my panties off me like they were paper. Then he jerked me up a little and spread my legs.

"*You fucker!*" I punched up at him with my almost useless right arm.

"You little cunt. I should have done this a long time ago.

You've always wanted it. Don't tell me you don't." His knee pushed my legs further apart, and his big hand leisurely smashed the side of my face. He laughed then, as if he liked the feel of my blood on his fist, and hit me again. I opened my mouth to scream, and his hand closed around on my throat.

"I'll give you what you really want," he said, and his whole weight came down hard. My scream was gaspy and low around his hand on my throat. He fumbled with his fingers between my legs, opened me, and then reared back slightly, looking down into my face with his burning eyes.

"Now," he said, and slammed his body forward from his knees. "You'll learn." His words came in short angry bursts. "You'll never mouth off to me again. You'll keep your mouth shut. You'll do as you're told. You'll tell Anney what I want you to tell her."

I gagged. He rocked in and ground down, flexing and thrusting his hips. I felt like he was tearing me apart, my ass slapping against the floor with every thrust, burning and tearing and bruising.

"God!" I screamed with all the strength I had. Not loud enough, not loud enough for anybody but me to hear, but he let go of my throat and slapped my mouth, crushing my lips into my teeth. He started a steady rhythm, "I'll teach you, I'll teach you," and pounded my head against the floor.

"You'll die, you'll die," I screamed inside. "You will rot and stink and cave in on yourself. God will give you to me. Your bones will melt and your blood will catch fire. I'll rip you open and feed you to the dogs. Like in the Bible, like the way it ought to be, God will give you to me. God will give you to me!"

All the time my left hand was flailing, reaching, scrambling for anything, something. Where was that knife? Where was Aunt Alma?

He reared up, supporting his weight on my shoulder while his hips drove his sex into me like a sword.

"Give me something! Give me something!" I begged. I

tried vainly to bite him, my teeth pushing up through my clamped-down lips. "Give me something!"

He went rigid, head back and teeth showing between snarling lips. I could feel his thighs shaking against me as my butt slid in the blood under me. "Oh God, help me, let me kill him. Please, God. Please, God. Let me kill him. Let me die, but let me kill him."

He went limp and came down on me, rag-loose and panting. His hand dropped from my mouth, but the urge to scream was gone. Blood and juice, his sweat and mine, my blood, all over my neck and all down my thighs, the sticky stink of him between my burning legs. How had it all happened so fast? I tried to lick my lips, but my tongue was too swollen. I couldn't feel my tongue move, just my lips opening and closing with no sound coming out. Red and black dots swam up toward the ceiling and back down toward me. Daddy Glen moved a little, mumbling something I could not understand. I saw past him the open door and the late-afternoon sun darkening. I closed my eyes, opened them, felt like I had passed out briefly. He was still on me, but something was different, some feeling in the air. I looked again to the door and saw her. Mama's enormous white face was moving toward us where we lay, toward me.

"Mama," I tried to say, but never got it out. Glen's body jerked above me and pulled back. The air hit me like a fist, all my wet and open places. I whimpered. He screamed.

"*Anney!*"

She hit him with something I could not see. Then she was grabbing things, canisters off the stove, pans, glasses, plates, anything she could throw at him. I smiled. The corners of my mouth tore, but it didn't matter.

"*No, Anney, no!*"

"*You monster!*"

"No, darling. No! It's not what you think."

What was it, then, I wondered, and flopped over on my belly. Pain. My shoulder, my knees, my thighs, my face—

everything hurt but none of it mattered. It was all far off. Rubbery and numb, my arm was under my face.

"*You!*" Mama screamed. There was more crashing, but I didn't look up. Would she think I wanted him to do that? Would she think I asked for it? What would he tell her? I had to tell her that I had fought him, that I had never wanted him to touch me, never. But the blood running out of me was stealing all my energy, all my air. I could not talk, could not think. For a moment then I wanted to be dead already, not to have to look into Mama's face ever again, and not his. Never his, never again.

Please, God, let him die, let me die, let someone die.

Don't let him hurt my mama.

"*You bastard! You monster!*"

"*Anney, please!*"

"*Don't you touch me. Don't you touch her!*"

I tasted tears, snot, blood that had run down from my ear. I spat and tried to push myself up. I had to get up, do something, get Mama out of there.

Mama's hands were on me now, feeling for the damage. My head cleared a little, and I looked up. He was across the room, face white and stricken, and she was down on her knees with me. A roar went up through me, and I gritted my teeth. We had to get out of there, get away from him. I got to my knees.

"Come on, honey," she cooed like I was a baby again. "I'm gonna get you to a doctor." Her hands smoothed my blouse, knotted the torn pieces together over my belly, dragged my pants up my legs a little at a time, covering me up.

"Anney, no, wait," he was saying, but she wasn't listening. That's good, don't stop. Keep moving, Mama. Get us out of here.

"Come on, baby," she said, and pulled me to my feet. I swayed on rubber-band knees, an empty bowl of pain for a belly. Those dots were floating everywhere. I looked over at Daddy Glen. His face was as empty as my belly. Icy terror rode up my legs to my heart.

Get out, we've got to get out of here. You don't know, Mama, you don't understand.

She was whispering, "Baby, baby," holding me tight to her hip as she started for the door.

A terrible clarity seized me. I was thinking way ahead of myself. Uncle Travis's shotgun was at his house, in Aunt Ruth's bedroom closet. If I could get there, get it in my hands, I'd hide it until he was there, right there, as he would be, certainly. At the door or standing in the living room, telling his version of things, explaining it all away, crying again or begging, or just holding Mama by the arms the way he had held me. I would have to be careful, not let anyone stop me until I could blow his head off, blow his neck open, his blood everywhere like a whirlwind. I had to do it. I had to, or he would kill me, me and her, someday, I knew, both of us. If I had to die, then that was the way it would be.

"Ruth's, Mama," I breathed. "Take me to Ruth's." If I could get my hands on that gun, I'd never let it go. Maybe I could just pretend I needed it the way Alma had needed her razor, just to hold it like a doll or something, so that they'd tell the cops, "We never thought she'd use it." Never.

"We've got to get you to a hospital," Mama said. No. Ruth's. But she wasn't listening to me. Was I saying it or just thinking it?

"Anney. Oh, Anney." Daddy Glen was right beside us, blood on his face. From her or me? I wondered. Something had hit him. I stared at his face like it was a road map, a route to be memorized, a way to get back to who I really was. After I shot him, there would be nothing left, no way back.

All right.

"Please, Anney." He sobbed like a child, and she pulled me tighter into her armpit. Her free hand snaked out and slapped him, drew back, made a fist, and punched him full on.

"*Ohhh,*" he howled. "Don't, don't." He staggered back, tripping on scattered dishes.

"Anney!" he whined like a little boy. "I don't know what

happened. I was just gonna talk to her, darling. I just wanted you to come home, for us all to be together again!"

Mama kept moving, dragging me with her, using her hip to open the door, half-carrying me down the steps. Not a pause, not a hesitation, across the yard toward her car.

"Anney, please! I didn't mean it. I went crazy. I went crazy. Honey, listen to me!"

I was dizzy. Everything hurt, but it was better, better. Strength was coming back, and with it thought. My muscles felt weak but no longer severed from tendons and bones. I could move now. There would be a way. Look how hurt I was. There would be a story we could tell. It would be self-defense. It would be justifiable. I grinned to feel the blood trickling down my neck. Look how hurt I was! Thank you, God.

"Anney!" He was following us. "Please, Anney!"

Keep moving, Mama.

Across the sparse grass and dirt, up to the car. Mama gasped into my ear, holding me against her trembling rib cage. She opened the door, eased me down onto the front seat, lifted my legs. He was still crying her name. I was thinking fast and slow at the same time. How could I do it? No shotgun here, not even a butter knife.

"Anney, please. Talk to me. Love, please. Please, Anney."

She dodged him, ran around to the other side of the car, and got the door open. He was right beside her, sobbing and wringing his hands. He pushed the door almost shut while she struggled to open it again.

"Anney, you know how I love you. I wouldn't have hurt her, darling, but I went crazy. I just went crazy!"

I pulled myself across the seat, trying to reach her and help, but it was back to being hard to move. The air had become thick as jelly. I had to push through it. I gritted my teeth and inched forward until I was leaning against the steering wheel, watching them struggle with the door.

"Mama."

She looked toward me, her face empty and strange.

I said it again. "Mama."

Mama slapped Glen again, with her open hand and then with her cupped fist. The sound of her blows was dull and horrible, but not so horrible as the mewling grunts he made as she struck him. "Let go," she said. He staggered, sweat streaming into his eyes. His mouth worked uselessly, all his features seemed realigned. "Let go," she said again. He wailed and dropped to his knees, his hands still clinging to Mama and the door. He bowed his head and whispered, "Kill me, Anney. Go on. I can't live without you. I won't. Kill me! Kill me!"

Mama jerked away from him, and the door slammed shut. "Oh, no," she whimpered. Her face became the mirror of his, her mouth as wide, her neck as rigid.

"Kill me," he said again, louder. "Kill me." He butted his head into the metal door, pulled back, and rammed again. He shouted every time his head hit, the thuds punctuating the cries. "Kill me. Kill me."

Mama was so close I could have touched her, but her head was turned away, turned to Glen. I could not reach her. "Oh, God," she cried, and I let go of the steering wheel.

"No," I whispered, but Mama didn't hear me.

"Glen!" she said. "Glen!" She moaned and covered her face with her hands. Her body shook as she sobbed. Mine shook as I watched her.

"Glen, stop," she said. "Stop." She grabbed his head, wrapping her fingers over his forehead to block the impact of his blows.

"Stop."

There was blood on her fingers. She was crying. He was still. I closed my eyes. "No," I said again.

He spoke once more, drowning me out. His voice was very calm, very soft. "Kill me, Anney. Kill me."

I tried to reach her with my right hand but the pain made me gasp. "Mama," I pleaded, but she still wasn't looking at me.

"Lord God, Lord God, Lord God." Her cry was low,

sibilant, painful. She was holding him, his head pressed to her belly. His bloody hairline was visible past the angle of her hip.

"Mama," I whispered.

"Help me, God," she pleaded in a raw, terrible voice. "Help me."

I could see her fingers on Glen's shoulder, see the white knuckles holding him tight. My mouth closed over the shout I would not let go. Rage burned in my belly and came up my throat. I'd said I could never hate her, but I hated her now for the way she held him, the way she stood there crying over him. Could she love me and still hold him like that? I let my head fall back. I did not want to see this. I wanted Travis's shotgun, or my sharp killing hook. I wanted everything to stop, the world to end, anything, but not to lie bleeding while she held him and cried. I looked up into white sky going gray. The first stars would come out as the sky darkened. I wanted to see that, the darkness and the stars. I heard a roar far off, a wave of night and despair waiting for me, and followed it out into the darkness.

21

Aunt Alma has a scrapbook full of newspaper clippings, with a few wedding invitations, funeral announcements, and baby pictures pasted down beside page after page of headlines. "Oh, we're always turning up in the news," she used to joke when she'd show people that book. Her favorite is the four-page spread the *Greenville News* did when Uncle Earle's convertible smashed into the barbershop across the street from the county courthouse a few months before it burned down. There are pictures of the front end of the car propped up on a barber stool just a few feet short of splintered silvered mirrors, another of Earle sitting on the curb leaning forward with his head in his hands, and a series of the barber picking through the remains of his shop with the help of a highway patrolman and Granny Boatwright. The barber looks funny, holding up his shaving brush and cup in fingers that blur a little so that you can see he must have still been shaking.

HE DIDN'T COME IN FOR A SHAVE, the headline reads under the picture of the car on the stool.

BOATWRIGHT captions the close-up of Earle's numb face.

In those pictures, Uncle Earle looks scary, like a thief or a murderer, the kind of gaunt, poorly shaven face sketched on a post office wall. In that washed-out gray print, he looks like a figure from a horror show, an animated corpse. Granny, my mama, uncles, aunts, cousins—all of us look dead on the black-and-white page.

"We look worse than other people ever seem to look," I once complained to Aunt Alma.

"Oh, piss," she said. "Watery ink and gray paper makes everybody look a little crazy." I think she was annoyed that I didn't take more pride in her scrapbook, but it seemed to me nobody looked quite like my family. Worse than crazy; we looked moon-eyed, rigid, openmouthed, and stupid. Even our wedding announcement pictures were bad. Aunt Alma insisted it had nothing to do with us, that Boatwrights weren't bad-looking seen head on.

"We just make bad pictures," she said. "The difference is money. It takes a lot of money to make someone look alive on newsprint," she told me, "to keep some piece of the soul behind the eyes."

I'm in Aunt Alma's book now.

As soon as I saw the picture of me on the front page of the *News*, I knew it would wind up in her scrapbook, and I hated it. In it, I was leaning against Raylene's shoulder, my face all pale and long, my chin sticking out too far, my eyes sunk into shadows. I was a Boatwright there for sure, as ugly as anything. I was a freshly gutted fish, my mouth gaping open above my bandaged shoulder and arm, my neck still streaked dark with blood. Like a Boatwright all right—it wasn't all my blood.

Coming back to myself at Greenville General, I kept my teeth clamped together, not even screaming when the doctor rotated my arm in the bruised shoulder socket, put a cast on my wrist, washed out the cuts, and then wrapped the whole tight to my midriff. Mama had been there, had carried me in from the car and made the doctor look at me right away. The nurse took me out of her arms, and Mama stepped back, her bloody knuckles still outstretched, touching my cheek lightly. I looked into the nurse's face and then looked back for Mama, but she was gone. Before she could give her name or mine, she had disappeared.

"Come on, honey." The soft-voiced nurse ran her fingers through my hair, then stroked lightly all over my head. I looked for her nametag but saw none. "Don't jump, now. You'll hurt yourself." Her fingers smelled of alcohol and talcum powder. She seemed kind. I wondered if she had children.

"Feeling for bumps or cuts," she told me while the doctor was still busy with my wrist. There was just the scrape on my temple and the cut along my ear, but those had bled all down my neck and shoulder. It was hard to believe all that blood had come from so few cuts. The nurse was gentle and slow. I let her touch me as she pleased, turning my head to follow her smile like an infant watching the nipple. I watched, but didn't speak. I didn't tell her how much I hurt. I figured she could see the bruises on my throat and my torn lips. She could certainly see the look in my eyes. The one glance I'd got at my face in the mirror-black pane of the examining-room door scared me. I was a stranger with eyes sunk in shadowy caves above sharp cheekbones and a mouth so tight the lips had disappeared.

"That shoulder's gonna ache for a while." The doctor didn't look at me when he spoke, just made notes on a clipboard. "And that wrist is badly sprung. It'll be a couple of months healing completely." The nurse was washing dried blood from my cheek with an alcohol swab. I watched her instead of him.

"We're going to have to wait a while before we give you anything." The doctor's eyes wandered up from the clipboard and down my body, pausing at the bruises on my thighs and sliding down to the swollen knees, one of which was scraped raw. He put his palm on my hip and squeezed slightly. "You tell me now if anything else hurts you."

It might have been a question. It might not. I looked up

at him with no expression. I kept wondering where Mama had gone. What had happened to Daddy Glen? I didn't remember the ride in from Alma's place, didn't remember Mama saying anything to me. Had she told them what had happened? Did anyone know? Where was Mama, and why wasn't she with me?

The deputy leaned against the door until the nurse brought him a folding metal chair he could prop back against the wall. He was a red-faced boy with sandy hair cut so short you could see his pink scalp under the fuzz. He reminded me of the twins when they came back from the county farm, stiff-backed, crew-cut, and proud of themselves. This one was proud of himself too; kept smoothing down his uniform shirt and pulling at the material so the sweaty wrinkles under his arms wouldn't show. His mouth was soft and his chin small, but when he looked at me, he would poke his lips out and try to make his face stern. Watched too much television, probably thought of himself as some public defender type. I tried to feel dangerous, but my eyelids were damp and swollen, my neck itchy, and my mouth too painful for me to frown. He kept fiddling with his shirt and looking over at me. After a while I began to feel more and more like a child, a girl, hurt and alone.

By the time Sheriff Cole came in, walking stiffly as if his big wide belt weighted him down and hurt his back, I felt so small I didn't know if I could talk.

"Ruth Anne." He greeted me by name.

He pulled a stool over beside the hip-high table I was propped up on, grunted as he shifted his butt onto the stool, then rolled his head so that his neck made a loud cracking noise. At the sound he grinned and put both hands flat on his thighs.

"You want to talk to me? Tell me what happened?"

I swallowed. Olive complexion, big nose, bigger ears, strong chin, and thin gray hair combed straight back off his face—Sheriff Cole didn't look like anybody else I knew. People said he came from Maryland and that he would never have made sheriff if he hadn't been such a churchgoing Baptist, a deacon, and well-off even before he married a Greenville girl. He looked more like a frycook than a sheriff, big-bellied, greasy, and soft.

I looked up into his wide, dark eyes. His voice was soft, almost lazy, his tone both polite and respectful. He made me wish I could talk, tell him what had happened, what I thought had happened. But it all seemed so complicated in my head, so long and difficult. How could I begin? Where would I begin? With Aunt Alma going crazy? With the moment Daddy Glen grabbed me and tore my shirt? I thought of that moment in the parking lot so long ago, waiting to find out about Mama and his son.

"You're not hurt too bad," he told me. "Doctor says you'll be fine."

I lifted my head, knowing fear showed in my face.

"No concussion, the doctor says." He took the little notebook out of his pocket, opened it. "You're a little shocky, need to be careful for a while. Some of your people are out there. I got the doctor talking to them."

"Mama?" My voice was a hoarse croak.

"I an't talked to your mama yet. Your aunts are here, though. We'll let you see them soon." He flipped pages, took out a pen, and looked at me. "Now, we need to know what happened, Ruth Anne. I know you're not feeling too good, but I want you to try to talk to me." His mouth softened, as if he were trying to look comforting. "You tell me what happened and we can work on getting you home soon." He put the point of the pen to the paper.

I closed my eyes. Mama hadn't talked to him. I felt suddenly so tired I could barely draw breath.

"They call you Bone, don't they?"

I said nothing.

"Bone, I want you to know that no one is gonna hurt you. No one is gonna be allowed to hurt you. We can see that you've been through enough. Just tell me who beat you, girl. Tell me." His voice was calm, careful, friendly. He was Daddy Glen in a uniform. The world was full of Daddy Glens, and I didn't want to be in the world anymore.

"Honey," the sheriff said again. I hated him for calling me that. He didn't know me. "We're gonna have to know everything that happened."

No. My tongue swelled in my mouth. I didn't want anyone to know anything. Mama, I almost whispered, but clamped my teeth together. I couldn't tell this man anything. He didn't care about me. No one cared about me. I didn't even care about myself anymore.

"Ruth Anne." He leaned forward, his face close to mine, his whispery voice too big in my ear. "I want to help you. I want you to tell me what happened, girl. I'll take care of everything. I promise you. You'll be all right."

No. He thought he knew everything. Son of a bitch in his smug uniform could talk like Santa Claus, promise anything, but I was alone.

"I want to go home," I said. "I want my mama."

Sheriff Cole put his hand on mine and sighed. "All right. All right, girl."

I looked at him, remembering what Raylene had said that night on the landing when I told her how much I hated people who looked at us like trash. What must it be like to be Sheriff Cole? What made him who he was? I'd think about that sometime, but not now. I didn't want to think at all right now.

The double door swung open. I turned eagerly, but the struggling angry figure there wasn't Mama. Raylene was wrestling with a nurse, pushing the woman away and almost losing her black pea coat in the process. "Let me go," she said in a voice bigger than the room. "You let me go." She shoved the woman away and came forward like a tree falling, massive, inevitable, and reassuringly familiar.

"Bone. Baby." Her words echoed hollowly against the stark white walls.

"Oh, my girl, what'd they do to you?" Raylene leaned over me, and the smell of her wrapped me around. I opened my mouth like a baby bird, cried out, and reached up to her with my good arm. I said her name twice and lay against her breasts. Her arms were so strong, so safe. Don't let me go, I thought. Just please, don't let me go.

"What are you doing to this child?" I felt her turn slightly, her voice loud and insistent above me. "You tell me what right you got to be in here with her alone, and keeping me outside?"

Sheriff Cole's voice was patient. "We need to know what happened," he said.

"You can see what happened," Raylene snapped. "Look at her. She's hurt and scared and don't need nobody hurting her any more. Were you gonna keep me away from her till you had her ready to jump out the window or say anything you wanted her to?"

"Miss Boatwright, I'm sorry, but there's been an assault. There has to be an investigation."

"She's just twelve years old, you fool. Right now she needs to feel safe and loved, not alone and terrified. You're right, there has to be justice. There has to be a judgment day too, when God will judge us all. What you gonna tell him you did to this child when that day comes?"

"There's no need—" he began, but she interrupted him.

"There's need," she said. "God knows there's need." Her voice was awesome, biblical. "God knows."

The notebook snapped closed. I looked sideways out of Raylene's embrace and saw Sheriff Cole glare at her and stuff his notebook back in his pocket. "You call me," he said. "You call me when she's ready to tell us what happened."

Aunt Raylene grunted contemptuously, and held me close as he stomped away. "My girl," she whispered in that strong voice, and stroked my hair back off my face. "Oh, my poor little girl, you just lay still. We'll get you home. Don't you worry. Don't you worry about nothing. I'll get you home and safe."

There was no stopping Aunt Raylene. When the doctor insisted I stay overnight, she planted herself in a chair by my bed and refused to move. She held my hand all night while I lay unsleeping and restless. My arm throbbed, and my mouth was so bruised I could only whimper.

"I can't give her anything," the nurse told Raylene each time she checked on us.

"I know," Raylene nodded. "Just give me a straw, why don't you?" She fed me sips of Coke and hummed quietly while I stared up at the ceiling.

In the morning, the doctor felt all over the back of my head while Raylene glared at him from her chair. I was numb with exhaustion and pain, couldn't even smile when he grumbled and signed the release forms. The nurse took me to the entry in a wheelchair. I could see the photographer waiting outside, but Raylene just harrumphed and picked me up like a baby doll, not looking left or right as she carried me out to her truck.

Raylene settled me close to her right hip before she started the engine, but I slid away, over to where I could hang on to the door and look out through the window. I could not look at her, could not listen to the words she kept trying to speak softly in my direction. Murmurs of comfort, meaningless phrases that did not register. The one thing I wanted her to say went unspoken. Where was Mama? What had happened to her?

When we pulled up in Raylene's yard, the sun was beating down on the muddy spring grass. The river ran flat and fast, and there was no breeze at all. I wiped sweat off my neck and watched a big unfamiliar yellow dog creep out from under the porch and stand by the steps with his head canted to one side. Raylene sighed and cut the engine.

"I need to say something to you." Raylene sounded uncertain. "The thing you need to understand, that's the one thing I'm afraid you're too young to hear." She didn't look at me. Her words came out in a rush. "But it's simple enough, and one day maybe you will understand it." She turned to look at me then.

"One time you talked to me about how I live, with no husband or children or even a good friend. Well, I had me a friend when I was with the carnival, somebody I loved better than myself, a lover I would have spent my life with and should have. But I was crazy with love, too crazy to judge what I was doing. I did a terrible thing, Bone." Her skin looked tighter over her cheekbones, as if her whole frame were swelling with shame. She shook her head but didn't look away from my eyes.

"Bone, no woman can stand to choose between her baby and her lover, between her child and her husband. I made the woman I loved choose. She stayed with her baby, and I came back here alone. It should never have come to that. It never should. It just about killed her. It just about killed me."

Aunt Raylene covered her eyes for a moment, then pushed

her hair back with both hands. "God!" She dropped her hands and turned back to me. "We do terrible things to the ones we love sometimes," she said. "We can't explain it. We can't excuse it. It eats us up, but we do them just the same. You want to know about your mama, I know. But I can't tell you anything. None of us can. No one knows where she's gone. I can't explain that to you, Bone. I just can't, but I know your mama loves you. Don't doubt that. She loves you more than her life, and she an't never gonna forgive herself for what she's done to you, what she allowed to happen."

Aunt Raylene gripped the steering wheel fiercely and stared at me. "I shouldn't talk so much. I've said enough." She wiped her mouth. "We need some time. You need some time. You know what you look like, girl?"

I turned away. I knew what I looked like. At the hospital when they had left me alone in the bathroom for a minute, I had looked at myself in the mirror and known I was a different person. Older, meaner, rawboned, crazy, and hateful. I was full of hate. I had spit on the glass, spit on my life, not caring anymore who I was or would be. I had wanted to laugh at everyone, Raylene and the nurses, all of them watching me like some fragile piece of glass ready to shatter around boiling water. I was boiling inside. I was cooking away. I was who I was going to be, and she was a terrible person.

"Ruth Anne," Aunt Raylene whispered. "Girl, look at me. Stop thinking about what happened. Don't think about it. Don't try to think about nothing. You can't understand it yet. You don't have to. It don't make sense, and I can't explain it to you. You can't explain it to yourself. Your mama . . ." She stopped, and I looked back at her. "Your mama loves you. Just hang on, girl. Just hang on. It'll be better in time, I promise you."

I promise you, she said. My mouth twisted. I stared at her hatefully.

Raylene looked at me as if my rage hurt her, but she said nothing, just climbed heavily out of the truck. She moved slowly, hugging her old purse to her bosom and stopping only to give the panting dog a quick pat on the head before she went up and laid the purse on the steps. She came back and took me up again as easily as if I weighed no more than that purse. She carried me inside the house, the dog following, and put me in her bed. The dog settled himself on the rug, comfortably. I lay still, ignoring Aunt Raylene's movements but thinking even so about the woman she had loved, the woman who had loved her child more. It was too much for me. I'd have to think about it some other time.

The dog turned to me with hopeful brown eyes, his tongue hanging down as if he wanted me to invite him up on the bed. Big dumb sad eyes waited on me. I wanted to beat my fists until bones splintered, kick my heels into raw meat, scream until my tongue pulled loose and split at the root, but everything was slow, words and feelings just moved across my brain. I was slow, numb, and stupid. The pain in my arm was comforting, the throbbing at my temple was a music I needed in order to keep breathing.

Everything hurt me: my arm in its cotton sling; the memory of the nurse's careful fingers; the light that glinted into my eyes from the flawed glass of Raylene's window; my hip where it pressed against the mattress. Most of all my heart hurt me, a huge swollen obstruction in my chest. Every time I closed my eyes there was a flash of Glen's face as he had looked above me. I kept turning my head as if Mama's prayers still echoed in my ears, and even the slow drag of that dog's eyes raked over my skin like a pitchfork cutting furrows in dust. I had seen my whole life in Sheriff Cole's eyes, contemptible, small, meaningless. My mama had abandoned me, and that was the only thing that mattered. When Raylene brought me some soup later, I refused to eat. "I hate her," I whispered through torn lips. "I hate her."

"You'll forgive her," Raylene said.

I pulled the sheet up over my mouth.

How do you forgive somebody when you cannot even

speak her name, when you cannot stand to close your eyes and see her face? I did not understand. If I thought of Mama, I thought of her with her head thrown back and her mouth open, Glen's bloody face pressed to her belly. I could not stand to remember that, could not watch it again. I turned away, closed my eyes, and prayed for the darkness to come back. I wanted to die. I refused to eat, refused to speak, covered my face, and would not let Aunt Raylene coax me out of bed. She left me alone, and I woke up with my eyes wet and my mouth open, but with no memory of dreaming. The only sound was the yellow dog's tail thumping the rug. My heart, the pulse that pounded in my head, beat to that rhythm. Everything in me said no, repeated it, drummed it, hummed and sang it. I had no more spirit of meanness than a bug had. I was just a whisper in the dark saying no and hoping to die.

Raylene came in the morning and fed me grits with a spoon. She let me be quiet that day, but the next, she picked me up and carried me out to the porch to sit on her rocker in the sun. I wouldn't look at her, wouldn't speak, but she didn't seem to care. She watered her plants, fed her dogs and chickens, and stood smoking on the steps until the cool air came up from the river. Then she carried me back to bed. The next day, grudgingly, I dragged myself up, ate a little on my own, and went out to the rocker on the porch. But it was not a surrender. I was willing to eat and sit up, but not to speak.

I stayed on the porch and would not talk to anyone, not to Raylene and not to Earle when he brought me his battered record player and tried to make me laugh. He played some of the same records I had listened to with Aunt Ruth, but I sat unmoving, dry-eyed and distant. Eventually he left me alone. Raylene didn't try to talk to me. She brought me beans to pick over, which I did with no interest. She also asked me to rip out the hem on some old curtains, but that I refused to do. Not that I argued with her. I just left them lying untouched on the dusty boards by the rocker. I would have slept in the rocker, but Raylene threatened to drag me out of it kicking and screaming.

"I an't gonna have you sleeping on the porch," she fumed. So I pulled myself up painfully and crept off to bed like an old lady, bent over and cramped. I did what I had to do so they would leave me alone. I heard Raylene talking to Earle about Mama. They were worried. No one knew where she had gone. No one knew where Glen was either, though the uncles were talking about paying a bounty to anyone who found him. Earle was adamant, Beau had bought a new shotgun, but it was Nevil who scared Raylene.

Nevil came out to Raylene's one evening and stood silently in front of me. He touched my bruised chin with one outstretched finger, traced my hairline, and leaned forward to kiss my left cheekbone with dry chapped lips. I wanted to speak to him but instead held my breath, looking into his dark hooded eyes.

"I promise," he said, and I saw Raylene cover her mouth with one hand. I knew what he meant, and I smiled. He turned and went down the steps abruptly, stomping with his bootheels. Raylene called his name, but he didn't pause. Fay told Raylene that Nevil had stopped sleeping at home. He was living in his truck, driving the county roads at night, searching.

"He'll get himself killed," Raylene told me, but I refused to say anything.

I didn't care anymore who got killed.

The night Mama came, Raylene was at the record player, listening to every record Earle had brought over. That music seemed to echo off the porch ceiling, the silvery river surface, and the night sky. The guitar plunked and became clearly Patsy Cline's voice singing "Walking After Midnight." The driving notes and the dark undertone of the drum paced her voice. I listened closely, heard the pause as the song ended, and then

Patsy's voice started again, taking up from the beginning, the scratches and popping of the worn record overwhelming that heartbreaking voice, making me wish I could still cry the way I had with Aunt Ruth.

The silence extended, the soft rustle of the river barely audible. A breeze swelled and died down. The music came back, the chords different. Not Patsy Cline. Kitty Wells. "Talk Back Trembling Lips." Her twangy voice shook and scolded, louder still than Patsy's drawl. Mama always said Kitty had a smoky voice, not as pure as Patsy's, but familiar. That raw accent, like Beau's or Alma's, flattened vowels and stretched-out syllables to fit the chorus. I rocked back and listened to the record play through. The next one was another of Mama's favorites, Patsy Cline telling the world that it wasn't God who made honky-tonk angels. Grief filled me.

I stared up into the pattern of rusty dried paint and spider-fine traceries on the porch ceiling. I opened my mouth to cry, but no cry came. Tears kept running down my face into my collar, but I didn't make a sound. Children cried. I was not a child. Maybe, I told myself, I should go stay with Aunt Carr up in Baltimore or go out to Eustis and visit Aunt Maybelle and Aunt Marvella. I closed my eyes and licked my lips.

The screen door swung closed with a thud. I turned my head.

Mama stood motionless in one of her old short-sleeved dresses, her arms crossed under her breasts and her head up. She was looking at me from slitted eyes. My heart raced at the sight of her.

Aunt Ruth had told her after Lyle Parsons's funeral that she would look the same till she died. "Now you look like a Boatwright. Now you got the look," she'd said. In all the years since, that prophecy had held true. Age and exhaustion had worn lines under Mama's mouth and eyes, narrowed her chin, and deepened the indentations beside her nose, but you could still see the beautiful girl she had been. Now that face was made new. Bones seemed to have moved, flesh fallen away, and lines deepened into gullies, while shadows darkened to streaks of midnight.

I breathed hard, feeling like I was underwater looking at her. She came across the porch, her face stern, her mouth set in a rigid line. The muscles in her neck stood out in high relief. I pushed myself up. She came straight to the rocker. My face felt plaster-stiff. The music was still playing. It wasn't God who made us like this, I thought. We'd gotten ourselves messed up on our own.

"Baby." Mama's voice was a raspy whisper.

I did not move, did not speak.

"Bone." She touched my shoulder. "Oh, girl."

I could not pull away, but still I did not speak. I wondered if she could see herself in my pupils.

She drew back a little and dropped down to half-kneel beside me. "I know," she said. "I know you must feel like I don't love you, like I didn't love you enough."

She took hold of her own shoulders, hugging herself and shivering as if she were cold. "Bone, I never wanted you to be hurt. I wanted you to be safe. I wanted us all to be happy. I never thought it would go the way it did. I never thought Glen would hurt you like that."

Mama shut her eyes and turned her head as if she could no longer stand to look into my face. Her mouth opened and closed several times. I saw tears at the corners of her eyes.

"And I just loved him. You know that. I just loved him so I couldn't see him that way. I couldn't believe. I couldn't imagine . . ." She swallowed several times, then opened her eyes and looked at me directly.

I looked back, saw her face pale and drawn, her eyes red-rimmed, her lips trembling. I wanted to tell her lies, tell her that I had never doubted her, that nothing could make any difference to my love for her, but I couldn't. I had lost my mama. She was a stranger, and I was so old my insides had turned to dust and stone. Every time I closed my eyes, I could see again the blood on Glen's hairline, his face pressed to her belly, feel that black despair whose only relief would be death. I had prayed for death. Maybe it wasn't her fault. It wasn't mine. Maybe it wasn't a matter of anybody's fault. Maybe it was like Raylene said, the way the world goes, the way hearts get broken all the time.

"You don't know how much I love you," she said, her face as stark as a cracked white plate. "How much I have always loved you."

My heart broke all over again. I wanted my life back, my mama, but I knew I would never have that. The child I had been was gone with the child she had been. We were new people, and we didn't know each other anymore. I shook my head desperately.

"Mama," I said, not wanting to speak but not able to stop the rush of that cry. I shuddered, and the word came out like a bird's call, high and piercing. The sobs that followed were hoarse and ugly. I grabbed the front of Mama's dress with my good arm, ignoring the pain in my shoulder as I pushed forward into her embrace. She caught me, pressing my face against her throat and whispering into my ear.

"It's all right, baby. You just cry. You just go on and cry." Her hands touched me gently, lifted, and came back down as if she were afraid she might hurt me but couldn't keep from reaching for me again. "You're my own baby girl. I'm not gonna let you go."

Over Mama's shoulder, I saw Raylene in the doorway, her face as red as a new apple. Mama's hands stroked my hair back off my face, cupped my head, held me safe. I pressed my face into her neck, and let it all go. The grief. The anger. The guilt and the shame. It would come back later. It would come back forever. We had all wanted the simplest thing, to love and be loved and be safe together, but we had lost it and I didn't know how to get it back.

The music stopped, and the sound of the river water filled the night. My crying eased and then stopped. Mama rocked back on her heels. A jaybird dropped off the porch lintel and streaked up into the darkening sky. The dog loped out to nose its track in the dusty grass. Raylene called Mama's name softly, then mine, her voice as scratchy and penetrating as the chords of a steel guitar, as familiar as Kitty Wells or a gospel chorus. Mama looked back at her and shook her head. She straightened and gave my hand on the rocker's arm a little pat. Her smell, that familiar salt-and-butter smell, almost made me cry again, but I felt empty. I just watched her.

Raylene had been right. I didn't understand anything. But I didn't want to understand. Seeing Mama hurt me almost as bad as not seeing her had.

There was an envelope on my lap. Mama had put it there. She leaned forward and kissed my cheek just below where Nevil had kissed me. The memory of his burning eyes startled me. He would not forgive. He was out there hunting. I almost cried out. Mama's finger touched my lips. Her eyes burned into me.

"I love you, Bone," she said. "Never forget that. You're my baby girl, and I love you." Her ravaged cheeks shone in the light from the house, her eyes glittered. She bent, kissed my fingers, and stood up. Aunt Raylene came through the door, but Mama backed away quickly, shaking her head again. We watched her cross the yard, heard her start the Pontiac in the darkness past the curve of the road.

"Damn," Raylene cursed. Her fist drummed on the doorjamb. "Damn," she said again, and dropped her hand as if she could think of nothing else to say, to do. I held the envelope and watched her shoulders. They were shaking, but she made no sound.

"Do you know where she's going?" I asked.

"No." The word was a whisper. Raylene lifted her hands slightly, dropped them again. She did not turn to me, and I knew she did not want me to see her face.

"California," I said. "Or Florida, maybe. He always talked about taking us off there sometime, someplace where they grew oranges and a man could find decent work." My voice sounded so rough and mean I barely recognized it. I felt old and chilled, though I knew the night was warm. I looked down my bandaged arm to the envelope. It was oversized, yellow, official-looking, and unsealed. I opened it.

Folded into thirds was a certificate. RUTH ANNE BOATWRIGHT. Mother: ANNEY BOATWRIGHT. Father: UNKNOWN. I almost laughed, reading down the page. Greenville General Hospital and the embossed seal of the county, the family legend on imitation parchment. I had never seen it before, but had heard all about it. I unfolded the bottom third.

It was blank, unmarked, unstamped.

I looked out into the dark night, past Raylene's hip and the porch railing. What had she done? I shook my head and swallowed. I knew nothing, understood nothing. Maybe I never would. Who had Mama been, what had she wanted to be or do before I was born? Once I was born, her hopes had turned, and I had climbed up her life like a flower reaching for the sun. Fourteen and terrified, fifteen and a mother, just past twenty-one when she married Glen. Her life had folded into mine. What would I be like when I was fifteen, twenty, thirty? Would I be as strong as she had been, as hungry for love, as desperate, determined, and ashamed?

My eyes were dry, the night a blanket that covered me. I wasn't old. I would be thirteen in a few weeks. I was already who I was going to be. I tucked the envelope inside my pocket. When Raylene came to me, I let her touch my shoulder, let my head tilt to lean against her, trusting her arm and her love. I was who I was going to be, someone like her, like Mama, a Boatwright woman. I wrapped my fingers in Raylene's and watched the night close in around us.

Also by

Dorothy Allison

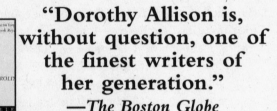

"Dorothy Allison is, without question, one of the finest writers of her generation."
—*The Boston Globe*

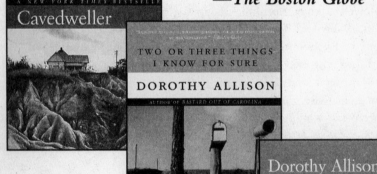

"A hell of a writer—tough and loose, clear and compassionate."
—*The Village Voice*